TWIST OF THE THREAD

The Lancashire Cotton Saga
Book Two

Christine Evans

SAPERE
BOOKS

TWIST OF THE THREAD

Published by Sapere Books.

20 Windermere Drive, Leeds, England, LS17 7UZ,
United Kingdom

saperebooks.com

ISBN: 978-1-913028-87-9

CHAPTER 1: OLD HOME

At the last house on Weavers Row, Jessie Overdale lowered her swelling body gratefully onto a chair in her old home. With a head full of memories, she glanced round the kitchen. The loud tick of the old wooden clock filled the room and she smiled to see its familiar face on the mantelpiece. Flanking it were two pottery spaniels with black ears and round staring eyes gazing out over the blue and white china jam pot that held useful odds and ends. Nothing seemed to have changed since her mother had been alive. There was a noticeable film of dust over the whole display though, and a tell-tale cobweb in the corner, something that would never have been allowed to rest during Nellie's lifetime. The sound of heavy footsteps echoed down the stairs and Jessie's father appeared at the door.

"Well, this is a nice surprise," said Jacob Davenport, smiling broadly.

"I knocked on the door but you must have been busy upstairs," said Jessie, struggling to her feet to give him a hug.

"No need to knock," said her father. "You might be living in grand style up at Overdale House, but this is still your home."

"Grand style!" said Jessie with a grimace. "Aye, I expect most folks would think it was. But that house is perishing cold in winter, I can tell you. Up on that hill the wind blows all across the Pennines. Still, it's cosy in here."

"I'll put t'kettle on. We'll have a brew," said Jacob, taking the blackened kettle out to the pump in the little scullery behind the kitchen.

"So, how are things?" asked Jessie, when the kettle was merrily bubbling on the fire. She'd noticed the cast iron range smelt of burnt grease and needed a good polish. "Are you coping all right?"

"Of course we are. Our Eddie's gone off to play football with his mates. We muddle along, you know."

"I could come up and help you sometimes," Jessie offered.

"You have enough to do, lass," said her father seriously. "And in your condition... Anyway, you ... you have to think of your position now."

"Oh Father, you know I don't think like that," scolded Jessie in exasperation. "If you need help…"

Jacob shook his head. "If I need help I'll get it, love," he insisted. "Anyway, Alice pops in now and again when her lasses are all busy at the sewing class. She's very good if I get in too much of a mess."

Alice Connelly lived in the first house on Weavers Row. A widow for many years, she took in mill girls as boarders to make ends meet. Her daughter Mary was Jessie's great friend, but even Mary seemed to be avoiding Jessie now she was married to the son and heir of Matthias Overdale, Master of the Invincible Mill.

Jacob looked for a moment as if he would say more but turned and began busily making the tea. "And how's that husband of yours? Is he treating you right?" he asked with a smile.

They both knew that Robert Overdale thought the world of Jessie, but he had been busy since taking over the affairs of the mill after his father's stroke.

Jessie sighed. "I'm a bit worried about his leg. It seems to heal well then it gets inflamed all over again, especially if he knocks it. I sometimes think he does too much with his Uncle Eli at the Municipal Works Committee. He gets very tired of a night, and his leg gets painful in bed so he can't sleep. But he won't listen to me."

The wound was a souvenir of Robert's entanglement in the American Civil War, where he had almost lost his leg.

Jessie shook her head at the frustrations of married life. "With Matthias ailing, Robert feels he has to shoulder as much of the responsibility as he can. Not that his father appreciates it. He interferes all the time. He opposes nearly every innovation that Robert suggests. Says we can't afford it. Matthias is terrified of bankruptcy after he was threatened with it during the war in America. He's hoarding every penny he can, instead of improving the machinery."

"Hmm," said Jacob thoughtfully. "Even Eli at the Endurance will invest in new machinery, and goodness knows we're not the most modern mill." The old mill at the end of the valley where Jacob worked as a master weaver had done steady business before the American Civil War, weaving cotton damask for the tables of respectable Victorian housewives who couldn't aspire to silk. "What about Taylor Walmsley?" asked her father. "I thought he'd bought into the mill during the cotton crisis. Couldn't he back Robert?"

Jessie fell silent for a moment. Taylor had pursued her before she'd married Robert, and had been coldly enraged when she resolutely rejected him. "I don't know," she said quietly. "We don't see much of him. He seems to spend most of his time travelling in India looking for cotton supplies. He comes home for a few months, takes a bit of interest in the mill and then swans off again. His big idea is to buy our cotton cheaper from the Empire instead of America. The trouble is that the Indian grades aren't as good at the moment. The staples are still too short."

"Aye, that Surat stuff was a beggar to weave," agreed Jacob.

"Taylor hired a botanist to travel with him last time, and they're carrying out experiments in different parts of the country. But it all takes time, and Matthias is grumbling about the cost, of course."

Jessie had been recently introduced to Crispin Pettigrew the botanist, a timid young man who looked as if he would shrivel away in the heat. He'd patiently explained the growing cycle of the cotton to Jessie and the efforts he'd been making to improve the length of the fluffy white cotton strands, or staple.

Taylor Walmsley had been invited to the dinner arranged by Jessie's mother-in-law too, but sat silently throughout the meal. Jessie had felt his pale eyes on her, but he'd looked away the second she turned her head in his direction.

Robert was very enthusiastic about Crispin's ideas, and even Matthias had reluctantly agreed that they should look for alternate supplies of cotton after the devastating war had left the mills of Lancashire without supplies and the people starving through lack of work.

Jessie turned her thoughts away from the problems of living with her in-laws and began to ask about the family. "Have you had any letters from Arden?" She relied on her father to give her news of her brother, who had been fighting with the Union navy. Now the war in America was drawing to a close, he was planning to secure work as an engineer on the transatlantic steamships.

"Aye. I had a letter the other day. He'll be coming over to Gorbydale when he docks in Liverpool next. He promised to call and see you."

"Oh good. Robert will be glad to see him too. I had a letter from Honora the other day. She says she saw him when his ship docked in New York last month. He seems very — well, ardent! I'm sure she's fond of him. I do hope they get together once she's finished her studies."

Honora was studying to be a doctor in New York, as women were not allowed to practise in England and there were no training places for them.

"And have John and Elsie been in touch?" Jessie asked, enquiring about her eldest brother and his wife living with their two children in a railway house in Doveton.

"Me and Eddie went over for Sunday tea last week and they're doing gradely," said Jacob with a smile. "They were asking about you."

"Did you say I'd like to invite them over for tea at Overdale House?" Jessie asked. "I'd love to see them all. You can see I'm not really fit to travel far myself."

Jacob hesitated. "The thing is, love, Elsie says she'd feel funny being waited on by her cousin Dolly. I suppose she still works there?"

Jessie nodded. Dolly Tate, the maid at Overdale House, was an irritating and truculent thorn in her side.

Her father carried on. "Elsie reckons she'd be frightened to death to have tea with Matthias Overdale. She knows she'd be too nervous to enjoy herself and drop things on the carpet and suchlike. And those kids! Well, let's just say I wouldn't trust 'em round fine china."

Jessie chuckled. "The children would have tea in the kitchen where everything is robust. I know what Elsie means, though. I was as nervous as a kitten myself when I first went to live there. That seemed to make me more clumsy. But Melissa is so nice, she wouldn't mind at all and she'd make them very welcome. It's Matthias who'd be tetchy. He gets very impatient. We moved our rooms to the back of Overdale House so he couldn't hear Robert cry out at night."

"He still does that, does he?" asked Jacob.

Jessie nodded. Though her husband was cheerful enough during the day, the horror of war sometimes came flooding back into his unconscious memory at night.

"So, living in luxury isn't all it's cracked up to be?" said Jacob, chuckling.

"Oh Father, I often think back to when we were all at home together, you and Mother and the boys and me. We'd be cosy in the autumn evenings round the fire, drinking tea and eating Mother's fruitcake." Jessie sipped her tea thoughtfully. She'd had few responsibilities then except to help her mother occasionally.

"Aye, and the boys squabbling if one of them got a bigger piece of cake than the other. Then young Eddie would fill his nappy and we'd all be horrified," said Jacob, laughing. "You're looking through rose-coloured spectacles, my lass. Life goes on, and anyway you didn't have your husband and a fine house to live in back then," he added. "Or a baby on the way."

"Speaking of which, I'll just stand up for a moment and stretch," said Jessie, placing her hands firmly on her back to ease her cramped body.

Strolling round the kitchen she wandered into the parlour. She was surprised how tidy the room was. It had been dusted and tidied, unlike the kitchen, and a faint aroma of beeswax scented the air. The wooden fire surround and the bookcase gleamed. A fire was set in the grate, which was unusual as the room was seldom used these days. The glass dome over the wax flowers glinted in the pale sun filtering between the heavy curtains and half nets. There was a posy of flowers in her mother's rose patterned vase, something which was also unusual in a male household.

"Have you had visitors?" she asked her father casually.

To her surprise Jacob blushed.

"Well, I have in a manner of speaking," he confessed, looking uncomfortable. "There was something I was meaning to mention. The thing is… I've been a widower for some time… I was devoted to your mother, you know that."

Jessie was instantly alerted. "Father, what is it? Have you met someone else?" she asked with a sly smile.

"In a manner of speaking," he said hesitantly. "It's hard being a man on his own, and with a growing lad in the house I can't always… And anyway, Alice and I have always been friends, and she was so good when your mother was ill…"

Jessie smiled at his discomfort. "So you and Alice have become more than friends," she concluded for him.

"It's all very respectable," he protested.

"I should hope so, as a good chapel man," said Jessie, laughing. "Father, I'm delighted for you. I always said Mary was like a sister to me and now it's all going to come true. So, you've been doing a bit of courting in the parlour?"

"In a manner of speaking. Alice's girls are always in and out at her place," he explained, speaking of his sweetheart's lodgers. "We've been talking things over like, and we have a bit of privacy at our house."

"You are going to get married, I take it?"

Jacob nodded vigorously. "When things are all sorted. Mary knows, and I think our Eddie suspects something's going on. And now you know, too."

"Oh Father, I know Mother would have been so pleased for you. She and Alice were the greatest of friends, and we all love her too. I can't wait to tell Robert."

"I don't mind you telling your husband, of course. But keep it under your hat for the present, if you don't mind. You know how people talk, and I wouldn't trust that Dolly Tate not to

11

spread it around all the gossips. I've not had a word with our John yet. I don't know how he'll take it. He was always close to your mother as her first born."

"You can trust me, Father," said Jessie, giving him a hug. "Anyway, I'd better get going. Give Alice my love and tell her I'm happy for you both." Then she remembered she had another snippet of news for him. "By the way, the Committee hope that the Park will be finished next month. They're planning a grand opening to cheer up the town. Eli is to be guest of honour for all the work he's done."

"Quite right, too," said Jacob, proud of his boss and old friend. "Th'owd lad has saved this town from going under. I did know, though. Being on the Relief Committee has its perks. You get to know the gossip before everyone else. Mrs Overdale and I are to be on the platform, I believe. You take care of yourself, love. Would you like me to walk home with you?"

"Perhaps to the bottom of the Row," said Jessie. "It's steeper than I remembered."

Arm in arm, they strolled down Weavers Row, surrounded by memories. It wasn't long before Jessie tired and paused to rest. This pregnancy business was harder than she had expected, and her growing lump made her feel ungainly and awkward. She wondered if she should have agreed to her husband's suggestion to take the trap and pony to her old home. Deep down though, she still felt an outsider in her in-law's large house and didn't like to put them to any trouble.

At the end of the Row, she waved goodbye to her father and glanced back with wistful affection at her old home and life. The Overdales were thrilled with the impending news of her first child. If it turned out to be a son as Matthias hoped and frequently mentioned, she knew her place in Overdale House would be cemented forever. Perhaps one day she would become used to 'grand living' as her father called it. It certainly wasn't as easy and familiar as her old life, but she was determined to persevere for her husband's sake and for their coming baby.

CHAPTER 2: DOLLY

Dolly Tate, arms akimbo, straightened her back and stretched as she glanced round the room. This work was getting too much for her. Dolly felt as if Jessie suspected she'd pinch something. It was true she'd been caught posing in front of the cheval mirror clutching Jessie's new dress in front of her, but it wasn't as if she was wearing it. Stuck up bitch! Who did she think she was, putting on airs and parading round like a daughter of the house when everyone knew she'd been just a common mill hand like the rest of them?

That husband of hers was no better — Robert Overdale, with his gammy leg. He'd told Dolly off a couple of times too. She'd have to be careful though. She didn't want to be turfed out on her ear with no job to go to. Now that the war in America was grinding to a close, the mill was sure to come back into production and cotton supplies would start trickling in. She didn't want to go back to working there. That had been hard graft.

Still, she had to bring some money into her old home. Her mother was bringing up Dolly's fatherless child, Albert, as her own, although Dolly's father still grumbled about it. Maggie loved Albert though. He was a good little chap with his fiery red hair. But with Seth and Tommo for male role models, it wouldn't be long before the boy turned into a rough street urchin like the rest of the local kids.

Dolly sighed. Was this all her life would ever be, skivvying for others and watching her child grow as wild and useless as her father and brother? She gazed out of the big window of the billiard room, her eyes on the little white temple on the hill where she'd lost her senses and her virginity to that American visitor. Clement something, he was called. He was probably dead by now, lost in the war in America, she presumed. He wouldn't dare show his face in Gorbydale anyway after he'd tried to swindle old Matthias. Clement had arranged a deal with Matthias and other associates to illegally ship arms to the South. Matthias had been paid, not in the gold that had been agreed, but in worthless confederate dollars. The Invincible and Overdale House were almost lost as a result.

None of the local lads would look at her. Although her parents were bringing up her child, most people suspected that she was the real mother, especially after father Tommo and her brother Seth had charged up to the Davenports' house on Weavers Row when they'd discovered she was pregnant. The fools had shamed her by wrongly accusing Arden Davenport of being responsible.

The only men who showed any interest in her these days were Seth's mates, and it wasn't marriage they had in mind. Her brother had soundly beaten the one lad who had made a serious attempt on her, so the others had swiftly backed away.

She was still lost in her thoughts when the cook popped her head round the door and frowned at Dolly's perceived idleness.

"Haven't you finished that yet? You'll have to leave it and give me a hand in the kitchen. It's nearly dinner time and they'll be expecting summat on the table. You can finish it off tomorrow. Get a move on."

Skivvying and drudgery, that was Dolly's future until she was a dry old husk like her mother, worn down with life. Dolly picked up her brush and duster and trudged down to the kitchen, weary with it all.

She sweeping round the floor of the billiard room when Melissa Overdale bustled in with Jessie.

"Now, this would make the perfect parlour for you," Melissa told Jessie with a sweeping gesture round the room. "It's not as if Robert plays billiards anymore. And it's a lovely view." She patted Jessie's hand and smiled. "It will give you a bit more privacy," she decided. "Our Robert's been hinting at it and I know you have to retreat to your bedroom whenever you need a private chat."

Dolly, with one ear on the conversation as she carried on sweeping, thought it most likely that the young couple would want to escape from Matthias and his moaning.

"This would be lovely," said Jessie. "Are you sure?"

"I'm quite sure, Jessica dear. You will need more space when the little one arrives. Though I'm sure I'll miss you in the drawing room."

"Oh, you know you'd be very welcome in here at any time," said Jessie, giving Melissa a tentative hug.

Dolly, ignored in a corner, grimaced at the thought of the extra work.

"Now about furniture," began Melissa, thoughtfully glancing round the room. "Perhaps you and Robert could go to Manchester and… Or perhaps not. I'm not sure if Matthias would be happy with the expense… There is some old furniture up in the attic."

"Old furniture will be fine," said Jessie eagerly. "Perhaps Robert can go up there and see what he can find and we can buy anything else that is needed. We really don't want to put you to any expense."

"We could always reassemble the billiard table in part of the coachhouse, now that the coach has gone," decided Melissa.

"The boys only played billiards when Augustus came over from Liverpool, and that isn't very often these days."

Gus Kearsley, a shipbuilder's son from Liverpool, was Robert's oldest friend.

Dolly, quietly dusting in her corner, listened to the conversation with growing annoyance. She'd already had to help change over the bedrooms upstairs. Now there was to be more upheaval as the billiard room was turned into a parlour. It had been a huge waste of her time cleaning out this room, which would once again be full of dust as the carpets and furniture were moved. Her only consolation was that Jessie would probably want to keep the room clean herself. Jessie wouldn't trust her at all, especially after that dress incident.

CHAPTER 3: THE OLD CAPITOL JAIL

Gazing through a tiny barred window overlooking a railway yard, Clement Duplege scratched himself. The damned lice got everywhere; nobody was immune. He assessed his possibilities. Number 13 cell was three storeys up, so it was impossible to escape through a window, even if he managed to remove the bars from the crumbling building.

Who would have thought this was once the very heart of the nation, where all the business of government was carried out? Now it was a stinking rat hole, full of vermin, filth and disease, not to mention the hundreds of prisoners washed up by the war. He'd been there so long that the smell had almost become unnoticed. The parole arrangement and the exchange of prisoners between the Union and Confederate armies had ceased since black men had joined the Union. The South had refused to recognise that a black soldier's life was worth the life of a white one, so now there were no exchanges and there was no opportunity to be free that way.

He glanced round the room at his fellow inmates. They were as dirty and pungent as he was, yet they had been respectable men of the South once, as his fellow inmate Mahony frequently reminded him. The man was a bore about his rights and his complaints about being kidnapped by the state. Didn't he recognise that human decency was abandoned in war? Did he think that the South were treating their prisoners any nicer? Clement had been to one of the southern prison camps to interrogate a prisoner and he knew better.

Mahony was busy writing his journal at the end of a rickety pine table, the only piece of furniture in the room apart from the primitive beds, with their thin straw mattresses and scant covering. At the other end of the table sat the other three inmates, playing cards to stave off the monotony. Clement's fingers instinctively sought his watch and chain in the pocket of his tattered vest waistcoat. When he had been arrested at the Willard Hotel he had automatically tucked it deep into his trouser pocket. Of course the guards had demanded to know if he had any arms, liquor or contraband about his person when· he'd been dragged to the Old Capitol jail. The small pistol he'd habitually concealed up his sleeve had already been taken away from him at the restaurant. Then his pockets were checked and the watch brought to light.

"Why, sir, didn't you display this watch in your vest pocket?" the guard demanded.

"Why, so any damned Yankee could steal it from me while my hands were manacled?" growled Clement.

He grimaced to see his precious watch roughly handled by the guard. It was a fine French piece given to him by his father. The chime tinkled sweetly round the grim room as the man opened the case. He stared at the inscription.

"Leastways we know your name 'Clement', 'cher fils'. Ain't that pretty? Unless of course you stole the watch."

"That is my watch, a gift from my father and I'll thank you to give it back. I should hate to report to the Superintendent that it was stolen."

Clement spoke with a dignified authority to let the man know he was not intimidated. The guard shrugged and gave it back.

"No doubt you'll soon be trading it in to make life — let's say, more bearable," he said with a smirk.

Now in his cell Clement found the smooth cold metal of the case comforting in his hand. It was his last link with the Amiens plantation, his home in Louisiana. He would never trade his precious watch if he could help it, but the watch chain was another matter. Gradually he had detached several of the gold links for food and, more importantly to him, for playing cards. The rumours that he had been a riverboat gambler had never been confirmed. He had played cautiously for a game or two, betting small stakes, winning small sums, losing some. Then he would slowly build his stake and pounce like a mountain lion. That way he had built up a small store of useful items to bet with and regained most of his links, though the ones that had been paid for food had gone forever. He now had a pair of pearl cufflinks, a quarter bottle of rough whisky, a few candle ends and a jar of coffee that was much better than the swamp water served up by the prison. These would be good bargaining stakes in his plan. He had a blanket, a spare shirt and some socks without darns, items he had once taken for granted but were as good as gold in this bleak place. His fellow cell mates were beginning to avoid playing with him, but there were other cells where men of better means had not yet witnessed his skill. There were opportunities to mingle during the brief leisure times each day, and Clement was determined to use these opportunities. Some of these men would deign to visit Cell 16 where a rudimentary mess room had been assembled.

Clement smiled to himself. Soon he hoped to have enough stores and bargaining chips to enable him to escape this fetid hell hole. The first thing he would do when he was free was get even with the English bitch who had betrayed him as a

Southern spy to the Washington authorities. For a moment he paused and remembered something she had said before Pinkerton and his thugs descended on their table. There was a child, a boy fathered on some kitchen maid in some godforsaken northern town in England. He vaguely remembered the night, a moon and a little white temple up in the blackness. He'd had many women since then, but the unusual setting still lingered in his thoughts. It might be the only chance he'd have for a son now. A fight in a mean back alley in Baton Rouge with some man armed with a knife who'd accused him of cardsharping had had an effect on his manhood. Even one of his valuable gold links given to a whore for a fumble in the prison had made him doubtful of his potency. A boy, a child of his in England, could that be possible? Why had that woman, Honora Overdale he thought her name was, betrayed him to the authorities when he was helping her find her brother or some sort of relative? Had the man been a lover who had abandoned her to make her turn on Clement that way? She seemed quite convinced the boy was his son. 'Cher fils' said the inscription on the precious watch, 'my dear son'. Life was a mystery, but he suddenly became convinced that the unknown boy in Gorbydale was one mystery that would need to be checked on. He stroked the smooth gold watch case and was determined he should be free to find out.

Clement watched and waited like the spy he was, lurking on his bunk, silent as a spider waiting patiently for a fly to land in his web of intrigue. He observed and noted the tiniest of opportunities, the vaguest of chances that might help him escape. And there had been a new development in recent days. The grapevine soon informed everyone of a new woman prisoner, one known to him in the past. Belle Boyd, the famed spy and informant, was incarcerated somewhere on the floor below him. Known as La Belle Rebelle, every night before she retired she entertained her fellow inmates with a rousing rendition of 'Maryland, My Maryland' to the annoyance of the authorities. Clement was determined to contact her, although he knew she was closely guarded. He might need her help with some notions of escape that were brewing in his fertile mind.

CHAPTER 4: A LESSON IN ANATOMY

The object of Clement's malice, Honora Darwen, was gazing down at a pile of stinking giblets spilling out of a corpse on an operating table in the Geneva Medical College. The woman beside her stepped back with a small gasp, her hand over her mouth.

"Miss Darwen, will you point out the gall bladder to your colleagues please?" asked the tall man beside her.

Honora glanced up into piercing blue eyes under shaggy grey brows and saw a malicious challenge in their depth.

"Certainly sir," she said and pointed it out with bold accuracy.

Doctor Walgrave should know by now that a woman who had witnessed blood and carnage in a Washington military hospital would not be cowed by a neatly dissected corpse in a modern New York medical college. He seemed to take delight in disconcerting his pupils, as if to challenge their suitability to train as doctors. Honora's determination to become a doctor had grown with her as a child beside her father in the slums of Manchester. She had left a comfortable home with her relations in Gorbydale to study in America, and no mundane pile of offal would make her wither in her resolve.

"Very good," said her tutor in a clipped voice.

Honora smiled to herself as the lesson continued. There were only two women working at the operating table with the doctor and the rest were men. The remainder of the group sat high in the seats that rose up round the theatre and watched carefully as the body was dissected. Honora's friend Verity Cain composed herself and gingerly approached the table again. Walgrave then turned his attentions to her fellow student Ben Clark and began to interrogate him with malign vigour now that he had failed to discomfort Honora.

"I don't know how you stand up to old Walgrave," Verity confessed afterwards as the girls made their way to their shared lodgings. "It was the smell that overcame me. It was only the thought that old Walgrave would sneer at me if I fainted that kept me standing."

"I expected it," said Honora, laughing. "The stench is a shock though if it takes you unawares, and that body wasn't very fresh to begin with."

"I was so glad he didn't turn on me," said her friend.

Ben, walking beside them on his way to lodgings nearby, gave a terse laugh.

"He must like you, Miss Cain," he said. "I believe he is a friend of your father's."

"Yes, Doctor Walgrave and my father trained at medical school together. But do you really think that would make a difference?" asked Verity defensively.

She was well aware that her father had pulled strings to allow her to train.

"Most assuredly," Ben told her. "You see, Miss Darwen and I are outsiders. She is English as well as being a woman. And I'm quite sure that our beloved doctor does not like Jews."

"Are you Jewish?" asked Honora in surprise.

He seemed very different from the Jewish folk she had seen around Cheetham Hill when she lived in Manchester. They wore long black clothes and skull caps on their heads. The young Jewish boys had long spirals of hair down the sides of their faces and the men had ample beards.

"Dear Miss Darwen, my full name is Benjamin Gluckstein," he said with a smile. "My father changed our name to Clark when we came to America to escape the Russian pogroms."

"Oh, I see," she said, nodding with understanding, well aware that many Manchester people had disapproved of the Jews too.

They arrived outside their lodgings.

"Goodnight, dear ladies," said Ben with a small bow.

Honora thoughtfully watched his retreating figure for a moment. He was a nice man and had been very helpful to her when she had struggled with some of her studies. In return she had explained some of the emergency techniques used on the wounded returning from the battlefield. They worked well together.

"I think he likes you," Verity teased her.

"I like him too, but not in the way you're hinting," Honora playfully scolded her friend, though she thoughtfully watched his slim figure retreating along the busy street. He was certainly attractive with his air of intelligent kindness.

Back at the brownstone lodging house she found a letter waiting for her. The stamps showed Queen Victoria, so she knew it was not from Arden Davenport as she had hoped. He was serving with the Union navy somewhere in the Southern states. Could she call him her sweetheart? She was not yet sure he would endure the wait she had imposed on herself until she'd finished her studies. It was yet another letter from her aunt Melissa begging her to come home and hinting how disloyal Honora had been to desert the family with her uncle Matthias still recovering from a stroke. Smiling when she read that Jessie's baby was due any day and might even have been born by the time she received the letter, she decided to write to

Arden straight away in case he had not heard the welcome news.

His last letter told her that he was down in Louisiana with the Union Navy patrolling the Mississippi river. A great bluff rose up beside the river at Vicksburg, and the Confederate army were making a valiant and bloody effort to defend it. She prayed with all her heart that Arden would be safe, especially for his family's sake. She was very fond of Jessie, his sister. They had become close friends travelling to Washington to try and find Robert when he was missing during the Civil War. They'd finally found him wounded and weak in the military hospital where they were working. Honora prayed for her own sake too. Arden loved her, she was sure, but she was too determined to follow her calling as a doctor to allow herself the luxury of giving herself to love just then. This was her only chance to follow in her father's footsteps, as England would not yet allow women to train in the profession. Honora raised the letter to her lips and then quickly slipped it into her pocket, ashamed of her weakness. Did she love him? Surely she must do.

CHAPTER 5: FREEDOM

In the mean light of a candle end Clement Duplege was sewing. Around him his fellow prisoners snored rhythmically or made strange animal noises in their sleep. He shielded the light with his body in case a passing warden might notice it from the cell door and question his night-time activities. He didn't want anyone to discover what he was doing, knowing that the governor salted spies throughout the cells. He had a battered bible open beside him as an excuse to plead insomnia. He froze as a bed creaked and someone rose and staggered half-asleep to pee. A noisy stream of water hit the enamel pot. Clement didn't dare even to breathe until the stupefied body slumped back onto his bunk and began to snore again. His eyes tiring, Clement finished the seam and laid his head down, but his busy brain would not let him sleep.

There had been a breakthrough at the prison. Through a minor miracle Clement had found a way to communicate with Belle Boyd. At first she had tried to slip notes under her door but these had been picked up and destroyed by the guards. Bribery had not worked, but then she was moved to the cell directly underneath his. A hole had been burrowed through the floorboards so they could pass messages. She was surprised by Clement's requests and wondered why he should want a lady's veil. She assumed it was a gift for some sweetheart, but the length of silk that she begged the guards to purchase took some persuading. They were suspicious of the gold links she gave them for payment, knowing full well that the source was Clement. He had bribed the guards with the same gold for extra food. They did not suspect that the material would be carefully threaded through the hole into his possession. Clement was alert and waiting. He retreated into a corner with his purchases.

He was not a religious man but, to the surprise of his fellow prisoners, he began attending the Sunday services at the jail. Someone even remarked on the open bible they had noticed by his bed and nodded wisely. The minister and sometimes his wife came regularly to bring spiritual comfort to those incarcerated there. The service was popular with the prisoners as their only other taste of freedom was the monotonous exercise trudging round the prison yard. This gave them a chance to leave their cells.

But religion was the last thing on Clement Duplege's mind. Early on a cool Sunday as the mist from the river crept around the jail, he rose quietly from his bed and slipped a razor from under his pillow. Over the time he had been imprisoned, he had grown a large beard, bright red against his much darkened auburn hair. Now, in a small cracked mirror, he carefully scraped it away. The razor was not very sharp although he had tried hard to give it an edge. His skin felt raw and strangely exposed, but slowly his blotchy flesh appeared from behind the months of wiry growth. He looked like a stranger in the dark mottled glass. Then he carefully snipped away at his eyebrows until they were much reduced. He stared at himself. His chin looked pink and tender and he winced as he dabbed it with cold water, but at least he looked different.

Clement silently extracted a bag of a few things he had stored in readiness from his corner of the cell. As the jail slowly came to life he tried to make himself invisible among his fellow prisoners, keeping his face away from them. The fewer people who could remark on his transformation the better. Finally there was a general stumbling of bodies towards the Sunday service. Watching from behind a book, Clement finally managed to grab Mahony as he went to the door of the cell. The man stared at Clement's changed appearance and opened his mouth to speak. He was immediately silenced by his cell mate.

"Just shut up and listen," hissed Clement. "I need you to do me a favour. I want you to detain the preacher's wife after the service. I don't care how you do it. Ask her one of your interminable questions. Flatter her. Say you know she has influence. Say you are sure she can persuade one of her illustrious friends to help you get out of here."

"You know that's a mighty fine idea," began Mahony, his eyes lighting up with renewed zeal. "She must surely know that we men of good standing are being detained illegally by a corrupt…"

"Enough of that," growled Clement. "Just detain her in any way you can — away from her husband."

"Why should I…" said Mahony indignantly.

Clement slipped two gold links into his hand.

"Will that help? Or shall I take them back?"

Mahony's eyes gleamed as his fingers closed over the gold. He would help.

Whether religious or not, most prisoners attended the service for their small moment of freedom. They joined in robustly with the hymns. Clement watched and waited until the service finished and the men stood up to leave. There was always a general melee after the service. He saw Mahony pull the preacher's wife to one side. Then in a dark corner he put his plan into action.

As the preacher made towards the gate, a figure stepped beside him and linked him with a rigid grip. For a moment he assumed it was his wife eager to leave the jail. Then he felt something sharp in his ribs.

"Keep going. Don't look round," growled a voice.

The preacher's knees trembled as he staggered forward. Out of the corner of his eye he could see a veiled figure who he was quite sure was not his wife. Whoever it was held a kerchief to their face as if they could not bear the stench from the latrines.

"Bye, Reverend. See you next Sunday," said the guard at the gate.

The man was too busy carefully scrutinising the milling crowd of prisoners to take much notice of the departure of the preacher and his 'wife', who seemed overcome by the visit.

Once outside, Clement hurried his prisoner away from the jail. The man tried to protest but Clement tersely commanded him to stay silent. They had walked several blocks when he pulled him into an alleyway.

"Where is my wife?" wailed the preacher.

"She'll be safe enough," snapped Clement, his voice muffled by the veil. "Now if you go back and start raising the alarm, I'll tell them you were in on the plan, you just hollered out because you'd demanded more money."

"They wouldn't believe you, a common criminal…!" protested his hostage.

"Oh, they would when I'd finished with them," said Clement with a threatening leer. "Walk slowly back to the jail. You'll probably meet your wife coming to find you. No doubt she'll be in full flow as to why you abandoned her." He vaguely patted a pocket. "And don't forget I have a gun. I'll be watching you. If I see you running, I can shoot you in the back at fifty yards."

He watched the man slowly walking to the corner and tapped his pocket once again to encourage him to comply. But once the man was some way ahead Clement rapidly went into action, pulling the veil from his face and the silk neckerchief from his hat. Tearing off the silk roses he pulled it back into shape. From round his waist he dragged off the fine length of silk he'd fashioned into a long skirt, revealing his jacket tied round his waist to bulk out his behind. Slipping it on he strode quickly away, stretching his legs from the cramped walk he'd used to make himself smaller beside the preacher.

Although Clement was not welcome at the back door of one of his associates, he managed to threaten his way into the house and finally emerged from a bath feeling clean. He was free at last, from filth and from jail. He stayed in hiding with his nervous hosts for some days until he hoped the search for him had ceased to be so urgent. The guns of the Confederacy had been heard near the city and its citizens had more important matters on their minds. There was an exodus on the trains and the roads by the more nervous or those with more to lose or hide. The authorities finally assumed he had left the city. But Clement had one more errand before he left. In the dark reaches of the night, he stealthily made his way to a little white house at the edge of the city. He had a sharp knife in his pocket and a determination to find out more about a certain child in a far off Lancashire town.

The door wasn't as easy to open as he had hoped. Some sort of sturdy bolt barred his way. He finally had to knock loudly on the rough wood, glad that there were no near neighbours. A muffled voice demanded what he wanted.

"I need to speak urgently to Miss Honora Overdale," he called. "I have some news of her family."

"Honora is not here," called the woman. Clement hesitated but the accent was obviously American, and a Yankee one at that. "But Miss Honora is not called Overdale. That is the name of her cousin Robert, who has gone to England. Honora's name is Darwen. She has gone to New York to train as a doctor. I can send on a letter if you like."

"She's found Robert, you say?" Clement was stunned for a moment.

"Oh yes. Badly hurt but surviving. He has gone home to his family."

"I see," said Clement.

So that was why Honora had betrayed him as a spy to the authorities. She had known that Robert was safe and that Clement had abandoned him at sea.

"Do you have an address for me?"

The woman hesitated. "I can forward a letter if you wish," she repeated, obviously reluctant reveal Honora's whereabouts. The war made everyone unhelpful and suspicious.

"Very well," said Clement. "I will call back and give you a letter for her."

He had no intention of doing so. Honora and his revenge could wait. He urgently needed to return to Baton Rouge and then to the Amiens plantation in Louisiana to see how his old home had fared in the war.

The abandoned preacher, peering anxiously over his shoulder, hesitatingly shuffled to meet his wife coming from the jail. He was confronted with a hailstorm of complaints.

"Fancy leaving me alone with those … those barbarians," she snapped, grasping his arm hard and dragging him away from the scene of her perceived embarrassment. "I was waylaid by that interminable bore Mahony. Where were you when I wanted to get rid of him? I cannot conceive that you deserted me in that…"

He raised a trembling hand to try to silence her but, affronted by his feeble protest, she raged on until she decided she was due an apology. It was then that she noticed his distressed state and stared at him in surprise.

"I have just been forced to help a prisoner escape," he gasped. "He threatened me with a gun. I was terrified he or his accomplices might hurt you, my dear."

"But why didn't the guards stop him?" she demanded, her mouth dropping open as she tried to understand what had happened.

"He … he was dressed as a woman," her husband almost sobbed. "He was all swathed up in fabrics like a woman. His face was hidden in a veil."

"But I never wear a veil," she protested.

"My dear, I do not think guards in a prison of rough men notice such niceties."

"We must go back and tell them at once," decided his wife, swinging her husband round towards the jail with determination.

But he pulled her to a halt in panic.

"We cannot. We cannot. Oh, my dear, I might be arrested for helping him to escape. What will I do?"

They stared at one another, appalled by their predicament.

"We should go and tell the truth," she decided finally. "The guard must surely realise that two women left the jail. Surely you will be exonerated? When they finally do find the man missing, questions will be asked and the guard could remember that two women left. Then you will be asked why you did not say anything and that will make you seem guilty. But you must protest that your life was in danger and that you thought that mine was too and that we were in the hands of desperate men. Surely you will be proclaimed innocent."

Reluctantly they went back to the jail. The prisoners were still being herded back to their cells and all was as chaotically organised as could be expected for a Sunday morning.

Once the governor had been informed what had happened by a tearful preacher, interrupted by his protesting wife, a flurry of action was unleashed in the jail. The preacher was little help in identifying his captor. He was tall and he was a southerner was all he could tell them. This was not much use in a jail with a plethora of tall southerners. As the guards searched the cells and questioned the prisoners, they finally reached the decision that Clement was their culprit. The dogs were brought in, but the spy had taken all his possessions and had had the forethought to swap his pillow and mattress from another prisoner's bunk. The hue and cry was stalled as the confused animals continually milled round the cell and barked at the unsuspecting recipient of the bedding.

CHAPTER 6: A FETE IS PLANNED

Robert Overdale was exultant as he hugged his wife.

"Well, my dear, the Gorbydale Municipal Gardens are well and truly finished and the flowers and bulbs are budding beautifully with the spring. Uncle Eli is planning to have an official opening on May Day, with a maypole and maybe even a fair."

Jessie smiled, remembering how she had met Robert at a Wakes Week fair, although that encounter had almost blighted their relationship. It had ended with her slapping his face when he stole a kiss from her to win a bet. But somehow the twists of fate, not to mention the American Civil War, had brought them together.

"It will be a welcome celebration for the town, don't you think?" said Robert, rubbing his hands with satisfaction.

"I think it sounds like a wonderful idea. But what of the men who'll be out of work now that the gardens are finished?" asked Jessie, ever mindful of the jobless citizens of their town.

So many were out of work after the cotton trade with America had ceased and closed the mills during the war.

"There is still money in the kitty for more work on the latrines for the houses down by the river," her husband told her. "The work isn't so pleasant as you can imagine, but it is still work and will bring in a little money for the men."

The government Relief Fund was still sending money to Lancashire to help with the cotton famine while the war lasted. Robert had been set to work by his Uncle Eli requisitioning all the materials for the town's projects. Sometimes an unpleasant whiff of latrines clung to his clothes which made Jessie feel nauseous in her state of pregnancy. With his damaged leg, he could do little hard physical work but he could make himself useful as right hand man to his uncle, riding round on his little cob. Some grumbled about nepotism, but Robert took no more wages than the other workers and the work had to be done by someone who could bargain with the suppliers.

Jessie had an idea.

"The girls in the sewing class could sew bunting from the scraps of material left over. I'll mention it to your mother."

The Relief Fund was funding the workless mill girls in the sewing classes and Melissa, Jessie's mother-in-law, had gladly allowed them to use the billiard room at Overdale House, feeling that she was doing something to alleviate their poverty during the cotton famine.

"I'd just go ahead if I were you," said Robert with a smile. "You know she relies on you entirely to organise the class."

Jessie nodded. "But it's only manners. She is after all the head of the class, and I wouldn't like to upset her."

She still felt acutely that she was in the house as a guest, albeit one who was carrying the future of the Overdale family. Melissa was delighted with her idea, and Jessie's friends sewing in the billiard room began to delve into a big bag of scraps to organise their bunting.

"We could make a banner too for the sewing class," said her friend Mary.

An old much-patched sheet was found in the linen cupboard and decorated with fabric flowers and letters. 'The Gorbydale Sewing Class' read the legend together, beautifully embroidered and appliqued with bobbins and needles all worked carefully by the girls. The patches on the sheet were soon hidden with flowers.

"It beats hemming dishcloths," said one of the girls as they proudly raised their banner on a couple of clothes props.

"I hope I'll be able to attend," sighed Jessie.

Her growing belly made her feel awkward and tired. Melissa disapproved of her showing herself round the town, though Jessie felt she needed some exercise by walking to her father's house. She was coming to the conclusion herself that she might need to curb her activities.

Jacob called to see her when he could to tell her of his wedding plans.

"It will be a quiet affair up at the chapel," he said. "Though we'll have to go to the registry office first as we're recusants," he added with a chuckle. "Will you be able to come?"

Jessie was growing larger by the day and her movements slow and cumbersome.

"Oh, I do hope so, Father," she said.

CHAPTER 7: BATON ROUGE

In the cool light of a southern morning before the sun had burnt the mist from the river, Clement Duplege knocked softly on the back door of his own house in Baton Rouge. A cautious black woman opened it slightly and her hand flew to her mouth.

"Massa Clement," she gasped.

He put a finger to his lips.

"May I come in, Gemima?" he whispered.

"Massa Clement, this house is full of Yankees," she warned him urgently. "They's off these ironclad things what's patrollin' the river. If they catch you…"

"They won't catch me if you're quiet about it," he hissed, trying to edge his way in at the doorway. "Is Mrs. Domain around?"

"She's in her bed, but I'll go and warn her. I can't let you in though. Them Yankees is in and out of my kitchen, always lookin' for food all the time. You stay there and I'll go an' get her."

He waited impatiently by the back door. It was galling that he should be barred from entering his own house dammit, bought and paid for by… Then he remembered that he had actually won the house in a card game from Mrs. Domain's husband. She had stayed on as his housekeeper, as she had nowhere else to go when her husband shot himself. With that history between them, could he trust in her loyalty? He wondered what kind of reception he would have as an escaped spy when she was obviously playing landlady to a bunch of Yankees.

She arrived alarmed and flustered, wrapped in a shawl and with her hair in rags.

"Surely Gemima has told you how we are fixed, Mr. Duplege," she hissed.

"Thank you, Mrs. Domain, for your kind and gracious welcome," he answered sarcastically. "I trust you are charging these Yankees a fair rent, which I will no doubt collect in due course."

"You can count it as my wages for keeping your house intact," she snapped. "Anyways, the house has been requisitioned by the army and the men pay me for my services."

"Personal services, no doubt," said Clement with a snort.

"How dare you!" she said, her eyes narrowing. "Remember your position, sir. I have only to cry out and you will be sorry you ever said that."

"Madam, I apologise of course. It was only my little joke," said Clement, immediately backing down. "I have had a hard journey to be here, only to be prevented from entering my own house. You can imagine my chagrin to find it full of Yankees."

She looked him over.

"I could try to smuggle you up to my room, but it would be too dangerous. I suggest you go to Amelia Kay's house and wait there a while. She lives on her own nowadays. I'll come and talk to you as soon as I can."

"Bring me some clothes — if there are any left?" he asked, and she nodded.

"Yes, of course I will," she said, glancing at his much reduced figure, obviously doubting that his old suits would still fit him.

Clement was reluctant to leave his house but had no choice. He had once had a dalliance with Amelia Kay and was unsure of his welcome. But he slipped along behind the houses and gave Amelia as much of a surprise as he had Mrs. Domain. However, she drew him into her parlour and they spoke quietly about the happenings in the town and the arrival of the Union forces while waiting for his housekeeper to make her appearance.

Amelia was a practised gossip and soon filled him in on what had been happening in the town.

"Oh, Alice is quite taken with a major from Milwaukee," she giggled. "He calls most evenings. I can just see the house from my bedroom window."

Clement was impatient with her chatter and wasn't interested in his housekeeper's affairs, though it could make it awkward for him if she had Union sympathies. Surely she would not turn on him after all these years when he had offered her a home and a job after her husband's gambling folly? In his experience though, women could be unpredictable. He remembered Honora Darwen and her betrayal. When he was next in New York he would pay her a visit.

There was a discreet knock at the back door and Mrs Domain slipped into the house carrying a bag full of his clothes. She was brisk rather than hostile, but she soon informed him it would be impossible for him to come back to his old home.

"I'll have to go to the Amiens plantation then," he said. "I had hoped to have a base here, but I can see that that won't be safe for the present."

"I can tell you what little I know of your family," she said. "I had a letter from your nieces' old nurse, Hattie. I expect someone wrote it for her. She was asking if Clementina could come here to Baton Rouge. You know that your family went to Vicksburg?"

Clement nodded. A letter had found him at the home of an associate in Washington. His brother Henri and his wife and daughters had gone to Vicksburg, a high bluff on the Mississippi to be safe. The siege of the town had lasted many months but it had finally fallen to the Union army. Mrs Domain looked grave.

"I'm afraid, Mr. Duplege, that your brother and his wife are no longer with us. I do offer you my sincere sympathies."

Clement was shaken. "I had not heard," he said, swallowing hard. He had not expected such bad news and now it struck him with force. The pit of his stomach plummeted and he gripped the arm of his chair as his housekeeper continued, her eyes full of genuine sympathy.

"Hattie wrote me that your niece Delia had left before they reached Vicksburg. The family thought she had gone to find a man called Bartholomew who went over to the Union."

"The young fool," sighed Clement. "I guessed she might."

"Hattie went with the family to Vicksburg to look after them but Clementina is… She has had a very hard time what with the shelling and the starvation and watching her parents die. She is not quite…" His housekeeper paused as she struggled to find the right words. "I'm afraid, sir, that she has lost her mind."

Clement took a deep breath. "I see. What did you tell Hattie?"

"That it would be unwise for her to bring the girl to Baton Rouge. The house and town is full of men, soldiers, sailors. It would not be suitable for a girl with … problems. I advised her to take Clementina back to the plantation. She could be cared for there in peace."

"Yes, I expect that is the right advice," admitted Clement. "I shall of course go there myself, seeing as I am not welcome here." He gave his housekeeper a critical glance.

"It is not that you are unwelcome, sir, but that it is very dangerous for you to be here," said Alice Domain, raising her chin defiantly.

"Then I shall leave you to continue your dalliance with your major and go back to the Amiens plantation," said Clement, leaving her to blush.

She left, promising to write to him when things were more settled.

Clement left the town that night, unwilling to see his home abused by strangers and his enemy. He felt deeply sad about his brother Henri and his wife, remembering their carefree boyhood days on the plantation. He had hero-worshipped his older brother and always tried hard to keep up with him although Henri was older by several years. Though Clement had always roamed the country with his trade, he had always considered the Amiens estate his natural home. He was proud of it and had always been welcome there. Clement realised that, knowing his brother had no sons to inherit, he could now be the owner of the plantation. Unless of course there was a will leaving the property to Henri's daughters. He knew though that his brother was bound by tradition. Surely a male heir must inherit, and that man must be Clement.

Disguising himself as a preacher, Clement boarded a riverboat and sailed upstream. Despite his disguise, on the last evening before he disembarked, he sat down at a table to play cards. The man seated opposite him wearing a fancy yellow waistcoat had an air about him that Clement well recognised. He'd noticed it in the mirror each morning as he shaved. With his flair for observation he had also noticed a slight bulge in the man's waistcoat pocket. Adopting a look of bewildered innocence, he sat down and the man eyed the gold watch arrayed on Clement's sober dark waistcoat with satisfaction, sure that it would soon be in his possession. The other players were very helpful as Clement professed to be a complete beginner. As they dealt the first hand, he pretended to be confused but then cautiously grasped the play with their help. Then as they continued, he was guarded and lost the first hand with a modest stake. He made to leave the table but was persuaded to have another game by the man in the yellow waistcoat, obviously reluctant to let the gold watch escape. He offered him a drink of whisky, which Clement wisely refused.

"I do not touch strong liquor," he said with a mild smile. "In fact, I should not in conscience be playing these cards, but it helps to pass the time on such a tedious journey."

The wily spy won that game with affected protestations of beginner's luck. He won the next game for a greater stake, professing his amazement that one so unskilled should have such success. By the time he dragged his next pile of winnings towards him, his opponent was becoming suspicious.

"I think I'll retire to my bed now," said Clement, unwilling to take any more chances. "It has been a very busy and surprising day. But thank the Lord I shall now have enough to restore our meeting house."

The other players protested, hoping to regain some of their losses, but he was quite adamant and left to go to his cabin. He had reached the deck when a yellow waistcoat appeared from a doorway. "So tell me, *Mr. Preacher*, where did you learn to play cards like that?" he sneered.

"Why, you gentlemen were just so helpful to a pure beginner," said Clement innocently, suppressing a growing need to laugh.

"You don't fool me," growled the man. "You're an old hand at this game."

He was about to pull something from his waistcoat pocket, but Clement was ready for him. He grabbed the man's wrist and twisted it.

"And you should be ashamed of yourself, sir, trying to hoodwink a man of the cloth," said the spy and gambler with a hollow laugh. "You should know by now not to double-cross a double-crosser."

Wresting a miniature pistol from the man's waistcoat pocket, it hit the water with a splash.

"Goodnight sir," he said, releasing the man and pushing him against the handrail. "I warn you not to try anything further. Take your losses like a man. I have a gun in my possession and I am a very light sleeper."

Next morning as he left the boat at Natchez, the man was at the rail scowling at him. Clement gave a cheery wave and chuckled to himself as he went to find a stage coach.

After many days on the road he finally limped into sight of the plantation on a tired old horse. There had been few to choose from at the dealers, most of the good horseflesh having gone to the army, or even been eaten when times were hard and food short. The house was silent except for an odd crow flying in at the broken windows. The once proud and pristine mansion was as broken and destitute as the country, the garden overgrown, the paths broken. He heard some sound coming from the slave village so guessed there were some who had not deserted the Amiens estate altogether. As he approached the boarded front door a head bobbed up at a nearby window.

"Massa Clement! Massa Clement! I thought I heard a horse. Chile, it's your Uncle Clement. Come see. Come see your uncle Miss Clemmie."

As there seemed to be no response from within, the scrawny black woman hung out through the window.

"Front door's busted, Massa Clement. You can come through the garden door. Am I glad to see you," cried the woman.

Clement presumed that this was Hattie, though the Hattie he had known had been plump and looked much younger.

"Thank the Lord one of you has survived," she called, beckoning him with an enthusiasm he did not feel towards his home.

Clement stepped through broken glass to the back of the house. Hattie hurried to meet him and led the way into his home. It had been stripped of any comfort. Any glass that was left in the windows was cracked or jutting in broken shards from the frames. In the reception room the wallpaper hung in mouldering curls from the ceiling. A ruined piano squatted in the corner, denuded of most of its wood, its wires like the exposed ribs of a corpse. In the corner of the smaller breakfast room on a makeshift cushion sat his niece. She stared up at him, blank eyed.

"Hello Clementina," he said gently.

The girl opened her mouth but no noise emerged. Then she began to cry, whimpering like an animal.

"Been like this ever since her Mammy died," whispered Hattie. "Mrs. Duplege, she died 'cause there was no food. Massa Henri went first. He got a fever in them caves where they was sheltering away from the shellin'. They was in there together and the fever soon spread like wildfire. The fever sure weakened Mrs. Duplege."

"And you didn't get it?" asked Clement.

"They didn't want no black faces in them caves with white folks," said Hattie with a shrug, raising her eyes to heaven. "Looks like someone up there is lookin' after me."

"And you didn't starve?" he asked again.

"I ain't so particular about eatin' rats," said the former slave, giving him a knowing look. "I ate plenty before now and no doubt will again. They got mighty fat with all that was happening."

Clement felt queasy. He knew well what the rats might have been feeding upon.

"Once she got like this, Miss Clemmie didn't care what she was eatin' so I could feed her anything. I reckon that's how she survived."

"Thanks to you," he said wryly.

"I reckon so," Hattie told him. "I nursed those girls since they was babies. Ain't had no babies of my own. I wasn't going to abandon them if I could help it. Miss Delia though, she didn't get as far as Vicksburg. She met a man who knew the Bartholomew boy, swore he could get her to him. 'I's goin' to follow my heart, Aunt Hattie,' she says and off she goes. I ain't heard from her since. I just pray to the Lord she got there."

"So do I," said Clement with a deep and thoughtful sigh.

Hattie offered him some kind of stew mostly containing corn. He ate it gratefully and sank onto a spiky straw-filled mattress. Hattie and his niece seemed to be camping out in the breakfast room with any bits they could glean from the house. He was too tired to care about his surroundings. The jail had been little better. He fell into a deep sleep, knowing that at least he was home.

The next morning he rose and ate a porridge of corn, then set out to see what was left of the plantation. The few remaining slaves in the village stared at him with sullen defiance. Though Abraham Lincoln had declared them to be free, the war had not yet been won. Nobody knew their status in the South. In Clement's eyes they were still slaves, but all the same he wondered if he could persuade them to work for him. He had little money to pay them anyway. They had cultivated a thriving patch of corn and some greens for food. Clement stared at the decay and neglect around him and was overcome with despair. Like his niece, his home was a hollow shell. He had potentially inherited an estate, but it was not the once prosperous home that he had taken for granted. It was a wasteland and likely to be so for the foreseeable future.

He stayed for some days, prowling around the plantation, wondering how to begin the restoration. Though he had been brought up there, he had paid little attention to the growing cycle of the cotton. He had left the running of the estate to Henri and the overseers. They had long left to join the army and could well be dead on some battlefield. The priority of their former slaves was in growing food to feed themselves. He had no idea if there was cotton seed to be had or if the crop would seed itself or had fallen to all the various pests that would attack it. Now he recognised he was ill equipped to run a plantation. Making sure his niece was safe and secure with Hattie, he left them with some money and headed back towards civilisation where he could find news of the war. There was no way he could go back to Washington or his old home in Baton Rouge. With a growing and niggling idea in mind, Clement resolved to find one of his old comrades and see if there was any business he could perform for them in England. There was the rumour of a mysterious child in a Lancashire town that continually plagued his mind.

CHAPTER 8: A VISIT TO GORBYDALE

Landing in the Bahamas, Clement easily found a ship to Britain. On arriving in the bustling port of Liverpool he decided to take the train straight away to Gorbydale, the home of the little boy he suspected was his son. He avoided his old friends, the wealthy, shipbuilding Kearsleys who'd assisted him in arming the South. With the war looking increasingly desperate, and no doubt payments overdue, he was not sure of his welcome in their opulent home. He wanted to arrive late in Gorbydale so that he would not be recognised, especially by those he had swindled. Matthias Overdale had been glad to trade illegally with the Southern states to save his mill, but it was hardly Clement's fault that the British would not recognise the Confederate dollars the mill owner had been paid. All the same, he was cautious as he approached the darkening town on a hired hack from the station some miles away. Wondering where he might stay quietly and unnoticed so he could seek out the child the next day, he slipped into one of the few public houses that appeared to be open and enquired about rooms. The landlord looked him over suspiciously.

"You from America then?" he demanded, although Clement had tried to disguise his accent.

"Canada," he said pleasantly and easily found a lie. "I emigrated to look for work when the mills closed."

The man nodded. "Aye, I reckon a lot our lads left the same way. Let's hope there's enough folk to work the damn mills when they open up again. Are you back for good?"

"Just visiting family," answered Clement and smiled to himself. In a way it might be true.

"We've a room here we sometimes let out if you're interested," said the landlord, nodding over to his wife, who was taking a surreptitious interest in the conversation. "We had a bio… er … plant bloke in a couple of weeks back. He's off to India now and won't be back for a bit. It's not a large room."

"It will be fine," said Clement, unwilling to stay a moment longer than was necessary anyway. He followed the landlord up a grubby staircase to a room that was little bigger than the corner of his cell. It looked clean enough, though, so he dropped his bag on the bed to claim possession. "Is there anything to eat?" he asked.

"I'm sure my wife will have the odd meat pie somewhere," said his host.

Clement wondered what an odd meat pie might be. It turned out to be quite tasty, though short of meat, but it staved off his growing hunger, accompanied by a pint of beer. The pub was almost empty but he managed to fall into conversation with a couple of men on the next table, and they became quite chatty when he treated them both to a drink. His card playing on the voyage to Liverpool had provided him with a useful sum of money, and in their gratitude the men provided him with some useful information.

"I knew a gal — a girl locally. Worked at the Overdale house," he slipped into the conversation.

"That'll be Dolly Tate," said one with a laugh. "You don't want to get mixed up with her." He turned to his mate. "Remember when she tried to foist her little bastard onto Arden Davenport that time? I worked with him and he were a decent enough lad. His pal put it about it wasn't him. Said Arden swore he wasn't responsible."

"So she has a boy?" asked Clement.

"Her mam's bringing it up as her own," said the man. "But nobody is convinced."

This was good news to Clement. He had expected the boy to be in an orphanage somewhere and had planned to question Dolly as to his whereabouts.

"It's best not to say anything about it, though, in front of that father of Dolly's, unless you want your head kicked in."

That didn't sound like the ideal situation for his son to be living in. "So they're still living locally?" Clement asked nonchalantly as he gestured to the landlord to provide more drinks.

"Aye, down the old River Road as far as I can remember. My mate Tommy would know. He took an interest in Dolly himself, though he's had a lucky escape by all accounts."

Clement now had his information. Excusing himself that he'd had a long journey, he said goodnight to the men and rose to go to his room. A glance passed between his drinking companions as they looked at one another askance. He heard their murmured speculations as he ascended the rickety stairs. It would be seen as odd that someone all the way from Canada should inquire about Dolly Tate. But Clement didn't care what they thought about him. He planned to rise early next day, supposing the mentioned road would be near the river. He'd take a look at the boy and, if it looked likely that he was the father, he would try to persuade whoever was responsible that he should take the child back to America with him. Surely they would have no objection to removing an extra mouth to be fed.

"Cher fils," he murmured as he checked the time on his watch.

Next morning as the sun rose over the grimy houses of Gorbydale, Clement wandered down towards the river. What he found was a street of dilapidated back-to-back houses. The inhabitants were barely wakening, though those on the streets he'd passed through were busy about their morning routines. A small boy with a snotty nose was sitting on a doorstep. The lad's tears had left a pallid streak down his grubby face. Could this even be his son? Then he quickly calculated that the child was too old.

"Do you know where the Tates live?" he asked.

The boy eyed him suspiciously, taking in Clement's respectable clothes. "Give us a penny and I'll show yer," he said with a sniff.

Clement chuckled to himself at the boy's enterprise and delved into his pocket. "One penny," he said, tossing the coin into the boy's hand.

The child struggled to his feet and, beckoning to Clement, walked past a couple of houses. "That one there," he muttered, pointing to a house with a boarded window two more houses down. "Don't tell 'em it was me what showed you."

The boy watched from a distance as Clement tentatively knocked at the door. There was no answer. He knocked again louder. There was a loud string of curses as the door was flung open and a dirty grizzled man in a disintegrating vest stood glaring at him.

"What d'yer want?" he demanded. "Making all that bloody racket at this hour of the morning."

"Mr. Tate?" asked Clement, stepping back from the smell of sour beer.

"Who wants to know?"

"It's a private matter. May I step in? I was wondering if I could have a word with your daughter."

"Dolly?"

"Yes, Dolly."

Tommo Tate hesitated, staring hard at Clement.

"What do you want our Dolly for?" he demanded with a suspicious scowl.

"I've told you it's a private matter; a matter of some delicacy."

"She's not here anyway. She's up at the big 'ouse. You'd better come in," said Tommo finally, muttering 'bloody delicacy' under his breath.

The room smelt of sweat and old food. Even in the prison Clement had never seen such mess and dirt. The man bawled up a small flight of rickety stairs.

"There's a fella here wants a word with our Dolly. Sounds foreign. Hurry up and get down 'ere."

A skinny dishevelled woman of indeterminate age shuffled down the stairs, a ragged shawl clasped round a greying nightgown. Behind her crept a small child wearing nothing but a dirty vest, his legs pale and bare. He clasped the woman's clothes when they reached the bottom of the stairs and tried to hide behind her, peeping cautiously out at the stranger. Clement immediately noticed his red hair and fair skin. He was reminded of the portrait of himself as a child which had once hung proudly in the drawing room of the Amiens plantation house. The boy's eyes were a luminous blue, though, unlike his own eyes. They were the eyes of a woman he had once seduced in a mock temple on a hill overlooking the town.

"What's up? Is our Dolly all right?" asked the woman. "Is she all right?" she demanded urgently when she had no reply.

"This fella wants a word with her. Says it's delicate," said Tommo with a snort.

"What's she been up to?" said his wife anxiously.

"How the 'ell should I know? She's not here, as you can see. She's up at the 'ouse like I told you. You'll have to go there for her."

"I'd rather not, if you don't mind," Clement told him, unwilling to meet with the Overdales after he had once abandoned their son, besides trying to swindle them with worthless Confederate money. "Perhaps you could send for her."

"She has to work you know. She might not be able to get away."

Tommo was anxious that his daughter should keep her job, as she was the only one keeping the house running with her meagre wages and he did not want to lose his beer money.

"Perhaps I could write her a message?" tried their visitor, becoming exasperated. This was not going to be as easy as he'd planned.

"Aye — if she could read," Tommo said scornfully.

"There's a boy outside," said Clement. "Perhaps he could go and ask her to come."

Tommo glanced at his wife. She nodded vigorously, anxious to solve the mystery of this stranger in their presence. 'A delicate matter,' he'd said.

The boy from the doorstep was dispatched with the promise of sixpence and a message for Dolly. She must come home as soon as she could. There was a gentleman to see her. Canadian, he said.

CHAPTER 9: THE BARGAIN

Dolly stared in surprise at the grubby child at the door of the kitchen of Overdale House.

"All right," she whispered. "Tell 'em I'll be there as soon as I can."

Dolly thought fast. She was good at making up excuses.

"I'll have to go home," she told Cook, pulling off her apron. "I've just had a message from me dad."

"What about all the breakfasts?" demanded the cook. "Who's going to serve the master then? Did I hear that lad say 'Canadian'?"

"No, no," stammered Dolly. "He said 'can I er ... go home 'cos me mam's been taken bad.'"

"You'd better go then," said the cook with a sigh of exasperation. "Happen Mrs. Jessica can give me a hand."

Grabbing her shawl Dolly made her escape, wondering who this Canadian might be. Her father wouldn't have sent for her unless it was urgent.

Dolly hurried to River Road and met her scruffy young messenger just leaving her parents' door clutching his reward. She burst in and was confronted by a face that was somehow familiar. She stared hard at him and gradually came to a realisation. When she had last seen Clement Duplege he had had fierce auburn hair and abundant whiskers. Now it was darker brown and his face was bare of any facial hair.

"You!" she gasped, stepping back from his disturbing presence. "What the bloody 'ell are you doing here?"

"Not in front of the child, Dolly," said her mother primly.

"He's heard worse," snapped Dolly.

"Not from his mother he hasn't," scolded Maggie. "Anyway, who is this bloke? Do you know him?"

She and Tommo had tried to question the stranger but with little success. Instead of answering their enquiries, Clement had ignored them and been intent on coaxing the child from behind his mother-cum-grandmother.

"Well?" Dolly challenged Clement. "Are you going to tell her what you did, or shall I?"

"Is there anywhere we might speak privately?" he asked calmly and quietly.

"Does it look like it?" Dolly flashed her eyes round the room. "Anyway, what have you come for?"

"I heard about the boy. Honora Darwen kindly informed me."

"Oh, 'er. Interfering as ever," said Dolly with a grimace. "So what have you come here for?"

Tommo finally understood about the stranger. "So you're the bastard that…" he said, advancing with menace towards Clement.

Clement stepped back and Dolly placed herself between the two men.

"Get out of my way," snarled Tommo, about to push his daughter aside.

To Tommo's surprise, Clement coolly reached into his pocket and Tommo found himself staring down the barrel of a small gun. He edged backwards and had to content himself with growling menacingly.

"Can we talk about this sensibly?" said Clement. He hadn't wanted to act this way in front of the child but he'd had no choice. "I haven't come here to cause trouble. I just want to take care of the boy — if he's mine."

"Oh he's yours all right," scoffed Dolly. "Look at his flamin' hair."

"Then I'd like to take him back to America with me. He'll have a better life than this, I'm sure," said Clement, staring round at the poverty that surrounded the child.

"No!" cried Maggie, clasping the child to her.

"How much?" said Tommo.

Dolly stared at her father in disgust. Trust Tommo to want money. She looked with pity on her mother.

"We'll have to talk about it. I need to think about it."

"He's mine," whimpered Maggie. "He's registered as mine. I've brought him up from a babby. I'm the only mam he knows." She hugged Albert to her, her eyes filling with tears. The boy clung to her skirts in bewilderment. "How can you think of taking him away from me?"

The child's eyes filled with anxiety at all that was happening and seeing Maggie's tears.

"You must know, Mrs. Tate, that this is no life for Albert," said Clement gently. "He'll have a better life with me. I have a fine plantation."

He thought guiltily of the dilapidation he'd left behind in Louisiana and his niece who might be the true heir but was incapable of enjoying her inheritance.

"So who's going to compensate me for bringing up the lad?" tried Tommo. "Who's clothed him and fed him all these years, eh?"

"You'll get some compensation," snapped Clement.

"I think that'll be for me then. I'm the only one bringing money into the house," said Dolly with an odd gleam in her eye.

She looked at the man who'd forced himself upon her in her ignorance. He looked as if he had a bit of money. She glanced around the dirty room, at her father and his drink swollen nose and her mother worn down with life, her son pale and skinny. A vision of a different future came to her. Life could be different for her son. And if for her son, why not for her too? Her busy mind began scheming. Here was a chance to leave Gorbydale and drudgery and poverty and infamy.

"Look, for all you've got all this fine stuff, little Albert will still be a bastard. How will that go down in America? Can he inherit all that stuff if he's illegitimate?"

Clement's eyes narrowed. What was behind the girl's thinking? "I'm not sure," he said.

Her question had surprised him. She could not know that his right to the plantation was questionable, so it would be doubly so for his son. He'd thought his mission would be so simple, but he could see Dolly's mind working. He was suddenly faced with a scheming woman and he had not been prepared for that.

"If you married me, that would make it right," said Dolly, challenging him with an unwavering stare.

Clement looked astonished at her suggestion. He had been outwitted. Dolly assessed him with her shrewd gaze. She guessed he was thinking fast how he could do the deed and then somehow get rid of her on the other side of the Atlantic. It could be easily done. She knew that all he needed was a marriage certificate that would at least make Albert legitimate and safe. But Dolly had to take a chance or be forever a drudge in Gorbydale.

He hesitated. Tommo was glaring at him.

"Aye, you could at least make her an honest woman. That would save me having to kick your brains out."

Clement fingered his gun. He returned Dolly's shrewd gaze. In that glance, a bargain was made.

"Very well," he decided. "If you would do me the honour?" he added sarcastically.

Although she knew it was a business arrangement, Dolly's eyes lit up with prospects.

"We can get a special licence," she said, one step ahead of him yet again.

"Perhaps in Liverpool," suggested Clement.

Tommo immediately became suspicious. "I don't trust you. What if you abandoned our Dolly and took the lad to America without her?"

"You'll just have to trust me," said Clement.

"We'll do better than that," decided Tommo. "Me and the missus will come with you to Liverpool and, when t'deed's done, we'll see you all on the boat. How's that for trust?" he chuckled. "And better still, it'll all be done away from the nosy beggars around here."

Clement eyed him suspiciously.

Maggie was sobbing and clutching Albert. "You can't do it. You can't take him away from me. He's my baby."

"He'll be better off, Mam," said Dolly firmly. "We both will. You surely don't want him to be dragged up in this shit 'ole?"

"He'll be with people who love him," said Maggie vehemently, tears streaming down the ingrained wrinkles on her face.

Dolly lowered her eyes, acutely aware of the simmering resentment she'd felt against the boy. Now he was her key to escape the grinding poverty of Gorbydale and the monotony of her job.

"I'll love him. His dad will love him. He's his son after all. 'Course we'll love him. You won't live forever, and me dad and Seth won't love him, will they?"

Maggie glanced fearfully at Tommo. In her heart she knew her daughter was right. Tommo's temper was unpredictable. He might even kill the boy in a drunken rage. He'd always been jealous of the love and time she lavished on little Albert.

"All right then," she sobbed. She bent down to Albert, tenderly stroking his pale cheek. "You go with this nice man and be a good boy," she said and tried to wrench the boy from her nightdress. "Go with our Dolly."

Albert clung hard, his eyes wide like a cornered animal. Clement immediately became practical.

"Has the child got any clothes?" he asked, turning to Dolly. "Could you clean him up a bit?"

She hesitated. "I've got to get back to work. Me mam'll do it. When are we going to Liverpool, anyway? I'll have to tell them at the house that I'm leaving."

He grasped her arm. "Don't go back there. Tell them nothing. We'll go to Liverpool as soon as possible. I'll make all the arrangements and your mother can send a message to the Overdales when she comes back from Liverpool."

"But all my clothes are there!" wailed Dolly.

"We'll get you and the boy new clothes in Liverpool. Get Albert cleaned and dressed and we'll go."

Dolly's eyes lit up at the mention of new clothes. The house immediately became a flurry of bustle and arrangements. Clement headed back to the pub to collect his things and pay his bill. When he arrived back in River Road with a cab, he found the family looking surprisingly clean and, though shabby, relatively respectable. They piled aboard to head for the station and the train for Liverpool.

CHAPTER 10: A WEDDING

The cab pulled up at the Doveton railway station and Dolly and the family climbed out. They were all wearing their best clothes except Dolly, who appeared shabby in her working clothes. Clement caught young Albert from Maggie's arms and swung him down from the cab. For a moment he held him, his face softening. Maggie began crying again, knowing what was to come.

"Be quiet, woman. Don't say a word. Don't make a spectacle of yerself or I'll land you one," said Tommo gruffly.

To her annoyance, Dolly spotted her cousin Elsie strolling down to the station. She was clutching the hand of her small daughter, Eleanor, and carrying a baby wrapped closely in her shawl.

"Hello Dolly," she called. "Fancy seeing you here. I'm just taking our Jack his piece for dinnertime. I didn't have any time to make it this morning with these two."

"Oh, er … hello Elsie. How's things? Is that the baby? Are you all all right?" Dolly was babbling to prevent Elsie asking any awkward questions.

"We're fine," replied her cousin. "'Lo Auntie Maggie, Uncle Tommo and er…"

Dolly didn't wish to introduce Clement. To her relief, little Eleanor began tugging at her mother's shawl and, complaining loudly that her legs were tired, distracted Elsie.

"We'd better go," said Dolly, coaxing her family away. "We're going on a trip. We don't want to miss the train, do we? Take care of yourself."

Hampered by her child, Elsie could only watch and wonder as they hurried towards the station platform. Moments later a train whistle echoed over the valley and, before her cousin could reach the station, Dolly was on her way to Liverpool.

In the bustling city the relevant paperwork was obtained. Dolly immediately wanted to go and buy some new clothes, but Tommo insisted that the marriage was carried out first, much to his daughter's annoyance. The ceremony was brief and to the point and, when it came to signing the register, Clement discovered that his bride could neither read nor write. That might suit his purposes even better.

Tommo stuck like a limpet to his new son-in-law until he was sure everything was in order. He brusquely asked pertinent questions of the officials involved until he was certain his daughter was legally wed and would be on the ship to America and not back home to plague him.

Once all the necessary arrangements had been accomplished, they headed towards the shops. The shop assistants watched and wondered as Dolly spent a great deal of Clement's money on her trousseau, though she complained bitterly that she should have had a new dress to wear for her wedding. They added some basic clothes and a couple of outfits for Albert. Tommo would not let Clement leave until he had his hand on a clutch of bank notes given in recompense of his 'care of the child'.

"Don't spend that all at once," commanded Dolly.

"You mind yer own business," said her father with a smirk. "Anyway, yer Mam can go back to work cleaning now she doesn't have your brat on her hands."

Maggie could not stop weeping, moaning into a grimy handkerchief. She was so pitiful that even Dolly felt guilty about abandoning her mother and depriving her of the only comfort she had in the world.

The ship would not leave for few days, so Clement booked into the Adelphi hotel. To Dolly's annoyance, Tommo suggested they might stay too.

"Well sir, you now have enough money to pay for yourself," said Clement with a pleasant smile.

"I reckon we'll go home," said Tommo abruptly, to Dolly's relief.

The newly married pair with their son accompanied Dolly's parents to the station. Little Albert was a pale anxious shadow, although looking more respectable in a sailor suit. Despite Clement's attempts to make him interested in the steam train and all the things happening in the station, the boy's eyes grew wider in bewilderment and suspicion. As they stood on the platform to say their farewells, the child in Clement's arms stared at his weeping grandmother waving goodbye. His little face froze in fear when he realised what was happening.

"Mam! Mam! Mam!" he screamed, flinging his scrawny arms out in a heartrending plea. The other passengers watched the drama as Maggie collapsed against Tommo and was hauled onto the train. Dolly and Clement glanced warily at one other, strangers on a stranger journey.

Clement suggested they ate in their room at the hotel but, despite the poverty of her background, Dolly knew how to behave in company. She had watched the gentry at Overdale House long enough to be able to ape their table manners. However, she arranged for Albert to have something to eat in their room and tried to feed her grieving son. He ate little and finally sobbed himself to sleep. As Dolly managed to soothe Albert, Clement stared out of the window over the darkening city, wondering how he, with all his craft and guile, had fallen into this situation.

He glanced at Dolly. Of all the women he'd seduced, she would not have been his first choice for a wife but she was presentable enough in her newly bought outfits. He decided he could not easily rid himself of his bride until they had reached America. Once on the plantation, a stranger would not be missed. It would be quite easy to explain that his English wife had succumbed to the heat of Louisiana. For the time being Dolly seemed to be able to calm the boy and, as he had no experience whatever of small children, it suited his purpose.

Dolly was bubbling with excitement as they ate in the grand dining room. She felt wonderful in her new clothes and after a soothing bath. As their bedtime approached, she sobered up when she realised that this was her wedding night and that the bewildering fumble in the little white temple was the only experience she had of men. However, Clement was in no mood to satisfy her curiosity. After the meal, he accompanied her back to their room.

"I have noticed someone of my acquaintance in the dining room," he told her as he made to leave. "I'll just go down and take this opportunity to transact a little business."

Dolly stared through the window onto the wet streets of Liverpool. Clement had kept her and Albert quite secluded in a quiet part of the Adelphi dining room, but she'd thought she'd glimpsed Robert Overdale's friend Gus Kearsley with a group of men. Clement hadn't acknowledged Gus, though she knew they were acquainted. She certainly hadn't been introduced as his wife. She guessed Clement was ashamed of her and annoyed that he'd been tricked into marriage.

Dolly wondered if, despite her efforts, her future had improved. She was saddled with an uncaring and contemptuous husband. She was now responsible for a child and although Albert was her own flesh and blood, she hardly knew him. Nor did she have a clue how to care for him. Before her was a long journey by boat, and she had never travelled on the sea. Suddenly she felt fearful, faced with an unknown land full of strangers. Quietly she slipped into bed and lay awake listening to her son sobbing in his dreams. By the time she had drifted off to sleep, Clement had made no appearance or made any effort to consummate their marriage.

CHAPTER 11: MAGGIE

"Has that girl not returned yet?" demanded Matthias as Jessie placed a plate of meat pie in front of him.

"I'm afraid not, Father-in-law," she said quietly. "Perhaps we should send a messenger to ask if her mother is all right?"

"Messenger be damned," growled Matthias. "She should be sending messages to us herself, not having folk run round after a scullery maid. Who does she think she is — Duchess of Gorbydale?"

"Don't fret yourself dear," said Melissa soothingly. She was worried that Matthias' agitation might cause another stroke.

"We could enquire in the morning," suggested Jessie. "One of our sewing girls lives nearby. She might have heard something."

"Yes, that will be best." Her mother-in-law nodded gratefully. Jessie was always ready with a sensible solution.

"Is there any more of that pie?" demanded Matthias.

Jessie dutifully served him another helping. Melissa was tempted to remind him to say 'please', but thought better of it in his present mood.

The next morning, Melissa and Jessie were having their breakfast when there was a timid knock on the door.

"Maggie Tate is here to see you, ma'am," said the cook with a brief curtsey to Melissa and a brief nod to Jessie.

"Maggie Tate? I thought she was poorly?" said Melissa.

"Well, she's here now," said the cook, shaking her head.

"We'd better see what she wants then," decided Melissa.

A nervous Maggie was shown into the room. She bobbed a small curtsey, clutching her skirts tight with bony hands. She trembled, overwhelmed by her surroundings.

"Yes, what is it?" asked Melissa.

"Please, ma'am, I'm sorry, ma'am, but…" She hesitated, unsure how to drop her news.

"Yes, spit it out," commanded Melissa impatiently, anxious to finish her breakfast.

"It's our Dolly, ma'am. I'm sorry but she won't be coming back. She's er … gone to America with her new husband," stammered Maggie.

"Her husband!"

"Yes, ma'am. He's an American fella."

"American!"

"Is he named Clement something?" asked Jessie quietly.

"Yes, ma'am, Clement Duplege. Do you know him?"

"No, but I guessed as much."

Melissa was astonished. "Good grief. Clement Duplege and Dolly! I can't believe it. Matthias will be furious," she exclaimed.

"Well, this is a turn up for the books," said Jessie with a chuckle. "I must write and tell Honora the news."

"You mean that Clement Duplege has actually come to Gorbydale to marry your daughter?" said Melissa, quite bewildered.

"Yes, ma'am, and … and … he's took away little Albert as he was his son."

To their discomfort Maggie began to cry, big gulping sobs that she struggled to contain, wiping her nose and her eyes on her sleeve so pathetically that Jessie put a comforting arm around her shoulder and offered her a handkerchief.

"I expect you'll miss him," she said gently. "But it will be better for the boy. It'll be a new start for him. And he's with his natural mother and father."

Maggie nodded through her tears.

"I don't know what Matthias is going to say about this," said Melissa, ever mindful of her husband. "He'll be furious what with Dolly leaving us in the lurch and with that Clement Duplege for being so duplicitous. I do hope it doesn't bring on another attack. Perhaps we'd better wait until after his breakfast to tell him?" she appealed to Jessie.

Her daughter-in-law agreed. Matthias usually slept late while his mill was mothballed so hadn't been around to hear this curious news.

Maggie took a deep breath and composed herself. She obviously wanted to say something and was nervous as to how it would be received. "About our Dolly leaving, ma'am," she began tentatively. "I was wondering, ma'am, if you might need any help, ma'am, what with you being shorthanded like?"

She lowered her eyes as if expecting to be rebuffed. Melissa looked quizzically at Jessie, taken aback by the suggestion. Jessie looked surprised and shrugged.

"You could try her," she mouthed silently as Maggie stood with head bowed.

Melissa nodded. "Well, Mrs. Tate, all this is very bewildering. But as you say, we are shorthanded and my daughter-in-law cannot be expected to keep helping out. So we shall hire you for a trial period. I take it you won't be living in?"

Maggie's eyes lit up in delight and amazement. She looked as if she could have kissed Melissa's feet and would have immediately thrown herself on the carpet and done so. "No, ma'am. I've got a fella at home that wouldn't like it. But I'm an early riser, ma'am, and I'm a hard worker, ma'am. I promise you I won't let you down."

It was as well Melissa hadn't witnessed the dirt and confusion in the house on River Road.

"Very well," said her new employer. "But it is only for a trial period, you understand. You'd better go and see Cook, and she can tell you what you're expected to do."

"Yes, ma'am. Thank you, ma'am. God bless you, ma'am."

Maggie backed out of the room, bobbing curtseys all the way. Melissa and Jessie relaxed and looked at one another.

"Well! What do you make of all that?" asked Melissa eventually when she had digested what had just taken place. "And that scoundrel Duplege is involved too. Honora was right about him all along. She didn't trust him one bit. But Dolly Tate! I wonder what Matthias is going to say?"

Matthias, red-faced and furious, had plenty to say when he arrived down for his breakfast. "And you hired that … that … harlot's mother to work in our house. What were you thinking, woman?" he demanded.

"I felt very sorry for her," his wife defended herself. "She's just lost her daughter and what we were told was her little son too."

"It's no loss if you ask me," thundered Matthias. "If I'd have had a shotgun when I knew that scoundrel was in town, that slut would have been on her way to America on her own."

"Don't distress yourself, dear. You wanted her to leave anyway, didn't you?" Melissa poured her husband a soothing cup of tea.

"That's beside the point," he grumbled. "I'd have liked to kick her out myself. And as for that blackguard…" He muttered into his tea and spent the morning growling to himself.

Later, Melissa went down to speak to the stupefied cook. "Has Maggie Tate told you that she's to be on trial to see if she's suitable?" she asked.

"Yes, ma'am," said the cook. "She promised she'd work as hard as she could, and I told her she better had or she'd be out on her ear. Them Tates won't be very popular round here after what Dolly's done." She paused for a moment. "And I told her that she'd better keep that husband of hers well away from the house and all. And Seth too. I don't want him and Tommo Tate hanging round and nickin' stuff," she finished fiercely.

Melissa nodded. "Very sensible," she said. "You'll let me know how she gets on and if there is any trouble, won't you?"

The cook nodded.

When Maggie went home with her news, Tommo and Seth agreed that they wouldn't cause any trouble. Though Tommo was all for giving Matthias some grief when he found that Maggie would not be paid as much as his daughter had been. Matthias had made the excuse that the mother was not as young and strong as Dolly and so could not be expected to do as much work. But at least Maggie was fed and was given leftovers by the kindly cook to supplement her wages. All Maggie's wages went into the family's purse, unlike Dolly's, though every week she put a few pence aside in her secret jar. She was determined that one day she would visit Albert in America. She could not calculate that she would have to live well past her hundredth birthday to achieve her impossible dream.

As Maggie was more willing to work than her daughter, Melissa treated her with much kindness. She knew Jessie felt so much easier now she was rid of the thorn in her side that was Dolly.

CHAPTER 12: INCIDENT IN NEW YORK

Maggie's daughter, however, was not being treated as kindly. Clement had carelessly left a considerable amount of money on the hotel dressing table when he slunk into bed in the early hours of the morning. He noticed that Dolly was just about to examine it and hailed her in a voice gruff with whisky.

"Don't touch that," groaned Clement.

"Have you pinched it?" demanded Dolly.

"Pinched? Oh, you mean stolen?" said Clement, shielding his eyes from the light. "No, my dear. I simply relieved some fools of their money with a game of cards."

"Was one of them Gus Kearsley, Robert Overdale's mate?" she asked.

Clement gave a hollow chuckle. "The fool will never learn," he sneered. "He has more money than sense. Still, my winnings will enable us to purchase a bigger cabin on the ship."

Yet despite his winnings, Clement had been unable to secure a larger cabin with his hastily arranged booking to America. The cabin he'd managed to book aboard ship was small and stuffy. There were two cramped bunks and a smaller makeshift bed on top of a chest for Albert. This didn't seem to faze the child, and Dolly explained he'd always slept in the bottom drawer of a chest of drawers at Maggie's. However, despite the calmness of the sea, both Albert and Dolly suffered from seasickness at first.

Clement escaped to the deck whenever he could to avoid the fetid stench of the cabin. Gazing over the sea he wondered at his folly of bringing the woman and child on the journey. They were, after all, three strangers to each other. His original gratification at having a son was slowly dissolving. Albert was miserable. His continual sobbing punctuated the night, although he became quieter once Dolly had loudly berated him for disturbing her sleep. Nevertheless, his sobbing was as rhythmic as a heartbeat and inescapable in the confined space. Clement slept restlessly, disturbed by his fellow cabin mates resorting to the sick bowl. He recognised, however, that to bring his son home he needed Dolly to take care of him. This she did with a brusque efficiency which was very slowly softening towards the boy. Clement treated him with all the kindness he could muster, despite being irritated by Albert's constant whinging. It was not a happy journey.

During the day, though, they managed a semblance of normality in front of their fellow passengers. On deck Dolly's reluctant husband coaxed their son with a gentleness neither of them suspected. The journey continued in an uneasy routine. Gradually Dolly and Albert overcame their seasickness, except in the occasional rough sea, and Clement disappeared each evening to repair his fortune through gambling. Then one night he came hastily into the cabin long before his usual early morning return. Moments later there was loud banging and cursing behind the door followed by an argument with one of the ship's crew. Clement's gambling exploits came abruptly to an end. Even Dolly remarked that whenever the three of them walked upon deck to take advantage of the evening air, Clement continually glanced warily around him.

Clement's shifty behaviour continued once they had docked in New York. The hotel he chose was everything that Dolly desired. Leaving Dolly in their room with Albert, Clement warned her not to leave it and go out on her own. He lurked in the hotel lobby until he was sure that the receptionist was fully occupied with a fussy woman with a complaint. Then he slipped out into the city. He was on a malevolent mission with a score to settle. All he knew of Honora Darwen's whereabouts was that she was studying to be a doctor in New York. A cab driver took him to Bellevue Hospital Medical School where he politely enquired after Miss Darwen.

"We certainly do not train *women* here, sir," he was informed with utter distain by a pinch nosed man in a wing collar.

Clement thumped his fist on the counter and leant forward with a menacing glare. He was not going to tolerate condescension by a pasty-faced pen pusher. The man faltered.

"You might try the Geneva Medical College," he stammered. "They train young ladies there."

"Thank you, my man," said Clement sternly and swiftly left the building.

So determinedly set on his purpose, he realised he had become careless. At Bellevue he had got himself noticed and resolved to act more cautiously. With this in mind, he hovered for a long time round the medical school until he noticed two females accompanied by a young man approaching. They were too busy in an animated conversation to notice him. Both women had dark hair under their hats but one he knew instantly. The face of Honora Darwen was fixed in his memory as she feigned a look of surprise at his arrest at the Willard hotel in Washington. There was no doubt in his mind, though, that she'd betrayed him to the authorities. He remembered how very edgy she'd been and assumed it was because she was unused to the grandeur of her surroundings. The appearance of Alan Pinkerton and his cronies at her instigation had explained it all. Now many miles away from Washington he watched her movements, a spider weaving a subtle web. He cautiously followed her into the building at a distance. Tall and respectable, his hair close cropped and darkened and wearing a pair of spectacles, he was hardly noticeable among the doctors and lecturers moving about the building. He cautiously passed the room where the chattering students were hanging up their outdoor clothes, unaware of spying eyes. Then he left the building. He would await his moment to ensnare his victim.

"Where have you been?" demanded Dolly when he arrived back some hours later. "Little Albert has been starving. I have too. I asked that fella at the desk to get us something to eat. I got you nowt because I didn't know when you were coming back. Anyway, he says you can pay him later."

"I asked you not to leave the room," he said angrily.

"Your *son* was starving," growled Dolly. "Remember your son? He's not going to grow into a big strong lump if he's starving, is he?"

Albert sat wide-eyed on the bed, a smear of brown around his mouth. "Was starvin'," he murmured.

Clement's heart softened. He hauled the boy up into his arms with a smile. "Well, your Papa's going to get you something nice to eat. Can you wash his face or something?" he snapped at Dolly.

"Oh, come here," said Dolly, spitting on a handkerchief and rubbing the side of the boy's mouth.

It wasn't what Clement had expected, but he was becoming hungry by now and the brief cleaning would have to suffice. They went to a nearby restaurant and Dolly and Albert tucked into ice cream while Clement devoured a steak. Dolly spit on a napkin this time to mop the cream all round her son's mouth to the dismay of the waiter. Clement rolled his eyes. Dolly had a lot of manners to learn, but his son seemed contented enough with her ministrations.

They lived like this for some days as Clement disappeared each morning, telling Dolly he was 'out on business'. In the evening he disappeared 'to see old friends'.

"You wouldn't like them. They're very rough," he excused himself.

"You forget I've been brought up with the likes of my Dad and our Seth. I suppose you're off out gambling again," she added with a shrug.

Each day he staked out the Geneva Medical College and wandered its corridors. Then one morning he saw his chance. He noticed Honora alone in the cloakroom, her back to him. He recognised her dark hair in a chignon. He slid inside the room and quietly pushed the door closed behind him. She had taken off her coat and was about to hang it up when he slipped the garrotte round her throat. She let out a small squeak of pain as the choking piano wire squeezed the breath from her body. He pulled tighter, his anger fuelled by vengeance.

"Take that, you bitch," he hissed. "Nobody betrays me and gets away with it."

Her body fell limp against him and he let it slide to the floor. He looked down with a smirk of triumph. His satisfaction abruptly turned to horror as he saw the staring eyes in the lifeless face. It was not the face of Honora Darwen.

Clement was transfixed in disbelief. Then he came to his senses. Breathing hard, he quickly slipped the garrotte into his pocket and crept out of the cloakroom, closing the door firmly behind him. He walked as normally as he could out of the building, though his legs were trembling. He slipped his hands into his pockets to hide their shaking. How had he become so careless? Striding away from the scene of his foolish mistake, his eyes raked the side streets in search of an empty alley where he could dispose of his weapon. He must have walked miles before he could slip the garrotte down a grid unnoticed. Then he found a seat in a crowded bar for a much needed drink.

He had killed before, men that he thought deserved their fate. But he had never killed a woman, and a completely innocent woman at that. The look of the staring innocent blue eyes in the pale and pretty young face ground into his memory. Finally he roused himself and went to buy train tickets for Boston, wishing to leave the city as soon as possible. Somehow he would make his way home to the plantation with his son — and the wife that had been forced upon him.

CHAPTER 13: HONORA

The medical college was in an uproar. The body of Verity Cain had been discovered by another student who'd arrived late and raised the alarm. Honora stared down at the body of her friend, a mere lump under a blanket. She felt sick and weak. Verity had been her only real friend. The other women in training had decided that Honora was haughty, although it was her innate reserve and shyness that made her appear so. Ben stood beside her. They had both been summoned as Verity's closest friends and colleagues.

"Who would do such a thing?" she sobbed.

"Who indeed?" said Verity's father through gritted teeth. "We will find this … this evil murderer and he shall pay the price."

A detective knelt by the body and gently lifted a corner of the blanket. "Did your daughter have any enemies?" he asked, turning up towards Doctor Cain.

"Of course not," her father protested. "She is … was a lovely girl," he added, his voice breaking in anguish.

At the word 'enemies' Honora felt a sickening cold shiver through her body. How could her dear friend Verity make any enemies? Something stirred her thoughts. She had always thought that she had no enemies, but she remembered the urgency with which Detective Alan Pinkerton had insisted she leave Washington after she had betrayed Clement Duplege to the police. Surely Duplege was many miles away in jail? She tried to dismiss the thought from her mind but it lurked there like a malevolent shadow. A prison break in Washington was of no interest to the newspapers in New York and she could not know he was free.

"Perhaps it was someone who objected to the idea of women physicians," murmured the policeman, replacing the blanket. "There are such people, though I have yet to hear of one going to these wicked lengths."

He nodded to a couple of his officers who were waiting nearby with a stretcher and they swiftly removed the body to a waiting ambulance.

"I should like to speak to you both again," he said with a nod to Honora and Ben.

"We'll both do whatever we can to help," said Honora, and Ben readily agreed.

The detective stared hard at Ben for a second and then turned to Dr. Cain. "And I'm afraid I must speak to you and your wife, sir," he added with a formal bow.

They were all anxious to have the murderer apprehended and Verity avenged.

"I must go and tell my wife and family," said the doctor. "God alone knows how she will take it. I shall post a substantial reward to make sure this murderous villain is caught."

As Verity's father accompanied the policeman from the room Honora sagged against a partition, weak from grief. Ben put a comforting arm round her and she broke down and sobbed against his chest, comforted by the rough wool of his coat against her cheek. He was much shorter than Arden, but his shoulder felt comfortable and right. Over his shoulder she suddenly noticed the detective staring at her and Ben.

"No time for that," snapped Dr. Walgrave, coming into the cloakroom. "It is time to get back to work, despite this very unwelcome development."

He left the room sharply as Honora stepped quickly away from Ben, appalled by her weakness and her tutor's interpretation of it. Ben glanced down at her with kindly dark eyes.

"It is quite all right to grieve for your friend," he murmured gently.

"She was my only friend here," sobbed Honora.

"I hope I am your friend too," said Ben, his eyes searching her face in a way that surprised and troubled her.

She nodded, unable to speak, her feelings were so overwhelming.

Days later, she was surprised when Ben was summoned to the police station and questioned for hours about his whereabouts on the day of the murder. He looked drawn and weary when she met him at the station when she too was summoned to answer questions. Sitting in a stark room opposite the detective and another policeman, she was asked repeatedly if she was sure Ben had been studying with her on the morning of the murder.

"Yes, of course he was. All the other students can confirm it," she asserted.

"You know he's a Jew?" asked the policeman.

"Yes, of course," Honora said angrily. "What has that got to do with it? He's a very clever man and a good student."

"Clever enough to commit a murder and get away with it?" demanded her interrogator, leaning threateningly over the table.

"That's ridiculous," snapped Honora. "Why on earth would he want to murder Verity? She was his friend. She was a good friend to both of us."

"Yes, I notice he has a liking for Christian girls," said the man slyly. "Perhaps he had a grudge against Miss Cain because she rejected him."

Honora seethed with anger but was determined to keep calm. She had been used to dealing with pompous officials in the military hospitals in Washington, but she had hoped she had left such overt prejudice behind.

"That is a total nonsense," she said firmly. "Ben Clark is training to save lives, not to destroy them. He was sitting behind me in the lecture theatre and there are dozens of witnesses to that fact. You should go and check with them instead of making such ridiculous assumptions."

"So you have eyes in the back of your head, do you?" persisted the detective.

"I know he was there because I turned round to speak to him several times and also swapped notes. You would be better employed trying to find Verity's murderer than making totally false accusations against an innocent man."

The man leaned back in his chair. "Oh, you can be assured that we'll get our man, Miss Darwen," he said, his eyes narrowing.

Honora left the station feeling angry and upset. She made her way back to the Medical College, anxious to speak to someone. Who could possibly have killed her friend? Verity was such a kind and loving person. She surely had no enemies. The same niggling thought wormed its way once again into Honora's mind. Verity may have had no enemies, but she surely did.

It was some days later when she received a letter from her friend Jessie containing the astonishing news that Dolly Tate had run away to America with a surprising husband. Clement Duplege was free and on his way to that very country. It was growing dark, and for the first time in New York Honora felt afraid. Had her enemy already visited that city? Was he in the very streets around her? Had he mistaken Verity for Honora and carried out his revenge on the wrong person? Honora felt sick and guilty.

There was no one to speak to at the College and Honora walked home, anxiously glancing about her. She could not sleep that night, wondering if her theory could possibly be right. Would the detective dismiss it as fanciful or would they take her seriously? Next day she found Ben so anxious that he found it difficult to study, despite her assurances that she had confirmed his alibi. There were a couple of policemen asking questions of the other students. The students hung in groups, whispering.

"I couldn't remember if he was in the lecture theatre or not and so I told them," she heard one woman say as she passed. The woman went silent and looked embarrassed when she saw Honora glaring at her.

Finally she asked to speak to the detective and tentatively told him her theory.

"Clement Du... How do you spell that?" he asked, casually glancing up as he scribbled in a notebook. "And the detective Alan Pinkerton, you say? All this is a fiction, isn't it Miss Darwen? Is this to throw suspicion away from your beau?"

"Ben is not my beau," said Honora angrily. "My beau is an officer in the Union Navy and serving in the war as we speak. His name is Arden Davenport and I can show you his letters if you wish for proof."

The detective seemed annoyed when she insisted that he contact Alan Pinkerton. "Very well, if you insist," he said. "But this is all a bit farfetched. And of course it will take time. Perhaps we should arrest Ben Clark in the meantime to prevent him making a getaway."

"He has a firm alibi for the time of the murder," insisted Honora. "Several people walked with him to the lecture. I have spoken to them myself and they will verify the fact."

"Some of them were very doubtful if Ben Clark was present," he said. "We are still making enquiries."

"You should be concentrating on catching the real murderer. He might even strike again," she told him, her voice trembling with anger.

If her supposition was right, the next victim would be herself. She left the building in despair, with little hope that her theory would be investigated.

After a few anxious days when every dark corner seemed to hold some menace, Ben told her that he was no longer under suspicion.

"The police surgeon says they are looking for a taller man than I am. I know someone who works with him. He examined the angle of the cut from the garrotte on Verity's neck and…"

Honora shuddered.

"I'm sorry to tell you this, but it is very relevant to the case. It seems the murderer was about six foot," he added quietly. "It is fascinating what they can deduce from such small clues. I should like to work with the police surgeons for a while. I'm sure I would find it fascinating."

Honora, who had seen too many dead bodies in Washington, could not agree. She had no time or inclination to ponder on the manner of death of bodies destroyed by bullets, bombs or just plain old infection. She did want to help catch Verity's murderer though.

When she had summoned enough courage she decided to ask the police surgeon if she could see Verity's body, steeling herself not to cry. He agreed to her request but when he pulled back the sheet, she had to grip the mortuary slab to prevent herself slumping to the floor. This was no anonymous body but her friend, once pretty, lively and kind. Now Verity lay pale and cold as a marble statue. For a second Honora had a chilling vision of herself on the slab.

"Have you any clues who killed her?" she asked quietly.

"I suspect someone tall, over six foot at least," said the surgeon, pointing out the cruel line where the garrotte had bitten into Verity's pale flesh. "I found some black hairs on the back of her dress, so obviously a dark man. Maybe a Jew or a negro."

"May I see them?" asked Honora, trembling. She was anxious to confirm her suspicions.

He led her to a cluttered office and produced what little evidence he had. The hairs were trapped between two small glass slides. Honora stared at them, examining them minutely.

"They aren't curly, so it probably would not be a negro," she ventured. "And look…" She had spotted something that confirmed her dreaded suspicions. She pointed to the small colour change at one end of the hairs. "The hairs are a different colour at the root end — as if someone has dyed his hair to disguise it."

"I can't see it myself," said the surgeon with a shrug. "A man would surely not dye his hair. That's for you ladies," he added with a patronising smile. "Unless of course the murderer was a very tall woman. Perhaps a love rival?" he said, chuckling.

Honora was disgusted. Her blood chilled through her veins. He was not taking her seriously. But she knew a man who dyed his hair. She had witnessed it in Washington, where a disguised Clement Duplege had been working as a spy: a man who might look for vengeance for a betrayal. She decided to write to Alan Pinkerton herself with her suspicions. She could not be sure that the police would even bother to contact him. He had helped her once before as she had helped him. He would surely like to get his hands on Clement Duplege.

CHAPTER 14: AN UNEXPECTED ARRIVAL

"I feel the size of an elephant," said Jessie, hauling herself up from an armchair. She clutched her back and stretched to ease her bulk. The time for her confinement was some weeks away, but she was becoming increasing hot and uncomfortable.

"You certainly are very large, my love," said Robert with a fond smile. "This baby should be big and healthy."

"It'll be a sturdy boy," was what Matthias had decided on noticing Jessie's increasing girth.

"Or girl," she said faintly.

She was becoming anxious and feared complications. She didn't have her mother to advise her, though her mother Nellie's great friend Alice had reassured her that everything would be all right. Just then Alice was busy arranging her wedding to Jacob which was to take place a week or so after the municipal gardens were officially opened. Jessie really wanted to be present to support Robert's project at the gardens, but the plans were painstakingly slow with so many officials and groups wanting to take part.

"Why do they take so long to make any decisions?" Jessie asked in exasperation as her husband returned from yet another unproductive meeting of townsfolk. "If they don't set a date soon, I won't be able to come."

He put a comforting arm around her. "I shall insist they make a decision soon. I shall tell them our baby is eager to arrive but not before his mother has admired the sewing class banner unfurled," he teased her.

"At this rate our child shall have a full set of teeth before that happens," groaned Jessie. "And there's Father and Alice's wedding delayed because Father is on the Relief Committee."

The Committee had provided funds for the refurbishment of the gardens and Jacob was eager to represent them along with Melissa and Robert's Uncle Eli.

Jessie placed a protective hand on her swelling belly and sighed. Matthias was adamant that Doctor Braddock should be in attendance at the birth of his first grandchild, but Jessie was determined that Alice should be present too. She and Nellie had helped in many of their neighbours' home births. When Jessie herself had grown older, she too had been permitted to help. She'd been impressed by the quiet and efficient way in which the women worked. Doctor Braddock was not a sympathetic man. Jessie had been annoyed when Honora had told her how she'd been dismissed as a 'quack' and a nuisance when she had offered to help him in his work.

"I wish Honora were here," Jessie told Robert.

"I do too, my love," he said, stroking her lump. "I don't expect she'll come home until her studies are finished, though. Mother would put too much pressure on her to stay."

"I expect you're right," sighed Jessie, resigned to her fate.

Their baby was more eager to arrive than they expected. Jessie was about to haul herself into the carriage to drive with Melissa to the gardens when a cold rush of waters flowed down her leg. She immediately felt embarrassed.

"Oh Mother-in-law, I think I've wet myself," she murmured, close to tears.

Melissa stared at her. "Are you sure it's not your waters broken, Jessica dear?"

Jessie was confused. She had had an uncomfortable night as a ripple of pain had coursed through her. It had subsided and she had assumed it was a false labour pain as mentioned in one of the books she'd read. Now she recognised that it might be the start of her confinement.

"Perhaps I might have started," she admitted, as another trickle of water splashed onto her shoe.

There was immediate panic as they helped her back into the house. Robert had left early to help supervise the groups at the parade. Jessie tried to stay calm, despite the overwhelming contractions that shook her body at increasing intervals.

"I'll send for Robert," decided Melissa.

Jessie shook her head. "No. I'll be all right. He'll probably be home before the baby comes. This opening day is very important to him."

"If you're sure, dear?"

Melissa sent Maggie scurrying for the doctor. Jessie hauled herself to the kitchen and commandeered the cook.

"Send someone to get Alice at the end of Weavers Row," she said quietly and fiercely. "She might be at the parade, but find her. Say I need her here — urgently."

Cook nodded. "I've got you, ma'am. Don't worry. She'll be here in two shakes of a lamb's tale," she said with a wink.

Jessie hauled herself to her bedroom and lay down, exhausted. Melissa came and fussed around her, but she was too overwhelmed and fearful to care.

"Take the carriage to the gardens and go to the opening, please," insisted Jessie. "I'm sure to be here for some time. You can tell Robert not to worry."

"If you're sure?" said her mother-in-law, patting her hand. "I'll wait until the doctor comes."

Jessie nodded firmly.

Alice was soon beside her.

"What a time to arrive!" she said, chuckling. "Perhaps he wanted to see the parade."

"He nearly did!" said Jessie with a breathless laugh. "Or she. We'll find out soon enough. I'm so sorry you'll miss it."

The doctor arrived soon after. He gave Jessie a dismissive glance and, opening his black bag, began arranging a daunting array of instruments. Melissa took once glance at them and slipped away with vague excuses. She had had a hard time giving birth to her only son, Robert, and did not want to be reminded. Alice discreetly helped Jessie into her nightdress, while quietly murmuring encouraging words. It was some time before Jessie's labour began in earnest.

"Come along girl. You aren't the first woman to have a baby," said Dr. Braddock brusquely. "Give a good push."

"Breathe deeply," murmured Alice, "deep against the pain. Try to let your body relax. It'll be easier for you if you do. When I tell you to pant, just you do it."

Grasping her hand hard, Jessie nodded with a weak smile. She'd witnessed many births and helped deliver little Eleanor, her niece, so she knew the routine. But in the midst of her labour she could hardly think straight herself. She felt as if her whole body was about to burst.

"I can see the crown," said Alice. "Nearly there now. A couple of good pushes and... There, the head's out. Good girl. That's the worst bit over."

As the next great urge overwhelmed her, Jessie felt she could do nothing but push. With a burst of relief, she felt the rest of the little body slither into the world.

"Oh Jessie, it's a little girl," said Alice. "A lovely little girl. Well, not so little. She's a whopper."

Tears rolled down Jessie's cheeks. "Is she all right?" she whispered anxiously.

"She's fine. A healthy child," said the doctor, who had done little but examine his instruments. He picked up the baby and she roared into life. "She's a fine pair of lungs, anyway," he said. "We'll have a boy next time, eh?"

Jessie didn't care if the baby was a boy or a girl. Nor was she ready or eager to repeat the experience any time soon.

Alice took the child from him and, wrapping her in a small sheet, passed her to the new mother.

"She's going to be called Helen," said Jessie, touching the soft waxy cheek. "My brother John and Elsie already have an Eleanor, so it's the next nearest name to my mother's."

"Helen, that's lovely," said Alice. "Nellie would have been so proud."

"You did well there, girl," said Doctor Braddock. "I must say, I did have my doubts that all would be well given the size of you. I presume you will clean up," he told Alice.

"Certainly, doctor," said Alice, winking at Jessie.

Just as he was about to leave, Jessie gave a cry. "Oh Alice, Alice!"

"What is it pet?" asked her friend.

"I think… I don't know…" Jessie cried in panic.

"Just the afterbirth," the doctor dismissed her.

"No, no, something's not right," Jessie insisted as another burst of pain shook her.

Alice peered where the afterbirth might appear. "I'm sure I can see another crown," she gasped.

"Nonsense," said Doctor Braddock. "She can't be having twins. I have detected no twins."

"I think you'll find she is, though," insisted Alice. "Take a look for yourself."

A bloodied dome was slowly emerging, and Jessie cried out as yet another wave of powerful pain engulfed her. To their surprise and bewilderment, a small wrinkled body emerged onto the bed as Alice and the doctor stared at the second baby.

"Well I never. It hasn't survived, though, I'm afraid," the doctor said confidently. "It was a runt. It would have been a boy."

"I'm not sure. I don't…" began Alice. "I think I saw a little movement."

Jessie tried to sit up. "Give him to me," she insisted, bundling Helen into Alice's arms to put into the waiting crib.

Alice picked up the limp body. "If you're sure?" she asked.

"Give him to me," demanded Jessie again. She thrust out her arms urgently.

Alice handed her the tiny lifeless figure and grabbed a towel to wrap him in. Remembering one cold evening at a confinement at her mother's side, Jessie clutched the baby to herself. She wiped the baby's nose and mouth and held it to her own. Then with desperate determination, she breathed her life's breath into him. The small chest rose and fell. She blew again and yet again. The little body trembled and then, as everyone anxiously watched and willed, the chest slowly rose on its own. She turned the body over and patted and rubbed its back. A weak wail wracked the tiny frame. Matthew Overdale had arrived into the world.

There was a commotion outside the door.

"Jess, Jess, are you all right my love?" called Robert.

"I'm fine," she called back, crying and laughing at the same time. "We're all fine."

"Wait a moment, Master Robert," called Alice. "We'll have them sorted out in a moment. We've got a bit of a surprise for you." She stared at the doctor, who was glaring at the second child.

"It's not right," he muttered. "It might not survive. It would have been best if it was left to…"

"No, *he* wouldn't," growled Jessie fiercely. "He's my son and he should be given every chance."

"As you so wish," said Doctor Braddock. "But don't expect any miracles. I'll have a quiet word with your husband before I go."

Whatever the doctor said to Robert had alarmed him. The moment Alice called him into the bedroom he rushed over to his wife, demanding to know if she was all right.

"Of course I am," said Jessie, weakly smiling up at him. Her hair and face were damp with sweat and she was anxiously holding her child, but he kissed her fervently.

"This is our Matthew," she introduced her husband, revealing the tiny baby swaddled in her arms.

He glanced down at their son, but she could not read his face or know what the doctor had told him.

"And over there is Helen." She nodded towards the crib where their daughter lay. "We're going to have to get another crib too. This is all a bit of a surprise. No wonder I was the size of a house."

"Who would have suspected twins?" said Robert, staring in amazement.

"Well, certainly not Dr. Braddock," said Alice with a chuckle. "He was still denying it when it was obvious that your little boy was on his way." Alice gently took Helen from the crib and placed her in her father's arms.

"She's lovely," he said, laughing with relief. "Look, she hasn't got a wrinkle on her!" He showed Jessie their daughter and sat on the bed beside her. The difference between the two babies was obvious as they were held side by side: Helen plump and contented, Matthew wizened and struggling for every breath.

"We can call him Matty to avoid confusion," said Jessie.

Robert just nodded in agreement. She assumed that the doctor had voiced his opinion on the chances of their son's survival. She could not help wondering what lay in store for them all. With fierce maternal determination, she was going to ensure that her son would have every chance.

"I'll leave you two alone with your little family and go and organise a wet nurse," said Alice, practical as ever.

"I want to feed them myself," said Jessie anxiously.

"We'll see," said Alice wisely. "You've got two there, don't forget."

Despite Jessie's best intentions, Alice's warnings proved right. Helen would need much more milk than the faltering Matty, and a wet nurse was quickly found for her. Jessie struggled to feed her son for, though she had enough milk, he was very poor at suckling. Somehow he survived, though his head rolled on his shoulders.

Over the next few days, a succession of visitors came to see the new arrivals. Jessie watched as people cooed and congratulated her on Helen and mumbled embarrassed words of sympathy over Matty. Only her father was positive.

"My first grandson," said Jacob, cradling the tiny boy. "Come on little chap, you'll have to buck up if you want to grow as big and strong as your uncle Eddie here."

"What's up with him?" asked Eddie tactlessly.

Jessie fell silent and bit her lip, annoyed at the criticism of her son, but reluctant to scold her brother.

Jacob squeezed her arm in support. "Poor lad's had a bit of rough time when he was born, that's all. But don't you worry, he'll catch up," he told his son. "You were only a tiddler when you were born. Your mother and I put you by the fire in a shoe box. She was worried sick that you wouldn't survive." Then he changed the subject and talked about the opening of the municipal gardens. "Eli was the hero of the day for all the work he'd done," he told his daughter. "You should have heard the cheer everyone gave him. The brass band was a bit poor, like. Most of the lads had had to pawn their instruments to get by, so they haven't had much practice. But Eli paid their pledges to get them out. The tuba player has emigrated to Canada, and two of the trumpeters have left the town to find work. Old Jerry the drum player died in the workhouse last winter, and the lad who stepped in had all the rhythm of a broken clock, but they managed a bit of 'For He's a Jolly Good Fellow' and 'God Save the Queen'. A troupe of Morris dancers from Bacup arrived, and a couple of our own clog dancers did a performance. So it wasn't a bad do. It's a shame your mamma missed it when you decided to come early," he added to Matty, who was lying comfortably in his arms.

Matty never quite 'caught up'. While Helen thrived and delighted her father and grandparents, he fought merely to keep alive. A hasty christening was arranged. Few people thought the little boy would survive long. Robert had already asked Gus to be a godfather before the children arrived. Now there were two babies, and it presented a problem. Should Gus be godfather to the robust Helen or Robert's first but ailing son?

"He'd better be godfather to the one that'll survive," said Matthias bluntly. Jessie glared at him but he was oblivious to her disapproval.

"I could ask my brother John and my friend Mary to be godparents to Matty," she suggested to Robert.

He nodded in agreement, acutely aware of his wife's anger at his father's insensitivity. "That would be good. What about a godmother for Helen?"

With a shortage of female relatives Matthias suggested the vicar's wife, insisting his granddaughter should have someone of quality for a godmother. Even Melissa objected to that.

"She hardly speaks to me after our disagreement at the Relief Committee."

The vicar's wife had been especially ungenerous when handing out meal tickets to the poor laid-off millworkers, and she and Melissa had disagreed. Finally it was decided that they would ask Uncle Eli to stand for Helen and she should have two godfathers.

The christening was a quiet affair due to Matty's frailty. Helen roared lustily as the cold water trickled onto her head.

"They say that's the devil leaving her," said Melissa with an indulgent smile.

Matty whimpered but quietly went back to sleep.

The christening had taken place in the Gorbydale parish church, though Jacob was disappointed. "I can understand that you're now expected to fit in with your in-laws and worship at the Anglican church," Jacob told Jessie when they had a moment alone at the following celebration at Overdale House. "But don't forget us folks at the chapel."

"You know I wouldn't, Father," she said, hugging his arm. "I was raised in the chapel after all."

"I know lass, and I know where your heart lies."

Their conversation faded as Robert joined them.

"I think it's all gone very well," he said, smiling. "Our guests seem well satisfied despite the hurried arrangements."

"I wish Honora were here," murmured Jessie.

"Perhaps next time," said Robert, putting a comforting arm around her.

She gazed thoughtfully into his eyes. Although he'd been anxious at the time of her confinement, he didn't have a clue how hard giving birth to the twins had been. So many women died in childbirth or soon afterwards. Now he'd forgotten his fears completely. She hadn't, though. Her heart had almost broken to see the lifeless body of her tiny son on the bed. Hopefully it would be some time before she would face bringing another child into the world. They must see how they could cope with Matty first. Each snuffle and wheeze filled her with anxiety. Sometimes in the quiet stretches of a sleepless night she would lean over his cradle just to make sure he was breathing.

Matthias muttered under his breathe, words like imbecile and cripple that infuriated Jessie. She was left in no doubt that he thought the child should have been left to die. Ignoring her father-in-law, Jessie looked into her son's eyes and knew deep down there was an intelligence and a will to live. Despite his opinions, to appease his son, Matthias consulted Doctor Braddock, who promptly recommended a specialist. The man who arrived at Overdale House was little help.

"He'll never walk," he pronounced. "It's unlikely he'll develop any speech. I have seen these situations many times before. If I were you, I would find some sanatorium for him."

"He'll be living with us," said Jessie firmly. "Where else would he have better care than with his family?"

Robert backed Jessie, to his father's annoyance. He helped Matty whenever he could, but his wife knew deep down that he, too, had his doubts about the little boy.

As the children grew, Helen rolled on the floor and crawled and chuckled. Matty gave his lopsided smile and laboured to move his ungainly little limbs, but Jessie could see that he took notice whenever she spoke to him. Melissa gently hinted that she should spend more time with her daughter but Jessie knew that Helen, with her sunny disposition, would thrive in the world. She was forever charming the family. Though she loved Helen as everyone did, Jessie saved her special care for her struggling son.

Alice and Jacob's wedding was a quiet affair. Contrary to tradition, Mary gave her mother away and was also her bridesmaid. John was his father's best man.

There was all the hospitality that was necessary but also a quiet dignity about the occasion that suited the widow and widower. The wedding breakfast was held at Alice's house, and then the couple were going to live at Jessie's old home so as not to disrupt Eddie's life.

"You don't mind, do you love?" Jacob asked Jessie when he'd called to tell her the arrangements.

She shook her head and smiled. "And I don't think Mother would either. I know you'll both be happy wherever you live."

"If you'd like anything of your mother's things…?"

Jessie was about to say 'no' when she remembered her mother's red glass rose bowl. Her father was delighted that she should take it with her. It held so many memories of Nellie.

Mary was to live at the boarding house that she and her mother ran as a home for other girls from the mill. After the wedding, she linked Jessie's arm. "So we're sisters now," she said with a smile. "And I'm the eldest, so you'd better behave yourself."

"Only by three months," laughed Jessie. "So why don't you come up and see me more often at home? I do keep asking, but you haven't come yet."

"And bump into old Matthias? I see enough of him at t'mill, moaning and groaning all the time. But I promise I will call and see the children more often. I thought you might bring them today."

"They're too young really, and Helen has a good pair of lungs. I didn't want them spoiling Father's wedding," admitted Jessie. "Melissa couldn't cope with them on her own, though. We've got a young girl in to help us."

"Anyway, I'll see you at your Dad's," said Mary. "I've still not decided what I should call him. Mr. Davenport seems a bit formal, and I can't call him Jacob. It doesn't seem right."

"How about Daddy Davenport?" suggested Jessie with a giggle.

"You horrible girl!" Mary playfully punched her arm. "I think I should ask him all the same."

"What are you two girls up to?" asked Robert.

"Just sisters squabbling," said Jessie, laughing.

"Then of course you must be my sister-in-law," he told Mary with a gracious bow. "Welcome to the family. I never really liked being an only child."

Jessie could have hugged him. He had come a long way from the callow youth who had stolen a kiss from her for a bet at the Wakes Week Fair. He was sporting a newly grown moustache which he said made other businessmen take him more seriously, and his waistcoats had become more sober. His figure had certainly filled out since their marriage. She hoped with all her heart that he would not become as corpulent and grumpy as his father. Jessie put her mother's rosy bowl in pride of place in her bedroom. She often glanced at it whenever she had a difficult day with Matty, or Helen was fractious and headstrong. Memories of her old home when her mother was alive gave her a subtle strength.

CHAPTER 15: THE PLANTATION

The image in Dolly's head of a thriving plantation and elegant living slowly disintegrated as they approached the Amiens house. Even from a distance it looked derelict, the drive dusty and overgrown, the fences broken. All Clement's boasting had been hollow, and she knew she had been deceived. Her heart sank as they drove nearer, her dreams crumbling to the dust whirling round the cartwheels.

After their long and arduous journey, Dolly felt weary and defeated. There had been no decent seats on the long train journey carrying them towards New Orleans. It had been full of battle-grimed soldiers, disillusioned and bloody, returning to their homes. Many had been wounded and were groaning in pain as the train jolted onwards. After hours and miles of sitting on hard wooden seats they were all stiff, and the packed carriages had been hot and uncomfortable. Albert with his fair skin and red hair was fractious in the heat and Clement dismissive when she complained.

"What do you expect of a war torn country?" he'd growl as he turned away from the dereliction surrounding him.

At Jackson Clement gathered Dolly and his son together and they alighted to catch a riverboat towards Baton Rouge. He asked for news of the war at every opportunity, but what news he could glean was not favourable to the South. He heard of defeat after defeat and his mood plummeted.

Their last miles in a bumpy cart over rough roads had left her aching and bruised. Dolly had been longing to reach her new home. Now her heart sank. As a girl brought up in a bustling town, Dolly suddenly began to feel isolated. They had passed through the nearest thing to a town, which was Picardy Creek. That consisted of two ramshackle rows of buildings and was a couple of miles away along a dusty road from the plantation.

Aunt Hattie rushed out and greeted them with relief. "Thank the Lord you folks have arrived safely. I told Miss Clemmie when we received your letter and she is mighty pleased to hear her folks are coming home."

Clement scrutinised his niece with a doubtful eye. The broken, whimpering girl he had witnessed on his last visit had seemed incapable of being pleased.

"And this must be the new Missis," said Hattie, with a small bob to Dolly.

Dolly stared in bewilderment. No one had ever shown her any deferment before.

Clement took a deep breath. "Yes, this is indeed your new mistress. And here is my son, Albert." He glanced round for the boy, but the timid child had once again made himself invisible. Clement turned to Dolly. "Mrs. Duplege, this is my niece Clementine's nurse and companion, Hattie."

"Pleased to meet you, I'm sure," murmured Dolly with a tentative smile. She made a small bob in return.

"You don't bow to the servants," hissed Clement.

Hattie ignored him. She held her hand out to Dolly with a smile. "You come along of me," she said kindly. "You must be worn out with all that travelling. We'll find you something nice to eat, and this little angel too," she said with a big smile as she spotted Albert, peeping from behind his mother's skirts. "Why, look at all that golden hair! He's as bright as a sunbeam. Just like Massa Clement when he was a boy. Come to me, chile. Come and say hello to your Aunt Hattie."

Coaxed out by her kindness, Albert readily clutched at her hand.

"I'll be damned if that woman is an aunt to my son," Dolly heard Clement mutter through gritted teeth.

She'd had enough of his condescension and foul mood. "Why not?" she called back over her shoulder. "Kezia Amiens is by all accounts."

Jessie had informed Dolly that the freed slave who had accompanied her home from Washington was indeed Clement's half-sister.

Aunt Hattie's eyes opened wide in surprise. Everyone on the plantation knew that Clement's father had taken a shine to the house slave who was Kezia's mother, but no one had dared say aloud that the Kezia was half-sister to the Duplege brothers. She glanced at the young woman beside her, her nose pertly defiant in the air and holding Hattie's hand in a firm grip. It looked like things were going to change on the plantation, that was for sure.

Dolly was dismayed when she was introduced to Clementine. She had expected an elegant southern belle and had in fact been somewhat apprehensive to meet her. She had not expected this blank-eyed girl, whimpering on a pile of cushions, gazing out at nothing, seeing only some tormenting image in her head. Hattie had done the best she could for Clemmie. She looked washed and had on a clean though shabby dress. Her hair had been combed and tied back with a bright yellow ribbon. Dolly turned to Clement.

"You never told me that your niece wasn't right in the head," she accused him.

"Is all this something to boast about?" he snapped, turning away. "You were determined to come here anyway."

It was true. She had been so anxious to escape Gorbydale, that she had never considered the consequences. Dolly had listened to and remembered Clement's boastings over the

Overdale dining table and built a picture of wealth and plenty. She was faced with a son she hardly knew, a husband who did not care for her, a wreck of a home and now a witless girl. There was only Aunt Hattie between her and total despair.

"I did it for Albert," she said defiantly. "I did it for *your* son." It wasn't quite true, but it did no harm to remind him how he'd blighted her life.

There was a rustle from behind her skirts. Albert appeared and tottered up to Clemmie. He gently touched the ribbon in her hair.

"Nice," he said. He smiled up at his mother. "Nice."

Clemmie's eyes turned to the child and watched him curiously as he settled down on the cushions beside her, curled up and promptly went to sleep.

"Bless my soul," said Hattie. "What do you think of that now?"

"Nowt as queer as folk," said Dolly with a chuckle. "Did you say there was something to eat? I'm starving. I could eat a horse."

"Might just be mule," said Hattie with a shrug.

Dolly smiled and wondered if she was joking. She was so hungry she didn't bother to ask.

In the days that followed, the odd family fell into a routine. Despite all expectations, once Dolly was rested she proved a hard worker. She had habitually felt resentful and half-hearted when working for others. Now, as she was working for her own benefit, she set to with new heart. Her efforts to make the house habitable took on a renewed vigour. Hattie had made a makeshift bedroom for Clement and Dolly in one of the old reception rooms. They were sleeping on the floor on rough mattresses sewn from curtains stuffed with cotton wool, but even that was more comfortable than some of the beds they'd recently slept in.

Dolly waited and wondered, but Clement kept a firm distance between them. She knew she'd tricked him into marriage but had hoped to develop some sort of intimacy between them. However, he treated her no differently from Hattie and that was with an exasperated distain. Finally he found a smaller room nearby and just about habitable. He dragged his makeshift mattress there with the excuse that he would sleep better uninterrupted by Albert's sobbing.

Dolly, unimpressed by his previous unwelcome efforts at lovemaking, decided to ignore him and did what she could to improve the house, sweeping up the shards of glass so Albert would not cut himself and washing and drying the clothes and bedding with Hattie. She badgered Clement to have glass put in the windows but he continually reminded her that the country was at war. Dolly had to make do with makeshift screens that she and Hattie patched together with muslin from bits of old underskirts they'd found. Clement called a slave from the village to tack them up round the windows with broken shutters. It gave them more privacy and kept out some flying insects, though there was no one to see them anyway.

Dolly watched Clement as he tried to engage Albert, but the little boy stared silently up at him in awe. The child had had nothing but unhappy dealings with men. He burnt easily in the sun when his father took him round the plantation, despite the broad straw hat Clement made him wear. After days of prowling round the estate, Clement told her he was leaving for Baton Rouge. Dolly guessed he wanted to escape her continual harassment and demands. He mentioned business, but she suspected he was planning to gamble and gain some funds to improve their lot.

Meanwhile, Albert and Clemmie's natural bond had mutual benefits. Clemmie, intrigued by the little chap, slowly came out of her whimpering stupor. She began to have simple conversations with him. Happy in her calm company, he started to chatter away and the unlikely friendship grew to the advantage of them both. Albert began speaking in a Southern accent.

With Clement gone, Dolly decided to visit the slave village.

"You sure you want to go?" asked Hattie.

"Of course I do." Dolly was determined.

She had seen no one except Hattie and Clemmie since she arrived and had no desire to live like a hermit. Holding Albert's hand firmly, she and Hattie made their way through the overgrown paths.

"Why, just look at that!" said Hattie, glancing over her shoulder. "Miss Clemmie ain't put a foot through that door since she arrived."

Behind them trailed the fragile girl. She stopped and her eyes widened with fear. Then little Albert scampered up to her and caught her hand.

"Come on," he coaxed and led her up to where Dolly and Hattie were waiting. Then he urged them on with a nod. "Come on," he said again.

"A born leader!" said Hattie, laughing. "A born leader!"

Dolly was laughing too. It was the first time in weeks. "That child surprises me. I don't know where he gets it from." She watched her little son moving determinedly forward through the long grass, dragging Clemmie with him. His body was slender but wiry under his broad straw hat. "A born survivor, more likely," she thought.

The folks in the old slave village watched them warily. The war had still not officially ended, and though Abraham Lincoln had declared them free, they were still living in the Confederacy and weren't sure if they were legally so.

"This here's the new mistress at the house," Hattie introduced Dolly.

They had of course heard all about Dolly's arrival from Hattie, who came down to the village each day looking for food. They did not know though of Dolly's lowly origins.

"Missis Duplege," they said, bowing and curtsying.

"Hello," said Dolly naturally and bobbed to them in acknowledgement.

Clement might not think she had the correct manners, but she'd found that a little mutual appreciation went a long way. They found her the best chair they could muster and she sat and surveyed the village. The houses were primitive and huddled together, but the place was lively in stark contrast to the sterile dilapidation of the grand house. An old woman approached her slowly.

"Pardon me for asking, ma'am, but do you have any news of my Kezia? She is my sister's girl, you know, and I heard tell she went to England."

Dolly looked into the anxious dark eyes. She had met Kezia Amiens, the escaped slave from the plantation, when she stayed at Overdale House and knew her history. Kezia had been instrumental in saving Robert's life after he was wounded and stranded in Louisiana, and in gratitude Melissa wanted her to live with them. She had been invited to talk to the folk in the chapel at Gorbydale, telling them about life on the plantation. She'd spoken of the casual cruelties, the families wrenched apart through the slave trade. The people of Gorbydale had given her a great welcome. But feeling strange in a strange land Kezia had told Jessie, her friend, that she wanted to leave England.

"She's come back to America," said Dolly. "Someone told me she was teaching children in Washington. She came and told everyone at our chapel about how you lived here on the plantation. We had a collection for her to buy books for the children."

With the news that Dolly seemed to be on the side of the slaves, they visibly relaxed.

"God bless you, ma'am, for that welcome news," said the old woman, smiling contentedly. "I heard she lost her man in the war, but praise the Lord she's come home and is being useful to our people."

Dolly didn't feel she was worthy of being blessed. She'd been tempted to take a coin out of the collection in the pretence of putting one in, but she too had been affected by Kezia's harrowing tale simply told. It all seemed such a long time ago, yet it had been barely a couple of years.

It suddenly struck Dolly how astonishing it was that she should be here in that same slave village. The plantation had been abandoned throughout the war, the owners and overseers gone to hide or fight. The land was lying derelict, the people idle. Yet Lancashire was crying out for cotton and here was land that could produce it. A wild plan hatched in Dolly's busy brain.

She addressed the oldest man. "You know all about cotton, don't you?"

"Sure do, ma'am. I's been growing it all my life since I was the size of your little boy."

They glanced over to where Albert was playing with pebbles with a boy about his own age. They were engrossed in their game, watched by Clemmie.

"What's your name?" asked Dolly, touched by the sight of her son, playing in the dirt like any normal child.

"It's Barnabas, ma'am, same as in the bible. Folks call me Barney."

"So do you think we could grow cotton again here, Barney?" asked Dolly.

"I don't see why not, ma'am," said the old man, nodding thoughtfully. "Soil's laid fallow for some seasons. Cotton growing wild from the seeds," he added, pointing to the weedy plants round the edges of the parched field. "But it's hard work and not many of us left. The gin's all rusted up."

"Gin?" asked Dolly. The only gin she'd heard of was the potent spirit known in Lancashire as 'mother's ruin'.

"Cotton gin's the name of a machine that gets the seed and husks out of the cotton," he explained.

He led her over to examine it in a large hut. The solid mass of machinery looked as if it had seized up and would never work again.

"Could we get it going?" she asked.

"I don't know. My son Abraham was the one who nursed it like a baby," said the old man with a sad smile. "He died in the war, you know."

"He was married to Kezia," said Dolly in realisation.

The old man nodded. "That's right. He died a free man, fightin' for freedom," he said, his eyes misting over.

"I'm right sorry. But Barney, so what can we do now?" Dolly insisted.

"We still have an old hand-cranked machine. I'm mighty sure we could get that working again. It's hard work, though, like I was sayin'."

They examined an old wooden box affair with a handle at the side.

"I suppose we could take turns until we got the bigger machine working again," said Dolly thoughtfully.

The folk around her stared in disbelief when she said 'we'. It was ludicrous to think that a white man would do such work, let alone a white woman and the mistress of the house. Seeing the astonishment on their faces, she wondered if she was sane suggesting all these things herself. It would be easier just to go back to the mansion and potter round trying to fix it up. But Dolly Duplege, née Tate suddenly had a mission. She wanted to make a better life for herself and her son. This plantation had become wealthy on cotton. She was determined she could recreate its past glory and make it pay again.

"So what do we need to grow cotton?" she asked. "We could start in a small way."

"Seeds, ma'am. That's the first thing. All God's plants need seeds to grow."

"So where do we get these seeds?"

Barney looked thoughtful. "We have seeds here. Cotton loves to grow. But I don't know how good it is. It's been a long time since we planted any. We been growing food to feed ourselves with the family gone. And some soldiers came and took what we got anyway. Mr. Nathan Jacques knows. He's been planting cotton all through the war. He'll have good seeds. You could go and ask him — if he'll let you have any, though, is another matter. He and Master Henri didn't see eye to eye about slaves and all."

Clement's older brother Henri had been the master of the Amiens plantation. As he'd died in the siege of Vicksburg, Clement was now in control.

"I can only ask this Nathan Jacques and he can only say no," said Dolly with determination. "But he just might say 'yes'."

Next day she and Barney set out, Dolly sitting astride an old mule, wearing a very fetching white cotton cap against the sun.

Barney was leading her but began to flag as the sun grew hotter on the dusty road. She slipped off the mule.

"Come on, you get up for a bit," she said.

"I can't do that, ma'am," he protested in alarm.

"Well, you're no good to me if you pass out in all this heat. Then we'll both be in a mess," said Dolly reasonably. "Go on, get up. I don't have to order you, do I? Anyway, me bum's getting numb," she added, rubbing the offending part vigorously to restore her circulation.

Barney hesitated and stared at this mad Englishwoman. In all honesty Dolly was surprised at herself. She'd been enjoying all this 'ma'am' calling and the feeling that she had come up in society. Now the journey over rough roads sitting on the jolting mule had stiffened her and she wanted to stretch her legs. Dolly was practical above all things. All her life had been lived eking out what she could from her meagre prospects. Now she had a goal and this old man was going to help her. He couldn't help her by fainting at the side of the road. Barney reluctantly climbed onto the mule and Dolly led him in the way he directed.

When they were nearing the Jacques' farm, he insisted he should dismount for appearances' sake and Dolly climbed aboard the mule and rode, like a ramshackle Queen of Sheba, up to the house. She wore her best dress, now covered in the dust of the road, but her cheeks were pink and bonny under the snowy cap. A tall austere-looking man rose up from a chair on the porch. Beside him a younger version followed. The Jacques, father and son, came to meet her, puzzled by her appearance. For a moment Dolly felt daunted. Then she took a deep breath and held her hand out to Barney, who helped her down from the mule. With her heart thumping she was relieved that she managed to slip down in some semblance of a ladylike manner.

"Good morning," she said pleasantly. "I am Mrs Dorothea Duplege and I have come on business." She didn't think 'Dolly' sounded business-like and used the name on her birth certificate.

"Mrs. Duplege, Barnabas." Nathan acknowledged them both with a nod and an amused smile and introduced himself and his son, David. "I hear by your accent that you have come from England," he said.

"Gorbydale, Lancashire," said Dolly with a proud smile. The reminder of her home gave her courage. She was determined that she and her son hadn't travelled all this way for nothing.

"I have a friend in Gorbydale," said David. "Are you acquainted with Mr. Robert Overdale?"

"Oh yes, I know him. His Dad owns the Invincible Mill." Dolly suppressed a smile. Of course she didn't say she'd worked for the Overdales. Nor was she was tempted to say, 'Yes, and I've picked his smelly socks off the floor!'

"He visited us here some time ago and we are to conduct business with him again soon," said Nathan. "It's a small world. Would you like to come into the house and take some refreshment, Mrs Duplege? It's mighty hot out here."

Dolly took his arm. It was good to be treated like a lady, and she enjoyed every minute of it. Some workers nearby hailed Barney, and he was about to go and join them when Dolly called out to him in alarm.

"Oh Barney, don't go. I need you to help me." She turned to Nathan. "He's advising me on cotton seed," she explained. "I haven't a clue to be honest."

Disarmed by her candid confession, Nathan called Barney to join them. "You couldn't ask for a better advisor if you ask my opinion," he said with a smile.

Dolly felt she was among friends.

After a glass of lemonade on the porch and a brief chat about the Overdales and Clemmie, they got down to business.

"Is your husband content for you to come here?" asked Nathan before they started.

"My husband is away from home at present," answered Dolly with a quick glance at Barney. "I thought as how I'd get the cotton crop started to surprise him. Barney said you might help me with seed and such."

"I'll bet he'll be surprised," muttered David.

"We're only planning to plant in a small way," said Barney. "We ain't got the labour, as you know."

"And are you going to be paid, or are you still considered as slaves?" David asked him to Dolly's consternation.

This was something she just hadn't considered. She looked flustered and turned to Barney for an answer.

"Don't know how we's fixed Massa David," he said with a shrug. "The Missis here asked me for help an' I gave it. Don't know how we's fixed."

"When we sell the cotton, we'll all be paid," decided Dolly. She'd been paid a pittance herself for her work at the Overdales, but she knew her family would have starved without it. Besides, the folk in the village had been feeding her from their supplies along with Albert and Clemmie, and she had no idea if Hattie was being paid.

"And how are you going to pay me for the seed?" Nathan asked.

She suddenly felt very inadequate and wondered why she'd started this mad scheme. But Dolly was used to wriggling out of awkward corners. She thought quickly. "I was thinking that perhaps you could give it me on tick, neighbourly like," she said with a winsome smile.

"Tick?" The Lancashire word for credit puzzled the Jacques.

"Yes," said Dolly, warming to her task. "If you gave me the seed and I'd give you a note to say I'll pay you when I sell the stuff. That's how tick works, doesn't it?"

Or didn't work, as her family rarely managed to pay their debts. If they were threatened with the bailiffs, Tommo usually made veiled threats in return. In the end most shopkeepers hadn't bothered pursuing the Tates. Consequently, new shopkeepers in town were warned and so Maggie was rarely given credit in any of the shops.

"Oh, I see. Like a loan?" said Nathan.

Dolly nodded vigorously. "That's right. Neighbourly like."

Nathan relaxed back in his chair and scrutinised his unusual visitor. He had bales of his last crop in his barn awaiting shipment to Britain. Though he knew of the difficulties of shipping in the time of war, now the time of conflict was coming to a close he had heard that some cargoes had been sent to Liverpool and fetched a high price from cotton wholesalers desperate for stock.

"So your husband doesn't know of your enterprise?" he persisted.

Dolly wasn't quite sure what 'enterprise' meant, but she was certainly sure Clement had no idea what she intended to do. "I'm sure he'll be glad that I'm trying to get the plantation working again," she said firmly. "I do hope you can help me."

To her surprise, Nathan laughed. "Why not? Neighbourly like. Clement Duplege is no farmer. But you seem eager enough to be one, little lady. I'll sell you some seed — good seed too."

Barney beamed. "Thank you, Massa Jacques. We gonna make sure you gets your money."

"Well, I'm sure glad she's got you to help her, Barney," said Dolly's benefactor. "David, will you and the boys get me a sack of seed? Mrs Duplege here can ride home on the cart. I'm sure you don't want to go back home on that ole mule, Mrs Duplege."

"Call me Dolly," she said with a big smile.

To his surprise, she spit on her hand and held it out to shake his. Tommo always did that after sealing a deal and she was sure it was the right thing to do. Taken aback by this odd behaviour, Nathan took her hand anyway and shook it firmly. Dolly Duplege was about to become a farmer.

It was back-breaking work hoeing the sun parched earth to scatter the seeds. Dolly worked with her sleeves rolled up, sweat dripping down her neck. Barney worked beside her. He'd been questioned hard by his neighbours. Dolly listened to their conversation, pretending to be oblivious to their complaints as she hoed.

"Are we back to slaving for the Massa, you ole fool?" they demanded. Since the plantation had been deserted, they'd worked growing food for themselves.

"Mrs Dolly says we're gonna get paid when the crop is sold," said Barney with a shrug. "Well, I believe her, anyways."

"What happens when ole Clement gets back though? He ain't gonna want to pay us. We slaves in his eyes, no matter what old Abe says."

"I don't know," Barney said, leaning on his hoe. "But if he finds us sittin' back while his wife toils in the field, he ain't goin' to be happy. He might even throw us off his land. He was once mighty handy with that lash."

Reluctantly they found their hoes and mattocks and joined Dolly. Albert came out with them, making a game of picking up stones. Some of the little black children joined him. Clemmie sat and watched and finally took a hoe too. Though her work was haphazard, she tried to imitate Dolly and made her small contribution. Hattie brought water to slake their thirst. One of the workers began to sing and the others joined in, a slow methodical song that echoed the rhythm of their work. Dolly's thoughts flew back to her home and the girls in the sewing class singing old songs as they worked. Here on this sunbaked field, a vast ocean away, very different workers turned to song to relieve the monotony of their work. Perhaps people the world over were not so different after all. Slowly the field was being cleared. When the sun was at its highest, Dolly decided they'd had enough.

"We can't work in this heat," she told them, stretching her stiffened back. "We'll come back out when it's a bit cooler."

By evening, a large patch of ground was ready to be sown the next day.

They began early in the morning, Barney instructing them how to plant in rows so the workers would have room to pick at the due time. He'd been talking with the Jacques and observing the methods of their well-run farm.

The days passed in hard graft, but weeks later Dolly was finally rewarded with the sight of the green shoots pushing through the soil. A timely shower of rain nurtured them on their way, and Dolly and the workers danced like idiots with the rain coursing down their faces. Albert stared in surprise and then began to dance too. Clemmie hesitated then joined in with a lumbering gait, holding Albert's hand. Anyone who had once witnessed her graceful waltz at an Amiens party would have been shocked. Aunt Hattie stood on the porch, her arms folded and shaking her head in smiling disbelief.

Some days later a familiar figure rode up to the house. David Jacques shyly offered to take a look at their cotton gin. "I have some small skill at repairing machines," he said modestly.

"Sure have, Massa David," said Barney. "Was you showed my Abraham a thing or two 'bout this here gin."

Dolly watched David's broad back as he bent over the rusty cotton gin. Clement had been away for days. When he was there he barely tolerated her. As the green shoots struggled through the dusty soil, something stirred deep inside her too.

"Would you like a drink of water?" she asked.

David smiled and nodded. "That would be fine," he said. "Thirsty work in this heat."

She was about to turn when she remembered. "Would you like some too, Barney?"

Barney gave a slow smile. "I surely would, Mrs Duplege."

It was almost as if he was reminding her of her status. She was a wife but no wife. She was a mother but had become one by a foolish mistake.

By late afternoon the machine was fixed. To her disappointment, David refused Dolly's invitation to come into the house.

"I'd best be getting home," he told her.

She watched him ride away and turned to the house with a sigh. That night she could not sleep. She had become used to the endless sound of the crickets but that night they seemed louder, more insistent. All through the morning she watched the horizon, hoping to see the figure of David coming their way again. A thrill of excitement ran through her when she spotted a figure riding down the road. To her disappointment, when the figure became clearer through the heat haze it was her husband on a tired old horse. It ambled into focus and a surly Clement dismounted. He stared at the burgeoning field and the small figure in the large straw hat.

"What's been going on here?" he demanded. "Why is my son associating with these slaves?"

Albert glanced up and automatically dodged behind his playmates, trying to become invisible. Dolly rose to her full height and puffed out her chest, proud of all she'd achieved. "I thought you would be pleased that we're trying to bring your plantation to life again. I'm doing it for Albert and for our future. Gamblin' ain't goin' to do that, is it?"

Clement's eyes darkened, angered at her defiance and the way she'd spoken in front of the workers. For a moment he looked as if he would raise his hand to her, but he hesitated. He'd noticed Joshua, a young field hand, had raised his mattock just a fraction but it was enough to show his intent. Then Clement noticed the faces of all the workers. They were all willing and ready to defend Dolly.

"I think you'd better come into the house," he said sternly, "and tell me what you have been doing in my absence." He wanted to add 'and without my permission', but Dolly seemed to have been doing very well without it.

Clement demanded a glass, though all Hattie could find was an earthenware mug. He refused it and swigged a shot of whiskey from a dusty bottle he pulled from his pocket. Then he demanded water.

"So where did you get the seed?" he asked. "I wasn't aware there was any on the plantation."

"From Mr. Nathan Jacques. I promised to pay him when we sell the crop," explained Dolly.

Clement snorted. "I see."

"David, his son, was kind enough to mend our cotton gin," she added.

"Making sure they got their money," said Clement cynically.

"I'd prefer to think that he was just being a good neighbour," Dolly defended David. "Anyway, when we sell the crop we'll all get paid."

Clement looked wary. "All?" he queried.

"Yes, the Jacques and us and I've promised the village folk they'll have a share too."

"They're slaves," shouted Clement. "They don't get no share."

"Well, then they won't work," said Dolly. "You can't shoot them all. Mr. Jacques says this war will soon be over. The South is losing. Surely you know that. And then they will be free … free and ready to work for whoever pays them."

A purple-faced Clement looked as if he was about to explode into violence now there was only Hattie as a witness. Dolly defiantly folded her arms.

"We could soon be ready to sell our own cotton. Lancashire is crying out for it. We could make a fortune. We can't do that if we've got no workers."

He could not dispute her logic. Since the fall of Vicksburg the South seemed to have collapsed. There were skirmishes around Washington, but the South was as exhausted as he was himself.

"Albert should not be playing with those people," he growled. "They are animals."

"That's as much as you know," said Dolly. "They've been decent with me, and how do you think we get fed? Besides, who else is Albert going to play with? He's not a bloody hermit. Barney knows more about cotton than the lot of us. I'd

115

have been lost without him. And everyone else has worked hard too. It's to all our benefit to sell this crop."

Clement stared at this wife he had only married for convenience to legitimise his son. In spite of his absence, he had just witnessed the green shoots as his plantation rose again from the neglect of the war. She was right, 'gamblin" wasn't going to achieve that. Who would have thought that after that fumble in the dark in a small temple above a Lancashire village his fortunes might revive? He'd been along the Mississippi attempting to gamble, but his luck had deserted him. He'd fumbled trying to perform his usual tricks and only just avoided a couple of fights.

"I'm tired," he said wearily. "I need some food and I need a sleep."

Hattie smiled and went to find some food. Knowing Clement of old, she must have been expecting some violence. Dolly caught a glimpse of a rusty carving knife in the folds of her skirt.

CHAPTER 16: THE NEW BRIDE

"I've just had a note from Taylor Walmsley," said Melissa, waving it at Jessie. "He's home from India and wants to come and introduce his wife!"

Jessie was astonished. "His wife?"

"Yes, I'm surprised myself. She's probably the daughter of one of the officers or perhaps an official out there. I'd better invite them for dinner," sighed Melissa. "Would you nip over to the mill and let Matthias know? He and Robert are having a look at the machinery. There's a rumour that some more cotton has arrived in Liverpool, but the price is extortionate. I don't know how we'll afford it. But they want to be sure we're ready when the cotton comes back." She paused, looking troubled. "You don't suppose I'll have to invite Taylor's mother too, do you?"

"Oh no," Jessie reassured her quickly. The acidic Mrs. Walmsley was never a welcome guest. "The bride should be guest of honour, and his mother would never stand for that."

"Quite right," said Melissa and went off happily to make her plans.

Jessie had been too absorbed with her babies to bother with the news from the cotton exchange. Helen was thriving and could sit unaided, but Matty was still lolling against cushions. She was constantly trying to encourage him, though Robert didn't have the patience.

A young girl from the town was helping Jessie with the children. Lizzie worked for bed and board and a very meagre wage. Despite her poor reward, life was much easier for her at Overdale House, and she was a very willing worker. She was one of seven children living in a cramped and noisy terrace and, as the eldest, had all the experience of looking after her younger siblings.

Jessie stared at Taylor Walmsley's note. He had once made her a tentative proposal of marriage, and she'd been tempted until fate stepped in. As a former overseer at the mill and now a partner, he was too fond of being in control. She wondered what this new wife might be like and pitied her.

"Amy Parkinson," she murmured as she read the name.

The dinner wouldn't be a grand affair in the circumstances with just the family present, but Melissa made sure that everything was proper and respectable, even if the courses were fewer and the portions smaller. The family waited in the parlour for Taylor and his new bride to arrive. Maggie, in a crisp white apron and her scatty hair hidden under a neat cap, announced the visitors with a bob.

"Mr. and Mrs. Walmsley, ma'am … er … sir," she added hastily, unsure who to address first.

Taylor and his new wife appeared in the doorway. Melissa hurried forward to greet the new arrival and then paused in surprise. Mrs. Amy Walmsley was most certainly Indian although wearing western dress.

"How lovely to meet you, Mrs. Walmsley," said their hostess, remembering her manners and taking the girl's hand. "Mr. Walmsley, welcome home. And this is my husband, Matthias."

Matthias studied the girl carefully. "Pleased to meet you," he said abruptly. "Walmsley, glad you're back safe. What's the news on the Indian cotton crop? Is it coming along?"

"Oh Matthias, you can save all your business talk until after we've eaten," Melissa chided him. "Come and meet my son and his wife, my dear."

Melissa led the girl over to Robert and Jessie. Amy looked overwhelmed, but Robert gave a welcoming smile and shook her hand. Jessie took both hands and kissed both her cheeks.

"Welcome to Gorbydale," she said. "I'm Jessie, by the way."

"Amisha," said the girl with a shy smile.

"But we've decided she'll be known as Amy, haven't we?" Taylor warned her sternly. "When in Rome…"

The girl nodded, her eyes lowered at the rebuke.

"Amy is *Anglo* Indian. Her father Randolf Parkinson is an official on the railways."

"Oh, he went native, did he?" said Matthias with a chuckle.

Taylor glared at him, and everyone else shuffled and cleared their throats with embarrassment.

"Let's get something to eat," said Melissa busily. "Come along Amy, you sit next to me as guest of honour. You don't mind me calling you Amy, do you?"

The girl shook her head and they proceeded to the table. After Matthias's blunder, Taylor was in a defensive mood and the meal was awkward despite Melissa and Jessie's attempt at small talk. Robert coaxed Amy to tell them about her country, asking her questions, despite Taylor's grim face.

"I believe it's a fascinating place," said Robert. "I should like to see that great wonder, the Taj Mahal. I should like to travel there one day."

"Let's hope you have a better time than you did in America," said Taylor sourly.

"I'm sure I should," said Robert pleasantly, ignoring the jibe. He began to tell Amy about his escapades in the American Civil War and how he ended up with a damaged leg. "I fear I must go back there soon," he said, to Jessie's surprise. "I hope to buy the cotton from the Jacques estate like before. My father and I were just talking about it at the mill this afternoon.

The few cargoes of cotton arriving at the Liverpool exchange are way beyond our means at present, and it's obvious the brokers are making a big profit."

Jessie's heart sank. This was the first she had heard of his plans to leave for America, and she would be left alone with the two children, one of whom was not thriving as he should. Lost in thought, her small talk all but dried up and it was a relief when Melissa suggested they leave the table and let the men speak of business.

"I'm sorry that you heard Robert's news like that," said Melissa, taking her arm and patting her hand. "Matthias mentioned it to me in passing, and I thought Robert might have mentioned it to you."

Jessie knew she had been so wrapped up in little Matty and his problems that Robert might have mentioned his plans and she hadn't really been listening.

"And you have two small children?" said Amy, looking sympathetic.

"You know we'll look after you all if Robert has to go to America," Melissa reassured Jessie.

It was a kind and reassuring offer, though Jessie knew her mother-in-law would spend her time fussing over Matthias. She was quite happy to leave the children to Lizzie and expected Jessie to do the same.

"I should love to see your babies," said Amy with a shy smile. "I have left four young sisters behind in India. I do miss them."

The women went up to the nursery. Helen was sleeping soundly, her plump cheeks pink in the candlelight.

"How pretty," said Amy.

Matty was restless and disturbed by the light of the candle. He held out his puny arms and Jessie gathered him from his cradle and carried him through to the nursery. Lizzie was dozing with some sewing on her lap. She slowly awoke and stared in surprise at the visitors, then tried to struggle to her feet, despite Jessie signalling that she should rest. It was obvious even to Amy that things were not quite right with Matty, but she talked to him and coaxed a lopsided smile.

"I have a cousin who has the same trouble as your son," she said gently. "The doctor said he was born too slowly."

"We didn't expect Matty at all," confessed Jessie. "His sister was born first and seems to have taken up all my energy while I was expecting them."

"Have you tried massaging his little limbs?" asked Amy. "In India it is customary to massage a child's arms and legs to make them strong."

"I've never heard of it," said Jessie. "But it makes sense. I'd be grateful if you would show me how."

"I will call and show you soon," promised Amy. "It can do no harm. He is very alert. Look how his eyes follow you."

Jessie hugged her son and felt fresh hope. So Amy too had noticed Matty's intelligence. Robert might be going away and leaving her to cope on her own, but she felt she had a kindred spirit in Amy. It had been obvious throughout the meal that Taylor had not altered his controlling ways, and she was relieved she'd refused his offer of marriage all those years ago. For a moment she wondered if she should call Amy 'Amisha' as she had been named but decided against it. Taylor would no doubt see it as interference and it could cause awkwardness. All the same, Jessie was reluctant to let him get away with his bullying. The girl had a right to her own name.

They settled Matty back in his cot and he slowly drifted to sleep. Then they went down into the drawing room, asking

Amy about her marriage and her family. She had lived in a railway house in the hills.

"My brother John is an engineer on the railways," Jessie told her. "He has two children."

"I miss my parents and young sisters very much," confessed Amisha. "Our house was always lively, and we lived near the railway track. It seems very quiet in Gorbydale. And people seem to stare at me so," she added quietly.

Jessie remembered how people had treated her friend Kezia at first. Gorbydale folk had been intrigued by the appearance of a black woman among them but accepted her with kindness once she had spoken in the chapel and told the congregation of the hard lives of slaves on the plantation. Jessie hoped Amy would eventually be accepted too. With her gentle manner she would cause no offence. But even Jessie had to admit there were some folk who thought themselves superior and would never accept anyone different. Matthias was chief among them.

"Once the mill is back in full production, the town will come alive," she assured Amy. "We'll all be glad of a bit of peace then, what with the hooters going and the millworkers marching along with their clogs on the cobbles. It can be a right racket."

It wasn't long before the men joined them.

"I think we should be going home," Taylor told his wife. "We have taken up these good people's time for too long."

Amy meekly joined him and Maggie was despatched for the coats and hats. They all stood awkwardly in the hall, Amy murmuring her thanks.

"By the way, my mother sends her regards," said Taylor, giving Melissa a withering glance.

"Thank her and tell her I shall hope to see her soon," said Melissa politely.

Turning her back to take Amy's coat from Maggie, she gave Jessie a grimace. Jessie had to bite her lip to prevent a smile.

"I hope to see you soon," she told Amy warmly. "It would be such a help if you could teach me to massage Matty. I'm sure it would help him."

"My wife will be kept very busy in her new home," said Taylor tersely. "My mother mentioned that you have a crippled child. I expect you have found a good doctor for him. No doubt there are places where he can be sent."

It was Robert who defended his son. "Matty will be staying home with us. There is no place better to nurture a child than in his own loving home," he said, glaring at Taylor as he paraphrased Jessie's own words.

The family closed the door on the Walmsleys with a sense of relief.

"Thank goodness that's over with," said Robert, pushing his hair back from his face. "That man gets more insufferable."

"His wife seems nice. She was very gentle," said Jessie, wondering if poor Amisha would wither under Taylor's control. "She was very taken with the children."

"Looks like the Indian cotton isn't coming on as well as we'd hoped," Matthias told his wife. "It'll take a long time before the crop is up to Sea Island standard. We'll enquire about this trip to America. They say the war's all but over. You can trust the Jacques, you say?"

"I would trust them with my life," said Robert, slipping his arm round Jessie's waist. "I'm sorry my love, but I think I will have to go to America after all."

She nodded. It was inevitable. Their whole livelihood depended on the mill.

CHAPTER 17: AN UNWELCOME GUEST

Jessie hadn't realised that with finances so tight at the mill, the journey would be so soon. The next day Eli came over from the Endurance Mill and the three men retreated to Matthias's office.

"Uncle Eli says he's sold Primrose cottage. It's been lying empty for a while and half the money should rightly be my mother's. It hasn't been sold for what it's worth, but it will be something towards financing the trip," Robert told her afterwards. "The papers say Robert E. Lee has surrendered, though there's still a bit of skirmishing around the country. It should be safe enough to go, my dear." He held her close. "Will you be all right?" he murmured into her hair.

Jessie took a deep breath. "Yes, of course," she reassured him with a determined smile. "Lizzie is a great help."

Next day she spent some time with the children in the nursery before Lizzie settled them down for a nap. Finding herself at leisure, she wondered if she should go into the sewing class where Mary was in charge. Lately she'd found the girls falling silent whenever she visited her old friends. She'd overheard two of the girls talking about her.

"She's talking all la-di-dah these days, now she married to the master's son," they'd said.

It was true she'd modified her accent since her journey to America with Honora searching for Robert on Melissa's insistence. Mainly it was because the Americans she'd met had trouble with her Lancashire accent, and it was vital that the patients in the military hospital where she'd worked were able to understand her. Even Mary teased her about her new found status. Somehow, Jessie felt isolated from her old friends. Though she was now welcomed by the Overdale family, she was well aware that Matthias in particular thought that Robert had married beneath him. With a sigh she decided to tackle some mending. With lack of money her clothes were becoming shabby and frayed.

She found Robert in their bedroom looking through his wardrobe for some of the lighter clothing he'd worn in America. That too was in a shabby state after his ordeal. One leg of his trousers bore a stubborn brown stain from the wound on his leg. He tried them on but the waistband would not meet.

"That's thanks to your good care of me," he told Jessie with a chuckle. "How could you ever take a fancy to such a skinny fellow?"

"I was wondering that myself," she teased him.

They were interrupted by a knock on the door, and Melissa cautiously entered at their summons to "Come in."

She looked in dismay at Robert's clothes. "Oh dear," she said. "I don't suppose they could be revived. We don't have much money for this trip."

"I suppose I could fit a piece into the back seam," said Jessie, examining the trousers again. "But this stain on the leg just won't budge. Perhaps we could dye the whole suit and hope it doesn't shrink."

"Might Augustus have some old clothes he doesn't want?" asked Melissa.

Robert frowned at the idea of scrounging off his wealthier friend.

"More likely grown out of," said Jessie, laughing. "Gus gets stouter every time I see him."

Robert gave her a withering glance and she curbed her joking. He was very loyal to Gus.

"Your father proposes to sell his gold watch," said his mother. "But that will barely pay for the fare."

"I needn't travel first class," protested Robert. "Second class was quite adequate for Jessie and me — and of course Kezia."

They had endured much whispered disapproval on the voyage from America for travelling with a black ex-slave. As Dolly had told her aunt, Kezia had since returned to teach the children of her old community in Washington.

"I'll be quite comfortable travelling in second class," Robert insisted.

Melissa reluctantly had to agree. Jessie offered to go to Manchester and find some clothes for her husband's journey in the second-hand shops, an offer which the family gratefully accepted.

"The lad and the wife might be recognised," said Matthias gruffly. "I don't want folk to think I've sunk so low as to be buying second-hand clothes."

Jessie ignored him. She had never needed to buy old clothes for herself, but she was willing to do anything to help Robert — even if folks would think she'd 'sunk so low'.

Plans came together quicker than Jessie had expected. Tearfully she was preparing to wave him goodbye on the day of his departure when Maggie timidly approached them.

"I was wondering, sir… I'd be ever so grateful, sir… It's just that you know our Dolly went to America an' she took little Albert with her. She's never wrote nor nothin'. I just want to know he's all right. I know you know that Clement bloke. I'd be ever so grateful sir…"

126

Robert patted her arm. "I'll see what I can do, Maggie," he said kindly. "Though I can't promise anything. America's a big place, you know."

"Thank you, sir," said Maggie and scurried back to the kitchen.

"It's daunting to think how big America is," Robert told his wife, "but you know that yourself. But the war is coming to a halt, and I'll be safe enough."

Jessie fervently hoped he was right as Robert kissed her and the sleeping babies and headed for Liverpool.

With Robert gone Jessie felt restless and anxious. Her husband had assured her that America was safe, but she couldn't help but be worried. She was distracted by some visitors.

"You did invite me to call," Mrs. Walmsley told Melissa as she made herself comfortable by the fire. "And Taylor's gone to Manchester in our gig. My daughter-in-law agreed to accompany me to Overdale House. There are so many rough types hanging about the streets these days, you can't be sure."

"Yes, it's nice to see you both," said her hostess with barely a flicker at the lie.

"I'll arrange tea," suggested Jessie and, with a quick smile at Amy, escaped to the kitchen. She arrived back carrying the tea things.

"I see you are having servant trouble too," sniffed Mrs. Walmsley. "I can't seem to keep these young girls nowadays. They don't want to work, that's the problem. I have to rely on young Mrs. Walmsley to make tea for me," she added with a nod at Amy.

Jessie wasn't surprised that the dreadful woman lost her maids-of-all-work and felt very sorry for Amy. She was glad she hadn't found herself in that position.

"Maggie was busy preparing supper with Cook," she said with a smile. "So I thought I'd help." She busied herself pouring the tea and offering it round. "Would you like to see the children?" she asked their guests once they had finished.

Mrs. Walmsley declined, pleading that there would be too many stairs up to the nursery. Amy eagerly joined Jessie.

The moment she spotted them Helen held out her chubby arms, anxious to be picked up, and Jessie duly obliged. Amy knelt by Matty and stroked his arms.

"He seems to have put on some weight since I saw him last," she said with a smile. "How are you my little chap?" she asked as she held his floppy body to her. Matty gave her his crooked smile. "See, he recognises me."

"Have you got time to show me how to massage him?" asked Jessie. "I really want to help him, but I don't know how. I'm so afraid I might hurt him."

"Babies are very tough," said Amy with a laugh. "Look, I will show you." She placed Matty carefully on a sofa and curled his two small hands round her index fingers. He had a weak grip but automatically held on, and she began to pull him up. He came a surprising long way up before he began to falter. "See, this will strengthen his muscles," she told Jessie.

Lizzie came to watch too as Amy showed them how to massage the little limbs.

"It will benefit Helen too," she told them.

The girls were chatting and laughing as they practised their massage techniques on the babies when an imperious call echoed from downstairs and brought a halt to their activities.

"I think it is time we should be going," called Mrs. Walmsley.

"I'd better go," said Amy with a grimace.

"Please come back when you can," begged Jessie. "I'm so grateful for your help. I feel we've done Matty some good even in this short time."

Amy promised she would come when she could get away.

"Thank goodness that's all over," sighed Melissa as they waved off their visitors. "That woman! She was complaining to me about her new daughter-in-law. It sounds as though she has the girl working like a skivvy and then has the cheek to complain that she doesn't do things the right way."

"Poor Amisha," said Jessie. "Though I suppose I must call her Amy to keep the peace. But I like her. She was so gentle with Matty. She's promised to teach me to massage him some more."

"That's if Taylor Walmsley gives his permission," said Melissa with a snort. "I feel so sorry for that poor girl." She paused and gave Jessie a curious look. "Was he sweet on you at one time?"

Jessie blushed but didn't tell her mother-in-law that she'd almost married Taylor. "What makes you say that?" she asked cautiously.

"It's just the way he keeps looking at you whenever he refers to his wife. It was almost as if he was informing you he'd got a better deal. Can't say I agree with him," she said with a chuckle and a reassuring arm along Jessie's shoulder. "We get along all right, don't we dear?"

Jessie nodded happily. "We certainly do."

Despite her father-in-law being an old curmudgeon and Melissa's agitation around any infirmity, Jessie felt very fortunate that circumstances had prevented her from marrying someone as controlling as Taylor Walmsley.

CHAPTER 18: DOLLY HAS VISITORS

As Robert journeyed towards the plantation to buy the Jacques' cotton crop, Dolly's cotton was flourishing too. With Barney by her side, she felt confident that she could sell it. The news from the outside was sparse. David had called with the rumour that Robert E. Lee had surrendered. Despite Dolly's insistence that he take a drink, he declined politely, clearly feeling unwelcome with Clement at home. Clement, lounging on the porch in the heat, barely acknowledged David but rudely scrutinised the visitor from under his hat.

Later that day there was another unwelcome visitor to the plantation. A scrawny man in a tattered army uniform appeared, riding a mule. He dismounted and sneered at the workers. "I see you've been slacking since I've been gone," he called as he dismounted.

"Clucas," hissed Barney under his breath. "God curse him. He must be back from the army."

Dolly had heard the name mentioned before and it was always with pure hatred. She knew the man had been the overseer at the plantation before the war. His reputation was of cruelty beyond measure.

"Hey you there, yella gal," shouted Clucas. "You come here. I ain't seen you here before."

Dolly rose to her full height and glared at him. "I beg your pardon!" she said in her best Melissa tones. "What is your business here, man?"

"Who the hell do you think you are, missy?" demanded their visitor.

"I," Dolly declared loudly and paused for effect, "am Mrs. Clement Duplege."

The man looked shocked and visibly shrunk. "I'm sorry, ma'am. I din't realise, ma'am," he stuttered and grovelled as the workers secretly smiled to one another. "I came to see Mr. Clement. Need my old job back."

"You will find my husband up at the house." Dolly dismissed him and abruptly turned her back to continue surveying her crop with Barney. Then she thought better of ignoring him altogether. "I'd better go and see he doesn't get his job back. I don't want him here upsetting my workers. I've heard he's a horrible man by all accounts."

"Too right, as the scars on my back testify," said Barney, shuddering with memory.

She'd felt very threatened by the way Clucas had eyed her as if she were a piece of meat. She shuddered to think what he had done to the women of the plantation. Hurrying towards the house, she was just in time to see Clement come out onto the porch with their visitor.

"I take it you've met my lovely wife," said Clement with a sneer. He had been drinking and steadied himself against a post, trying to look casual. "Mrs. Duplege likes to work out in the fields like a common hand, as you can see. She's raising my boy like a piccaninny. Things have changed around here, Mr. Clucas, and not for the better. But I have no money at all to pay you. Seems these people are working 'cos they like it. You'd best find somewhere else where your talents will be more appreciated."

Clucas glared at Dolly. "Them English always did have weird ideas, Mr. Clement. Beggin' your pardon, ma'am. I guess I'll look elsewhere for my work. Things ain't easy nowadays for a man been fightin' for his country."

"I'm right sorry, Mr. Clucas," said Clement. "I lost most of my family too. Spent time in jail besides. Miss Clemmie's back here, but she ain't right in the head after all the things she's witnessed at Vicksburg. Look, here she is now, and here's my boy too."

Albert and Clemmie were curious to see who had arrived. Albert took one look at their visitor and hid behind his friend. Clemmie too looked anxious. Who knew what she had witnessed when Clucas had a whip in his hand? The man looked stunned at the change in her.

"Guess little Missy has been through a lot by the looks of her," he said. "Shame, though. She was a right pretty little thing as I remember."

Dolly scowled at the sneering way Clucas talked of Clemmie. Even Clement looked displeased.

"Don't like him," said Albert, watching Clucas ride away, kicking his mule in fury. "Don't like him. Bad man. Nasty man."

The workers in the field watched him go with relief.

"Praise the Lord," said Barney fervently to his friends as the overseer disappeared down the dusty track. "And God bless Mrs. Dolly."

CHAPTER 19: THE COTTON DEALER

Days later their next visitor was more welcome, at least to Dolly.

The workers froze when they saw a figure emerging from the heat haze, anxious that Clucas might have returned. But as Robert came into focus they relaxed, and Barney came to see what his business was.

"I'm mighty glad to see you, Mr. Robert. Glad to see you survived too. Didn't like the look of your leg when you was last here," he told Robert.

"Well, I'm back and I've been staying over at the Jacques' house, buying their cotton. I've come to see Mrs. Duplege. The Jacques told me she and her son are living here. Albert's grandmother was worried about him."

"The little boy is fine," said Barney with a grin. "The Master and Missis is up at the house."

With a newly practised eye, Robert glanced over the field. "You've cotton?" he asked.

"Got half a barn load of it ready to sell, ginned and bailed," said Barney with a grin. "Best see the Missis about that."

"Dolly?" asked Robert in surprise.

"That's right. Mrs Dolly has seen the plantation reborn. It's a pukin' baby just at present, but you jus' wait and see what she'll do next."

Robert chuckled at the idea. This didn't sound like the truculent servant girl he'd known at home in Gorbydale. Now he was intrigued. "I'd better go and talk to her then," he said and turned his horse towards the house.

Dolly was out of the house like a flash, her face wide with surprise. "Master Robert! What the hell are you doing here?" she demanded, a broad smile lighting her face at the sight of someone from her old home. Then her face fell. "Is my Mam all right?"

"She's fine. Honestly, Maggie's fine. She was anxious to know if little Albert was all right, and I promised I'd come and find out for her. I've been over at the Jacques plantation doing business, buying their cotton. You should have written to her, you know."

"Can't write, can I?" she said with a shrug and a glance towards the house. "And I didn't want to ask that drunken lump to write a letter for me."

Robert glanced up as Clement slouched out onto the balcony and propped himself against his usual pillar.

"Well, well, well! If it isn't the son and heir risen from the deep," he drawled. "You caused me a lot of trouble, boy. That damned sister of yours informed on me to the Yankees. They kindly entertained me in one of their damned jails thanks to her."

"Honora is my cousin," said Robert stiffly.

"Cousin, sister, damned sneaky whore, it's all the same to me," snarled Clement.

Robert bridled at the slur on his cousin but said nothing, anxious to avoid an argument.

"Anyway, what do you want?"

"I came to see your son. His grandmother was worried about him," began Robert. "But I see you've cotton to sell."

"Nothing to do with me." Clement threw up his hands in despair. "Ask that bitch there."

Dolly sighed as her husband lurched back into the house.

"Are you all right?" asked Robert. "He seems a bit…"

"If I could handle Tommo, I can handle him," said Dolly with a shrug. "Somewhere deep down he's still a gentleman. He's been a miserable sod since Robert E. Lee signed the surrender, though. He knows the South are sunk — but there's something else eating at him, like a little maggot in his brain. Anyway, do you want a drink? Then we can talk business."

"I haven't much money," started Robert.

"I haven't much cotton," said Dolly, laughing. "How's my Mam? By the way, did you bring the wages I was owed?"

Everyone had been surprised when she'd left in such a hurry, and no one had given her wages a thought. Robert stared at her in confusion for a moment but relaxed when she began to laugh at him and punched his arm.

"Got you there then! Anyway, if you remember the wages, you can give the money to my Mam."

Robert promised he would and she knew she could trust him. Still laughing, she led him into the house.

Clemmie and Albert shyly appeared. Robert looked taken aback by Clemmie's appearance for a moment and then graciously bowed to her.

"Miss Clementine," he said. "I'm very pleased meet to you once again."

She looked bewildered for a moment and then began to cry. Some deep memory stirred in her traumatised brain and she gave a little curtsy. Dolly smiled with gratitude, and even Clement nodded in approval at Robert's courtesy to the much altered girl. Then Robert automatically knelt down to the little boy.

"Hello Albert. Your grandmamma asked me to come and say hello to you."

The little boy looked bewildered.

"He means Mam," explained Dolly.

Robert nodded. "Of course."

Albert beamed. "Mam!" he said with a big smile.

"I'll tell her you're very well, shall I?"

Albert nodded happily. "An' a big kiss," the little boy murmured.

"He's doin' fine here," said Dolly. "Better than down on River Road, anyway. I want that big drunken lump to get someone to teach him reading and writing. I don't want him to be an ignoramus like me."

"That 'big lump' will get around to it, see if I don't," said Clement, bridling at her insult. He stared at his son, and some glimmer of recognition lightened his drunken haze. "Yeah, I'll do that. You don't do so bad for an igor… ingor… ignorant woman yourself."

Robert accepted a drink of water, politely refusing a drink from the bottle that Clement had just taken from his mouth. Then he and Dolly went to examine the cotton. Though there wasn't a lot of it, it was good stock, almost equal to that from the Jacques plantation. Dolly explained how David and Nathan had helped her and Barney.

"Next year we'll put more land to cotton," she said. "We're hoping that more of the ex-slaves might come back to the village to see their families and some might settle back home if there's work for them."

He told her that her mother was working at Overdale House in her place.

"I hope she's a better worker than me," said Dolly with a wry smile.

"From what I hear and see around me, your work is fine." Robert glanced round the field of cotton.

"I'm working for me and Albert now," Dolly assured him. "It makes a difference."

"You know I haven't much money after buying the cotton," explained Robert. "But I could take your stock to the Exchange in Liverpool and sell it if you wish. Cotton's at a premium at the moment, and a lot of the manufacturers will pay a good price. They're eager to get their mills rolling again. It will take longer to get your money, though."

Dolly spit on her hand and a hesitant Robert shook it to seal the deal.

"Wait 'til I tell them at home," he said with a smile. "Dolly Tate — I mean Dolly Duplege — as a cotton farmer! Your mother will be very proud."

"Tell her our Albert's fine. Tell her it was for the best."

"I will," he promised.

They arranged for Dolly's cotton to be sent to the Jacques plantation and shipped with their crop.

Robert left with the memory of Dolly and Albert waving from the porch with Clemmie beside them. He was determined that when he returned home, he would reassure Maggie that her daughter would do well in America and that Albert was thriving. He would tactfully omit the state of the plantation house and make Jessie promise to keep the secret too. However, Robert could not dispel the surly figure of Clement lurking behind his wife and son, still clasping the bottle.

Robert was treated as a hero when he returned to the mill with the laden wagons. He sold the surplus of Dolly's cotton as he'd promised in Liverpool, and for a good price. He was tempted to sell some of his own cargo for extra money but knew the Invincible was desperate for the work the cotton would bring. His Uncle Eli too would have some of the bales to send to a spinner who produced finer thread than the Invincible Mill to weave his cotton damask.

Robert sent Dolly the proceeds of her sale, although he had only been given the details of Clement's bank. Then he wrote her a letter to explain what he had done but as he posted it he remembered that she'd said she couldn't read. Deep down he was hopeful that Clement would give his wife what she was owed but, with a sinking heart, wondered if that was likely. As insurance he quickly wrote a note to David Jacques asking him to help his illiterate neighbour.

Jessie hugged her husband as if she would never let him go. Then he noticed Maggie hovering anxiously for news.

"I must tell Maggie about her grandson," he murmured to his wife.

Jessie reluctantly released him.

To his embarrassment Maggie fervently kissed his hand when he told her how he had found Albert and that the boy was fine.

"God bless you, sir," she said and hurried away to the kitchen, wiping her eyes on her apron.

"It must be very hard for her, being parted from her loved ones," said Jessie, hugging his arm. "I know how hard it was when you left and I was not sure you would return. To have lost her daughter and her grandson…"

Robert chuckled. "Oh, she forgot to ask about Dolly."

Jessie listened intently as he told her all he had witnessed at the Amiens plantation. She was especially shocked to hear that the once lazy maid had been working hard to become a successful cotton farmer.

"I can only hope that husband of hers gives her the money she's owed," he said with a heavy sigh.

"I expect he's turned to drink since he's lost the war," said Jessie. Brought up in a temperance household she was still wary of drink, despite the decanter on the table each night.

CHAPTER 20: A GUILTY CONSCIENCE

It wasn't the South's defeat that was troubling Clement. He hadn't been sleeping well. So many times, he closed his eyes to see the glassy staring eyes of the woman he'd strangled in New York. He'd killed men as slyly and as callously as he'd killed her, but she'd been an innocent victim and a woman. There had been thousands killed in the war and he'd witnessed many dead bodies, but this one frail girl haunted him. He'd got away with it. No one would ever find him in the backwoods of Louisiana, but somehow her reproachful spirit had followed him there, crying silently for vengeance in the haunting hours of the night. Drink could not dispel her; inaction was troubled with her presence. He decided he must find something to fill his time. His wife was running the plantation effectively without his help and he was reluctant to interfere. He wondered if Barney and the rest of the ex-slaves would work for him in the same selfless way they worked with Dolly. 'With Dolly' — those were the key words, he realised. Despite that realisation, he swore he would never bring himself to stoop so low as to work in the fields with slaves.

It was only the news that Abraham Lincoln had been assassinated that roused him from his drink soaked lethargy. The village folk were all devastated by the news, and Dolly, who knew little about politics, was moved to tears by their grief.

"Well, I ain't goin' to mourn him," grumbled Clement. "Things ain't goin' to change for the South with that Andrew Johnson in charge either." He'd decided to head to Baton

Rouge to find out more and thought up an ideal excuse. "I'm going to advertise for a tutor for Albert," he told her.

She glanced up from the mending she was doing, assisted by Hattie. Dolly, who once had been barely able to thread a needle, was learning how to sew from necessity rather than pleasure.

"That would be good," she said with a satisfied smile, pleased that at least one of her suggestions had wormed its way into Clement's whisky soaked brain. "He's growing up a proper street Arab — though there's no streets round here!"

Clement and Hattie looked puzzled by her Lancashire saying.

"A young ruffian — and urchin," she explained.

Hattie shrugged and went on with her work.

"Would you like a man or a woman?" asked Clement, consulting his wife for once.

Dolly considered for a moment. "A woman would be nice. Someone I could talk to." Then she reconsidered. An educated woman might look down her nose at one who couldn't read or write. Clement might take a shine to a younger and better educated woman and be tempted to replace Dolly with her. "A man might be best," she decided.

"You could be right. Too many women around Albert will make him soft," said Clement.

He watched his son playing out in the sunshine in his large floppy hat and bare feet. The growing boy had outgrown the shoes they'd bought for him in Liverpool and said they hurt his feet. Clemmie was sitting on the porch, watching him. She said so little, but what she did say was to Albert. It was as if she'd appointed herself his guardian.

"Perhaps an older man," suggested Clement. "I don't want you playing fast and loose while I'm away from home."

Dolly shrugged. "That's a bit unlikely." But surprisingly the thought of David flitted into her mind. "Anyway, do what you think best. Albert must learn to read and write. He mustn't be ignorant, running an estate like this." She immediately noticed Clement's look of outrage. "If anything happened to you, of course. None of us are immortal," she added to appease him.

She little knew how close she'd come to being dispatched herself. Clement may be haunted by the unknown dead woman, but he had at one time thought he would have to rid himself of an unwanted wife.

"I'll make enquiries in Baton Rouge," Clement decided. "I have some business to attend to there, so I'll be gone for a few days."

"Have you any money?" asked Dolly. "There are dozens of things I need, especially for Albert," she added quickly. "Perhaps Robert Overdale will have sold my cotton by now."

"That money will take an age to come through," Clement told her. "It's only been a few weeks since he left."

Next day he patted his son's head as he left. "I'll bring you something good when I come home," he told Albert. "Perhaps a toy gun — just like a real soldier."

"Don't like guns," muttered Albert. "Like a ball, and I can play ball with Jim and Lukey and Maisy."

Clement grimaced. He did not approve of his son's friends among the black children, though it didn't seem to bother Dolly. If he could not find a suitable tutor for his son, the boy would have to be sent away to school as he had once been by his parents. There had been a school run by an order of religious brothers in New Orleans where he and Henri had been sent. He wondered how his wife would be reconciled with that idea.

141

CHAPTER 21: CLEMENT VISITS OLD FRIENDS

Clement set out next day with a list of instructions from Dolly, instructions he did not intend to carry out, though he had agreed to keep her quiet. He called on one of his old acquaintances on the way to assess the news from Baton Rouge and was persuaded to stayed overnight. The man's home was in a better state of repair than his own, and they spent half the night drinking and reminiscing about the old days before the war. They ended in bitterness about the state of the South in defeat. The rumour was that the Union army and navy were gradually leaving, but Clement knew he had to be careful. He wondered if the authorities would still be pursuing him after his jailbreak or if his exploits would just be forgotten in the messy aftermath of the war.

Unaware of what was happening far away in New York, Clement rode his tired old horse along the road past his former home in Baton Rouge. He stared in surprise at the building work in progress on the front of the house. Mrs Domain his housekeeper may have commandeered his home as a boarding house for Union officers for the duration of the war, but he was surprised to find her making alterations without his permission now it was over. He tied his horse further up the street and strolled back as casually as he was able.

"That's a fine job you're doing there," he called to the black workers erecting a porch over the front door. "I was looking for a couple of good workmen myself."

"Afraid we'll be workin' here for some time, Mister," said one of the men. "Fella that's bought the house wants it all fancied up — at least his wife does."

"You say the house has been bought?" said Clement in disbelief. "Are you sure?"

"Sure as anything, Mister. The lady that owned it has gone east with her soldier husband."

Clement was shocked and then angry.

"Say Mister, ain't you the one they called the Gambler as lived here before the war?" said the older man, looking closely at Clement's face.

"I lived here one time," said Clement cautiously. "Say, who sold the house for the soldier's wife?"

The two men looked at one another and shrugged.

"I reckon it could be Applebaum and Sons," said one. "He's the nearest one selling houses round here at present. You could ask there, Mister."

"Thanks, I will."

Clement strode back to his horse in a rage. That woman had swindled him. First she had filled his house with Union soldiers, and now it looked as if she had married one and moved away with the proceeds of the sale of Clement's house. Anyway, he was sure it was not legal and went in search of Applebaum and Sons. He found their office some streets away and marched in.

A prosperous looking older man looked up from a wide mahogany desk and glanced over his spectacles. "Good morning sir, and what can I do for you?" he asked, beaming. "Are you buying, selling, renting or leasing?"

"I'd like to know if you recently sold a house," snapped Clement and gave him the details.

"Ah, Mrs. Domain's house, now Mrs. Corcoran, of course. A delightful woman, a pleasure to do business with," said Applebaum.

"Except that the house was not hers to sell," growled Clement, leaning over the desk in a threatening manner. "That house was mine, and she had no right to sell it."

Applebaum looked alarmed and leant away from his desk. "But I can assure you, sir, that her deeds to the house were in order. She showed me the original deeds in her husband's name and his death certificate and his will. There can be no surer proof than that, sir. If you have any proof otherwise, sir…?"

To his horror, Clement realised he did not. He had won the house from Mrs. Domain's husband in a card game. The man had shot himself in despair and a guilty Clement had asked his widow to act as his housekeeper. As he was often away from home, he needed someone to look after the house in his absence. It had been his one solid asset, but he had never bothered to change the deeds into his name. He had figured that it could not then be sold to cover any debts he accrued. Now he realised that he had been too clever for his own good. Mrs Domain had taken advantage of his caution and with her copy of the deeds had sold his house.

"I don't suppose you have her address?" he asked.

The man shook his head anxiously. "I just know she's gone back east with her Yankee husband. New Hampshire, I think she said."

Clement suspected he would never have told him the address anyway. Fuming and feeling thwarted, he stormed away from the office, furious at his own stupidity. He had trusted the woman, even taken pity on her when she'd lost her husband, conveniently forgetting that he had cheated her out of her home and all that she and her husband had worked for. Life was a gamble — and he had lost.

He called into a bar for a drink and a think. He decided to call on Amelia Kay, an old friend of his former housekeeper who might at least know her new address. The door was opened by another familiar face.

"Good morning, Gemima," he said to the black woman that answered the door.

She was as surprised to see her old master as he was to see her. "Massa Clement! Mrs. Kay said as how you might call one day. You better come in."

"You might guess I am looking for the whereabouts of your last mistress," snapped Clement.

"All I know is New Hampshire," said Gemima warily. "She knows I don't write, so ain't no use givin' me an address."

"How convenient," said Clement, glaring at her. "Anyway, where is your new mistress?"

"In bed," said his old servant with a shrug. "Don't expect her much afore noon."

"So you have life easy here," said Clement, glancing round.

"Certainly a lot easier than chasin' round after a lot of them soldiers. Some was all right — for Yankees," she added as if to appease her old master.

The conversation downstairs must have alerted Amelia, and she appeared on the staircase wrapped in a splendid silk robe.

"Ah, Clement! I knew you'd arrive someday. Have you been offered a drink?"

He shook his head and was about to say he'd had a drink at a bar but decided he'd have another one anyway.

"Whisky for Mr. Duplege — unless you'd prefer brandy?"

"The drink of my ancestors. I'll have brandy, a large one," he told Gemima.

"I'll have one too," said Amelia and ignored Gemima's pointed glance at the clock. "So you're here to pursue the runaway?"

"Runaway with my money," added Clement. "I want to know where she's gone."

"New Hampshire," said Amelia promptly. "That's all I know. She knew you would go looking for her, so she wouldn't tell me the address."

"And her husband is called Corcoran and he's in the army. I'll find her."

"Lots of Corcorans in the army," said Amelia with a shrug. "I wish you luck. But maybe you're wasting your time. It was thanks to you that her husband Fred killed himself anyway. Maybe she thought you owed her one."

"That's not how gambling works," said Clement. "He was a sucker. If it hadn't been me who won his house off of him, it would be some other man. At least I offered her a home and a job."

Amelia did not seem convinced.

Changing the subject, Clement told her he must find a tutor for his son. "You know the people round here. I thought you might be able to help."

Amelia thought for a moment and then mentioned an old preacher that she knew had lost his wife and whose two sons had been lost in the war. "Jeremiah Leach is a good man," she told him. "The chapel where he preached was destroyed in the war and there's no money to rebuild it. But if he doesn't find some occupation soon, I'm sure he'll turn to drink."

Clement drained his own glass. "So I'll go and see this Leach. I'll bid you goodbye for now then," he said with a sigh. "Thanks for the drink. If you hear anything of…?"

"I won't," she said firmly.

146

Finding his horse, Clement duly called on Jeremiah Leach. A middle-aged man with a balding head and small pebble glasses opened the door. He looked like his house, grubby and neglected. Clement hesitated for a moment, then briefly explained his business. He was not invited into the house. The smell that wafted through the open door was of dirt and stale food. Clement wanted to get the business over with, especially as he didn't know how he would pay the man anyway. Jeremiah thought for a moment, perhaps reviewing his circumstances.

"A little boy, you say?" he asked. "I well remember my son when he was a little boy. Full of curiosity he was, just full of…"

"Yes, well, I have some business to do in town, Mr. Leach," Clement cut him short. "So I'll have to be going."

"Very well. I'll be happy to teach the child," said Jeremiah with a contented smile. He began to call down many blessings on Amelia's head. "Well, bless the Widow Kay for thinking of me. And will there be any more little children to teach any time?" asked Clement's new employee with a twinkle in his eye.

Clement almost ground his teeth. "I'll leave that in the Lord's hands," he said sharply. "Goodbye for now, Mr. Leach."

The preacher promised to ride out to the plantation as soon as he had settled his affairs in town.

Clement wandered towards the bank to see if there was anything for him. The Confederate government had promised him funds for his espionage work, though he doubted if there would be anything for him now. Instead there was a sum of money arrived from England and also a letter in Dolly's name. He casually opened it and smiled.

Trust that idiot Robert Overdale to write to a woman who could not read. He withdrew most of the money and wondered where he might meet up with some of his old gambling friends. On the way to one of his old haunts, he passed a shop selling clothes. Remembering the list that Dolly had impressed upon him he paused, then went inside and a helpful assistant folded the required purchased items in a neat pile and wrapped them in a parcel for him. He also found a shop that sold toys and bought Albert a wooden train on a string.

Feeling virtuous that he had done most of what Dolly had asked of him, he now felt he could spend some of her money on a little game of cards. After all, he might double her money and have something for himself. The room behind the bar was dim, and the few men poring over the card table greeted him half-heartedly. One or two left the table with a disdainful glance his way, his reputation being no guarantee of fair play. The others dealt the cards as he slipped into a chair by the table.

The cards did not go well for him that day. There was a younger, sharper man than him at the table and stare as he might Clement could not fathom how he was cheating. With one last stake he tried again. He stared at the revealed cards in disbelief. He had lost. Searching in his pockets, all he could find was his watch. He flicked it open as though he was finding the time. It tinkled merrily in the tense atmosphere of the room. He saw again the ornately engraved 'Cher fils' and, biting his lip, closed the watch with a snap and left the table. He had lost all of Dolly's money.

It was getting late and he begged a bed for the night at Amelia Kay's house. She protested that it would ruin her reputation, but Clement ignored her. Dropping wearily onto her chaise longue, he promptly fell asleep.

"You'd better get a blanket to throw over him," Amelia told Gemima. "Just make sure he's gone in the morning before I get up."

For once Clement slept without a care in the world, despite the restrictions of Amelia's chaise longue, confident that one of his misdemeanours would surely never be brought to his door.

The murder of a woman at a far distant medical school was never far from his mind, but he was certain he could never be connected with it. He could not know that there was a very persuasive letter on Alan Pinkerton's desk. Honora had sent that letter, stating her suspicions that she had been the intended victim and that the hair found on her friend's body had been dyed. There was a substantial reward for the capture of Verity Cain's murderer, but that was not why Honora Darwen was pursuing the matter. She wanted justice for her friend. She received a reply from Pinkerton advising her to enquire at the shipping offices to see if Clement Duplege really had arrived from England as Jessie had mentioned in her letter. When she had some time between her busy studies, she did as the detective suggested and went to the docks.

By pleading that one of her relatives should have arrived in America, Honora was shown a ledger of the relevant dates by a very helpful shipping clerk. Slowly she had read down the numerous columns, but to her frustration she could not see Clement's name. Desperate for some answer she tried again. Slowly her eyes scrutinised every entry in the ledger, then something in her memory made her pause at the name 'Clay Davies'. Trying hard to remember, she became convinced that this was one of the aliases she had heard he used in Washington. It was certainly his initials as he had used in his other aliases. Below him on the list was a Mrs. Dorothea Davies. Could that be Dolly, Honora wondered? Then just below that was a very familiar name, 'Albert'. The date was just a week before Verity's murder. Honora felt a cold stab of fear in the pit of her stomach. It could have been her lying on that icy mortuary slab. Hurrying home, she immediately wrote back to Alan Pinkerton with her information and waited eagerly for his intervention in the case.

CHAPTER 22: A DISAPPOINTED

Dolly was alerted by the workers as her husband rode wearily back to the plantation, little suspecting that she had had a visitor during his absence. As Robert far away in England had hoped, David had received his letter and had called to alert Dolly of the imminent arrival of her money.

Clement had convinced himself that Dolly would never know that her money had arrived from England and that as time passed, would no doubt blame Robert Overdale for pocketing the money from the sale of her cotton himself.

"Your letter should have arrived before mine," David had told Dolly. "It will have taken a few more days to reach our plantation."

"I hope Clement has it with him when he comes home," said Dolly happily. "Then I can pay you back and let the lads and lasses have some money for all the work they've done."

He smiled at her quaint Lancashire expression. 'Lads and lasses' brought to mind a pleasant rural village green, not a decaying plantation in the Deep South.

"Thank you," she said simply, touching his arm.

"You're welcome," said David, smiling into her eyes.

She watched him ride away with a deep and hopeless longing in her heart.

So when Clement finally arrived back at the plantation and handed her the parcel of clothes and the toy with a smile, his welcome was not as warm as expected. When he told Dolly to expect their son's new tutor in the coming days, it was positively frozen.

"He might have turned to drink, you say? Are you sure he's all right?" she demanded to know. She was very tempted to say that one drunk on the plantation was enough but kept her peace, waiting for better news.

"Amelia Kay reassures me that Jeremiah Leach is a perfectly respectable man," Clement told her.

"Let's hope so then," Dolly said with a sigh.

Patiently she waited for Clement to tell her about her delivery from Robert. He said nothing and greeted his son with the toy train.

"Say thank you to your Dad," Dolly told Albert, determined he'd grow up with some semblance of manners.

Clement knelt by his son. "Say thank you to Papa," he said, stroking Albert's silky hair. He began to show his son how the little train worked.

"Thank you, Papa," said the little boy with a shy smile and, dragging the train behind him, hurried off to show Clemmie.

Though touched by this small scene of affection, Dolly waited for some news from her husband. Then she realised that it was not forthcoming. "So haven't you got a letter for me?" she finally demanded, hands on her hips. "Are you playing about or what, because I don't think it's funny."

"What letter? What are you talking about?" Clement defended himself.

"Robert Overdale has sent a letter to your bank for me. He also sent one to David Jacques to tell me what he'd done. His letter arrived last week. So where's mine?"

Clement looked stunned by this unwelcome revelation. He had to think fast. "I have no idea what you're talking about," he said, getting surly. "There was no letter waiting at the bank. There's a war on, woman. Post can get delayed. Payments can get delayed. I'm still waiting for the damned government to pay up."

"Well, there is no damned government now, is there — except in Washington. So you can go and whistle for your money. But where's mine? Robert Overdale wrote that he had paid a remittance into your bank. I need to pay the Jacques. I need to pay the workers."

Clement took refuge in attack. "This is a fine welcome home. I'm no sooner in the house than you're demanding money. I ain't got no money. I spent what money I had on the boy. You've only got Overdale's word that he sent you the money. The price of a letter is a damn sight cheaper than all the money he'd pocket."

The forget-me-not blue of Dolly's eyes narrowed to iced steel. Her lips tightened to an implacable line. "I'd trust Robert Overdale before I'd trust you," she hissed. She was so filled with fury she felt she could explode, as Clement casually destroyed all her plans. "That money was for your son's future — for the future of the plantation. No doubt you've got your filthy hands on it and squandered it on booze and gambling. Don't forget I've watched you and your damned dirty dealings."

He raised a hand to hit her, angry that she had spoken the truth.

"Go on, hit me," she spat at him. "Add hitting a defenceless woman to your thieving. That's goin' to help, isn't it? That's goin to get your precious plantation out of the shit! Striking a woman's going to help."

Faced by her implacable anger, to her surprise Clement's arm dropped like a stone. "I need a drink," he said and swiftly left her.

Dolly felt like crying. Her overwhelming anger dissolved into despair. She'd felt so proud of everything she'd achieved. All that she and her fellow workers had earned had vanished. She felt sick and ashamed. What was she going to tell everyone? She'd promised them so much. They'd surely desert her now. Why would they work just to line Clement's pockets? Hot tears welled in her eyes. Hattie slipped through a doorway. She was holding her rusty carving knife.

"I heard what happened," she said, looking anxious. "Is all the money gone?"

Dolly shook her head. "I don't know, Aunt Hattie. I just don't know. I suspect it has. He won't tell me — the thieving rat. I don't know what I'm going to do. What will Barney and the others think? We've worked so hard — so hard for nothing, nothing at all."

With that she dropped to the floor and sobbed until her heart ached. Clemmie and Albert crept into the room. Her son slipped down to sit beside her, patting her arm as if she herself was a small child to be comforted.

"Don't be sad, Mam," he whispered.

She smiled through the tears and stroked his bright copper head. It was the first time he'd ever called her Mam. "I've been doing it all for you chick," she said. "You and me and everyone. But your Dad is…" She stopped herself from swearing. "He doesn't help. He's spent all our money what Mr. Overdale sent us."

She was inconsolable all that evening; tears constantly stung her eyes. She went through the chore of routine living like an empty husk, drained of everything but tears. Clement, with some semblance of shame, stayed out of her way. When he fell asleep on the porch in a drunken stupor, even Aunt Hattie refused to put a blanket over him. Dolly slept badly. In the morning she knew she had to face the workers, and she could imagine the disbelief and anger in their faces. She had to face the Jacques family too and tell them that their loan might take longer to pay.

A small steely determination crept into her mind when she awoke. She was going to learn to read and write. She was going to manage her own affairs. In the meantime, she was going to search the house and find something she could sell. There were dresses in her trousseau that she would never wear, isolated as she was on the plantation. There were some small pieces of inexpensive jewellery. The frenzy of buying in Liverpool when they had money in their pockets would hopefully pay dividends. Albert had grown out of his sailor suit and other things, and they could be sold too. She glanced at her wedding ring. She was not a wife except in a legal sense, and she toyed with selling it. The only thing it gave her was an air of respectability. As she passed the door to Clement's bedroom she noticed that it was open. He was still on the porch. She glanced at the upturned crate by his makeshift bed and a gleam of gold caught her eye. It was his watch. She picked it up and was just about to open it when she realised that it might chime and alert him. Beside it was a pair of pearl cufflinks. She slipped them all into her pocket. Then she summoned Barney.

"I suppose you've heard what's happened," she said wearily.

"Surely did, Mrs Dolly. I don't suppose there's any hope?"

She shook her head. "I don't think so. But I'm so very sorry about what's happened." Tears stung her eyes again and Barney felt her distress. "But I'd like to go into the town with some things to sell," she told him. "Will you come with me? I'd likely get lost."

Clement, after two nights of uncomfortable half-sleep, was still avoiding his wife and slipped away to his bedroom to have a proper sleep. Barney saddled Clement's old horse and the mule. Dolly gathered her things to sell in an old carpet bag and they rode along the winding neglected ways into Picardy Creek, their nearest town. She hoped to reach their destination before the heat of the day drained all energy from them, but the horse seemed to go slower with each step.

She had time to think as she clung to the plodding horse, willing it on with every breath. It was an age away from Gorbydale. She'd hoped for great things in America, listening to Clement's boasting around the Overdale's table, but here she was again, selling her possessions to stay alive. She glanced at the loyal Barney beside her. Dolly had felt herself superior to Kezia, the escaped slave who'd visited her own town from this very plantation. She remembered with a wince how Jessie Davenport had furiously pulled her hair for daring to feel Kezia's hair. Now she knew she could not have survived without these good people who had helped her grow the cotton. She had badly let them down. She had been a fool to think Clement would have given her the money due to her and everyone else. It was her foolishness and ignorance that had always let her down. She was determined to make use of Albert's tutor herself when he arrived.

Finally they passed a row of battered houses, some derelict and dilapidated, others with listless owners lounging on their porches. A mangy dog chased up to them and barked at Barney, snapping at his heels.

"Call your dog off, before I shoot it," shouted Dolly in her most commanding voice.

A skinny boy ran up and grabbed the hair on the back of the mutt's neck. "Come on Rebel," he pleaded and stood staring at the pair plodding slowly into town.

"Have you got a gun, Mrs Dolly?" asked Barney in surprise when they were out of earshot.

"No, Barney, but they don't know that," said Dolly with a chuckle.

There were few shops in the small town nearby, just a general store and a few dealers. At the end of the two dusty rows of buildings there was a saloon that grandly called itself a hotel. Luckily there was also a shop that bought and sold second-hand goods, and Dolly dismounted to go inside.

"Are you coming, Barney?" she asked.

He shook his head. "Don't allow no negroes in there," he said grimly. "You go ahead now, but don't take the first offer. You bargain hard."

"Oh, I will," she assured him with a wry smile. She had been in many pawn shops in her young life. With her wide pleading blue eyes and fair hair, she had mastered the ability to act as a poor helpless waif. Wily Dolly was the one Tate guaranteed to get more for her pledges. Tommo and Seth had learned the hard way that bullying and bluster had much less effect than the appeal of a pathetic looking Dolly.

A small man appeared from a door behind the counter when his loud doorbell clanged. "And what may I do for you, my dear?" he asked.

"I've got some things to sell," said Dolly, her eyes wide and soft as dew.

"Let me have a look then," he demanded and she displayed her wares from the shabby carpet bag.

"Ada!" called the little man as Dolly displayed her dresses. "My wife," he explained. "She deals with ladies' clothes."

A woman with a bird's nest of hair appeared from somewhere behind the counter.

"A lady here has some clothes to sell," said her husband, fingering a lace collar.

The woman shrugged and dragged a skirt aside as if it were a rag. However, a canny Dolly had detected a ghost of a gleam in her eye.

"They're quite new," she almost cooed. "I've hardly worn them."

"How do I know you've not stolen them?" demanded the woman.

Dolly had dealt with people like her before and produced the receipts from a Liverpool store with a flourish.

"Hmm. So they're English are they? They're not bad. This little sailor suit ain't too bad. How much do you want for them?"

Dolly named a sum that was more than she expected. If she was going to haggle, she wanted to start high.

"Too much," said Ada. She named an insulting sum.

Dolly didn't hesitate. She promptly swept all the clothes back into the bag. "Never mind then," she said with a rueful smile. "I'll be going to Baton Rouge later this month. I might take them there. I really didn't want to cart them all that way with me, but needs must."

She was about to swing the bag from the counter when the woman placed a restraining hand on it. "Don't be too hasty now. I'm sure we can come to some arrangement."

"Such as?" Dolly was alert, the mild blue eyes focussed and piercing.

A quick haggle and Dolly had what she wanted. Once she had the money in her hands, she searched in her reticule and pulled out the watch and cufflinks. The man's eyes lit up.

"They're gold," said Dolly firmly. "Proper gold, not just plated." Her brother Seth had once explained the little essay marks to her on some watch he'd stolen from a drunk.

The man slipped an eyeglass into his eye and opened the watch. It tinkled prettily around the shabby shop, and the man's eyes lit up in admiration. "A very fine watch," he murmured and began to study it carefully. Of course he noticed the inscription. "Clement?" he queried. "Would this be Mr. Clement Duplege of the Amiens plantation? He's the only Clement I ever heard of."

Dolly nodded in confirmation.

"What are you doing with his watch?"

"I heard he'd married an English wife," said his wife. "Is that you? Your clothes are from England."

"Yes, I am indeed Mrs. Clement Duplege," said Dolly, lifting her chin. "My husband is of course a very proud man. He felt too embarrassed to come here. I agreed to sell his watch for him. It's French, the best quality."

"You understand this here inscription will lower the price," said the man with a smirk.

"Oh, surely a man of your talents could have that polished out," suggested Dolly. Living with the light-fingered Seth had certainly left her with a lot of useful information.

"The inscription is very deep," he insisted, peering deeply into the watch case. "It could be difficult."

"Fair enough," said Dolly, holding out her hand. "I can take it to Baton Rouge with me. Thank you for your time."

"No, no, I'm sure we can come to some arrangement."

She'd known he was taken by the beautiful watch. He named a sum.

"I was expecting much more than that." Dolly held out her hand firmly. "As you say, it is a very fine watch. I'll take it to

159

Baton Rouge like I said. I'm sure they'll appreciate its quality there."

The man lovingly fondled the gleaming gold case, reluctant to let it go. It would be a rare thing to find to have such a watch thereabouts, and Dolly was well aware of its appeal. The man glanced at his wife. She held out her hand and her husband passed it to her. Again the little tune chimed out.

"Very pretty," she agreed. "We could offer you a little more."

"Oh, I'd need a lot more," said Dolly firmly. "That is a rare and fine watch and of great sentimental value. My husband would be most angry if I sold it for a pittance."

He was going to be furious anyway, but Dolly was determined to pay her debts before he took his anger out on her.

Finally they agreed on a price which was more or less to Dolly's expectations. She then produced the cufflinks as a bonus and, although he was reluctant at first, Dolly had correctly predicted that he was a vain little man who couldn't resist a bargain. She glanced again at her wedding ring but decided that the status it gave her outweighed its value. She would doubtless need its value in the future. After buying some things for Albert, who was growing tall, though he was still skinny, she left the shop satisfied that she had a tidy sum which would go some way to replacing the money that Clement had stolen.

CHAPTER 23: DOLLY PAYS HER DEBTS

Outside the second-hand store, Dolly found Barney resting in the shade.

"You all right, Mrs. Dolly?" he asked.

"I'm fine. How are you? I'm sorry to have left you so long out in this heat. Let's find somewhere we can get a drink."

Barney gave a slow smile. He wasn't used to be apologised to by white folks. Mrs. Dolly was certainly a woman to be reckoned with.

"Ain't no place in this old town for a cup of tea, Mrs. Dolly. The hotel sells nothing but liquor. Wouldn't let me in anyways, unless I was waiting on folks. Best we can do is buy a bottle of something and drink it in the shade."

Dolly went into the general store and bought two bottles of sarsaparilla. At her insistence they sat on the porch of the store in the shade while they drank it. People stared at them as they passed. Everyone in the town knew by now that Clement Duplege was back from the war saddled with an eccentric English wife and a mad niece. Now the word was slowly circulating that he was strapped for cash and his wife had been selling what valuables they had left. Many of the folks in the town had witnessed the grandeur of the Amiens plantation, the parties and the fine furnishings, the lavish spending at the general store. All this had now vanished in the aftermath of the war. The furniture in the mansion had been burnt by marauding troops and rootless rebels alike and most of those who had danced in style and luxury at the parties were scattered or dead. Now the townsfolk stared at the eccentric wife sitting here in their town drinking soda with a black man on the porch of the general store. The fall of the house of Amiens was complete.

Finally the store keeper came out and demanded that Barney get off his porch.

"Fair enough," said Dolly sarcastically, rising as high as she was able. "I wouldn't want to be seen dead on your scabby porch anyway."

"Oh, I don't mean you, Mrs. Duplege. I am sure you will come to be a much valued customer."

Dolly confronted him. "I doubt it," she said grandly. "Come along, Barney. Let us shake the dust from our sandals and leave this godforsaken place."

No doubt her biblical reference was lost on the shopkeeper, but something of her visits to Gorbydale chapel had actually sunk in.

"Yes, Mrs. Duplege," said Barney meekly as he followed her, trying not to smile.

They passed the houses with the angry dog but his young owner had spotted them coming and was clinging to his pet, anxious for its safety. A figure rose up from the porch.

"Good day, Mrs. Duplege," he called. "Afternoon, Barney. Hope you folks have a safe journey home," he added with a cackle.

"Clucas," hissed Barney. "I thought we'd seen the last of him."

Dolly hadn't liked the sound of the man's mocking voice, heavy with threat. She was wary, wondering if the man would release the dog on them. Hopefully her threat that she had a gun was sufficient to prevent it. All the same, she was relieved when they finally came into sight of the plantation. Now she had to face a threat of a different kind.

Before they completed their journey Dolly sent Barney on ahead to the village. She sent him with some of the money and asked him to send one of his sons over to the Jacques' house with it.

"Tell him to ask for a receipt," she said. "I don't want Mr. Duplege to get hold of it before our debts are paid."

She waited a long time in a clearing, glancing anxiously about her. All was silent but for the buzz of insects and the occasional mournful cry of a bird. The depth of the woods was hidden by the shrouding fronds of the moss draped trees. Nearby a sluggish creek trickled away into the trees. Remembering Clucas's nasty smirking face, she peered among the shadows in the trees. Then she noticed bits of ropes hanging from some of the branches and, though at that time she had no idea why they were there, she shuddered despite the heat.

"Please hurry back Barney," she whispered urgently into the silence.

Peering nervously around to make sure she had no witnesses, Dolly divided the money in a way she thought was fair. Then she pushed a tidy sum firmly down her corsets. There had been many things hidden in Dolly Tate's corsets. Before her job with the Overdales, she had secreted contraband inside a similar pair when out and about with Seth. Her brother had found it very useful to toss stolen goods to her after he'd fleeced someone. Into the corsets had gone the bacon she'd smuggled home from Overdale House. She patted her stomach in the knowledge that her money was safe as she waited. It was with great relief she saw Barney arrive back into view on the plodding mule.

"Zeb's gone to do as you ask, Mrs. Dolly," he assured her.

Now Dolly felt able to go home. As they drew nearer the house, a pair of mismatched figures appeared in the heat haze along the dusty road. Finally they came into focus, and Dolly recognised them at once. "Albert, Clemmie, what on earth are you doing out on this road?" she called as they came nearer.

Clemmie's eyes were wide with anxiety. Albert had the stain of tears on his grubby cheeks. Barney dismounted from the mule and held the boy up to his mother. She sat him on the saddle in front of her.

"What's the matter, pet?" she asked kindly.

"Papa," he murmured. "Papa's shouting. He can't find his watch and he shouted. He said was I playing with it. We come away 'cos we was frightened."

Clemmie nodded her head vigorously to confirm what the little boy had said. Dolly wondered what she had brought on the family. Clement's rage was an unknown quantity. So far he had managed to control himself before he'd done anything drastic. At first filled with fear, she grew angry herself that he had frightened their son. Barney too looked fearful. There was no saying what Clement might do to someone who had aided and abetted his wife.

"The watch was taken in payment," said Dolly stubbornly. "If he didn't want to pay his debts, he shouldn't have stolen *our* money in the first place."

All the same, her hands were trembling as she held the reins and urged the weary horse forward. Unless she turned and ran, she would have to face the consequences, and she had just enough money to run. But Dolly Duplege was a very different woman from Dolly Tate, the girl with a thousand excuses.

Clement charged out of the house the moment he spotted Dolly and her little entourage arriving. Aunt Hattie slipped out behind him. She had something folded in her arms which Dolly suspected was her carving knife.

"Where the hell have you been?" he bawled. "Where the hell is my watch?"

"It's in the second-hand store," said Dolly calmly, though her heart was beating like a brass band drum. "I sold it to pay *our* debts." She stressed the 'our' to try and make him realise how important that cotton money had been to her.

"You had no right, you thieving bitch," he snarled and would have dragged her from the horse, but the frightened animal backed away from him, leaving him clutching at thin air.

"And you had no right at all to take my money, you thieving bastard," hissed Dolly. "You didn't do a hand's turn in those fields. We slaved all day to make that money, and you did nothing — nothing at all. Well, I've got my payment now."

"Give it me," demanded Clement. "I'm gonna get my watch back."

"A bloody watch — you can't eat a bloody watch. Albert can't eat a watch, and he shouldn't be relying on other people's charity to live. If you want your watch back you'll have to work for it, same as we did. I've paid the Jacques most of what I owe them, and Barney and all those who worked with us are due a share of the rest."

"This is my land and…"

"Is it?" Dolly stared at him hard.

Clement was taken aback at her challenge. She wasn't even sure of her facts, but there had been talk in the village of the Duplege family, a hint of the claims to the land of Clemmie and Delia the eldest daughter who had run away with her lover to the north. Dolly had listened and learned, gleaned and stored snippets of rumours and opinions to gain ammunition for the claims of her son. Now in desperation she fired it.

Clement turned pale. Much as she wanted her son to be heir to the Amiens plantation, Dolly suspected that Clement's claim to the land was indeed slender and tenuous. And the pallor of Clement's face showed he thought that too.

Dolly thrust out the wad of notes that she'd separated from what she owed the workers. Clement snatched it and anxiously counted it.

"I doubt you'll be able to buy your precious watch back with what we've got left," said Dolly.

Clement was dumbfounded. The treasured gift from his father had gone; the one thing that he had kept despite gambling debts and prison and shipwreck. "What are you staring at?" he snarled at the others, and they backed away in fear. "I'll pay you back for this," he snapped at Dolly. "Just see if I don't." With that he stomped away to the house.

"Maybe you'd best stay in the village while the Master's as angry as a bunch of hornets, Mrs. Dolly," suggested Barney. "Maybe he'll have calmed down by the mornin'."

She hesitated, but something told her that he was right. She would not be able to protect little Albert if Clement did her any harm. Dolly reluctantly agreed that Clemmie and Albert should be safe enough staying in the house so as to cause them little disruption. Hattie escorted her charges back into the house with many reassurances, but Albert's anxious face as he looked back to his mother struck her to the heart.

Dolly sank wearily down in Barney's shack and hoped with all her being that she'd done the right thing. What had she done to her son? He'd whimpered to stay with her, but she had a glimmering of hope that Clement might calm down when he realised his responsibility to his son.

Safe in the shack, she delved into her corsets and gave Barney the money that she'd secreted away to distribute to the workers. Dolly was relieved that she'd managed to save it. Later that evening the village folk thanked her shyly.

"First wages I ever had," said Zeb proudly.

"It's little enough for the work we've done. We should have had more," Dolly told him. "But you must know why we haven't. Let's hope we can earn some more when we get the plantation working again."

It was her great dream now to bring the land back to its former glory, though she hadn't a clue as to what the future held. Surely Clement would come to realise that gambling held no hope for them and would help her work the plantation. It could be his future too, whether the land belonged to him or not.

Later that evening Hattie arrived with some nightclothes for her and the news that Clemmie and Albert were settled and that Clement was in the process of drinking himself into a stupor. Despite the uncomfortable and cramped surroundings and the image of Albert's tearful face in her thoughts, Dolly slept soundly after her long day. She knew she was in the midst of friends.

Dolly rightly guessed Clement would ride away next day and with his stake try to replenish his money by gambling. She doubted he'd manage it. He kept telling her he had lost his luck since meeting her. Well, she wasn't so lucky either. She'd worked all season for absolutely nothing at all.

CHAPTER 24: GROWING PAINS

Away across the sea in Gorbydale, the Invincible was back in business. The big boiler was being stoked up, a head of steam building in the engine and a stream of workers queueing at the factory gates. The mill was not yet in full production, as a continual supply of cotton was not yet certain. Many workers had left the district, some to go to Australia and the colonies to make a new start; some to America to rebuild after the devastation of the war. Down the valley the loyal workers at the Endurance put down their paint brushes, their trowels and their spades and went back to their looms. The whitewashed walls of the machine room were pristine for the present. There were flowers and vegetables growing in the mill grounds and the walls and building of the old mill were in great repair. Until the smoke and corroding grime from the mill chimneys filled the valley again, an inkling of prosperity began to emerge in the town.

Matthias Overdale headed for his office. He was leaning heavily on his walking stick but his heart was light. "Are you right then?" he called to Robert. "You've a lot to learn and we'd better get started."

Robert leant and kissed Jessie as he left the breakfast table.

"Best of luck," she whispered.

"Will you be all right sorting out our parlour?" he asked anxiously.

"Of course I will. I'll manage fine without you under my feet," Jessie chided him with a smile.

The sewing class had been disbanded and the billiard room was now free for its transformation into a parlour for the young family.

She called up into the nursery first and helped feed her twins. Lizzie the nursemaid was busy with Helen, who was supping greedily at a spoon. Jessie gently lifted Matty from his cot and held him to her breast. He still struggled to feed, although she had plenty of milk for him. His efforts to suckle seemed to tire him out, and he was gaining little weight.

"Perhaps I could try Matty with some of Helen's porridge," she suggested to Lizzie. "It seems thin and smooth enough."

The nursemaid passed over a small bowl for him to try, but still Matty struggled to swallow.

"I'm going to lose you if you don't eat up," Jessie gently scolded her baby son. "Just look at your sister eating everything around her."

"Babies are all different," said Lizzie with a smile. "Our Jimmy was a poor eater and he's taller than me now." As the second eldest of eight children, Lizzie had much more experience of babies than the young mother herself.

"So there's hope for you yet, you little scallywag," Jessie teased Matty, kissing his forehead.

He gave her his lopsided smile that told her there was intelligence lurking beneath his tiny skull. She worried so much about his physical health, though. She'd tried some of the exercises that Amy had shown her, which seemed to be easing his tight limbs, but his feeding had not improved.

"Hand him to me," suggested Lizzie.

Jessie hesitated. She had jealously guarded the care of her ewe lamb. Now, as he refused to thrive, she was willing to try anything. Lizzie held the baby and gently coaxed him to eat a little from the spoon. He stared up at her in surprise at first and then began to try, tasting hesitantly and then trying some more. Helen complained loudly that she was not being fed and Jessie hauled her onto her lap. The little girl soon finished her own food then tried to reach for the bowl prepared for Matty, greedily trying to take the spoon. Jessie laughed with delight. It was a pleasure to feed her daughter, though she had loyally concentrated all her efforts on Matty. Meanwhile, Lizzie was making good progress with him despite all Jessie's previous patience.

"Why wouldn't he feed for me?" Jessie asked.

"Perhaps you were too anxious," suggested Lizzie shyly. "Some babies seem very sensitive to things like that."

"He seems to be doing very well now," the young mother reluctantly admitted.

Though she felt disappointed she had made no progress with her son herself, she was just glad he was taking some nourishment from gentle Lizzie. Thereafter Lizzie fed Matty, and Jessie learnt to express her milk into a feeding bottle to give to her baby son. At first she felt a failure, but he gradually began to put on weight. Even Matthias noticed an improvement in his grandson.

"Perhaps we might make something of him yet," he admitted grudgingly.

Despite that meagre response, Jessie was still annoyed that her father-in-law rubbished Matty.

Working hard with the help of the groom, Jessie shifted benches and chairs to be removed back to the mill or the attic. Gradually she formed a comfortable living room for her little family in the billiard room with furniture gleaned from round the house. She stepped back to admire her work and was pleased with her efforts. Some of the furniture was very old and dark and had been brought from Melissa's old home at

Primrose Cottage. Jessie had polished it until it gleamed. She brightened up the settle with bright flowery cushions and placed a large carved chair beside the fireplace. Robert was delighted with it.

"It was my grandfather's chair," he said, his arm round her waist. "Father didn't like it. He said it was old fashioned, but I think the real reason was because he and Grandpapa didn't get on."

The room was large and sunny, though a draught blew through the French windows whenever the wind gusted up the Gorby valley. Later Jessie made some long thick snakes out of old curtains, complete with big eyes and forked tongues to the delight of the children. In later days the snakes were to be more often incorporated into their games than sealing out the wind.

"I think this is the nicest room in the house now," said Melissa, coming to admire the work after it had finished. "It's so light and airy."

Her own main rooms were heavy with the ornate furniture Matthias favoured.

Now she had her own corner in the house, Jessie hoped her own family would call to see her without disturbing the rest of the Overdales. Jacob began to pop in to see his grandchildren more often. Eventually her brother John, with his wife Elsie and their two small children came to have tea. Elsie had been a Tate and was Dolly's cousin. She had been nervous of visiting the house while Dolly was employed there.

Maggie was a different matter altogether. She attempted to be formal when bringing in the tea to her niece but Jessie, taking the tray from her, invited her to have a cup of tea with them.

"We're all family here," she reassured Maggie.

"Oh, I couldn't," murmured a nervous Maggie. "The Master would be ever so annoyed if he found out."

Jessie, though feeling justified in inviting her to tea in her own space, didn't press her. She didn't want to get Maggie into trouble with Matthias.

"Why's Matty got a wobbly head?" demanded Eleanor, their daughter.

Her parents looked shocked and embarrassed at her question.

"He got a bit squashed by Helen in the doctor's bag when he was delivered," said Robert with a chuckle.

They all laughed nervously and Jessie hugged her husband's arm, grateful that he'd dispelled such an awkward situation. Thereafter that was always the joking excuse they gave when someone questioned Matty's disability.

Every now and again Amy Walmsley tapped, quiet as a shadow, on the French windows as if her visits must be a secret. When that happened Jessie knew that Taylor would be away from the town on business. At the mill he and her husband had been trying to blend some Indian Surat cotton with the Sea Island American staple to improve its spinning quality and eke out their supplies. It would be some months before they could get their hands on more American cotton, and they were trying to keep the mill going. Taylor had made great efforts to improve the Indian cotton, and his botanist, Crispin Pettigrew, arrived back from India with more samples for them to try. They discussed it over the dinner table at Overdale House.

"It's a damned waste of time if you ask me," said Matthias rudely. "The American cotton is nearly back on tap. The price'll come down any time now."

"I'll write to the Jacques about their next crop," suggested Robert. "But perhaps we shouldn't put all our eggs in one basket like before. If the American crop ever fails, we'll all be out of work again. The situation is still very unstable over there, I hear."

"Damned waste of time," muttered his father under his breath.

Jessie gave Robert a warning glance and Melissa caught the mood and changed the subject.

"I expect it's very hot out in India, Mr. Pettigrew."

"It is I'm afraid, Mrs. Overdale," he told her. "Mrs. Walmsley will tell you," he added, smiling at Amy. "Most of the East India Company head for the hills at this time of year."

Amy nodded in agreement but said hardly a word. Taylor listened to the conversations in brooding silence, affronted that Matthias should disparage his efforts to improve the stock.

Later, when Melissa was out of hearing, Amy quietly admitted to Jessie that she was anxious that Taylor didn't find out about her visits to Overdale House. She'd been frightened of saying something that might make him suspicious. Jessie promised to say nothing. She felt very sorry for Amy.

"I'm glad that's all over," said Matthias once their visitors had left. "The Walmsleys aren't exactly the ideal guests. They hardly open their mouths."

"Mr. Pettigrew was certainly very interesting, dear," said Melissa, trying to soothe her irascible husband.

Jessie quietly admitted to Amy, when Melissa was out of hearing, Robert might sometimes unknowingly treat his wife as if she was somehow beneath him but she was quick to correct his ideas with an apt reminder. Even living in Robert's family home, with his belligerent father, Jessie felt she had as much freedom as she wanted.

On another secret visit Amy had confided in Jessie. "The trouble is that Mrs. Walmsley has begun to come over to our house most days, especially when Taylor goes travelling. Although she has always complained about her ill health, I have noticed she is actually getting frailer. I have a dread that my husband will invite her to come to live with us."

"Oh dear, no," protested Jessie.

"You must think me very ungrateful," said Amy, bowing her head with guilt. She seemed close to tears.

"No, I do not!" Jessie told her firmly. "You are entitled to your own life without that interfering old…"

"In India it is customary for families to live together," said her guest, raising a smile at Jessie's vehemence. "But I am afraid she will interfere too much with my marriage. She keeps hinting that I should have a child by now and I do not know what to say. I should very much like a child of my own."

"And you'd be a good mother too," her friend reassured her. "You are so good with my two and especially Matty. In God's good time you will be one."

"I do hope so," said Amy. "I should like a little family of my own. Then perhaps Taylor's mother would begin to accept me."

"More likely begin to take over her grandchildren," thought Jessie to herself, though she didn't voice her doubts out loud to further distress her friend.

She didn't enquire any more into Amy's marital circumstances. She felt very sorry for her, alone and parted from her family in a strange land. The poor woman was even prevented from using her own name, Amisha.

Jessie reflected on the past, remembering how Taylor had once pursued her and how she had very nearly married him. Even her late mother Nellie had wished to see her settled with

Taylor. Jessie was sure he resented her marriage to Robert even now. What would Matty's fate have been with a father like Taylor Walmsley? No doubt her poor son would have been locked away in an institution. She thanked the fates that had prevented her marrying the man as she watched him silently but obviously quash his gentle wife. A life with old Mrs. Walmsley's malign presence hanging over her would have been intolerable.

CHAPTER 25: PROGRESS

Clement's luck hadn't deserted him entirely. He'd found a group of men at a Baton Rouge hotel who were ripe for fleecing at cards. It was later, as he talked to a waiter, that he realised why a bunch of Northerners were in town. The rumour was that they were eager to buy up land and abandoned plantations cheaply for investment. There were plenty of estates whose owners had been left penniless by the war, or whose sons had died in the conflict. He left the table glad that he'd deprived the speculators of some of their funds and wasn't tempted to try his luck again. Content for the moment with his winnings, he invested in a new horse and a pony for Albert.

Before Clement headed back home, he stopped at the second hand store in Picardy Creek. As the doorbell clanged noisily, the shopkeeper hurried to the counter with a gleam of approaching profit in his eye. He hesitated when he saw his customer's face.

"I believe you have a watch of mine," said Clement, leaning over the counter with obvious menace.

He was determined to have his precious watch back safely in his own hands. The man's eyes opened in alarm. Everyone in the town knew of Clement and his reputation. The shopkeeper hastily slipped his hand into his waistcoat pocket, paused for a moment but noticed the determination in the gambler's face. Slowly a round gleam of gold emerged.

"My watch," demanded Clement, thrusting out his hand.

"I was very uncertain about its purchase, Mr. Duplege," protested the dealer, hesitantly clutching it lest Clement should snatch it away without paying. "But your wife assured me she had your permission. She's very plausible."

"Oh, she's plausible sure enough," said Clement wryly.

Of course he had to pay more for the watch than Dolly had given to him. Though outraged at the price, despite haggling the man down, he was desperate to have his precious heirloom back in his possession. Opening it with reverence he heard again the sweet tinkle of the familiar chime with profound relief.

"Thank you kindly," he said with a leer as he left the shop.

It was as well he'd saved some of his winnings, as an unfamiliar trunk sat in the hall when he arrived home. He found Dolly drinking tea with Jeremiah Leach. In the trauma of losing his watch he'd forgotten all about the tutor he'd hired for his son.

Mr. Leach was very agitated. "I hadn't expected your plantation to be in such a … such a … a neglected state," he said.

"You might have noticed there has been a war on, sir," said Clement dryly.

"Yes, yes, of course. Your good lady wife has been explaining that you will of course provide a suitable room for me. Believe me, sir, if I'd known about the state of my lodgings I would have stayed in Baton Rouge."

"Why, sir, I assumed your lodgings would be an improvement on your old ones," Clement smirked.

Jeremiah hesitated as if remembering the state of affairs at his old home. Clement had not entered the house but witnessed its dilapidation and unwholesome smell.

"I'm sure we can accommodate you, Mr. Leach," said Clement wearily. "You are of course free to go at any time."

Dolly's eyes opened in surprise as he deliberately took out his watch and examined the time. He raised his eyes to her in a hard stare and she knew he had been gambling again and somehow won. "I wasn't expecting Mr. Leach," she said. "But Aunt Hattie is at this moment arranging a room with Clemmie's help. Would you like some more tea, Mr. Leach?"

"That would be nice. Well, I shall of course stay for a while and see what can be done. I can only try my best," said the schoolmaster, shaking his head in disbelief at the state of affairs.

"I hope you've got some money to pay him," Dolly hissed as she passed Clement to fetch more tea. "Let's hope he stays." She pointedly glanced round the room. Though time marched on, they were still virtually camping out in the semi derelict building despite the valiant efforts of Dolly and Hattie. On one of his winning streaks Clement had managed to purchase some sticks of furniture from a cotton estate which was being sold. He and Albert were now sleeping in proper beds, though Dolly preferred the comfort of her cotton stuffed mattress on the floor. Clement had not invited her to join him in his bed. Nor did he seem able to rouse himself into any enthusiasm for the work.

"There is of course a schoolroom?" asked Mr. Leach confidently.

Dolly stifled an incredulous laugh, and the two men glared at her. "Sorry," she muttered. "Tea went down the wrong way."

"We will do our best to provide one," Clement reassured him with a warning glance towards his wife.

Aunt Hattie hovered at the door.

"Yes, what is it?" barked Clement.

"Would the gentleman like to see his quarters?" she asked politely.

Dolly breathed a sigh of relief and grinned at her mentor. "That would be lovely, Aunt Hattie," she said gratefully. "Do you know where Albert is? He must come and say hello to Mr. Leach, his new teacher."

Hattie nodded. "I'll find him, ma'am."

The new arrival did not seem impressed at the makeshift bedroom with muslin windows. Albert's bed had been brought in, but that was the only furniture in the room apart from a homemade stool. Jeremiah's attention was distracted by the arrival of Albert, newly scrubbed and anxious.

"He seems very young," said Mr. Leach.

"He's small for his age," Dolly assured him. "But he's as bright as a button. Aren't you, love?"

Albert nodded, though his new schoolteacher didn't seem impressed.

"You just need to teach him to read and write for now," snapped Clement. "He can pick the rest up at school."

Dolly clutched her son to her. She had done little to raise him, but he was her flesh and blood and her only family on this side of the Atlantic. Now she didn't want to be parted from him, her only link with her old life. "He'll learn all right," she said firmly and felt a surge of determination that she would learn too.

Recalling the miserable state that Clement had found him, Jeremiah Leach soon settled down to his task.

CHAPTER 26: LESSONS BEGIN

Over the next few days, at a makeshift table, Jeremiah began to teach his pupil. He seemed disconcerted, though, to find his pupil's mother continually hovering round. He couldn't guess that Dolly was secretly trying to absorb the lessons herself. Mr. Leach was very patient with Albert, and the little boy soon learnt his alphabet. Dolly watched carefully when her son proudly showed her what he had learnt on his slate. It was late one night when Mr. Leach found her struggling over one of the books by candlelight. Beside her was a slate with some rudimentary writing that she had been practising.

"So you cannot read, Mrs. Duplege?" he asked gently.

Dolly stared up in confusion and then sought refuge in defence. "I never had the chance, did I?" she retorted. "I was working in the mill as soon as I was able. Us part-timers were supposed to be taught, but there were so many of us in that class that no one noticed if you couldn't pick up the lessons. I can reckon up all right."

"Reckon up?" he queried, unable to understand her Gorbydale vernacular.

"You know, numbers and that," she answered with a grin. "Us Tates are fine if there's anything to do with money."

Jeremiah Leach gazed at her in the candlelight. He'd been intrigued by her and wondered how she'd arrived in a Louisiana backwater from England. He'd been impressed by her progress in the proceeding weeks, watching her assessing the fields with Barney, struggling over a needle with Hattie. The schoolmaster had noticed her patience, tinged with a brusque cajolery with Albert and Clemmie. Now he admired her determination to better herself, despite what she had revealed about her poor upbringing. "I can teach you alongside Albert if you like," he suggested.

"I can't afford to pay you any more money," she murmured. "And I don't want my husband to know."

Although he'd been intrigued by the odd relationship he'd noticed between Dolly and Clement, this came as a surprise to Jeremiah. He pondered for a moment. Would Duplege resent the schoolmaster's interference in his wife's education? Might he be dismissed? Suddenly Jeremiah didn't care. Learning was learning, and this young woman wanted to learn. "I'm sure we can work around that, Mrs. Duplege," he told her with a shy smile.

To his surprise, she reached up and kissed him on his cheek. "Lovely!" she said. "I'll try my best."

"I'm sure you will," said Jeremiah.

They both went back to bed, smiling and satisfied with their deal.

Everything was growing, the cotton and Albert especially. The boy's knowledge was burgeoning too, thanks to Mr. Leach. Jeremiah had taken a liking to the boy with his gentle nature and willingness to learn. He had felt bereft without his family. He and Dolly were becoming friendly too, despite their very different natures. In their little chats she'd coaxed him to talk about his wife, and his eyes had filled with tears as he spoke of his sons.

"Two fine boys," he said, dabbing his eyes. "What a waste of my two fine boys. Don't even know where they're buried."

To his dismay Dolly began to cry too, overwhelmed by his sadness. "I miss my Mam," she sniffed through her tears. "I didn't think I would, but I do. Who'd have thought I'd be crying like a babby for that shit hole."

Jeremiah patted her hand in sympathy and blew his nose on a tatty handkerchief. Dolly wiped her nose on the hem of her dress. Fortifying themselves with deep breaths, they turned their attention back to the children's book she was attempting to read.

"We're a right couple of 'apporths," she teased him to lighten their woes. "Anyway, your home's here with us now and we're glad to have you."

"I have no idea what 'apporths are," said Jeremiah with a chuckle, "but I'm sure they are something very important."

"I expect it's something like a dime," she explained.

"Yes, you have very strange currency in England, counting in twelves and twenties I believe," he said. "It is much easier to teach young Albert about American currency counting in tens."

"I reckon you're right," said Dolly, laughing. "Though funnily enough, I never had much trouble counting money — just with getting my hands on it!"

The schoolmaster's life had purpose. Albert was happy in his company and Jeremiah treated him like a missing grandson. The boy was quick to learn. Dolly, too, was progressing nicely.

"You know, letters just seemed a jumble to me at one time and made no sense. Thanks to you, I can make my way though some of the writing. I'm right pleased," she said, hugging Jeremiah's arm after a lesson.

There were some things that Jeremiah could not teach Albert, though. Clement had told him that he wanted his son to learn to ride, and the schoolmaster was an indifferent horseman at best. Albert loved his pony, which he called Gorby in a vague memory of his days in his grandmother's house near the Gorby river. Much to Clement's aggravation, his son was reluctant to ride the animal, preferring to treat it as a large dog.

"Perhaps you might teach the boy to ride yourself?" Jeremiah ventured. "You are an excellent horseman, if I may say so?"

"What am I paying you for?" growled Clement, avoiding the fact that he hadn't yet paid the man. "Anyway, I haven't the time," he excused himself.

Clement had played little part in their progress. He sometimes went out hunting to supply meat for them to eat, complaining that he was fed like a chicken on corn. Dolly and Barney had grown corn and sugarcane to supplement their diets.

Finally Clement rode off to satisfy his gambling habit. The mood of the plantation lightened without his ominous presence.

"Would you come to town with me so I can open a bank account?" Dolly asked Jeremiah. "I wouldn't know where to begin, and my writing's not great. You can explain things to me."

"Where would we go?" he asked, anxious that they might bump into Clement.

"I think we'd be safe enough in Baton Rouge," said Dolly. "I reckon Clement will be out on the river by now, playing his tricks."

So they set off with a will and stayed overnight with Jeremiah's sister. With his help, Dolly opened her bank account. Then on his further advice, she wrote to Robert Overdale with a suggestion he buy her cotton again when it was ready. She told him to send the payment to her new bank, safely out of Clement's clutches. Proudly she added a note for Maggie.

"What would I do without you?" Dolly said to Jeremiah. "You're my guiding star."

He accompanied her over to the Jacques plantation to be introduced.

"With the cotton trade disrupted nowadays, many of the plantations are joining together to share shipping costs for their bales," Nathan told Dolly as they sipped drinks on their porch. "Perhaps we could do the same, like last time?"

"That would be grand," Dolly agreed. "I'm sure to have a better harvest next season. And now I have my own bank account, Clement can't get his hands on our money. All thanks to Mr. Leach," she added, smiling at Jeremiah.

He noticed that she beamed her warmest smiles at David and wondered why she would reveal her husband's betrayal so easily. Jeremiah admitted to himself, though, that most people knew what Clement had done. The gossip spread as quickly and steadily as a forest fire between the plantations, and visits to the town would embroider the tale still further. Though he had not been at the plantation when the deed took place, the schoolmaster had heard all about Dolly's trip to the second-hand store.

Jeremiah smiled to himself. Despite his initial dismay, he had gradually become content to be absorbed into the ramshackle family at the Amiens mansion.

CHAPTER 27: MOTHERHOOD

Robert showed Dolly's letter to Jessie. "Well, well. Our Dolly's becoming a cotton magnate," he said, laughing.

"You must show the letter to Maggie," said Jessie. "You'll have to read it to her, but she'll be so pleased. Does Dolly mention Albert?"

"She's written 'All here are well'," Robert told her. "'Albert has a teacher now called Jerm' (that's crossed out) 'Mr. Leech. Albert is learning to read and write. I am learning too.'"

Maggie was indeed pleased and blessed Robert to heaven and back. "Fancy our Dolly being able to write," she said, looking at the letter in wonder, though she couldn't understand one stroke of the writing.

"I can write a letter for you if you'd like," suggested Jessie. "It looks as if Dolly will be able to read it for herself now."

"Oh, would you, Mrs. Jessica? That would be lovely," said Maggie, clutching the letter to her heart in gratitude.

Jessie went to fetch pen and paper, glad to help. She much preferred the biddable Maggie to her daughter, although her cleaning skills left something to be desired.

Jessie's life had fallen into a predictable routine. Most of her days were spent with the children in the nursery, mostly caring for and encouraging Matty. Now that the mill was grinding back into action, Robert spent long days learning the trade with his father. Though cotton prices were falling, they were still high and would be until the industry recovered from the devastating war in America. Robert was in touch with the Jacques with the promise of their next crop. Matthias depended on his son more and more and often came back early from the mill, tired and tetchy so that Jessie had to keep the children quiet. She found a twin baby carriage in a second-hand shop so that she could take the children to her father's house.

"You're not taking them out in that thing, are you?" demanded Matthias when he saw her ready with the pram for her visit. "What will people think?" He glared hard at Matty.

"They'll think I'm a young mother taking my children out for some fresh air," said Jessie defiantly. She thought wryly that the air wasn't so fresh now the mill was back in production, but she resented her father-in-law's overt suggestion that Matty shouldn't be seen out in public.

"Would you like me to come with you?" Lizzie the young nursemaid murmured.

Jessie shook her head with a smile. "No, Lizzie, we'll be fine. It's only to see my father. It's not far. Why don't you pop out and see your Mam while I'm gone? I'm sure she'd like to see you."

Lizzie slipped on her shawl and accompanied Jessie and the children as far as the bridge over the Gorby. Then they parted ways as Lizzie headed for the poorer part of town and her large family.

"Thanks, Mrs. Jessica," she called as she headed home.

Jessie may have come up in the world, but she was glad she was in a position to do small favours to help others.

Her old home was further away than she'd remembered, though. As Jessie pushed her heavy pram, her thoughts turned to Dolly's letter and her new life so far away. She remembered her own unexpected travels in America and all the things she'd seen. Her work with Honora in the military hospitals had been gruelling but rewarding. How amazed and relieved she'd been to find Robert broken in a makeshift hospital bed, and how overwhelming his feverish kiss of recognition had been. Now Honora was studying hard to continue her work while she immersed herself in family life. She had tried to push aside the memories of suffering she'd witnessed, though sometimes they invaded her dreams. Now she smothered their unsettling misery with everyday thoughts of her children and plans for the future. Though she'd been glad to come home, she felt bogged down with domesticity. She loved her son but had to admit he was hard work. Now the hill up Weavers Row loomed steeper than usual. Luckily, Alice spotted her pushing the heavy pram and came to help.

"It'll be quicker on the way down," she joked. "Make sure you hang on tight or the kiddies might end up floating down the Gorby river."

"What's the gossip on Weavers Row?" asked Jessie.

She was puffing with the effort but filled with a sense of achievement as they reached the Davenports' home.

"Has Mary spoken to you?" asked Alice. "She has a happy bit of news."

"I haven't seen her in ages," said Jessie sadly. "I seem to be stuck at home with the children these days, and I know she doesn't like coming to Overdale House with grumpy old Matthias about."

"Perhaps I should wait for her to tell you." Alice looked thoughtful. "But you'll get to know anyway, what with your Father and Eddie around. Mary's going to be married."

"Married! I didn't even know she had a beau. And we used to be so close," she added sadly. She felt cut adrift from her old life, flotsam among the Overdales. Although she was living with them, she knew deep down she was not one of them. Helen had anchored herself firmly to their family with her inherent sense of entitlement, but she felt Matty was as tentative a dependant as she was.

"I know she would have told you when she had a chance," said Alice. "It's all happened quite quickly, really." She patted Jessie's arm in sympathy, probably assuming that the young mother's quiet sadness was because she hadn't been told Mary's news.

"Who's the lucky man?" asked Jessie, rousing a smile.

"Well, you know Myfanwy from Wrexham, one of our girls?"

Jessie nodded. Most of Alice's boarders had been with her a long time.

"Her brother Dilwyn came to see her. He's on the railway like John. Well, one thing led to another. He and Mary had been writing for a couple of months and then he popped the question. It will probably take place in a few months."

"So soon?" asked Jessie.

"They say they're so sure of one another, they don't want a long engagement. The wedding will probably be a quiet affair," said Alice. "They can marry as soon as Dilwyn gets a transfer to the Doveton line so Mary can keep running the boarding house. He says he'll miss Wales, but one lot of hills is very like another."

"I'm very happy for her," said Jessie. "Give her my love and tell her congratulations."

"I certainly will. Come on, let's get these little ones in the house," said Alice, hauling Helen out of the pram. "Your Father will be glad to see you."

The tot staggered off through the door on sturdy legs, shouting, "Gran, Gran."

Jacob was pleased to see Jessie and the children, and she was soon made comfortable with a cup of tea. Matty was propped up with cushions beside her on the horsehair sofa. He eagerly watched his twin making herself at home and playing tea party with some old cups Alice had given her. He giggled as his grandfather pretended to drink the imaginary tea that Helen had made, extravagantly declaring it the most delicious he had ever tasted.

"There's not much wrong with the lad's brain," said Alice, watching him. "Just look at him laughing at their antics."

Matty did have trouble, though, when Helen offered him one of her cups and he could not grasp it properly. Jessie prevented a mishap with a deft catch.

Days later, Mary called to see Jessie. She glanced round the shabby splendour of Overdale House and linked her friend's arm. "Let's go out in the garden," she suggested. "It's a nice day, and I don't fancy bumping into old Matthias."

They headed outside and raised their faces to the sun.

"Mam says you were a bit upset that I hadn't told you about the wedding," said Mary, giving Jessie's arm a hug. "I know I should have told you myself, but things have been so hectic lately. I expect you know I haven't been back to the mill. There's enough to do running the boarding house, especially with Mam looking after Jacob nowadays."

"Don't worry about that," Jessie reassured her. "I hardly have any time to visit myself these days, what with the children."

"But we're still friends?" asked Mary.

"And sisters," laughed Jessie. "You'll have to bring Dilwyn to see us. What's he like, then?"

"He's quite shy, surprisingly enough," said Mary, chuckling. "I got to know him better through his letters. But he said he knew what he wanted and went for it!"

"I like the sound of him already," Jessie said with a chuckle. "He's got good taste, anyway." She hesitated for one moment, not wishing to appear too grand, but hospitality was vital. "I'll send for tea," she murmured and went inside to ring a bell.

"Hark at you," said Mary.

Jessie shook her head. "Oh, I know. It would be much easier if I could just make a brew myself here. I mentioned getting a little spirit burner to Melissa, but she said it would be too dangerous with the children around. I suppose she's right, but I feel such a fraud calling for Maggie every time I want a drink. Life was much simpler on Weavers Row."

"But you don't regret marrying Robert?"

Jessie looked thoughtful for a moment. Her life was so different now. "No," she said firmly. "Remember when you helped to make the nosegays for our wedding? I promised to do the same for you and I will. There are some lovely flowers in the gardens. I'll get my scissors out when it's time for you to get wed."

The wedding day wasn't to be the quiet affair that Alice had planned. Although Jacob was nominally Mary's stepfather, Alice was to give her daughter away at the altar. Most of Alice and Mary's lodgers had returned to Gorbydale now that the mill was in full production once more. They insisted they would be her bridesmaids at their own expense. Even those who had left her house on Weavers Row to be married would not be left out and wanted to accompany her to the chapel.

"You won't be taking your children to this wedding, will you?" asked Matthias, with a pointed glower at Matty.

"Yes, of course," said Jessie. "They'll want to see Mary married, and she is Matty's godmother."

The precocious Helen would not be excluded and was to be a flower girl along with her cousin Eleanor. Jessie gave a wry smile as she took the cousins shopping in Manchester for their outfits. Although she was barely four years old, Helen insisted on wearing pink and would not be satisfied until she had precisely the right amount of furbelows. Fair, timid Eleanor meekly accepted anything her bold cousin chose. Robert had insisted that Jessie too must have a new dress, although she had tried to save money by having an old dress altered. She chose a simple sailor suit for Matty, which she could alter to fit him. With Helen's demands, she had barely time to make her own choice in mauve taffeta before they caught the train back to Doveton station where the Overdale's trap met them. Jessie politely refused a cup of tea with her sister-in-law as she dropped Eleanor home.

"I'd better get home," she said reluctantly. "It's been a very tiring day with this madam."

Helen bridled at her mother's pointed glance and Elsie became apologetic.

"I hope the girls haven't been too much trouble," she said.

"Oh, Eleanor's been no bother at all," Jessie reassured her with a smile. "I'll take her shopping anytime."

Helen sulked all the way home but Jessie ignored her. She only wished that the children's grandparents wouldn't give way to her daughter's tantrums. She arrived home to find the house in an uproar. Matty had run over his grandfather's foot with his new walking frame. She quickly carried the distressed child up to the nursery, though he was now getting very heavy for her. The callipers he was wearing on his legs added to that weight. The nursemaid Lizzie followed behind carrying the walking frame, apologising all the way.

"Mrs. Overdale insisted that Master Matty come downstairs so she could show him some nice books in the library," she said tearfully. "You know how he loves pictures. We thought the Master was out of the way at the mill, but he came home because he was tired. Master Matty just wanted to say hello to him and he shot off before I could stop him. He bumped into his grandpapa's foot and then it was all hell to pay."

"Oh, it's probably the Master's gout," Jessie told her. "He's always cranky when that flares up. You don't have to keep calling him Master Matty, you know, Lizzie."

"I know you said so, Mrs Jessie, but his grandmama's been saying it all day and I just got into the habit," Lizzie excused herself. "I expect they'll insist on it now he's older, so I'll probably keep saying it."

"If you think so," said Jessie with a sigh. "I expect you're right." Matthias was always conscious of his status and that of his family.

Her young son was making good progress, though he'd struggled to walk with his condition. His legs were weak and so Jessie's brother John, an engineer on the railway, had designed the callipers to strengthen his legs. He'd arranged for a friend in the railway's forge to make them. These had been a great help, and he could now struggle round the furniture. John had come up with another solution to help his nephew. He'd designed the circular walking frame with wheels to support Matty and to help him walk further. His friend had helped him build the original model and as Matty had grown, they'd adapted the design so that longer struts could be added. It had a rim of padded leather to prevent him from being injured. Though it had taken him some time and many bumps to get used to it, Matty was now quite proficient on his frame and his legs were getting stronger. His pale face sweated with determination as he struggled to keep pace with his boisterous sister. Helen seemed oblivious to his problems as she involved him in her games.

Matty loved colour and pictures, though his eyesight was poor. Eventually he would wear spectacles, though his parents had not yet seen his difficulty. As Helen was forever finishing his sentences, his speech was slow but progressing. Matthias, though, ignored his namesake's progress and was forever muttering about institutions. Jessie, furious at his suggestions but feeling impotent to argue when she was under his roof, pointedly mentioned the expense and the subject was dropped. She was Matty's fiercest defender and the reason he was progressing well despite his disabilities.

Amy Walmsley rarely visited anymore, and whenever Jessie met her shopping in the town it was in the grim company of her mother-in-law. Jessie truly pitied Amy, knowing the older woman was hankering to move in with her son and daughter-in-law. She remembered how Taylor had pursued her and how nearly she'd been tempted. Listening to Amy, Jessie knew she'd had a very lucky escape. Amy nodded politely when Jessie invited her to tea with a pointed and sideways glance at the older Mrs. Walmsley.

"My daughter-in-law is kept very busy these days," sniffed Mrs. Walmsley. "And my rheumatism is playing me up, so I can't walk far," she added, despite the fact she hadn't been included in the invitation. "I expect you're kept busy yourself with your idiot son."

Hot anger flared in Jessie. "My son is not an idiot, Mrs. Walmsley. He has problems with walking but not with his intelligence. And I'll thank you not to spread such malicious gossip."

Mrs. Walmsley bridled at the challenge. "I'm sure I was misinformed."

"I would never have said such a thing," said Amy quietly. "Matty is an intelligent little boy."

"No, I know you wouldn't," Jessie told her, firmly placing the blame on Taylor. "I'll bid you good day Mrs. Walmsley, Amy."

She was bubbling with anger for the rest of the day and, unfortunately for Matty, his exercises with his mother were more rigorous.

CHAPTER 28: MARY'S WEDDING

Robert and Jessie took their children in the Overdales' gig to the wedding. Jessie was aware of the curiosity shown in her son by the other guests. Her children were now almost five years old. Helen had grown sturdy and pretty, with a mass of dark curling hair, tamed into ringlets for the occasion. She was livelier than her older but blonde and delicate cousin Eleanor, who was nervously clutching her basket of petals. Robert carried his son, awkwardly shaking hands with his father-in-law and Jessie's brothers. Matty gave everyone his lopsided smile and shook hands with his uncles, who welcomed him as one of their own. He whispered his greetings shyly as Jessie had instructed him.

"Hello, our lad," said Jacob, shaking his hand. "And welcome to me and your Aunty Mary's wedding. I'd best not kiss thee today, as you look proper grown up."

"How do you do, Grandad?" said Matty softly with a giggle at his own formality. Concentrating hard, he held out his small curling hand.

Robert looked at Matty with a dawning realisation. He had been so wrapped up in the mill, working long hours with his father, that he hadn't noticed the improvement and growing confidence in his son. The children were often in bed when he dragged himself away from the mill. Matty's speech may be halting and quiet and usually overwhelmed by Helen's chatter; his arms and legs would not always do as he asked; and his walking was unsteady and needed support, but he was not the 'dummy' that Matthias constantly referred to. Robert decided at that moment that he would not be ashamed of his son. The little boy was struggling bravely and needed his support.

"Come on old chap, let's get you seated," he said with a smile. "You're getting to be a bit heavy. You'll be carrying me soon."

Matty smiled. "Yes, Papa," he whispered with a giggle.

Jessie noticed their tentative bond with immense relief. Deep down she had feared that Robert might one day reject Matty, as her father-in-law kept hinting. She continually fought against sending her son to an institution and tried to ignore Matthias's snide remarks. Though now she strongly suspected that she might once again be expecting a child, with all the complications that might bring. By encouraging Matty to be independent, she had avoided lifting him in recent days so as not to damage any child she was carrying.

The little family were soon seated in the chapel. Moments later, the harmonium wheezed into melody and Helen came bouncing down the aisle, liberally strewing petals, followed by her nervous cousin. Alice smiled proudly at her family of Davenports and Overdales as she ushered the flower girls into the bench and took her daughter's posy.

Jessie felt calm for the first time in months as she listened again to the age old words she had spoken herself some years before. Though she chafed at times living with her in-laws and Matthias' tetchiness, she never regretted marrying Robert. His gratitude for her saving his life had mellowed into deep affection and love. Though she sometimes felt neglected with the children while he toiled away re-establishing the mill, she knew she was his rock and their bond had grown through their adversity. Beside her, the children wriggled in the seats as her husband listened attentively. She wondered how he would take the news of a possible addition to the family. Melissa would be pleased of course, as she had always wanted a large family herself. Matthias would moan about the extra expense with another mouth to feed. None of that mattered. A new life would come into the world and would live and love and struggle and worry just like the rest of them. That was all in God's hands, and there was nothing she could do about it. You could only try your best.

She smiled as the Welsh contingent behind Mary's new bridegroom filled the little chapel with joyous fervour as they sang the hymns. Then Dilwyn gave Mary a chaste kiss and they turned to receive the congratulations of all their friends, as enthusiastic as it was prolonged. Then they all retreated to the Sunday school for the wedding breakfast.

Soon there was little left of the hearty spread in the schoolroom, and the toasts had all been drunk and short but heartfelt speeches given. Matthias and Melissa had been thanked for their contribution to the feast. They had not attended, though they had been invited. Matthias had deemed the occasion as unsuitable to be merrymaking with his mill hands. For her part, Jessie had baked and cooked many dishes to supplement the wedding breakfast with help from Cook and Lizzie. She'd overheard Matthias complaining about her activities to his wife, but Jessie ignored him. She knew he was peeved because Melissa hadn't given him her full attention as she minded the children while the others were busy. Cradling her son to her as they trotted home in the gig, she wondered if her little family would ever have their own home.

Helen was still wide awake, chatting about the wedding and the dancing and her new dress.

"I doubt she'll sleep tonight," said Robert with a smile. "But I was very pleased with Matty. Everyone said how well he was doing."

Jessie stroked her sleeping son's forehead and wondered what the future held for her children. And there was the small matter of yet another one on the way.

She waited another week until the excitement of the wedding had died down and she was sure in her own mind that she was pregnant. Standing on the terrace one warm evening, Robert slipped an arm round her waist.

"You're growing quite bonny, young Mrs. Overdale," he teased. "Is this thanks to contentment with your lot?"

"Our lot might just well be growing, young Mr. Overdale," she told him with a smile. "I think we have another little Overdale on the way."

"Oh!" Robert looked stunned as this piece of news sank in. It was a moment before he finally smiled and said, "How wonderful." Then he added anxiously, "Do you think it will be all right?"

"If it isn't squashed in the doctor's bag," said Jessie with a wry smile.

Robert chuckled, but his brow was wrinkled. "Let's pray he — or she isn't."

CHAPTER 29: SISTERS

Dolly had now sent two consignments of cotton to Gorbydale and her bank balance, though small enough and safe from Clement, had enabled her to make some improvements to her home and the plantation. One of Barney's numerous relatives was a handy carpenter. He had made some rudimentary beds for Dolly so that at least the family weren't sleeping on the floor. He had also fashioned a chest from some old floorboards in an unused part of the house and carved her initials on the lid along with those of Clement. There had been an awkward moment when the boy enquired how large Dolly's bed should be. There had been rumours around the village about the state of the Duplege marriage, but Dolly insisted on a double bed, knowing that though her husband would probably never grace it, Albert sometimes crept in there after a bad dream.

Most of Barney's family had stayed loyal, as had most of the other ex-slaves. Though some younger ones had left to join a co-operative growing cotton, others had returned to their old homes and were helping in the fields. During the war, with no slave masters to order them around, they had cultivated their own plots for food. As they had been feeding Clement's family too, he mostly ignored the encroachment on his land. Now and again he moaned that they were living rent free, but Dolly soon reminded him of their reliance on Barney and the rest of the workers.

Albert was progressing well under the tutelage of Mr Leach. After his initial misgivings the teacher had settled down and, though his ability was limited, was even helping in the fields in loose cotton clothing. He'd finally abandoned his rusty black suit in the heat. Dolly was an able student too. With Jeremiah's help, she wrote glowing letters to her mother about her life and Albert's steady progress. The picture she painted was magnificent but blurred. No-one reading her letters would recognise the plantation on a visit there. Maggie was unlikely to visit and so with Jessie's help, she wrote how very proud she was of her daughter and how happy she was that Albert was thriving.

If Jessie and Maggie thought that Dolly's life was progressing smoothly, they would have been mistaken. Inside Dolly chafed that she wasn't a real wife, longing for some love or even just a smattering of affection. Deep down she wasn't really bothered that Clement had made no advances to her after that quick and confusing fumble in the Overdales' folly. He was more interested in whisky and occasional disappearances to Baton Rouge and pursuing his gambling with intermittent success. When he won, he was generous, especially to Albert. When he lost, he retreated to the porch with his whisky bottle.

"Your winnings might improve if you left that damn stuff alone," said Dolly, picking up another empty bottle in disgust. "I'm sure it befuddles your brain."

"I have no idea what your 'befuddles' means, but you may be right," sneered Clement with a shrug, taking a swig from another bottle.

Often she made any excuse to visit the Jacques plantation, glancing secretly and longingly at David. Her dreams and aspirations were filled with his image. Frustratingly, he treated her with the kindness of a brother and seemed unaware of her secret longing. So Dolly took refuge from her yearnings, ploughing her energy into improving the plantation, unaware that her life was about to change.

One hot afternoon, a cloud of dust reared up on the road and the beat of horses' hooves echoed in the still, hot air. Dolly came out to see who would arrive, eager for any visitors. She could not know the three people arriving by carriage were bearing a threat to her endeavours. Clement rose from his habitual chair on the porch.

"I know that face," he said, staring at the woman in the fashionable hat seated in the dusty carriage. He moved to meet it, puzzled. Dolly followed him, somehow anxious.

"How do you do, Uncle Clement?" said the woman, rising from her seat.

"Delia? Delia my dear, this is a pleasant surprise," said Clement smoothly, opening the carriage door and holding out his arms to help her down. "I'm afraid you will find us sadly underprepared for visitors, but you are surely welcome. This is wonderful news that you are still alive. We had no news of you at all. You should have written."

"I did not know if there was anyone at the plantation," she excused herself, looking embarrassed as she glanced round. She turned to the man beside her. "You know Johnny, my husband, of course."

Clement stared at the tall man who had just dismounted. Taller and older and now with a bristling moustache, he was still recognisable as the raw youth who had rode away to join the Union army.

"Bartholomew," Clement acknowledged him with a brief and somehow disapproving nod. "I must congratulate you both. Your sister will be thrilled to see you."

Delia looked confused. "Clemmie? Clemmie is alive?" she stammered.

"She is indeed," said her uncle. "She survived that hellhole in Vicksburg. Though I think you must prepare yourself for some sad news."

"Oh, I know Ma and Pa are dead," said Delia, lowering her eyes in modest sadness. "We saw where they were buried in Vicksburg." A sharp-eyed Dolly noticed she soon raised her eyes and glanced round, assessing her surroundings. "But Clemmie?" Delia's eyes brightened. "Dear Clemmie has survived, thank the good Lord. Where is she? I must see her."

Clement laid a restraining arm on her enthusiasm. "She is a little altered," he said tactfully. "She has been through a harrowing time."

"She survived thanks to Aunt Hattie's good care," Dolly told her firmly. "But she's recovering nicely."

"And who is this woman?" queried Delia irritably, taking in Dolly's plain dishevelled dress and sunburnt face.

Clement took in a deep breath. "This *lady* is my wife, Dolly. And you will soon be pleased to meet my son Albert too, your young cousin."

Delia stared at Dolly, then condescended to give her a brief nod, followed by a glance of obvious disapproval. "Things have certainly changed round here," she said, staring around, her sharp eyes alighting finally on the mansion.

"You hardly expected the old place to be the same after the war," said her uncle. "The South lost, dear girl, which will no doubt please your husband. You joined the winning side and now you see the consequences of your actions. Your old home is in ruins. There are no slaves to do your bidding. The plantation is struggling."

"We have a cotton crop in the fields, though," Dolly interrupted with a confident smile.

"Yes, thanks to my wife we have the cotton at least," said Clement, giving Dolly an unfathomable look. It was the first time he'd acknowledged her sterling contribution to the plantation. Clement turned his attention to the other man now stepping down from the carriage. He vaguely recognised his face. "Are you going to introduce me to this gentleman?" he asked.

"This is Mr. Crowther," said Johnny. "He is a land agent," he added hesitantly.

Dolly felt nervous as a surge of anger reddened Clement's face. A carpetbagger! A man who had come to try and snap up the surrounding failing estates for a pittance.

"Mr. Duplege," he said smoothly, offering his hand. Clement ignored it.

The visitors were saved from any further embarrassment as Delia gave a cry and rushed past her uncle with her arms outstretched. "Clemmie!"

Her sister had emerged from the house holding Albert's hand with Mr. Leach a few steps behind them. Further back Hattie hovered, screwing her apron in anxious hands.

Delia clasped her sister to her and began weeping rapturously, though strangely there were no tears visible on her cheeks. "Oh Clemmie, I thought you were dead. Thank the Lord. Thank the Lord."

The bewildered girl, her arms held stiffly by her sides, stared at the newcomer.

"She gets a bit confused," explained Dolly. "But she'll get used to you in a bit. This is your sister Delia, Clemmie, come specially to see you and with her husband too," she added gently.

"My sister knows who I am," snapped Delia. Faced with the blank and fearful face of Clemmie, this was patently untrue. Albert came and squeezed her hand.

"Say hello to Delia, Clem," he coaxed. "She's your sister. Wish I had a sister — or a brother. They could be my friend and I could play with them then."

Clement avoided Dolly's look of scepticism.

Clemmie relaxed. "I'm your friend," she whispered to the boy.

Delia was as confused as Clemmie. She glanced round in consternation. "Has she seen a doctor? Can anything be done? Johnny, we must get her to a doctor."

"I'm afraid she is a casualty of war, my dear lady," said Jeremiah Leach courteously. "I have witnessed the phenomenon many times before. With patience and the care of dear friends, she may recover. Your good doctor would no doubt have her assigned to an asylum, where I'm afraid good friends and patience are in short supply."

"I'm sure I know what's best for my sister," Delia snapped at him.

"Do you now?" muttered Clement.

His niece glared at him and an argument was sure to ensue when Dolly intervened. "Will you be staying?" she asked carefully. "Some of the bedrooms are dry at least, and the weather is good. Hattie and I can make up some beds. It's a bit primitive I'm afraid, but we didn't expect company."

"I'm sure Mr. and Mrs. Bartholomew can have my room," said Jeremiah graciously.

"That's so good of you, Mr. Leach," said Dolly, smiling at her ally.

"We hadn't decided to stay," sniffed Delia. "But I'll see what you have to offer." She marched into her old home with the others trailing behind. Clement watched everyone go before him, tight lipped and looking ominous. Sensing the awkwardness, Mr. Leach began politely asking the other two men about their journey. Dolly consulted the hovering Hattie about bedding and provision as they gathered in the mansion. They all stood alert as Delia emerged from one of the rooms.

"It's a wreck," she protested stridently. "The whole place is a wreck. We surely can't stay here. We'll have to go back to the town to the hotel. At least they have beds. I won't sleep on the floor."

"Perhaps we can discuss business in the morning," said Johnny, with an embarrassed smile.

"What business?" demanded Clement.

"Well, with her father and mother dead, surely Delia is heiress to the plantation?"

"I have no copy of my father's will at present. Henri must have surely taken his with him to Vicksburg. But I was always given to understand that the eldest male heir inherits the estate," said Clement firmly. "And as you know, that is myself. And I do have a son," he added, glancing at Albert then glaring at Delia and her husband.

"I had no idea if any of you were alive," protested Delia. "And anyway, as my father's daughters, Clemmie and I are entitled to a share of the estate."

"What estate?" demanded Clement. "There is nothing here but a ruin of a house and derelict fields. If it hadn't been for my wife and her workers, there would be no cotton either. You are entitled to a share of nothing, my dear. And I have made a home for Clementine."

"The land must be worth something," insisted Delia. "We will of course consult our lawyers. What is your opinion, Mr. Crowther?"

The man smiled obsequiously but gave a wary glance towards Clement, as if he had somehow recognised him. His frozen smile betrayed his suspicion that Clement might be dangerously unpredictable. "You must of course consult your lawyer, Mrs. Bartholomew," he murmured.

Delia snorted. "Of course we will. Perhaps you will be good enough to drive us back into town, Mr. Crowther."

"Would you like a drink before you go?" asked Dolly.

"No thank you," snapped Delia, although Johnny looked as if he was about to accept. Without another word, his wife marched towards the carriage, climbed aboard and waited for the others to join her.

"Good day, Mr. Duplege, Mrs. Duplege," said Johnny Bartholomew, discomfited by his wife's behaviour. "I hope to see you in the near future."

"Mr. Bartholomew," Clement nodded. "Is your father well?"

"Worn down by the war," admitted Johnny. "He has moved to Philadelphia to be nearer to us. I expect you heard he sold his practice."

"I had, and I was very sorry for it. He was a good doctor. The South needs good men right now. Please give him my regards," said Clement.

With that Johnny climbed beside his wife and gave a tentative wave as they drove away. Delia didn't even glance back.

"They didn't even have a drink," said Dolly, staring after their visitors as they drove away.

"She was always headstrong. Never mind, more whisky for me," snorted Clement with a shrug. "I recognised that blackguard Crowther, though." He gave a sharp, triumphant laugh. "I fleeced him and a gang of carpetbaggers of a pile of money at poker the other night in Baton Rouge. He'll have less of a stake to buy up our land anyhow."

They turned to see Hattie with tears in her eyes.

"I raised her from a baby," she murmured, "just like Miss Clemmie. She seems so hard now."

Dolly put a comforting arm round her shoulder, ignoring her husband's disapproving frown. "The war has changed a lot of people," she murmured, glancing at Clement.

He'd been eager to pounce on her in that lonely little temple at Overdale House. Since he'd returned to Gorbydale to claim his son, he hadn't laid so much as a finger on her. "She was always headstrong," he repeated, shaking his head. "Perhaps I'd better consult my lawyer too."

"Did your brother not leave a will?" asked Dolly. Her family never had anything to leave in such a document, but she knew they were keenly sought after in the gentry.

Clement shook his head. "My father's will stated that I should inherit the plantation if my brother died without male heirs, but where that paper is now I do not know. Like I said, I assumed Henri had taken it with him when he went to safety in Vicksburg, but where it is now is anyone's guess. Probably in ashes in some Vicksburg pit."

"But wouldn't your lawyer have a copy?" asked Dolly, anxious to secure her son's future.

"Maybe. He is the son of my father's lawyer and works in the same offices. But what does someone like you know of wills and copies?" he demanded to know, annoyed that he hadn't thought of it himself.

Dolly gave him a scathing glance. "'Cos I kept my ears and eyes open when I was skivvying for the gentry, that's why. Do you think servants are deaf and dumb?"

Clement grunted. "Skivvying, eh! I suppose that's another of your heathen Gorbydale words."

Dolly ignored him. He was forever underestimating her, but he would come to realise that she had a native cunning that surprised him. Now that he'd discovered she was reading and writing, he was becoming wary of her. She was quietly triumphant that he hadn't been able to get his hands on any of her cotton money and suspected he had a grudging respect for her ingenuity.

"I'll do as you suggest and see if my lawyer has a copy of my father's will," he told her. "Maybe in a day or two."

CHAPTER 30: FIRE!

Dolly could not sleep that night. She could see everything she had worked for slipping away. She tossed in the humid heat and, when she did doze, disturbing dreams flooded her tired brain. She was chasing a piece of paper which tossed and fluttered in the air, a fingertip away from her grasp. Her dream changed to one of clinging to David Jacques as he turned away. She called him but he could not hear her frantic shouts, and when he turned towards her he had the face of Clement. She woke with a start and went to the window to feel the cold air through the muslin. The night was silent except for the continual chirrup of the cicadas. They had driven her to distraction once, but now their persistent noise had faded with familiarity. Then she tuned her ears more finely. For a moment she thought she had heard the distinct beat of hooves nearby. She listened closely but heard nothing more. Exhausted by heat and anxiety, she lay back on her bed and drifted into a fitful sleep.

It was in the middle of the morning that Barney hurried up to the house in a state of distress. "Master Clement, Master Clement, your niece Miss Delia has been hurt in a fire. The hotel went up in smoke last night. She and Mr. Johnny got out just in time. They blamin' the poor boot boy Joey for smokin' near the wood pile. They dragged him out and hanged him, though he was screamin' he ain't done it. The whole town is in an uproar."

As Dolly listened, a cold trickle of dread slowly filled her. She turned to Clement, whose face was unreadable.

"How did you find out?" he demanded.

"Josiah went over there early this morning on the mule on an errand for Aunt Hattie. They took Miss Delia to the store where they let a room for travellers sometimes."

"This is terrible," said Clement, suddenly animated. "I must go and see if Delia and her husband are safe."

"They say her arm is badly burnt," said Barney. "Master Johnny, he all right, but her nightgown caught fire and burnt her. The staircase was burning when he carried her out and her sleeve caught fire."

"Poor woman. Shall I come with you?" asked Dolly.

Clement studied her for a moment. "I don't think my niece would welcome that. She obviously does not approve of our liaison."

"You mean our marriage," snapped Dolly.

"Exactly. If she is badly hurt, she might not welcome your presence."

"Suit yourself," said Dolly, turning back to the business of the day. "I've got plenty to do here. Anyway, I hope they're all right."

"They may need to come back here," Clement decided. "There won't be much room at the store. It all depends how badly she is hurt."

Dolly stood with Aunt Hattie as Clement rode away. "I suppose we'd better prepare for their arrival," she said with a sigh. "Have we enough bedding?"

"Miss Delia won't come here," said Hattie quietly. "She ashamed of us now. She a grand lady now in Philadelphia. She only wants the money that the plantation will bring if it's sold. She'd sell her home for thirty pieces of silver like Judas. She'd sell over her sister's head if she could and put that poor girl in some filthy asylum."

"It won't happen," Dolly reassured her, though she felt anything but confident herself. "Clement won't let it happen, Aunt Hattie. But I wonder what happened to Crowther?" she added as an afterthought. "Perhaps Josiah or Barney will know."

Barney was in the machine shed, oiling the cotton gin in anticipation of the harvest. He straightened up as Dolly came in. "This is a bad business, Mrs. Dolly," he said. "Miss Delia and Mr. Johnny could have been killed. Josiah said that Jacob the boot boy was screaming he was innocent something awful when they dragged him away. God help that poor boy."

"Did somebody see him smoking there?" asked Dolly.

"That Clucas, he say he saw him. He say Joey was always smokin' out there. Jemima in the kitchen say that boy don't smoke. Who they gonna believe? It's surely a bad business, Mrs. Dolly." Barney shook his head and bent back to the machine.

"Do you know what happened to that Crowther man that came here?" asked Dolly.

Barney looked up from his work, his face tight with suppressed emotion. "Josiah didn't say. I never thought to ask. 'Course he knew about Miss Delia and her man. They say no one was killed, though. Seems Joey raised the alarm 'cos he was up late polishin' their shoes before the mornin' and he smelt the smoke. That poor boy, he saved their lives and look what happened to him. A bad, bad business."

Dolly went slowly back to the house, her mind in turmoil. An awful suspicion was growing in her mind. If Delia and her husband had died in the fire, the plantation would be safe in Clement's hands. The vague memory of the hoofbeats in the night haunted her. Surely Clement would not put his niece's life at risk when there was every chance that a will would be found, naming him as the beneficiary of the estate. Aunt Hattie stared as Dolly slumped onto a makeshift stool. The gnawing ice deep inside her made her feel sick, and she held her stomach to quell the rising bile.

"You all right, Mrs. Dolly?" asked Hattie, alert to her obvious queasiness. "This is a terrible shock. Enough to make anyone sick." Then she smiled. "Or are you maybe expecting a little gift from heaven?"

"She suspects I'm pregnant," thought Dolly with a wry smile. "No, Aunt Hattie, I'm not," she said. "But you're right. All this business at the hotel has upset me. Barney is really upset too. I've just been to see him."

"That boy Joey was his cousin's son," Hattie told Dolly. She sniffed hard then dissolved in tears. "His cousin was sold before the war. Barney always kept an eye out for the boy. A good boy."

"Oh no! No wonder's he's so upset then," said Dolly, her eyes filling with sympathy. "Poor Barney. If that fire was set deliberately it was a wicked, wicked thing to do."

"Pray God it was just an accident," sobbed Hattie. "That's an awful thing right enough. But who would do such an evil thing as set fire to that hotel? One thing's for sure. It weren't Joey. Joey was a good boy. They just killed an innocent boy for nothin', God rot their wicked souls. That Clucas will surely burn in hell for his wicked lies."

The thought that Clement had a hand in it would not quit Dolly's churning thoughts. And if he would risk his niece's life, why would he hesitate to get rid of a wife who was no use to him? True, she was the mother of his son and he had needed her to look after Albert on the journey from England. Now they were here at his home in Louisiana, Aunt Hattie was doing a fine job of looking after Albert as Dolly worked hard trying to revive the plantation. With Jeremiah Leach educating him, Albert could easily grow up without her. Dolly had never felt so fearful and uneasy about her continuing survival.

Her only value to Clement was as the saviour of the plantation. She could not envisage the ex-slaves working for Clement. He could of course sell the estate to a land agent as Delia had planned. It might fuel his gambling habit for a while. But Dolly knew that deep in Clement's dark soul was an unshakeable attachment to his home. His family pride ran deep as his blood. Dolly now realised what a terrible risk she had taken when she sold his watch. Clement would never have sold it, not even to pay for his gambling. The Amiens plantation and its splendour had been foremost in his boasting when he had sat at the dinner table of Gorbydale House all those years before. Dolly had been listening when Melissa read aloud from Robert Overdale's letters of the luxury he'd witnessed during his visit to the plantation. Clement's home on the plantation had been the one stable anchor in his ramshackle life. While she devoted herself to its improvement, she would be safe. But she could never be sure. Restless with insomnia, in the isolation of a black night, she strained her ears, trying hard to recall if she had actually heard those retreating hoofbeats.

CHAPTER 31: FAREWELLS

Dolly could not settle to anything for the rest of the next day. Her eyes and ears were alert for any movement on the road. She watched Barney exert all his energies on the cotton gin, his face grim in the fight to curb his emotions. She distractedly helped Hattie by rearranging the makeshift bedrooms in case Delia and her husband came to stay. In the late afternoon Clement rode up to the mansion. He was filthy from the dust on the road and smelt of smoke.

"How is Delia?" called Dolly, hurrying to meet his horse.

"Give me a chance to have a drink, woman," he growled as he slid from his horse. "Where's Barney? Get him to take my horse."

"But…" Dolly tried again, anxious for news.

"A drink," snapped Clement.

He had drained a large glass of whisky before he spoke to anyone. Dolly, Aunt Hattie and Jeremiah waited nervously, reluctant to rouse his anger. Finally he began to relate what he'd found. "Delia's arm is in a bad way," he told them. "She wants to go home to Philadelphia. Johnny is bruised but otherwise unhurt. That land agent has left. He says he wants nothing to do with the case. I offered her a place here to recover, but she won't hear of it. She wants to go home. I called in at the lawyer's. He's looking for some will, but his office was ransacked during our recent troubles and he'll need some time to find a copy of my father's will and Henri's too if it exists."

"If either of them exist," Dolly thought darkly to herself. "Maybe in desperation, Clement has tried another kind of insurance to ensure his inheritance."

Her unease would not leave her over the next few days. Clement rode daily into town to see his niece. Before Delia left for Philadelphia, Dolly suggested that she might take Clemmie into town to see her sister.

"She won't want to see you," snapped Clement.

"But I should go with Clemmie and take Albert too to calm her. I needn't see Delia. I could wait outside."

Reluctantly Clement agreed. He had no desire to accompany Clemmie into town where the local population were intrusively curious about the terrified girl. It had been a good suggestion from Dolly that Albert should accompany them. The little boy had a touching and pacifying effect on his friend. Clemmie took some persuading to go, though. They rode into town on the cart with Barney driving. He was grimly silent on the journey, despite Dolly's efforts. Albert chatted happily to Clemmie as they jolted along. Listening distractedly to his prattle, she clutched his hand for support.

The little group caused plenty of interest as they rode down the dusty dirt street. In a prominent position loomed the blackened shell of the hotel, and a heavy reek of smoke still pervaded the air. Barney averted his eyes and pulled the cart up outside the store. Dolly wondered what to do next, but Johnny Bartholomew helpfully arrived to greet them, all apologies and concern.

"Do not let that woman near me!"

Dolly heard the screech from the open window. Johnny went red and pretended not to hear his wife.

"I thought perhaps Mrs. Bartholomew might like to see her sister Clemmie before she travels home," said Dolly politely, ignoring the insult and summoning up manners and a refined accent she'd adopted from Honora in Gorbydale. "I won't come in myself so as not to distress her. How is she?"

"She's in terrible pain as you can imagine," he spluttered. "It has mightily affected her patience as you can understand."

Dolly bit her lip and nodded in sympathy, thinking it unlikely that Delia had much patience to begin with.

"Luckily it is her left arm that is burnt," Johnny stammered on. "I don't exactly mean lucky but I... Well you know and I... This has been a great shock to both of us. I think it best that we travel home, where my father can treat her and advise her. She will be happier there."

"Of course," said Dolly. "If there is anything we can do...?"

Johnny shook his head.

"Perhaps you would escort Clemmie and Albert to see her," suggested Dolly and added in a whisper, "Be very careful with Clemmie. She is of a very nervous disposition, as you can see. Albert will look after her."

"Thank you, thank you," said Johnny with relief. "I am sure she is well cared for at the plantation."

"We do our best," said Dolly proudly.

He gently helped Clemmie down, and she stood stricken on the road until Albert hopped down and grabbed her hand.

"Howdy, Miss Duplege," said a bystander loudly. "Nice to see you in town again."

The pretty Duplege sisters had been a welcome sight in town before the war, especially as they had loved to spend money. Clemmie looked instantly afraid, and Johnny and Albert hurried her into the store. A shriek of delight echoed from the sickroom.

"Oh Clemmie. Dearest Clemmie."

"Aunt Hattie says Miss Delia wanted to put her sister into an asylum," muttered Barney, unimpressed by Delia's loud declaration.

Dolly was silent. She hoped it wouldn't come to that but until a will was found, the future was an unknown and worrying problem looming before her.

CHAPTER 32: A LETTER FROM AMERICA

Jessie was sitting with the children leafing through one of Robert's old picture books. She never tired of looking at the pictures herself and wished she'd had such books when she was small. Her parents, struggling with three small children and only her father's wage coming into the house, reluctantly found picture books were an unnecessary expense. Robert, the spoilt only child of indulgent parents, had had plenty of books and their children were using them now. Though some favourites were tatty and well read, the pictures were still bright. Matty curled up beside her as she pointed to the pictures of animals.

"What's that, sweetheart?" she asked, pointing to the picture of an elephant.

"A lellyphant," said Helen, glancing over, although she had been looking through another book.

"Let Matty answer for himself," Jessie chided her with exasperation. "He's not daft."

Matty peered at the book. His parents had not yet realised how bad his eyesight was. "A lellyphant," he murmured.

"It's an *elephant*," insisted his mother. "Say el-e-phant."

Matty smiled and repeated the word.

"Good boy," said Jessie.

"I knew it first," said Helen. "Grandmamma says I'm a clever little thing."

"I'm sure she does." Jessie watched her daughter confidently leafing through her book. She knew she was sometimes hard on Helen, but Matty might never improve if his sister forever answered his questions for him. "Perhaps Papa will take us to

Manchester to see the zoological gardens at Belle Vue so we can see a real elephant," she told them.

Helen dropped her book and danced round the room, clapping her hands and singing, "a lellyphant, an *elephant*, yes, yes, yes." She waved her arm in front of her nose like a trunk and Jessie and Matty laughed.

Matty clapped his hands in his own awkward and disjointed manner. His mother promised them she would ask their father that evening. He would not refuse a request from his daughter, though taking Matty might cause some problems. Jessie had found a pushchair in a second hand shop. She'd cleaned it up and painted it. It was mostly used to take her son up to see his grandfather at Weavers Row. Helen walked on her sturdy little legs but complained and wanted a ride in the pushchair on the way home. Jessie wondered what Robert would think about taking the chair out in public. That evening, seeing the children's excitement, he happily promised a visit to the zoo.

Robert spent many hours at the mill now that more reliable supplies of cotton were arriving in England. His father was tetchy and interfering, though insisting that Robert was now in charge of the mill. Taylor Walmsley busied himself with the business side of things.

On one of her visits to see Jessie, Mary gleefully repeated the gossip from her lodgers. Taylor had been an unpopular overseer and when he had ventured into the mill, he found that many of the mill hands were surly towards him, resenting his presence. Though a partner now in the Invincible, he'd guessed that the spinners were sniggering at him behind his back. They'd made snide remarks about his elevated position and his attempts to improve the cotton supply.

Jessie knew his experiments with Indian cotton had not been a success despite his extensive travel, and now the American bales were returning once more. With Matthias ever interfering in the mill, Robert mentioned that Taylor felt happier away from it, selling the finished thread. Taylor had mentioned his successful profiteering during the American Civil War and wondered if his talents were better served elsewhere.

Amy, his Anglo-Indian wife, seldom visited Jessie these days. Once, she had frequently slipped into Gorbydale House to help with Matty and massage and exercise his little limbs. Jessie was delighted when she arrived one morning just after breakfast.

"I apologise for coming so early," she said, then lowered her voice. "Taylor has left for Manchester, and I thought I might leave the house before his mother arrives. She seems to appear these days whenever Taylor is out of town. I suppose she's lonely," she said kindly.

"More like she wants to keep an eye on you to see you don't come gallivanting up here," said Jessie with a chuckle. "I can't abide that woman."

"She is difficult," admitted Amy. "She still keeps hinting that I should have a baby of my own."

"She should mind her own business," Jessie growled. "Old bitch."

"What's a bitch?" asked Helen, gazing up innocently at her mother.

Jessie and Amy bit their lips so as not to laugh.

"It's a lady dog, dear. A gentleman dog is called a dog, but a lady dog is called a bitch. But you mustn't say it in front of your grandmamma, because it's not polite," she explained, trying to keep a straight face.

Amy left before they had their midday meal, and that afternoon Jessie had some time to herself. The children were having a nap, and so she was pleased when an envelope arrived bearing an American stamp. She recognised Honora's writing at once and settled down to read the news.

At first, after the usual enquiries about the family and the children, Honora wrote of her progress in her studies. She mentioned Arden's infrequent visits. Though still with the American navy, he was planning to find a berth on a British ship as an engineer. Jessie's usual source of news about her brother was from the letters he sent to their father. This letter was an unusually long one. After Honora had written all her news, Jessie came to a separate sheet, and when she began to read it a disturbing chill fell over her.

I do not wish to disturb you with what I must tell you next. You will remember when I wrote and told you that my good friend Verity Cain was murdered in cold blood at the hospital. Her father is an eminent physician and though he has offered a very substantial reward, there is still no one arrested for her murder. My dear friend Ben Clark was suspected and arrested, but I suspect only because he is Jewish. He had a cast iron alibi and so they had to set him free. I have had a very deep suspicion about someone else for some time, but the police will not take me seriously. I must write to you as my dearest friend so that if anything should happen to me, you will be able to take my suspicions to the police.

Jessie stared at the letter and tried to remember when the murder had taken place. She was sure it was some years before. She wondered about Ben Clark, Honora's 'dear friend' and hoped she was not going to jilt her brother Arden for him. Putting her worries aside, she continued to read.

You may remember that I betrayed Clement Duplege to the police in Washington. I do not think he is a man who is willing to forget these things. By coincidence he was in New York at the time of the murder. I only found this out because of your letter telling me of Dolly's elopement. I checked with the shipping agents, and sure enough he was in the city at that time. A hair was found on my dear friend's body that was not one of her own, and I am convinced it was dyed.

I do not think you met Duplege in Washington, but I can assure you that he did dye his hair as a disguise. I am convinced that he murdered Verity, mistaking her for me. We were of similar build, and our hair was similar too. She was strangled from behind so that he would not have seen her face.

I took my theory to the police, but they dismissed it as a fantasy. They were sure I was only trying to save my friend Ben. I have, however, written with my suspicions to Detective Alan Pinkerton, who is now in Canada.

I received a brief reply saying he would look into the matter, but as yet nothing has been done. I expect he is very busy, but I do hope that something will eventually be investigated. I am worried, though, that Duplege will return to exact his revenge when the case has long been forgotten in New York. I have said nothing of this to Arden, and I hope you will keep my confidence. I am sorry to burden you with my problems, but I was desperate to confide in someone.

I mean to write again to Detective Pinkerton and plead my case. He will surely have contacts in Washington, though I am afraid the war has drastically destroyed any trust between North and South. Louisiana, where I'm sure Duplege has retreated, is a long way from New York.

Please do not trouble yourself about this letter. It is merely an insurance policy should anything happen to me.

She ended with the usual endearments on a separate page so that Jessie could show most of the letter to the rest of the family.

Jessie stared at the sheaf of paper on her lap and felt afraid for her friend. She took the separate page and, folding it, placed it underneath some papers in an old oak bureau she and

Robert had rescued from the attic. She had only glimpsed Clement Duplege a couple of times in Gorbydale, an exotic presence in his light coloured suit and foxy red hair. If he had murdered an innocent girl as Honora suspected, then surely he would stay in Louisiana out of the way of the authorities. And what of Dolly, his wife? Did she know or even suspect that her husband could be a murderer?

Jessie did not mention Honora's extra page to her husband, unwilling to burden him with his cousin's worrying suspicions. Robert had enough to worry about with the mill and his father's irritability. Now she had told him about her pregnancy, he was also becoming concerned about its outcome. He was continually anxious about her health although she felt fine. Melissa was of course delighted when she heard her news. Matthias grudgingly congratulated the prospective parents.

"Let's hope it's a healthy boy this time," he muttered.

Jessie really didn't care about the child's gender as long as it was healthy.

CHAPTER 33: A TRIP TO THE ZOO

The following Saturday was bright and sunny, and Robert decided to take the morning off from the mill to take his wife and children to Belle Vue as he'd promised. He'd noticed that Jessie seemed distracted, falling into reverie at odd moments. He assumed her anxiety was something to do with the expected baby.

"We'd better go to Belle Vue before you become too big to enjoy it," he teased her, squeezing her waist. "Will you be all right to travel so far?"

"Of course I will," she protested, unwilling to miss the visit. When she was younger, lots of her friends had visited the zoological gardens and funfair near Manchester, but her father had deemed it too frivolous for chapelgoers. Now Jessie was a wife and mother she could choose for herself. She had been mildly sick in the mornings but was determined not to miss the treat. Early that morning they loaded Matty's pushchair onto the trap, despite Matthias' suggestion that the boy be left at home. "Matty's not going to miss our outing," said Jessie firmly.

"I'd have come myself if I'd been a bit younger," said Melissa, helping Helen aboard the trap.

Matthias left them to it with a snort but arrived back to wave them off.

The crowds all dressed in their best had begun arriving from the city by the time the little family arrived. They were met with a happy mass of visitors and had some trouble manoeuvring through the crowd.

"Fancy bringing a child like that," Jessie heard some woman remark and was about to turn to berate her.

Robert touched her arm and smiled. "Some people are very ignorant," he said loudly. "They have no manners at all."

The woman tutted and moved quickly away.

"Please don't get upset, Jessie, every time someone makes a remark about Matty," he murmured, so the child wouldn't hear. "Just mark it up to their ignorance. We know what a brave little boy he is."

Reluctantly she agreed with him but was sorry she hadn't been able to give the woman a piece of her mind.

The rest of the day was a success. The children were delighted with the animals, laughing in delight at the monkeys. Helen was disappointed that there was no elephant but soon forgot once she had seen the lions, kangaroos and rhinos.

"Like Noah's Ark," said Matty happily, remembering one of his colourful picture books.

"Good lad," Jessie told him, well pleased he had noticed.

On a bench in the gardens they enjoyed the picnic that the cook had prepared for them. Melissa had insisted they bring their own food, saying that food bought in the gardens would be adulterated. Some people did stare at Matty in his trolly, but Jessie learned to ignore them as Robert had suggested. Helen shouted at one boy who called her brother a dummy.

"Dummy yerself!" she called. "You're just higorant."

As the afternoon wore on, they reluctantly left for home and arrived tired but elated just as the sun was beginning to set.

"We must do that again. Perhaps you should come with us, Mother," Robert told Melissa.

Jessie smiled, knowing it might be some time before they could take three children and a pushchair and Robert's mother in the trap. But she had really enjoyed her day. Despite the small incidents with Matty, all the pleasure of seeing her children enjoy themselves was worth the effort.

CHAPTER 34: THE END OF A DREAM

Dolly was edgy. Delia and her husband had returned to Philadelphia with a veiled threat to consult a lawyer. Clement shrugged when Dolly asked him about his inheritance.

"My lawyer will find a will anytime soon," he said nonchalantly. "In any case, it is her word against mine. Do you suppose a woman who has deserted her country to marry an enemy of the South will convince any judge around here that she is entitled to the plantation? How little you know," he added with a sharp laugh.

All the same, Dolly was uneasy. She could hardly concentrate as she walked the fields with Barney, anxiously looking for signs of disease or infestation. The cotton was weeks away from being ready to process, and her mentor was continually warning of the disasters that could befall their crop. Besides her unsettling suspicions, she felt listless in the heat.

Albert fretted as Aunt Hattie kept him confined in the shade. His ramblings around the mansion had nearly ended in an accident as some floorboards on an upper floor had collapsed under his weight. Clement had investigated and found most of the upper floor unstable and the roof riddled with holes.

Delia had been gone several weeks, and Clement's lawyer had still not discovered a will. Finally he left the plantation to find some amusement on a riverboat and, despite his continual neglect of her anyway, Dolly felt lonely.

"I think I will ride over to the Jacques' farm and see what arrangements they've made to ship our crop," she told Barney casually.

"I'm right busy at present, Mrs Dolly," Barney told her with an apologetic glance. He had always been available to comply with her requests, but he had been trying to fix the roof of his shack while he had a little time before the tumult of the harvest.

"That's all right, Barney. I know the way. I can go on my own," said Dolly confidently.

"Too dangerous for a lady to ride on her own round these parts," said Barney in alarm. "If you just wait a day, Mrs Dolly, I'll go with you and…"

"Barney, I'll be fine," Dolly stubbornly assured him. She headed for the stable as Barney followed her, pleading with her for patience.

"I'll go tell my folks," said Barney, turning to go, but Dolly ignored him and carried on tightening the saddle on Albert's pony.

Albert wasn't happy for his mother to ride Gorby but watched sullenly as she prepared to ride away.

"I'll be very careful with him," she reassured him. "He needs the exercise or he'll get very fat." Dolly was eager to get away, and even her son's reluctance and pleading eyes could not stop her. The heat had taken hold of Dolly and a flame had slowly smouldered until it was burning in her whole body. She badly wanted to see David. He had always been kind and courteous towards her, but in her fevered state his kindness had grown in her imagination to something akin to love. A letter from Robert Overdale about the cotton crop had given her an excuse.

"Mrs. Dolly…" pleaded Barney.

"I'll be fine," she said again.

"They's all sort of bad men hanging 'bout since this war, Mrs. Dolly. Please wait for me."

"Oh Barney, don't be an old woman," Dolly scolded him.

He stepped back as she scrambled aboard the pony. Then he had an idea. Grabbing a riding crop from a nail, he handed it to her. "Take this, Mrs. Dolly. Take it and use it if you must."

Dolly took it to please him and headed off out into the heat. She was grateful for the broad straw hat that her workers had made for her when she was out in the fields. But she needed to see David. She didn't know what she would say when she saw him, but the desire just to look at his face overwhelmed her. There was always the excuse of cotton if they asked why she had arrived alone. The dust whirled from the pony's hooves as she trotted on. She had never travelled on her own so far, and in the silent heat she began to glance nervously around. It was with great relief that she spotted the roof of the Jacques' house appearing through the trees.

She was met with astonished hospitality by Nathan. "Why have you ridden over on your own, Mrs. Duplege?" he asked. "What was Duplege thinking of, to let you come so far? Why isn't Barney with you?"

Dolly laughed with relief as she glanced slyly around to see if David was about. "Mr. Duplege is away from home," she said gaily. "Barney wanted to come, but I told him not to as he was busy." She hoped Clement wouldn't find out about her bold move as Barney might get into trouble. "I thought I'd come and ask about our cotton before it ripens. I've had a letter from the Overdales."

"We have too," he told her with a smile. "But the cotton is the last thing on our mind at the moment. My son David is going to be married after the cotton's gathered in, and we've been sure looking forward to having a woman about the house again." His wife had died many years before, and Nathan had brought up David on his own.

229

"Married?" asked Dolly in a daze.

"Sure. He's been courtin' a neighbour's girl for a while now. Jassy O'Neill has finally decided she's old enough to leave her Mammy," he said, laughing. "I'm sure there's an invitation for you folks on the way."

"That's … that's … wonderful news," said Dolly faintly. She felt sick as her dreams shattered and tumbled about her feet. She wanted to cry.

"Are you all right?" asked Nathan.

"I think it must be the heat," she murmured. "Did you mention a drink? I'd be surely grateful."

He led her into the house, and a smiling young girl came into the room beside the Jacques' cook. She looked barely out of school, her hair in a big gingham ribbon which matched her dress. "Howdy do?" she said brightly when Nathan introduced Dolly. "You mean you rode all that way on your own? That sure is brave. An' folks say you're married to Clement Duplege?" Her eyes opened wide in alarm. "Why, my Mammy says he's the very devil. You truly sure are brave."

Dolly wanted to laugh aloud. Her emotions were in turmoil, and here was this fresh-faced country girl telling her how brave she was. Her heart gave a jolt as David came into the room and slipped an arm round his fiancée's trim waist.

"Why hello, Mrs. Duplege. Someone told me you'd arrived. Have they told you the news? I hope you all will be coming to the weddin' — if Mr. Duplege is agreeable, of course."

"Oh, if he's not agreeable that's too bad!" said Dolly with a frivolous laugh. "But I would be honoured to come to your wedding whether he comes or not."

The young couple smiled at one another, tearing another strip off Dolly's wounded heart.

"I've come about arrangements for our cotton to be shipped," she said with a deep breath.

"And she came all on her own," said Jassy with a look of envious admiration.

"The O'Neills have decided to send their cotton to England alongside ours. Robert Overdale says he'll buy as much as we can send," Nathan told her.

Dolly hardly paid any attention as they discussed their business. She had already sent cotton crops to Gorbydale and was sure she knew the routine. Now she didn't wish to stay long, needing to be alone with her bitter disappointment. Rising from her chair she made her excuses, but to her dismay, David and Jassy insisted on accompanying her in their gig to the edge of the Amiens plantation. Though Dolly protested, she had no choice but to agree. As they drove along, Jassy was full of excitement about the coming wedding. She happily told Dolly all her plans: the satin, the lace, the aunties baking cakes.

"And how did you meet Mr. Duplege?" asked Jassy coyly, obviously eager to discover how Dolly had ended up with 'the very devil'.

"Oh, he was in Lancashire on business," said Dolly faintly.

She glanced at David, wondering if Robert Overdale had told him of all the sordid details of her marriage. She remembered the brief civil ceremony in the Liverpool registry office, wearing her work clothes. Tommo Tate had been standing by with his arms folded, grimly determined that Clement would do right by his daughter; Maggie had been sniffing into a grubby handkerchief. No lace or satin for Dolly, just a drab, greasy dress with sleeves rolled up to hide their frayed ends. She was relieved when the lovers waved goodbye and headed home, their heads together as they drove away.

If Dolly had felt lonely before, she certainly felt it now as she headed home along the empty road. She slumped dejectedly on the pony as she realised what a fool she'd been to build her dreams around David. It was obvious now he'd never even thought about her. And what a tangled and frightening mess she would have caused if he had. Clement would never have let her run away with her son. The folk on the plantation would have been abandoned to the likes of Clucas. Worst of all would be Clement's anger. He surely would have killed them both.

CHAPTER 35: CLUCAS

Wrapped in her thoughts, she hardly saw the road. Now on familiar territory, the pony plodded steadily on towards his stable. Gorby started in surprise when a man emerged from the trees and grabbed his bridle. Dolly tightened her grip on the reins to steady herself and glared at the intruder. It was almost as if she'd conjured him up in her misery.

"Let go of my horse, Clucas," she snarled.

He tightened his grip. "Well, if it ain't Missy Duplege come to visit," he said with a mocking grin, his teeth black and crooked.

"Let go," she repeated in a hiss. "I'll tell my husband."

"Husband, eh!" he said with a hollow laugh. "Well, you can tell your 'husband' that I want my money."

"I don't know anything about your money. Let go of my horse." Dolly suddenly remembered the riding crop Barney had tucked at the side of the harness. She reached and grabbed it.

Clucas leapt back in surprise as she lashed out. He clutched his face and stared in horror at the trickle of crimson on his filthy hand. "You bitch!" he yelled and lunged for the pony again.

Dolly was too quick for him. She slashed at his hand as she urged the little pony into a panicked gallop away from danger.

"I want my money," Clucas yelled after her. "You tell him the hotel ain't the only thing that's gonna burn if I don't get it."

Dolly was trembling as she forced the pony on. It was tiring under her weight, but Clucas was far behind. Why had Clucas been so scathing about her 'husband'? What had Clement said about their empty marriage in his whisky clouded visits to the hotel? Surely he wouldn't admit to being so unmanly?

Then, as yet more sickening fear seeped into her trembling body, she wondered why Clucas was owed money. She remembered Aunt Hattie telling her that it was Clucas who said he'd seen Joey smoking near the woodpile. His accusations had caused an innocent boy's death. Had Clucas himself set that fire and, more terrifying still, was it on Clement's instructions? The echoes of the hoofbeats on the night of the fire filled her brain. The destruction of his niece would surely have solved Clement's inheritance problems. A fearful notion struck Dolly. If Clement could destroy his niece, then he would have no conscience about getting rid of his sham wife too.

What had begun with a pleasant ride to the plantation of a man she thought she loved was now turning into a nightmare. Dolly and the pony were near to collapse when a familiar figure came into view. She froze with fear until she saw it was Barney on the mule. Then grateful relief flooded away her terror.

"Mrs. Dolly, are you all right?" he asked, staring at her in concern as she breathed hard in her wild agitation.

She pathetically held up the riding whip as her fear dissolved into tears. "Oh Barney, I'm so glad to see you," she sobbed. "I had to use the whip on Clucas. He came and grabbed Gorby and I had to drive him away."

There was a smear of blood on the whip. Barney noticed it with surprise. "You must've hit him pretty hard, Mrs. Dolly."

"With all my might," she said vehemently as her weeping began anew.

"Master Duplege will have something to say about this," he said solemnly, shaking his head.

Dolly groaned. "Do we have to tell him, Barney? You warned me not to ride out alone, and I stupidly took no notice of you. I'm really, really sorry. I don't want you to get into trouble for letting me go alone. Perhaps we shouldn't tell him." Dolly was once again trying to extricate herself from trouble. She thought she'd come a long way from that hapless girl in Gorbydale, always ready with an excuse. Now here she was wheedling an old friend by insinuating he would be the one to be punished for her folly. Barney watched her face carefully, almost as if he could read her thoughts, and she blushed under his scrutiny. It hadn't been so long ago that he would never have dared to look a white woman in the face, but he trusted her and she knew it. Dolly felt guilty for even suggesting her subterfuge.

"I don't know, Mrs Dolly. That Clucas is a very bad man. Master Clement will surely get to know what happened one way or another. If we lie, we'll surely be in more trouble."

"Clucas's face might have healed by the time Clement gets home. Oh Barney, Clucas said he wanted his money. He said to tell Clement that the hotel wasn't the only thing that was gonna burn if he didn't get it. Oh Barney, I was so frightened."

Barney stared at her again as he digested what she had just said. "He said he wanted his money or he'd burn us down," he repeated for confirmation.

Dolly nodded vigorously and wiped her nose on her sleeve.

"That's a different matter altogether, Mrs. Dolly," said Barney, his eyes narrowing. "My cousin's boy Joey was hanged for that hotel, and Clucas was the man that accused him. Looks like we found the real culprit." He paused and looked at Dolly steadily. "And seems like Master Clement is in on it too."

"Oh Barney, that's what I suspected too," whimpered Dolly, her eyes wide with fear. "What do we do?" She had caused such a tangled thread of trouble with her foolish ride out to see her phantom lover. How could she have been so stupid and headstrong? She thought hard. Clement would have to be told, if only to warn him. Dolly would have to give him Clucas's message without implicating Barney in any way, perhaps saying that Barney was with her. If Clement wasn't told, the plantation might burn down. Barney reluctantly agreed with her when she told him what she planned.

"You must say I was just a ways from you and I didn't hear what Clucas was sayin'," he advised. "But don't say anything about all this to Aunt Hattie or the folks at home until Master Clement gets home."

Dolly promised she wouldn't and tried to compose her face.

"I don't like lying, but it's the only way," said Barney.

It turned out that it was not the only way.

CHAPTER 36: A KIND OF JUSTICE

Some days later, just before Clement arrived home, the sodden body of Clucas was found in a nearby creek. Zeb saw the body as he rode the mule to town in the early morning on an errand for Aunt Hattie. He hurried back to the plantation with the news and then rode into town for the sheriff. No one wanted to touch the body until he arrived, then they dragged him from the water. On the bank lay an empty whisky bottle.

The sheriff arrived with his deputy and questioned everyone, but nobody had seen Clucas for days until he had been found that early morning.

"Must have drowned during the night," ventured Zeb. "People walking and riding this road all day yesterday and he wasn't there."

The deputy immediately began to fire questions at Zeb until someone mentioned the whisky bottle. Dolly immediately noticed that it was the same brand of spirits that Clement drank. She had gone with Barney to the scene. It was barely two hundred yards from the mansion. Clement brought in his whisky from Baton Rouge. She sincerely hoped that if anyone else noticed the label they would just assume that Clucas had somehow taken it from the Amiens plantation or been given it by Clement. Though the deputy was all for arresting Zeb, the general verdict was that Clucas had drowned in the creek in a drunken stupor. Dolly feigned surprise when she was questioned by the sheriff, who arrived at the house to enquire if the folks there knew anything.

"Someone from the store said that ain't a bottle they sell," he said, looking at her sternly. "Said your husband might know where Clucas got it from. Seems it's fine stuff."

"I wouldn't know," she asserted primly. "I don't touch Mr. Duplege's whisky. He's away from home and I'm not sure where he keeps it. My husband should be home in a few days. Maybe he'll be able to tell you if he gave Mr. Clucas a bottle of the whisky. I'm sure I don't know. Clucas was hanging round here a few days ago. Maybe he stole it, but I just don't know."

Clucas and his sour ways had made as many enemies in the town as on the plantation. There was no one likely to mourn him.

It was later that day that Clement arrived home in a foul mood. He muttered something about a bad gambling session. Dolly kept silent about the encounter with Clucas on the dusty road. She noticed, though, how his mood lightened when he heard that Clucas was dead and the verdict that he had drowned while drunk on Clement's whisky.

"What I don't understand, though," he said, "is what Clucas was doin' with a bottle of my whisky. I know how many bottles I got, and I'm sure there ain't one missin'. You didn't give him a bottle, did you?"

"Of course not," protested Dolly. "Like I told the sheriff, I don't even know where you keep your whisky. It's certainly a puzzle," she added slyly. "Perhaps you gave it to him for some favour when you were drunk yourself."

"That whisky was good stuff, bought when I had my last winning streak," snapped Clement sourly. "I wouldn't waste it on the likes of Clucas."

"It's certainly a puzzle," repeated Dolly innocently.

Clement gave her a guarded glance then fell silent. He stared out onto the road leading to town and skirting the creek where

Clucas had drowned. Dolly could guess where his thoughts lingered. She felt secure, though, that he could not suspect that his wife and Barney now held a deadly secret about the fire at the hotel.

Barney's mood had lightened too. Dolly caught him singing as he finished the work on the roof of his shack. He looked down from his ladder as she approached. "Afternoon, Mrs. Dolly. You hear anything more about ol' Clucas?"

She shook her head.

"I reckon justice has been done regarding that ol' devil," he said quietly. "Most justice, anyway. An eye for an eye, a tooth for a tooth and all that."

She nodded silently. They never spoke of the incident on the road again.

"I called at the Jacques place while you were away," Dolly casually mentioned to Clement a couple of days later. She was worried that he might find out anyway. "We are to be invited to a wedding. David Jacques is marrying Jassy O'Neill, one of their neighbours."

"That simpering ninny," said Clement scathingly. "So you're gonna lose your beau?"

"I don't know what you mean," protested Dolly, hoping she wasn't going to blush.

"Don't think I haven't noticed you mooning over that … that damn fool."

"Anyone would think you were jealous," his wife defended herself by goading him.

Clement snorted. "Don't make me laugh. Anyway, don't expect me to go to the damn fool wedding."

"I shall make your excuses then," said Dolly, lifting her chin in defiance. "Perhaps I might have a new dress for the occasion."

"Please yourself," growled Clement.

That was precisely what she was going to do, despite the fact that it would hurt her to witness the end of her dreams. "The O'Neills will be sending their cotton to Gorbydale too," she told him as she left him to his thoughts.

Clement shrugged. He didn't seem interested in the cotton at all now that he was unable to get his hands on the proceeds. His wife hadn't yet convinced him that cotton was the only way to improve their future.

Dolly surveyed her wardrobe and, as she'd suspected, found the clothes she had left were past mending to look respectable. Most of her Liverpool trousseau had been sold, and her one remaining good dress had been altered for Clemmie, who had left Vicksburg with hardly anything. Dolly decided she should take a trip with Barney into the town and look in the general store for something suitable.

The women nodded to her in brief acknowledgement as she went into the store, head held high against their scrutiny. The men stared resentfully. The wife of the proprietor was cool, which was hardly surprising considering their last encounter. To Dolly's disappointment, there was nothing in the store but serviceable cotton. She decided to spend some of her precious cotton earnings to buy something that would not put her to shame among the planned silks and satins of the wedding. Repairs to the house would have to wait. She also wanted to escape the plantation for a while. The death of Clucas and her suspicions about Clement's involvement in the fire continually haunted her thoughts.

"How far is it to Baton Rouge?" she asked Clement.

He stared at her. "And why would you want to go to Baton Rouge?"

"I'd like a new dress for the wedding," she told him. "I didn't have one for my own. You wouldn't want me to look like a pauper among your neighbours, would you?"

"I don't give a damn either way," he growled. "You'd save yourself some money by staying at home and looking after your son."

"I was thinking of taking Albert and Clemmie with me," she said. "We're all desperate for clothes. Clemmie's dress is patched with an old flour sack."

"She'd be in fear of her life in that hell hole," said Clement. "Look how she was when she went to visit Delia."

"Not if Albert is with her. I can't buy her clothes without her. She's much taller than me."

Clement relaxed back in his sagging cane armchair, his hands folded on his stomach, and regarded her with interest. "Baton Rouge, eh? You're determined to go to Baton Rouge with a small boy and a half-witted girl, a town teeming with the dregs of the Union army and navy."

Dolly hesitated. She hadn't thought about the details, imagining only a taste of civilisation with grand houses and shops. "There's nothing suitable for us to wear in this godforsaken town," she said.

"Very well, then. You will need to take the wagon and spend at least a night there. Perhaps Jeremiah could go with you to keep an eye on you. Seeing as you're so determined, perhaps you could deliver a message for me while you're there?"

"Yes, of course. Give me the address and I'll do that," Dolly agreed.

Clement wrote down several addresses for her: one for a reasonable hotel, another for a store that would provide her with all she wanted. He took her to one side so that Jeremiah and Hattie could not hear. "This note is to be delivered to the house of a gentleman on Grandpre Street in Beauregard Town. Someone will show you the way. Be sure you give it straight into the man's hand," commanded Clement. "Explain that you are my wife, and it might help if you have Albert with you."

"I expect you're asking him for money," said Dolly.

"For money I'm owed for my work for the South," growled Clement. "It is often polite to remind your friends what they owe you for services rendered. Leave Clementine with Jeremiah and go on your own, you understand."

Dolly smiled as she assured him she would. She could easily play a needy wife with a sickly child. Though Albert was in rude health, he was naturally pale and slim in contrast to most of the local white children in the town.

CHAPTER 37: DOLLY IN BATON ROUGE

Jeremiah was more than happy to accompany them to Baton Rouge. He had a widowed sister there that he wished to visit. "I haven't seen her since I came here," he told Dolly. "I should like to see how she is. She was very good to me when my wife died, though I didn't always appreciate it."

They set off very early one morning in a holiday mood, Dolly and Jeremiah taking turns with the reins of the wagon and Clemmie and Albert seated on sacks filled with cotton at the back. Clemmie was fearful at first, but lulled by Albert's chatter she relaxed as they travelled on through new sights. He had been much younger on the journey to the plantation, and they had all been too weary by the end of their ordeal to take much notice of their surroundings. Now he eagerly drank in all these new experiences with sundry comments from Jeremiah.

Many of the plantations they passed were derelict, but some were bustling with new life, mostly from sharecroppers, black and white folk who were dividing the larger estates between them and building new dwellings. They stopped many times for a word or two with people they met on the rutted road.

"A lot of the old estates are being bought up by carpetbaggers," Jeremiah told Dolly. "Plantations, that have been in families for years, were brought low by the war. The Yankees are the ones with the money. They rent out parcels of land to these folk they call sharecroppers."

Since Delia's visit, Dolly had heard a lot about the northerners who were taking advantage of the situation.

Clement usually concluded his news with a curse and a derisory spit.

It was late afternoon when finally they rolled, weary and aching, into the outskirts of Baton Rouge. Jeremiah's sister Margaret lived on the way, and so they called in for a drink. She welcomed them in and greeted her brother with great pleasure, hugging him and saying how much better he looked. Then she made a fuss of Albert.

"So this is your pupil," she said, stroking the boy's fiery hair. "And a fine boy too. Do you like your lessons?"

Albert nodded solemnly. "Ma too," he said simply.

Margaret didn't quite understand this, and Dolly gave Jeremiah a warning look to safeguard her secret.

"Your brother is a very good teacher," she said warmly. "And we're very glad he came to the plantation."

When Margaret discovered that Clement's wife wasn't quite the grand lady she had envisaged, she insisted they all stayed with her for the night. "It'll be a treat to have company," said Margaret, bustling about to accommodate her guests.

Dolly helped as best she could. She was well pleased to stay as, by avoiding the expense of the hotel, she could eke out her savings. Next day with thanks and farewells they headed early into town, promising to call on the way home.

The main street was bustling with every kind of humanity. They soon found the store that Clement had recommended, and Dolly first settled Albert with a new outfit. She bit her lip as the shop assistant scrutinised her son's scruffy clothes and boots with a contemptuous eye.

"Boys, eh!" joked Dolly. "You can't keep 'em clean for a minute."

The woman sniffed. Though Albert had been well scrubbed by Aunt Hattie and his clothes were clean, there was no disguising the age and wear of his outfit, mostly cut down and resewn from Clement's wardrobe. They finally settled on a suit that was several sizes too big but with luck would see him through several growth spurts.

Clemmie's clothes proved harder to purchase. She had grown stout on a diet of starch and greens and had had little exercise until Albert had arrived. Also, she wasn't happy to try on anything offered to her. She cowered in a corner of the changing room, whimpering in terror. The saleswoman was horrified when Albert went in to help his friend.

"Madam," she protested to Dolly, "this is most improper in a ladies' dress shop."

"Do you want to sell us a dress or not?" Dolly challenged her.

Finally Albert helped Clemmie to try on a flower print dress. "Pretty," he declared. "Very pretty."

And so Clemmie was satisfied with her choice. Dolly also bought a cheaper cotton dress of the same size so that Clemmie need not try it on.

While Albert worked his charm on his friend, Dolly had noticed a dress of deep pink on a rack. She glanced at the price and hesitated. Buying the dress would eat a large chunk of her savings. She looked at the saleswomen. They had been sniggering among themselves at the pantomime the Duplege family were creating. She guessed they'd be glad to see the back of her little group. She beckoned a young saleswoman over.

"I wonder how much you might sell this dress for?" she asked.

"The price is on the ticket, ma'am," said the woman snootily.

"Oh, I can see that," said Dolly nonchalantly. "But surely you might make a reduction for a good customer. We've already bought several garments."

The woman went towards a senior colleague, and Dolly could see the older woman sternly shaking her head.

"I'm afraid…" she began when she arrived back.

"Fair enough," said Dolly. "I'll try that one on." She pointed to the first dress on the rack. It was obviously too big for her.

"But ma'am…"

"I would like to try it on," Dolly demanded loudly.

The woman led Dolly to the changing cubicle, carrying the dress.

By this time, a mother and her daughter had joined them in the salesroom. They glanced curiously at the shrinking girl and the little boy sitting in one corner.

"May I help you?" asked the older saleswoman.

Before the pair could answer, they heard loud complaints emitting from the cubicle as the hapless sales assistant tried to help Dolly dress.

"You've pulled my hair," squealed Dolly. "Oh, you've pinched my arm. This dress won't do at all. Albert! Albert! Fetch me the next dress."

Her son was too small to reach the hanger on the rack, and he stared helplessly at the older saleswoman.

"Perhaps we should come back later?" suggested the mother. "I can see you are busy."

"Oh no," said the woman, almost grabbing her arm. "My colleague has the situation in hand."

No one seemed convinced as more howls were heard.

"One moment," said the senior saleswoman. She stuck her head into Dolly's cubicle and named a reduced price for the pink dress.

Dolly beat her lower.

"Very well," said the woman through gritted teeth. "Now please be quiet."

Dolly smiled and placed a finger to her lips.

"Thank you for being so patient," said the smiling saleswoman, returning to her new customers. Seconds later, the other saleswoman emerged then disappeared back into the cubicle with the pink dress. Dolly emerged all smiles and paid for her purchases.

"Thank you for being so patient," she said graciously, mimicking the saleswoman. "I'm afraid I am a little sensitive. Come along Albert, Clementine. Thank the nice lady."

"Sensitive my…" The saleswoman's last words were swallowed in silent anger, but Dolly read their meaning in the grimace on the woman's face. She had her bargain, though, and had made sure she would look splendid at the Jacques wedding.

As she paid for her purchases, she was approached by a smart looking woman. The saleswoman had asked for Dolly's name for the receipt.

"I beg your pardon, but did I hear you say your name is Duplege?" the woman asked.

Dolly nodded.

"Are you by any chance related to Mr. Clement Duplege of the Amiens plantation?"

"I'm his wife," said Dolly simply.

"Oh, I see. I hadn't heard he was married. I am Mrs. Amelia Kay, an old acquaintance of Clement's. And how is he finding life down on the farm?" she asked with a smirk.

From her manner, Dolly deduced she had been more than 'an acquaintance'. "The plantation is slowly coming back to life," she said with a confident smile. She omitted to add that Clement had no part in its transformation. "My husband is very well, thank you."

"I'll look forward to seeing him whenever he is back in town," said Amelia.

"I'm surprised you haven't seen him recently," Dolly told her. "He has visited Baton Rouge several times in the past months — in search of a little excitement with the cards."

"Ah yes, he was ever a gambler," Amelia purred, with a look that said volumes about Clement's gamble on marriage to Dolly.

Dolly played her trump card. She turned and pulled Albert forward. "And this is Albert, our son. Say hello to the lady, Albert, there's a good boy."

"How do you do?" said Albert politely. He might look a waif in his scruffy clothes, but Dolly had drummed some manners into him, and he had the unmistakable Duplege hair.

"We must be going," said Dolly grandly. "We have Albert's tutor waiting for us in the carriage. I'll tell my husband you were asking after him. Come along Albert, come along Clementine."

They found Jeremiah with the wagon. He had been talking to an old acquaintance but seemed relieved to see them.

"I need to deliver a letter for Clement," said Dolly. "Would you stay with Clemmie while I go and find his house?"

"We'll be happy to accompany you," said Jeremiah.

"No. It's something private," decided Dolly, "but if you could drive me and Albert in the general direction, that would be good."

CHAPTER 38: A PAYMENT AND A WARNING

They enquired about Beauregard Town and drove for several streets. Then Dolly alighted from the wagon and helped Albert down too. She was directed by a passer-by to Grandpre Street nearby and stared up at the imposing houses. Clutching her letter and firmly holding Albert's hand, she approached the address on the letter. The name written on the front was Jameson. The door was opened by a smartly dressed black butler.

"I'd like to speak to Mr. Jameson," she said. "I have a letter for him from my husband."

The butler held out his hand for the letter, but Dolly shook her head firmly.

"I have to deliver it personally," she insisted.

The man scrutinised the pair. Though their hands and faces were clean, their clothes were travel soiled, and Albert's was the same tatty outfit he'd worn at the store. Dolly was saving his new clothes for the wedding.

"May I ask your name?" asked the butler. "Please wait here a moment, ma'am," he said when she'd told him. He closed the door firmly.

"So much for southern hospitality," Dolly muttered to little Albert. "He probably thinks we'll pinch the silver."

The door was opened a moment later, and a plump balding man appeared beside the butler. Like his manservant, he scrutinised them doubtfully. "You'd better come in," he said, glancing both ways down the street. He led them into a fine room, heavy with ornate furnishings. "I am Mr. Jameson. I didn't know Duplege was married," he said. "Please sit down. Now, what can I do for you?"

"We won't pinch the silver," Albert told him earnestly.

Dolly burst out laughing and the man smiled.

"I see he has inherited his father's wry humour," said Jameson.

"Oh, the apple doesn't fall far from the tree," said Dolly, stroking her son's head. "My husband asked me to deliver this letter to you personally. As you can see, we are living in poor circumstances. I think he's hoping you'll pay him for past services rendered."

"I see," said Jameson, opening the letter. "As you say." He paused and reread the letter. "I'm afraid, Mrs. Duplege, that I do not have the sum your husband mentions to hand. However, I can give you something. Wait a moment." He went to the door and called, and the butler arrived promptly. "Can you take this boy to the kitchen and find him something to eat?" he asked. "His mother and I would like a word in private." He turned to Dolly. "Your son is a bright boy, and I don't want him repeating what I have to tell you."

"Off you go, Albert, and get something nice to eat," she told her son.

He looked doubtful for a moment and then slipped his hand into the butler's.

"Mrs. Duplege, I take it you know the nature of your husband's previous business?" said Jameson, settling back in his chair.

"He's a gambler, I know that," snorted Dolly. "And I know he was doing something for the South in the war. He came to England to do some business for the South."

"I see. Mrs. Duplege, your husband is a wanted man. He escaped from a prison in Washington by kidnapping and threatening a preacher. Of course, after this war there is much confusion, and I doubt they will bother to pursue an escapee from prison, especially as most of the prisoners of war are being released anyway. Here in the South we do not give up our veterans easily. But one of our mutual acquaintances in Washington had a letter from some detective in New York enquiring about your husband's whereabouts. He of course replied that he had no idea where your husband was. But I think Duplege should be warned."

"I'll tell him," said Dolly thoughtfully. She was just about to mention that they had arrived in New York from England and stayed several days, when something warned her to keep quiet. She did not know this man and by the look of him, he might easily give up Clement's whereabouts to keep his life of luxury intact.

"I'll get the money," he decided and left her alone in the room.

There were several silvery knick-knacks on little tables. Dolly's fingers twitched and she clasped her hands to crush the temptation to slip one into her pocket. Luckily Albert arrived back, his mouth smeared with crumbs and a beaming smile on his face.

"Thank you," she said to the butler. "He looks as if he's enjoyed himself."

"Sure has, ma'am," said the butler with a grin.

Jameson returned with a clinking leather pouch and handed it to Dolly. "You must tell your husband that there will be no more to add to this. The war has impoverished us all."

Glancing pointedly around the room, Dolly implied that she did not quite believe his claims. She wondered if he, too, was profiting from the devastation of the South like the carpetbaggers Clement despised so much. She took the pouch and pushed it deep into her bag. "Thank you very much," she told Jameson, "and I'll mention to my husband what you have told me."

They found Jeremiah waiting patiently with the wagon where she had left them. Clemmie had fallen asleep on the sacking and woke up confused when Albert climbed aboard. With that they left town and headed back to Jeremiah's sister. It was getting late in the afternoon and, other than Albert and his cake, they had had nothing to eat. They hungrily ate the soup and bread Margaret offered them and decided to stay the night.

"I don't fancy driving down those godforsaken roads in the dark," said Dolly. "We might end up in the creek like Clucas." She shuddered, and the feeling of unease stayed with her through a restless night. Why had Clement been in prison? Now she'd been told he'd kidnapped and threatened a preacher to escape. Where had he been when he had left her alone with Albert in New York? She heard again those hoofbeats in the night before the hotel had burned down. And Clucas, who had given false testimony against an innocent boy, was drowned, unable to tell tales.

Dolly was tired and wary when they returned home next day. Clement snatched the pouch and groaned with disappointment when he saw the contents. She had taken the liberty of extracting some money for herself, having checked that there was no mention of the total sum the bag contained. Jameson was hardly likely to check with Clement.

When she arrived home, Clement barely seemed to listen to what she had to tell him, as if her news did not bother him. For a moment Dolly was annoyed that he was virtually ignoring her. He just shrugged when she mentioned Amelia Kay, saying she was a friend of his housekeeper. She was tempted to ask more questions about Mrs. Kay and wanted to know more about the preacher and Clement's spell in jail. Then she noticed the intense concentration on his face. Though he was pretending to be absorbed in a newspaper Jeremiah had brought back with him, she knew instinctively that he was listening to her every word. He did not question her further about Jameson's revelation. It was obvious he did not want to discuss what she'd discovered.

In the following days as Dolly concentrated on her plans for the Jacques wedding, all the time she thought about what she'd found out about Clement. Her husband made no comment at all about what she'd told him.

CHAPTER 39: A FRIEND LEAVES TOWN

Jessie was pleased one morning when a shy tap came on the French windows of her parlour and she found Amy waiting outside. She was edging from side to side and seemed agitated, glancing over her shoulder, an unusual thing for a young woman who was normally quite calm. Jessie just assumed it was cold outside. Dropping her mending onto a chair, she hurried to admit her friend.

"This is a nice surprise," she said, taking Amy's hand and leading her into the warm room.

Jessie was tempted to ask if Taylor was away from home but decided against it. Amy seemed nervous enough about her visits, and Jessie didn't want to give the impression that she was encouraging a conspiracy to make things worse.

"It seems ages since I saw Matty," said Amy. "Oh, and of course Helen," she added quickly.

Jessie smiled. She was sure she loved both her children equally herself, but like Amy she always had a soft spot for her struggling son. "Lizzie's just getting them ready. I'll go up and fetch them," she told her friend. "Would you like a cup of tea? I've got my own little kettle and stand now. I can pop it on and then we'll have a brew when I come down."

"Oh no!" said Amy quickly. "Please don't bother. Perhaps later. I'd love to see the children, though."

"See you in a minute then," said Jessie, heading for the stairs.

Lizzie had finished dressing Helen and was putting the finishing touches to Matty's clothes, so it took a few more minutes to have him ready.

"Auntie Amy's here to see you," Jessie told them.

Helen was off like a shot, calling Amy's name as she slithered down the stairs. Lizzie carried Matty carefully downstairs, knowing Jessie was expecting a baby. All the family were treating her like a china doll now that she and Robert had told them their news. They were all anxious that the coming child should not be harmed in any way. Helen was too small to reach the door handle so had to wait for her mother but, the moment Jessie opened the door, Amy appeared flustered and hurried to conceal something in her bodice. Jessie was sure she had seen the flash of white paper, but her vision was hampered as Helen threw herself at her mother's friend in an enthusiastic welcome.

"Auntie Amy! Auntie Amy!" Helen paused. "Have you brought me any sweeties?" she enquired politely.

Amy laughed as Jessie scolded her daughter. "Not today, sweetheart," she said. "Perhaps next time — whenever that may be," she added with an infinite air of sadness.

Jessie was immediately alert. "Is everything all right?" she asked.

Amy nodded with a wistful smile. "Oh yes, everything is fine, hunky dory as they say. Look at how Matty is growing," she said, quickly changing the subject.

"Me too?" demanded Helen.

Jessie felt uneasy, left with the impression that things were not as 'hunky dory' as Amy wanted them to appear. It was obvious her friend didn't wish to confide in her, so she joined in with playing with the children. It was at the end of the visit that her unease returned.

They had just finished a cup of tea, though keeping the children well away from Jessie's new kettle, when Amy reached for her shawl and slipped it round her shoulders. "I'd better be going," she said.

"Will Taylor be home soon?" asked Jessie, as this was the usual signal for Amy's departure.

Amy shook her head. "No, he's had to go Leeds for a few days," she said quietly. She took Jessie's hands.

"Thank you for being a good friend to me. I think I should have gone mad without your friendship in a strange land with no friends."

"I'll always be your friend," Jessie assured her. "You're so good with the children, and you've been so much help to Matty."

Amy squeezed her hands. "You may not always wish to acknowledge me as your friend," she murmured.

"Don't be daft," Jessie insisted. "Amy, what's wrong? You can confide in me."

Her friend shook her head, tears brimming in her eyes. "I'd better be going. Take care of yourself, Jessie. And do not worry. This next child is going to be fine." With that she slipped through the French windows and disappeared with a fleeting wave.

Jessie sat down, puzzled by her friend's manner. It was almost as if she would never see Amy again, though she knew that could not be true. Taylor hadn't given the Overdales any hint that he would be leaving the district. Surely if Amy were ill in any way she would have confided in Jessie.

Still perplexed, her attention was claimed by the children and she forgot about her friend for the moment. It wasn't until three days later that her suspicions had their answer. The family were eating their supper when a loud knocking echoed through the house.

"Who the hell's that at this time of night?" growled Matthias.

Robert leapt up to open the door as Maggie had left for home. Jessie's blood ran cold. She immediately thought that something had happened to one of her family. Then she heard the angry voice of Taylor Walmsley.

"Where is she? Is she here?" He burst into the dining room, followed by a bewildered Robert. Taylor faced Jessie. "Where is she, then? I expect you have something to do with this."

"I don't know what you're talking about," Jessie protested. "Is it Amy? Has something happened to Amy?" she added anxiously.

"Well, don't you know? She's not home at any rate. The girl says she's not been home for days, and my mother hasn't seen her either. I thought you'd have something to do with it, teaching her to be bold and disobedient."

Jessie gritted her teeth. "I can assure you, Mr. Walmsley, that I have nothing whatsoever to do with your wife's disappearance. Hasn't anybody seen her? Has she left you a note or something?"

"I've not found one if she has," said Walmsley, halted in his anger by Jessie's vehement denial.

"You have no right coming in here accusing my wife of hiding or colluding with Mrs. Walmsley," said Robert stiffly.

"Well, she's the only one I know that knows my wife. What else am I to think? They're thick as thieves, them two. My mother reckons…"

"If your mother had been more of a friend to Amy, she might not be missing," said Jessie. She clapped a hand to her mouth as an awful thought hit her. "She might be lying somewhere hurt. Might she go for a walk in the hills on her own?"

"You'd know more about that than me," said Walmsley, his eyes narrowed.

They were interrupted by a frantic tapping at the door. Robert again went to open it and was followed back into the dining room by the little maid from the Walmsleys' house.

"I'm sorry Master, but the old Missis said I should come with this," she said timidly, holding out a white piece of paper in a shaking hand. "She found it in the bedroom."

Jessie felt angry that Taylor's mother had the cheek to go rooting in the Walmsley bedroom but she said nothing. Taylor hesitated then opened the note. Even in the dim candlelight he turned pale as he read. He sat down heavily on a dining chair. "She's gone."

"Gone where?" demanded Jessie.

"I'm surprised you don't know already?" he answered with a hollow laugh.

"My wife has already assured you that she doesn't know anything about this business," snapped Robert, defending Jessie. "Just exactly where is your wife?"

Taylor glanced at the clock with a sneer. "I expect she's on the way to India by now with that … that blackguard Crispin Pettigrew. That worm, that snake in the grass. Well, she's gone and done it now. Her family won't have her back. She's a disgrace, a slut. And I definitely won't have her back."

There was a break in his voice as he spoke. He scrunched the paper into a tight ball, his face a mask of black anger. Jessie almost felt sorry for him. Taylor must have instantly regretted revealing his bitter secret in front of the Overdales, especially her. But knowing what she did, she guessed Amy wouldn't ever want to come back to her domineering husband anyway. She knew she should be shocked by such a drastic step but couldn't raise any feelings of condemnation of her friend. Amy had been driven to act so scandalously against her nature. Jessie was surprised at the botanist, though. Crispin Pettigrew had seemed such a respectable and upright young man. Then she recalled the kindness and consideration he had shown her friend. Had that deepened into such strong emotion that he and Amy should forsake everything, including their reputations, to escape Taylor Walmsley? She just hoped Amy would be safe and Crispin Pettigrew would stand by her.

"I'm going home," said Taylor, wearily rising from the chair. He turned to the Overdales, glaring directly at Jessie. "I don't want one word of this to get out, d'you understand? Not one word. If it does, I'll blame you. I'm going to tell folk she's gone to visit her family in India and that's the end of it. Right?"

"I can assure you, Mr. Walmsley, that no one here in this room will breathe a word of your wife's disappearance," said Melissa calmly. "I feel very sorry for you indeed. But I'm afraid you must warn your mother to be as silent. Do not let her use this opportunity to blacken the girl's name among her friends, or the scandal will soon get out."

Taylor looked about to protest at the slur on his mother, but a look of red realisation suffused his face. "Aye, I reckon you're right," he said with a grimace. "I'd better warn her. I'll say goodnight then."

Robert escorted him to the door. "I'm very sorry about all this business, Walmsley," Jessie heard him say. "If you want anything or need anything, you know we'll be only too glad to help."

Jessie could have hugged her husband. He had no need to be kind to a man who continually treated him with contempt, yet Robert had held out a hand of support in Taylor's troubles. It confirmed again her choice in marrying her Robert, despite their difficulties.

"Thank you, Overdale, but I'll be fine," Taylor Walmsley replied. "I'll be fine," he repeated, as if to reassure himself as he went home to face his mother and warn her to keep silent on his betrayal.

Then Jessie truly did feel sorry for him.

A couple of months later, she received a letter from India. Robert and Matthias were at the mill, but Melissa noticed and waited expectantly for Jessie to open it. Jessie was tempted to slip it into her pocket to read later but, seeing her mother-in-law's obvious interest, she broke the seal and read it to herself.

My dear friend Jessie,

You may not wish to think of me as your friend after what I have done and the shame I have brought upon myself and my family. Please believe I have not done this thing lightly. Crispin was so kind to me. I was so deprived of any kindness and affection in my life it was very easy for me to love him. We are very happy together. We are living as man and wife now in India, and I do so with all my heart and soul. Please forgive me if you feel I have betrayed our friendship. Your kindness to me was my one pleasure in Gorbydale. I hope that you and your children are well and continue to thrive.

I do not write an address with this letter. I should not wish Taylor to come searching for me, though I doubt he will after what I have done.

Your dear friend,

Amisha

Jessie smiled as she noticed that her friend had reclaimed her own name. She noticed Melissa waiting patiently. "It's from Amisha," she told her.

"I thought as much," said Melissa. "What does she have to say for herself?" She had a definite note of reproach in her voice.

"She apologises for betraying my friendship," began Jessie.

"So she should, leaving her husband like that and implicating you in her behaviour," retorted Melissa with a frown.

"But she sounds happy with Crispin Pettigrew. I suppose she must have been very desperate to have been driven to such an act," Jessie defended her friend.

"Still, vows are vows. 'For better or worse' you say when you get wed," insisted her mother-in-law. Then for a moment she softened. "Still, it can't have been easy being married to Taylor Walmsley with that mother of his. But vows are vows." She gave a sigh. "I won't mention it to Matthias just yet. He's that riled up about everything at the moment. Taylor Walmsley's threatening to pull out of the mill, and we can't afford to pay him off without increasing the mortgage."

"Robert hasn't mentioned it," said a surprised Jessie. She and her husband often discussed matters about the mill, especially if Robert was frustrated with his father. She was dismayed by this piece of news.

"Happen they hope Taylor is just bluffing with all this business with his wife unsettling him. Things will probably calm down now that she's well and gone and the mill's getting back into full production," decided Melissa.

"Let's hope so," said Jessie with a sigh. She'd hoped that when the mill was working full time, she and Robert might think about finding their own home. Another mortgage on the mill to pay off Taylor Walmsley was the last thing they needed.

CHAPTER 40: THE JACQUES WEDDING

"Are you sure you won't come to David Jacques' wedding?" Dolly asked Clement. "You have been invited, and it would look very unneighbourly. We've still got time for you to change."

"Why do you imagine I want to go to some hick wedding with people I despise?" growled Clement.

"I just thought you might like to escort Albert and me and go as a family," said Dolly with a shrug. "It'd be better than mouldering away here, clutching your whisky bottle. Anyway, please yourself."

"I intend to, without you and the brat annoying me all the time." Clement sank into his familiar sagging chair on the porch and reached for the bottle he usually kept to hand. He threw it away in disgust as he found it empty. His mood was definitely deteriorating if he included his son in his tirade.

"Come along then, Albert," coaxed his mother. "Let's go to this nice party and let your Papa stew in his own drunken juice."

Aunt Hattie and Dolly had decided that the occasion might be too much for Clemmie, and she had clammed into herself, shaking her head vigorously, when they had asked her. She and Hattie stood on the porch to wave them off.

Albert skipped towards the cart, proud in his new suit, although the trousers had a rather deep and chunky hem. "Bye, Papa," he called without a backward glance.

Dolly preened herself and glanced towards Clement, wondering if he would take any notice of her in her new outfit.

There was nothing but a small cracked shaving mirror in the house, but she knew she looked fetching from her memory in the mirror of the fitting room at the Baton Rouge store. She had struggled to do something with her hair in that tiny mirror, but, newly washed and with a natural bounce, it had been curled into a fetching style by Aunt Hattie. Clement paid her no attention at all and Dolly felt deeply disappointed.

"You both look very fine, if I may say so," said Jeremiah, smiling as he helped her up onto the cart.

"Thank you, Jeremiah," she said, returning his smile. Then with a scornful glance towards her husband, she added, "at least someone has noticed our efforts."

Barney was wearing a clean white shirt for the occasion and had arranged a couple of seats for his passengers at the back of the cart. Dolly complimented his appearance.

"Had an old three cornered hat from my pappy when he was coachman at the plantation," he told them. "But they laughed at me in the village when I tried it on and said I looked like somethin' out of a history book."

"You look very smart as you are," Dolly told him. "At least we won't disgrace ourselves when we arrive."

Dolly had never been to the O'Neill plantation before, but Barney knew the way. It was a short distance on from the Jacques plantation. After travelling some way they began to join a trail of miscellaneous wagons, carts and buggies heading for Jassy O'Neill's home. They weren't in the shabbiest vehicle in the procession. Some farm vehicles were creaking with their load, and Barney stopped and offered a lift to three sturdy young boys to lighten the burden of one poor horse. They scrambled aboard with the thanks of their parents and a stout grandmother sitting on a heavy armchair.

"We all struggled to put that chair on the wagon," murmured the youngest boy. "But the old nuisance insisted we bring it 'cos of her bad back."

"And Mamma insisted we couldn't go without Grandma," said another.

"We'll soon be there, boys," Barney told them and on the way they entertained Albert with reports of the good things they would soon have to eat.

"Better get to the table before Grandma," said one of the boys, "or there'll be nothing left."

They all started laughing, and, glancing back at the following wagon with the old woman fanning herself in the armchair, Dolly could well believe them. "She looks like the Queen of Sheba on her throne," she said, and the boys set off laughing again.

"You certainly had a fine time on your wagon," said the boys' father, helping Dolly down when they arrived. "We could hear you all laughing. Mighty obliged to you for helping us out."

"Barney guessed you were struggling," said Dolly, giving her driver the credit. "We were happy to help."

"You must be the English lady that Clement Duplege has married then?" said the man on hearing her accent.

Dolly nodded, pleased to hear herself called a lady.

"Mighty pleased to meet you," he said, shaking her hand. Then he introduced the rest of the family.

Grandma snapped her fan closed, offered three fingers in greeting, and scrutinised Dolly. "English, eh? And married to Clement Duplege? Is he here with you?"

Dolly gave the fingers a brief tweak. "He's sorry to miss the wedding, but I'm afraid he is otherwise engaged," she lied. "I hope you had a comfortable journey on your thr… armchair," she added pertly.

The boys and Albert started to giggle, and Grandma gave them a withering glance.

Nathan Jacques came to welcome them, looking very smart in a white shirt and jacket. He offered Dolly his arm as he escorted them all into the house.

"Glad you could come, Mrs. Duplege. David will be pleased you and your boy made the journey."

"I'm afraid my husband…" she began.

"That's all right. We didn't expect him," said Nathan with a shrug. "Come on in and have a drink. The O'Neills will be glad to see you — and looking very fine, if I might say."

"You don't look so bad yourself," she teased. "I almost didn't recognise you without your old dungarees and straw hat. You look very handsome."

He smiled down at her and patted her hand.

As she was welcomed by the O'Neills, Dolly guessed she was as much an object of curiosity as a welcome guest. Nearly everyone enquired about Clement, and, in the murmuring that followed her around the room, she frequently detected his whispered name. Determined to act the lady, with chin held high she met everyone graciously. Albert followed her with polite and modest 'how do you dos' and charmed all the mothers there. Then he slipped off to be with his new friends.

Finally as all the guests assembled outside the house, Dolly braced herself to watch the wedding. Her heart faltered as David gave her a polite smile as he approached the preacher. A beaming Jassy entered clutching her father's arm, looking young and fresh and so pretty that Dolly had to bite her lip with disappointment. She barely heard the vows as she held herself tensely, battling hard not to cry. A sigh of relief flowed from her as the groom gave the bride a tentative kiss. Recalling the rushed and hollow ceremony of her own wedding, she could not remember if Clement had even touched her. How could she have been so foolish as to think that David might care for her, a soiled and insignificant skivvy from the slums of Gorbydale with a barely legitimate child? Then the old Dolly spirit reasserted itself. Taking a deep breath, she congratulated the bride and groom with the other well-wishers and braced herself to speak to her neighbours.

She found Nathan at her side as he guided her through to the wedding feast. "I really appreciate you coming, Mrs. Duplege," he murmured. "I know this must have been an ordeal for you."

She glanced up at him in surprise.

"I think we both know how you felt about David, Mrs. Duplege. A father can see things that his son doesn't always notice. But everything has turned out for the best, I think you'll agree."

She didn't deny his suggestions. "Yes, I hope they'll be very happy," she said sincerely and meant it.

He stayed by her throughout the rest of the celebration, fending away any intrusive questions from some of the more inquisitive women. Albert was enjoying himself with his new friends under the watchful but discreet eye of Barney. Finally as others began to leave, Barney suggested they too should go before it got dark. Though the days of summer were long, they had some way to go. Again they gave the three boys a lift until the two wagons were due to part company. The boys were all tired and quiet, and Albert drifted off to sleep.

Barney slowed down as they approached a crossroad and waited for the other wagon to catch up. The boys roused themselves and clambered down, then squeezed onto their wagon beside their Grandma, snoring loudly on her throne.

"I hope they manage to get home," said Barney, amid calls of goodbye and invitations for visits. "If that axle goes, they'll have to abandon Grandma's chair."

"I think those boys would be willing to abandon Grandma too," chuckled Dolly. "She was certainly keen to find out about Clement — nosy old bitch."

Tired but satisfied that everything had gone well, she was filled with gratitude for Nathan's protection. She'd been anxious about this wedding day but had been determined to face it. These people were her neighbours, and with no support from Clement she knew that she might need them.

CHAPTER 41: BOUNTY

Arriving home in the misty twilight, they were met at the door by Aunt Hattie clutching a lantern. "I's so glad you're home, Mrs. Dolly," she said anxiously. "Master Clement, he's packed his bag and rode away. The storekeeper's boy came with a message, and next minute Master Clement's up and gone. Then this fancy fella arrived looking for him, but I told the man he'd already left. I don't think he believed me. He kept looking round to see if Master Clement was hiding somewhere. Says his name was Bancroft. Then he was askin' for you. I tried to stop him, but he started asking Clemmie some things and she got all riled up. You know how she is. I only just got her settled."

"Bancroft? Never heard of him," said Dolly. "I wonder why he came looking for Clement out here."

"Don't rightly know, Mrs. Dolly," said Aunt Hattie, lifting a very sleepy Albert down from the wagon. "Says he's coming back to see you in the morning."

Dolly shook her head in disbelief. She had only been gone a day and everything at home was in confusion, but she was too weary to figure out what was happening just then. "Let's get to our beds," she said wearily. "We can sort it out in the morning. If this Bancroft comes early, he'll just have to wait."

"Did you have a good time?" asked Hattie.

"We had a fine time," said Dolly with a chuckle. "Didn't we, Barney?"

"Oh, a fine time was had by all," he told them. He'd been well entertained and fed at a table with all the other workers.

Though colour did not trouble the Jacques, in the South inbred customs would take a long time to change.

Dolly sank onto her lumpy bed, exhausted, but sleep evaded her. Clement often left home without telling them where he was going, but from what Aunt Hattie had said, it looked as if he'd been warned that this Bancroft was looking for him. Perhaps Clement owed him money. Anyway, she was not about to pay her husband's debts from the secret stash she was squirrelling away under a floorboard.

Dolly emerged from her bed feeling weary after her restless night. Aunt Hattie had made her a drink of coffee and pointed to the porch where Bancroft was already waiting. Jeremiah hovered nearby, ready to intervene if the stranger should cause trouble. The man rose awkwardly from Clement's sagging chair, a tall man wearing a suit which was smart but dusty. A fancy waistcoat flashed out from under the jacket.

"Good morning, Mrs. Duplege," he said smoothly. "I trust you slept well?"

"No, I didn't," Dolly told him abruptly. "I believe you've come looking for my husband."

"Well yes, I have. My name is Ezra Bancroft, but I'd like to talk to you too if you would be so kind."

Dolly tried to assess him through narrowed eyes. "Depends what you want to know, Mr. Bancroft," she said.

"I have been talking to an acquaintance of yours, Mrs. Duplege, Miss Honora Darwen."

Dolly exploded. "Honora Darwen! What the hell has she got to do with my husband?"

Bancroft looked startled by her outburst. "So you do know Miss Darwen?" he attempted.

"What's she been saying?" demanded Dolly. "What's she doing interfering again in other people's business?"

"Interfering again, you say?" asked Bancroft cautiously.

Dolly realised she might have said too much. "I used to … er… I was living in the same house as Miss Darwen." Dolly tried to make her position as vague as possible. Skivvying at Overdale House was not something she wanted to admit to. "That was when Miss Darwen began snooping into my business," she added, looking very offended. "I didn't appreciate it."

"So you think Miss Darwen is interfering with your husband's business?" tried Bancroft.

"I didn't say that," protested Dolly. "Anyway, who are you? Are you a policeman or something?"

"I am something of a private enquiry agent," he admitted. "I am enquiring into a murder that was committed in New York several years ago."

"New York? Is Honora all right? She hasn't been murdered, has she?" Dolly remembered that Honora was studying in New York, but she didn't know what that had to do with Clement.

"Miss Darwen is fine. I am making some enquiries on her behalf. I believe you were in New York with your husband at the time the murder was committed. You would have just arrived from England," said Bancroft with a smile, scrutinising her face.

"I haven't the faintest idea," Dolly told him firmly. "That was years ago. We've been here for ages now. Anyway, my husband was with me all the time when we were in New York."

"So he didn't go off — say, gambling, while you were there?"

"It was a long time ago. I hardly think so. He stayed with me and our son. We couldn't be left alone in a strange city now, could we? Anyway, what has Honora Davenport got to do with this murder?"

"The victim was a good friend of hers," Bancroft told her. "The lady in question, Miss Verity Cain, was the daughter of a doctor, a wealthy man. He has offered a reward — a substantial reward — to find her killer."

"So you're a bounty hunter," declared Jeremiah from the doorway.

"Well, yes," the man admitted. "But I would like to discover the murderer along with Miss Darwen and Miss Cain's father. I'd like to see justice done."

"And claim the reward," Jeremiah insisted.

Bancroft ignored him and concentrated all his efforts on Dolly. "An old colleague of mine was contacted by Miss Darwen, a Mr. Alan Pinkerton. He contacted me. I went to see her myself to talk to her. She has the idea that her friend was murdered by mistake; that it was she who should have been the victim, but no one in the New York police is taking her seriously."

"So what's all this got to do with my husband?" demanded Dolly.

"When she and Mr. Clement Duplege were both in Washington, Miss Darwen betrayed your husband to the authorities. Mr. Pinkerton has confirmed that to me. She reckons Clement Duplege was out for revenge when he mistook Miss Cain for herself."

"It's all very fanciful. I'm not surprised no one is taking her seriously," scoffed Dolly. "It sounds like a load of nonsense to me. She never liked Clement. She argued with him when she met him in Gorbydale. So some woman who happened to be a friend of Honora Darwen was murdered and she's trying to blame him. My husband was with me and our son all the time we were in New York. Why would he bother to murder Honora Davenport for revenge? It's all a bit farfetched." A flicker of doubt crossed her eyes as she remembered Clement's outburst to Robert Overdale cursing Honora. She thought about the fire at the hotel and Clucas drowned in the creek. The watchful Bancroft noticed that flicker. "I think you've had a wasted journey, Mr. Bancroft," said Dolly, trying to dismiss him. "Anyway, we have things to do, so you'll have to excuse us."

"Perhaps you will think about what I've told you, Mrs. Duplege," Bancroft insisted. "Maybe I'll call in again to see if you've remembered anything while I'm in town."

"Please yourself," said Dolly with a shrug. "But like I say, it was a long time ago and my husband was with me all the time. Good day, Mr. Bancroft." With that she turned her back on him and went into the house.

Jeremiah waited for a moment to watch Bancroft head back towards his horse. Moments later he gave a cry of protest, and Dolly hurried out to see Bancroft crouching beside Albert, obviously questioning the boy.

"You leave my son alone. I'll thank you to get off our land, Mr. Bancroft," she yelled. He stood upright and was about to apologise, but she ignored him and grabbed Albert's arm, dragging him away from the bounty hunter. "And don't bother coming back," she snapped. As Bancroft rode off, she knelt to Albert. "What did the nasty man say to you?" she asked gently.

"He asked where Papa had gone," he told her, looking puzzled.

"And what did you say?"

"I said he'd gone to hell," answered Albert. "You told Aunt Hattie 'he can go to hell for all I care'. So I told him I thought he'd gone there."

Dolly burst out laughing. Jeremiah, who had joined her, chuckled too.

"Perhaps I should teach the boy more of the Bible, Mrs. Duplege," he said. "I don't think the boy has any idea what hell is all about."

Dolly sighed, despite her amusement. "What do you make of all that, Mr. Leach?" she asked.

Over time, Jeremiah had become a friend and a trusted advisor. "I'm not sure, Mrs. Duplege. I have to say that Mr. Duplege certainly disappeared in a hurry when someone came from the store to warn him about his visitor. I thought perhaps Mr. Duplege might owe him money. This reward must be a substantial one for Bancroft to come all this way."

"I know, Mr. Leach. I thought all of those things myself," said Dolly, taking Albert's hand. One thing she had thought but didn't divulge was that Clement had been frequently absent from her and Albert in New York. "Gone to hell — that just about sums it up." She started chuckling again as they headed for the house to tell Aunt Hattie what Albert had just said.

CHAPTER 42: A WANDERER RETURNS

Late one afternoon, back in Gorbydale, Jessie was intrigued when Jacob sent her a note telling her to expect a visitor. She was thrilled when a tall, handsome figure appeared at the door of Overdale House.

"Arden," she cried and flung herself into her brother's arms. "Why didn't you let me know you were coming?"

"It all happened very quickly," he said, laughing. "When I left the Union navy, someone told me there was a chance to work as an engineer on the Scotia with the Cunard line, and here I am. I wrote to Father to say I was coming home, but I've arrived before the letter anyway."

"It's just so good to see you," she said, giving him another hug.

"I see you've been busy while I've been away," he said, squatting down to greet her children, who had crept into the hallway to see what the commotion was about. "Hello, you two. This fine chap must be Matthew, and our pretty young lady is surely Helen."

"I'm Helen, he's Matty," declared Jessie's daughter boldly, approaching her uncle. "We're twins, you know."

"Oh, I do know." Arden smiled at her self-assurance. "I've heard all about you. Very pleased to meet you."

"Come into my parlour and I'll make you some tea," said Jessie, linking her brother and pulling him into her room. "Tell me what you've been up to. I'm so glad you've left the navy. We've been so worried about you."

"I'll admit I've had a few hairy moments since we last met," he told her. "We were at the Red River Campaign. Did you hear about it?"

"Father told me something about it," she admitted. "Matthias has a habit of taking his newspapers to the mill office nowadays, so I don't always get to read the news. Was it very frightening?"

"It was when we were trapped in our ironclads at the Alexandria falls with the Confederate army bearing down on us. Luckily our side had the sense to dam the river and flood it so we could escape, but it was a shambles from beginning to end and we ended back on the Mississippi. Still, here I am to tell the tale."

"And we'll see much more of you now you're on the transatlantic run," she said, and added with a smile, "and so will Honora." Jessie was surprised to see her brother's face tighten. "Is something wrong?" she asked cautiously. She'd been so pleased that her best friend and her brother seemed destined for one another, despite their separation.

Arden paused as if struggling for words. "Honora has recently had a visit from a detective about her friend Verity Cain's murder," he said. "You might know she wrote to Alan Pinkerton some time ago, but he was in Canada. Anyway, this acquaintance of his came to talk to her, and he's heading down to Louisiana to speak to Clement Duplege. It seems he was in New York at the same time as the murder, and Honora seems to think he has a grudge against her."

"Yes, she did write to tell me her suspicions," said Jessie. "I shouldn't like to be in Clement Duplege's shoes. But I shouldn't like to be in Honora's shoes either, if Duplege has a grudge against her. Think how he came all this way to fetch little Albert from the Tates. Poor Honora must be worried about it all. It's a good thing she's got you to support her."

Arden was silent for a moment. "I'm not sure if our romance is going anywhere to be honest," he said at last. "Honora informed me at our last meeting that she does not feel as strongly for me as I do for her. She tells me she has felt deeper emotions for someone else, and it wouldn't be fair to me to hold me to our tentative promises. She confessed she has not felt those deeper emotions towards me. So make of that what you will."

Jessie felt distressed for her brother as he fell silent and struggled to master his emotions. She linked his arm and hugged it to her. "Oh Arden, I'm so sorry. Did she say who it was?" she murmured, though she had strong suspicions.

"No. Nor did she admit that she had an attachment to whoever it was — just feelings for him. As far as I can tell, she hasn't revealed her feelings to him," said her brother, taking a deep breath. "Anyway, how are things with you? You're looking well. Positively blooming."

"I'm expecting another child," said Jessie, smiling. "So I'm positively expanding as well. Oh Arden, perhaps you'll be home this time and can be a godfather to our child."

They sat and chatted by the fire, and Arden made a fuss of the children. Helen hogged the limelight as usual, but her uncle made sure that Matty was included in their banter. Melissa arrived and insisted he stay for supper so that he could see Robert and Matthias when they returned from the mill. All was friendly and warm over the meal, and Jessie's husband and father-in-law were eager to hear of Arden's exploits in the war and especially how the aftermath was affecting cotton supplies.

But Jessie often glanced at her brother and saw a shadow of sadness in his eyes. She was disappointed that he and Honora would not sit with them as a family, perhaps with children of their own. She wondered if Honora's 'dear friend Ben Clark' had anything to do with her change of heart.

CHAPTER 43: A CONFESSION

Jessie was right in her suspicions. Honora had indeed fallen in love with Ben but was too embarrassed to write to her friend about it. Nor had she said anything to him, as she was determined as ever to finish her studies without any emotional entanglements. Despite her resolve, she had a hard time keeping her feelings to herself. She was relieved when he sometimes didn't attend the same lectures. Although she felt she could concentrate better, she wondered where he was and longed to see him. Ben, however, gave her no hint of his feelings. He was his usual friendly self, ready to help her with her studies when she asked. Then he began to make excuses when she asked for help, and she wondered if she had been doing so more than she needed.

Since Verity's death she had become friendly with Martha O'Brian, a tall raw-boned woman who had moved into Verity's rooms at her lodging house. Martha was nursing at the same hospital and knew them both. She listened with sympathy on hearing Honora's faltering confession that she had released Arden from his obligations.

"You let a good man like that go?" she said with disbelief. "You're crazy, Honora. He won't marry you, you know."

"I don't understand what you mean," said Honora, puzzled.

"Ben Clark. He won't marry you." Honora was about to protest despite seeing her friend had discovered her secret longing, but Martha carried on. "I'm not blind, Honora. I've seen the way you moon about Ben Clark. I thought it was just a silly infatuation, that you were missing Arden and that you would come to your senses."

"I don't…" Honora stammered but could not honestly deny her feelings.

"Ben's Jewish, you know that. I've talked to him. I worked in a Jewish hospital once. He's very devout, though he doesn't show it openly. It doesn't pay to be openly devout when so many people don't like Jews. You know that too. You've seen it with some of the tutors."

Honora nodded and had to admit that some tutors were openly offensive to Ben and another obviously Jewish student.

"But Ben won't marry you. The Jewish line comes through the mother you know — and you ain't Jewish."

"I really think you're mistaken, Martha," stammered Honora. "Ben and I are only good friends."

"Oh Honora, I've seen the way you look at him. Don't tell me he hasn't seen it too," said Martha with an exasperated sigh. "You mentioned the other day that he seems to be avoiding you. Don't you think that's his way of telling you that you're becoming too close to him? He's a nice man, a kind man. I'm sure he doesn't want to hurt your feelings."

Honora was silent. She'd struggled to hide her feelings from Ben, determined to concentrate on her studies, but it seemed she hadn't managed to conceal them from Martha or Ben, and surely others might have noticed too.

"Ask him yourself, if you don't believe me," said Martha. "You could save yourself a lot of heartache if you know the truth."

"I should," decided Honora. "Perhaps…" She hated to admit the truth. Surely there was some glimmer of hope for their love to shine. Had she really mistaken his kindness for something deeper? She resolved to speak to him and know his mind. Martha could be wrong.

At the end of a tiring and complicated day she glimpsed Ben in a cloakroom, very near the women's cloakroom where Verity had been murdered. "Would you like to come for a cup of tea?" she asked.

"I have a lot to do this evening," he said, without even glancing at her.

"Ben, I'd like to talk to you."

He caught the seriousness in her voice and gazed for a moment at her earnest face. "Very well then," he said quietly.

A fine rain misted the busy street as they walked along to a nearby café, not touching, nor speaking.

"I think I know what this is about, Honora," he said finally as they settled down in their seats. "Before you say anything, I want you to know that I value our friendship, but friendship is where it must remain." So he had guessed her feelings and wanted to spare her.

"But what if I love you?" she whispered. It was too late to conceal it. Frustrated with the sleepless nights and the longing, she wanted to know at last how he really felt.

"My father once told me that love has many faces," he said, patting her fingers over the table. "When he was a young man he was in love with a girl from his village in Russia, but of course they were parted by the pogroms, though he never forgot her. Then he met a girl in Austria, but that too was hopeless. Her father was rich and he wasn't. When he came to America he met my mother, and now she is the love of his life. Love has many faces, Honora. One day you will find the face that you wish to see over your breakfast table. And so will I. Perhaps a nice Jewish girl that won't break my parents' hearts. They have sacrificed so much for me to study to be a doctor. How can I disappoint them?" He straightened up and took a deep breath, looking at her seriously as if some revelation were due. "Anyway, soon I will be moving nearer to them to finish my studies."

"You're going away?"

"Yes. I feel it is my duty. My father isn't a well man, and they need my support. It will be easier now that more medical schools are opening their doors to Jewish students. This war has shown people that there is an urgent need for more doctors, whatever their religion. There are so many veterans returning with battle injuries that must be cared for. You understand, don't you? It will be for the best."

Honora nodded, too miserable to speak.

Arden had once quoted an Elizabethan couplet to her, one written on glass by Sir Walter Raleigh to the queen: *Fain I would rise, yet fear I to fall*. Elizabeth had written beneath it: *If thy heart fails thee, rise not at all*. Honora had dared to rise, but she was falling now. She felt broken and it hurt bitterly. She had thought that when she declared her love to him, Ben would have the courage to defy convention. She'd been very wrong.

"I'd better get going," she said, rising awkwardly from her chair in the crowded café. "I hope everything goes well for you. I might see you tomorrow."

Out in the street, her tears mingled with the rain as she walked blindly towards her lodgings.

Martha glanced up from the sitting room as Honora headed for the stairs. "Is everything all right?" she asked, seeing her friend's distress.

"Not really. I asked Ben about his feelings as you suggested. I was anxious to know. Of course you were right. He's looking for a nice Jewish girl to please his parents and as you said, 'I ain't Jewish'."

"I'm so sorry, Honora," said Martha, full of sympathy. "But it's better you find out now instead of eating your heart out for years. Perhaps it's not too late to get in touch with Arden Davenport and tell him you've made a mistake. I've seen how he thinks the world of you."

"*Thought* the world of me," said Honora with a sob. "I couldn't go back to him now and tell him what a fool I've been. I don't know if he would believe me anyway. I don't know how I could face him. I don't even know my own feelings for him anymore."

"Best sleep on it," suggested her friend.

Honora rushed upstairs and collapsed in heart-rending sobs. She cursed herself for being so foolish. If she had kept her secret perhaps she could have lived, heartened by her illusions. Perhaps Ben would have grown strong in his resolve to love her. But she knew deep down that he had already decided to move to be near his parents. Exhausted with grief, she still couldn't sleep, nor could she concentrate on her studies the next day. Her distraction incurred the wrath of Doctor Walgrave, who picked on her all through his lecture. She managed to hold her emotions together, though she was very tempted to flee from the class. Ben avoided her, and she missed his usual words of sympathy when Walgrave was on the warpath. In a week he had left for his new medical school. He'd said a brief goodbye when she was among a group of her fellow students, but deliberately avoided her eyes.

After another sleepless night, she decided to pour her heart out to Jessie in a letter but begged her not to tell Arden. Then she shredded the letter into tiny pieces. She had alienated her dear Aunt Melissa by her decision to stay in America to study; now she felt she would upset Jessie too by rejecting her best friend's brother. Honora felt very alone. She struggled to push her misery aside and threw herself into her studies.

"You work too hard," said Martha, finding Honora on the wards long after the other students had left for their homes. "You look tired. You'll make yourself ill. Go and get something to eat."

Honora didn't feel like eating, but she forced herself to do as her friend suggested. Staring into the sinking flames of the small fire in her room, she assessed her life. Ben's rejection hurt bitterly. And now that the support of Arden's love was missing, she felt empty. His intermittent visits had sustained her, and he'd been so excited when he'd told her of his new position on the transatlantic sailings. At last he'd be able to see her more regularly, he'd told her. And she'd let him down; told him she loved another; trashed his dreams with her flimsy longings. Their fracture could never be healed. She thought about her father and his dedication to healing the sick and poor of Manchester and decided that was where her life's dedication must be too.

CHAPTER 44: THE WOMAN OF BUSINESS

Clement had been gone for some weeks, though that hadn't bothered Dolly unduly in the past. A few days after his disappearance, Bancroft hadn't given up his quest and came snooping again around the plantation. He'd been asking questions of some of the children from the village before approaching Dolly. She berated him for spying on them and insisted again that Clement wasn't at home. She repeated that her husband had been with her all the time they were in New York. Finally, he realised that Clement was indeed missing and rode away in exasperation.

Now, though, Dolly began to wonder why her husband had made his escape before the visitor arrived. She rode into town with Barney with the excuse that she needed to buy some supplies. Leaving Barney with the wagon, she found the storekeeper's boy.

"What exactly did that Bancroft fella come askin' about?" she inquired, tantalisingly playing with a few coins in the palm of her hand.

"He was askin' Pa if he knew where Mr. Duplege was livin'. Asked if Mr. Duplege was away from home some time. He was askin' lots of questions. He said did Pa remember when Mr. Duplege arrived home with his new wife. Pa said he remembered all right, 'cos you came a hollerin' in the store and sat drinkin' on our porch with your negro. Pa couldn't remember just when it was though, but I was just ten and I remembered and told him."

"You would!" muttered Dolly. "So your Pa told you to come and warn Mr. Duplege?"

"That's right. The man wanted a drink and somethin' to eat, so while he was doin' that Pa told me to head on over to your place and warn Mr. Duplege."

So Clement had scarpered and made himself look guilty. And maybe he was.

"Thank you," she told the boy and dropped half her coins in his grubby outstretched hand.

She was so engrossed in her thoughts, she almost forgot her groceries. She reached the wagon and then remembered and turned back to go into the store. They eyed her suspiciously as she made a few purchases and drove home with Barney.

"You awful quiet, Mrs. Dolly," he said.

"It's not surprising, Barney. Clement's gone, and I don't know when he'll come back. I don't know what to do."

"Harvest coming up soon, Mrs. Dolly. Plenty to do there."

"You're right as always, Barney," she said with a smile. "Best concentrate on getting the plantation back on its feet. That needs to be done with or without Clement. He doesn't help anyway."

Over the next few weeks she tried to forget her missing husband and all the problems that went with him and gave all her attention to her crops. It was fruitless to speculate, and the thoughts that snaked around her mind were going nowhere. On the plantation they had had a good season. As they had cultivated more land there was more work to do and the crop was much better. In the heat of the day she toted her sack with the other workers, filling it with the creamy heads of the cotton. As the last sack of cotton had been cleaned through the gin, she had a visitor.

Nathan Jacques arrived with an offer for her workers. "I've more land to harvest this year. If any of your workers would like to earn some more money, I've work over at my place and at the O'Neills'."

Some of the younger men and women took the opportunity to earn some money. At the Amiens plantation they would not be paid until Dolly had received payment for her cotton, and Nathan was offering outright wages.

"I think I've had enough, Mrs. Dolly," said Barney. "Takes me all day to pick what I could in a few hours. Thank the Lord that you don't wield a whip like that bastard Clucas." He spit vehemently on the ground.

"I'd never do that, Barney," Dolly told him. "I hope I value our workers, though I wish I could pay them more." For the first time she noticed with concern that his hair was going a grizzled grey. Though she worked with him nearly every single day, she didn't even know how old he was, and he had had a hard life. She didn't know how she would cope without Barney. Dolly linked his arm. "Come on, let's go and have a drink. Are you coming too Nathan … I mean, Mr. Jacques?"

"Nathan will do fine," he said, laughing.

She told him how she had scandalised the town by drinking with Barney on the store's porch and how they had remembered it. They all went laughing onto the porch, and a smiling Aunt Hattie met them with a jug of lemonade.

"And how are the happy couple?" Dolly asked.

"Oh, happy enough, and the new little wife is set on rearranging everything in my house," said Nathan with a wry smile. "You could say that's why I'm visiting, to avoid the ruckus. I have to admit I've been set in my ways since my wife died. All the same, it pains me to see the home we set up together being shuffled about and some of her favourite gewgaws boxed away to make room for the new wedding presents."

"Oh dear," said Dolly. Her family never had any gewgaws to rearrange due to the numerous times they 'did a moonlight flit', moving one step ahead of the rent man. Her mother had one pot spaniel that always found a place on the mantelpiece. There had been two until Seth broke one in a drunken rage, and Dolly had luckily caught the remaining one when her father hit Seth for breaking the other. Her mother had been heartbroken over that one cheap pot dog. She glanced round her barely functional home and vowed to have some ornaments of her own one day. "You're welcome, anyway. Especially with Clement away," Dolly added with a chuckle. "It's a disgrace that he can't be more neighbourly."

"Duplege and I never did see eye to eye," admitted Nathan.

"I'd better get back to work," said Barney, rising to his feet. "You'll find my boys are good workers, Massa Jacques."

"I don't doubt it, Barney." Dolly had expected Nathan to leave as Barney left, but he seemed quite comfortable on the porch and began to chat about her crop. "I reckon we should have a good cargo of cotton to send between us all. The O'Neills' crop is a fine one too, though they had a mite of trouble down by a swampy patch. I told them not to plant there, but folks take no notice."

As he talked on Dolly noticed his work hardened hands on the rough wood of the porch chair. She looked up at his earnest face gazing out over her fields with a practised eye. He reminded her of David in a way, the shape of his head, the jut of his whiskery chin; David but mellowed with time. Like David, he had been kind to her. He had escorted her round at his son's wedding, not left her abandoned among strangers. Nathan had realised how she felt about his son but not laughed at her. Perhaps he felt lonely as she did. He must miss his wife, though she had been dead for some time, and now he was becoming a stranger in his own home.

"Your advice is very important to me," she said warmly.

He gave her a thoughtful smile and patted her hand. "I'm glad I can be of help," he told her, reluctantly getting up from his chair. "Expect I'd best be going. I've enjoyed our little chat. It's been nice just sitting here talking to a woman, 'specially one as determined as you. You've made a big change to this place."

"Both me and Barney with your help," said Dolly loyally. "You know you're welcome to visit any time if you want to escape the 'ruckus' at home."

He shook her hand and held it for a moment. "I'll remember that," he said with a smile and a friendly wave as he went for his horse.

Dolly watched him leave, and felt alone and abandoned in the world. She hoped he would call again. Then she was claimed by Albert and his shadow Clemmie and dragged back into the whirl of domesticity.

CHAPTER 45: WEAVERS ROW

If Nathan was facing change in his home, so too was Jessie. One afternoon, before she became too tired to climb the slope to Weavers Row, she decided to visit Alice. The children were having an afternoon nap, so she slipped out before they woke and demanded to be taken with her. All the way she was met by women she had once worked with at the mill. Yet instead of a friendly "Hello Jessie", she was greeted with a polite bob or a nod and "Good afternoon Mrs. Overdale". She smiled to herself and wondered at her change in circumstance. She was still the same woman with the same fears as all the others, and she missed the careless banter and easy relationships of the old days. Then she had just been Jessie Davenport, ready for a laugh and a bit of teasing; now she was part of the Overdales and the subject of grudging respect.

There were changes too in her old home. She was ashamed that circumstances prevented her from visiting more often. If the children were around, they wanted to come too and, though it was easy enough to bring the boisterous Helen, Jessie needed help with Mattie as he grew and became heavier. The pushchair was now more difficult to manoeuvre and, though he could walk some way, it was a great and laborious effort for him. Rarely Jessie would ask Melissa if she could use the gig, but she didn't like to ask for the favour with Matthias so tetchy and watching every penny.

Finding the rising Row difficult to climb, Jessie had to rest for a moment, but soon enough she was knocking on the door of her old home.

"Oh Jessie, how lovely to see you," said Alice, throwing open the door and giving her a hug. "Why didn't you just come in? You know the door's always open."

Jessie couldn't explain why. She only knew that this wasn't her home now. Inside, things had been subtly altered. The parlour had been newly decorated and the furniture moved around. The curtains were brighter too, letting more light into the room. Some pieces had gone altogether and a dresser she recognised from Alice's old home now stood in pride of place. Alice saw her glancing up.

"I gave your Mother's pot dogs to Elsie," she said quietly. "She always admired them, and the new dresser wobbles a bit on the flags. I was worried we might break them. I hope you don't mind?"

"Not at all, Alice," said Jessie warmly. "This is your home now."

"Look, I have her prism lamp by the window," said Alice, pointing to the cut glass oil lamp, sparkling in the sunlight.

"That looks so pretty there," said Jessie, her eyes alight as a small draught sent tiny rainbows glittering around the room from the prisms.

"Would you like it?" asked Alice anxiously.

"Oh no, she'd love for you to have it." Jessie was anxious to reassure her. "Besides, I've got Mother's rosy bowl on my mantelpiece. I always think of her when I see it. We had such happy times here in this room, didn't we all?"

"We did indeed until Nellie's illness," said Alice, glancing round. "Remember John's wedding to Elsie? I changed the parlour around for your Dad's sake, really. I know in his heart he could see her lying there whenever he came into the parlour."

"I know what you mean," admitted Jessie. "The parlour looks better for the changes."

"Oh, and Eddie and his pals come in here to do a bit of homework of an evening. At least that's what they say they're doing!"

"How's he doing at the grammar?" asked Jessie. She felt she had sadly neglected her young brother.

"He's doing all right. We had a bit of a to-do last year, but he's pulled his socks up with a stern warning from your Dad. Jacob's hoping Eddie will train as a schoolmaster, so fingers crossed."

"Father'll be pleased," said Jessie with a smile. "He was always prodding me in that direction, but that didn't quite work out."

Eddie was always itching to call Jacob 'Dad', but she couldn't quite get used to the idea herself.

"Anyway, how about a cup of tea?" suggested Alice. "I'm forgetting my manners."

They sat and chatted about the family and neighbours, and the conversation finally came to Jessie and her impending confinement.

"Will you come and be with me?" she asked Alice.

"Of course I will. I wouldn't miss it. I hope it's not as traumatic as last time," said her stepmother, laughing. "I hope you're not going to produce another surprise baby."

"No wonder I was the size of a house," chuckled Jessie. "But I'm not as big this time. Doctor Braddock's nephew Dr. Andrew has joined him at his surgery. He said he could only hear one heart."

"At least he seems to have more idea than that deaf old fool," Alice told her with a sigh. "He still wouldn't believe me when I told him I could see the second baby's head."

"I just hope this baby will be all right," said Jessie, stroking her swelling tummy.

Alice patted her hand. "Of course it will be. They say it's a lot easier to give birth to your second child (or in your case third!) than a first. Not that I could swear to it, as I only ever had Mary. But I'll be with you, don't worry." Alice accompanied her back down the Row and over the bridge as she left for home. "I'll pop and see you long before you're due," she told her. "And please don't worry. This baby will be fine."

Jessie walked slowly up the drive towards Overdale House. It was a bit of an effort, but she perked up when she saw the familiar figure of her husband hurrying towards her. His limp became more noticeable as he approached her. Though the American Civil War was far behind them, they had a daily reminder in the deep slice out of Robert's leg.

"What are you doing walking out on your own?" he demanded. "Why didn't you ask for the gig?"

"I wanted to see Alice, and I needed the exercise," Jessie excused herself. "Here, let me have your arm."

Linking each other they walked slowly towards their home, each quietly worried what the coming child would be like.

CHAPTER 46: HARVEST TIME

Many weeks had passed, and Clement had still not appeared at the Amiens Plantation. The cotton harvest had been baled and loaded onto the Jacques' carts and shipped to Britain, and Nathan called with an invitation to Dolly and the rest of the workers.

"We're going to have a party to celebrate the harvest," he told her.

"Like a harvest festival in England," she said, clapping her hands in pleasure. "Not that there was much harvest to celebrate in Gorbydale. Most of the hills were for sheep. But before the cotton ran out, the local churches used to collect for the poor after the harvest."

"You're all welcome," Nathan told her, smiling at her delight. "Mr. Leach too."

"You're most kind, Mr. Jacques," said Jeremiah. "Most kind."

"Will Miss Clementine come too?" asked their neighbour.

Dolly and Jeremiah glanced at the girl who was at a makeshift table nearby, looking through a book with Albert. As they looked anxiously at one another, Albert popped his head up. He missed nothing.

"Are you coming to a party with me?" he asked Clemmie.

She nodded happily, and Aunt Hattie clapped her hands.

"We'll see on the day, shall we?" suggested Dolly, and Aunt Hattie nodded. "She gets a bit anxious in company," she murmured to Nathan. "But if we can persuade her to come, Aunt Hattie can come too."

"That will be fine," agreed Nathan. "There'll be plenty to eat for everyone."

When they had waved him off home, Aunt Hattie began making plans. "We'll have to make some good things for the party too," she decided. "I'll get Ida from the village to help. She used to help Massa Henri's French pastry chef make some mighty fine gateau. She's gettin' old now, but you don't forget a skill like that."

Dolly went to assess her meagre wardrobe. She didn't want to wear the same dress that she had for the wedding, but she had no choice. Albert's suit fitted him better, as he had sprung up during the summer. Jeremiah's suit was a rusty black, and their attempts to smarten it had little effect. Then Dolly found one of Clement's silk neckties, which made some improvement to his outfit. They were all looking forward to the harvest party.

Nathan sent one of his wagons over to collect the folks from the Amiens plantation. Only the oldest and the youngest were staying at home. It was a lively crowd that set out to the Jacques' home, the workers in their finest clothes, Dolly in their own wagon with Jeremiah, Clemmie and Albert. Aunt Hattie sat upright in the rear on a small nursing chair. It was she who had insisted that they travelled separately to uphold their status.

"Besides, we don't want to upset Miss Clementine by sitting with that rabble," she said sternly when Dolly suggested they all travel together.

Dolly had to smile and guessed that it was Aunt Hattie's status that must be upheld.

Ida had produced a fine gateau with her help, and Aunt Hattie sat with it on her lap. They had also baked some trays of dainty small cakes, and Jeremiah was guarding these against Albert and Clemmie's hopeful glances.

They were all welcomed onto the Jacques plantation. Nathan arrived to help Dolly down from their wagon as Jeremiah and Albert dealt with Clemmie. Barney and some of the others hurried to relieve Aunt Hattie of the cakes. She graciously condescended to be hauled down from her lofty height, though not without some difficulty. Soon they were all seated round a large horseshoe of tables for the feast. A cacophony of fiddlers enlivened the proceedings as everyone tucked into the plentiful food.

Dolly, seated beside Nathan to the annoyance of some of the O'Neill relatives, felt that at last this was a life she aspired to. There may be no grand ballroom, no mirrors and drapes, but in the glowing circle of happy faces shining in the lamp light, she felt honoured and fulfilled. Even Clemmie's face was alight with pleasure. Sitting between Albert and Jeremiah in a corner, she seemed to gaze back in memory to the days when she was a young and petted daughter of the Amiens plantation.

"I hope you are enjoying yourself, Mrs. Duplege?" asked Nathan. "Would you like some wine? Perhaps some julip?"

"No thank you," said Dolly politely. "I have a very light head."

Many times she had witnessed the drunken rages of her father and brother Seth, raging mad as if the booze had taken a grip of their senses. She never wished to be in that state, always staying sober and alert to protect her mother from Tommo's excesses. She'd seen Maggie take a sip of gin and dissolve into maudlin weeping. And then there was Clement with his mood changes as he drank. No, Dolly avoided alcohol as if it were poison, and it had certainly poisoned her family life.

A black choir began to sing a lively song, and some of the children began to dance. A couple of the crowd produced banjos, and the adults joined the dancing too.

"Is Clement kind to you?" asked Nathan.

Dolly had to think about that. "He's not unkind, I suppose. He just ignores me until I annoy him, and then he's as mad as hell. But he's never laid a finger on me, if that's what you mean?"

"I suppose it is," said Nathan. "You're a fine woman, Dolly. You deserve better."

"Not really," Dolly admitted. "I'm just a skivvy from the rough end of town and doing the best I can for myself and for Albert."

"You're more than that. Much more." Nathan smiled at her, and she filled with deep affection for him.

Dolly watched him as he fulfilled his duty as a host and spoke to each of his guests. Everyone beamed as he approached — all except Grandma O'Neill, whose continual sour expression never varied.

Dolly found herself next to Jeremiah as they watched the whirling dancers. By the hazy smile on his face, he had been liberal with the Jacques' julip.

"It's a fine party, Mrs. Dolly," he purred, his words slurring a little, "a fine party."

"Have you seen Albert and Clemmie?" she asked, suddenly missing her son from the crowd.

"Last saw them going that way," he told her, pointing towards the side of the house. "P'raps going for the er … faslilitities … fasl… er … you know."

"Yes, I do. I might look for them myself," she said, chuckling. "Go and sit down Jeremiah, before you fall down."

He grinned at her and swayed off to find a chair. Shaking her head but smiling to herself, she headed round the house to find her son and Jeremiah's facilities. As she reached the corner of the house, she almost bumped into a couple entwined in the darkness. They sprang apart and apologised.

"I'm sorry I disturbed you," she whispered with a giggle and left them to themselves.

Dolly thought that it must be so satisfying to be young and in love. She had never had that luxury. No one had wanted to love her after she had fallen pregnant with Albert. Perhaps she just wasn't loveable. She had almost reached the back of the house when she bumped into Nathan.

"Mrs. Dolly, what are you doing here in the dark?"

"I came to find Albert and Clemmie," she said. "Have you seen them?"

"No, but I'll come and look with you." He offered her his arm, and she slipped hers into the crook of his elbow. A feeling of warmth and rightness flooded her. When they reached the velvet shadows at the back of the house she paused, holding him back. She could see the pale oval of his face glancing down at her in the fragile moonlight.

"Dolly?" he asked quietly. She could not speak, overwhelmed with a desire that she could not explain. He seemed to understand. "I'm a lot older than you."

"I know."

"I'm not David."

"I know. You're a lot kinder than David. More thoughtful," she whispered.

"Are you sure?"

She nodded, hoping that he could see her face in the dim night. He led her slowly and gently towards the stables at the back of the house, pausing to ensure she had not changed her mind. She had not. The horses shuffled in their stalls as Nathan and Dolly crept into a stall filled with fresh sweet hay. Awkward at first they embraced, unsure and hesitant. Then with growing confidence they lay down and lovingly entwined until Dolly burst with joy and relief. Moments later, Nathan gave a deep moan of pleasure. They lay for moments staring at the rafters above them, wondering at what they had done. Dolly could not regret it. For the first time in her life, she felt like a complete woman.

"Are you all right?" asked Nathan.

"Very," said Dolly. She did not have the words to explain how wonderful she felt, fulfilled at last and cured of a nagging yearning that had plagued her. Then she came to her senses. "I expect we'd better go before anyone misses us," she murmured.

"You'd better slip away before me," said Nathan, stroking her cheek. "I don't want anyone to see us together and…"

"Are you ashamed of what we did?" she asked, staring into his eyes as she adjusted her clothes.

He shook his head. "No," he told her. "Not one bit. It seemed the most natural thing in the world. But you are a married woman, Dolly, and I don't want any gossip to get back to your husband. There is no saying what he'd do."

"He'd kill us," said Dolly, starkly facing reality. "He'd kill us, no messing."

Honora Darwen immediately sprang into her mind, reminding Dolly that Clement may have mistakenly murdered a poor innocent girl for revenge of Honora's betrayal . A wife's betrayal was so much worse.

"Then this must be our secret. I'd risk plenty for you, Dolly, but I would not see you harmed. Go quietly and…"

"Don't worry," she said, taking Nathan's hand and kissing it. "I'll be discreet." Quickly and quietly she slipped round the back of the house and, turning a corner, found Albert and Clemmie sitting on the side porch in the quiet shadows. "What are you doing here?" asked Dolly.

"Clemmie was worried with all the people," said Albert. "We're having a quiet sit."

"Are you coming back now?"

"What d'you think Clemmie?" asked her protector.

"All right," she said, taking his hand for reassurance.

The three of them emerged to blend into the guests watching the entertainment. Nathan appeared from the opposite side of the building, adjusting his trousers as if he had been to relieve himself. Dolly resisted the temptation to look at him. Her heart was full of quiet joy. She felt a complete woman at last. The years of frustration had melted away. She had longed to be loved, though deep down she had feared it too. Dolly could not know that Nathan deliberately would not glance in her direction, but would smile to himself at their sweet interlude.

In the early hours of the morning, the company began to fade. Many of the children had been carried to their beds by their parents. Dolly took a lantern and found Albert and Clemmie huddled together, fast asleep in their sanctuary by the side of the house again. She shook them gently.

"Time to go home, sleepyheads," she whispered.

Clemmie awoke and gave a lazy smile. "I liked this party," she said quietly.

For once Dolly saw a light of understanding, free from fear, in the girl's eyes. It was as if memories were awakening as Clemmie remembered the excitement of the Amienses' parties when she was young and carefree.

Albert was still half asleep, and Clemmie hauled him up into her arms and carried him towards the wagon. Barney hurried over and relieved her of his weight. Many of the men had helped themselves liberally to the drink on offer, and some of the Amiens workers were snoring loudly in the back of the big wagon as the women protested loudly at their drunken state.

A beaming Jeremiah was unsteady on his feet. "Best party ever," he slurred and with a lopsided grin added, "My sister would kill me!"

"I'll take the reins," decided Dolly.

Nathan came to see them off. He took one of Dolly's hands in his. "Thank you for coming, Mrs. Duplege," he said formally. "And thank you all for coming," he called to the rest of the Amiens party. "Did you enjoy yourselves?" The enthusiastic cheers and thankyous he roused from those still awake assured him of that. "I may call and see you in the next few days, Mrs. Duplege, to discuss our shipping arrangements," he added quietly, gazing into her eyes.

"That would be helpful," said Dolly primly, hoping no one else would notice the deep yearning in them.

She drove home alight with euphoria while Jeremiah babbled nonsense beside her. Next day he was apologetic, but she told him truthfully she hadn't minded a bit.

CHAPTER 47: AN OLD ACQUAINTANCE

Three days later, Dolly saw Nathan approaching the house. She had discreetly watched the road, longing to see him. But when he arrived, he was quietly formal.

Aunt Hattie thanked him profusely for the party. "Best time I had since I was a girl," she told him as she poured him a glass of lemonade.

When he had finished drinking, he proposed they go and look at the fields.

"Shall I send for Barney?" asked Aunt Hattie with a curious glance at Dolly.

"No need to disturb him," said Nathan. "I saw him working on his house as I drove up."

Aunt Hattie nodded cautiously.

Dolly was impatient to speak with him, but what he told her gave her little pleasure.

"Dolly, what happened at the party was very precious to me, but you know that we can't repeat it. Much as I would want that, if Clement ever finds out what we did he would surely kill us, as you know yourself. For myself I don't care, but I don't want anything to happen to you. You have your son to think about. And I hope to God you don't have another little one to think about, because that would take some explainin', especially with Clement away for so long."

Dolly felt like crying, but she knew deep in her breaking heart that Nathan was right. "I suppose you're right. He never touches me anyway," she said quietly.

"You mean he never...?" Nathan looked astonished.

"No, never."

Nathan slapped his hand on his forehead. "We'll just have to hope and pray that you don't fall with child," he said. "Oh Dolly, what have we done?"

"Something lovely," she said, laughing. "Something absolutely lovely."

Nathan smiled ruefully. "I know. Let's hope Clement never finds out. I'm so sorry I put you to such a risk. I'm much older than you. I should have known better."

"I'm not sorry," said Dolly defiantly. "And if it never happens again, I'll always remember it. But I don't want you to get hurt either. Clement's vengeance would be awful. I suppose we have to be sensible — for the first time in my life."

"You're the most sensible woman I know," said Nathan. "Look what you've done on this plantation."

"I just wish Clement would never come back. I wish he were dead," Dolly whispered.

"Don't wish that on anyone," he told her.

But deep down that was exactly what Dolly wished.

They walked back to the house, Nathan talking loudly about fields and yields and what they might plan for the next year. Aunt Hattie wasn't fooled, though. After they had waved him off from the porch, she took Dolly's arm. Glancing about to make sure no one was listening, she spoke quietly and earnestly. "I hope Massa Clement never hears any rumours 'bout you and Nathan Jacques. The Lord knows what he'd do." Dolly was about to protest, but Hattie shook her head. "Might have only been me saw what was happenin' the other night, but that old Ma O'Neill is one nasty shrew, and she has a nasty mouth too. You be very careful, Mrs. Dolly."

"I understand, Aunt Hattie," sighed Dolly, "and Nathan does too. I think maybe it was just one night of madness."

"I knows you get very lonely, Mrs. Dolly, but better be lonely than dead. Believe me that Massa Clement has one evil temper, and I may not always be around to save you."

"Thank you, Hattie," said Dolly, hugging her protector with tears of bitter disappointment streaming down her face. "Thank you so much. What would I do without you?"

Hattie was like a mother to her, protective and caring. Her own mother had been cowered to the ground by Tommo. Provision and protection had been left to Dolly. She had always been left to muddle through the best she could.

That night she could not sleep. If Aunt Hattie had noticed her feelings for Nathan, no matter how discreet they had been, who else might have noticed? What would happen if she found herself pregnant? All night long a lurid vision of what Clement would do if he found out haunted her and stoked her fear. Despite her longing to be loved, she knew she must not indulge it. She rose next morning drowsy and despondent but firm in her resolve to quell her love for Nathan. Above all else, she wanted to protect him.

The following days seemed long and listless. For some engagement to take her mind off her dilemma, she walked the fields with Barney, planning their next crop. He chatted about the party and didn't seem to suspect that anything was amiss. The sugarcane was growing high, and they wondered how they might get the money for machinery to process it themselves. For the moment it was an impossible dream.

As they talked, Dolly heard the faint rumble of a cart and looked eagerly towards the drive. Sure enough, the vehicle came into view and her first thoughts were that it might be Nathan. Eagerly she hurried to meet the visitor with Barney trailing in her wake. She stopped short in surprise when she came nearer. There was a familiar figure beside Barney's son Zeb, who was the driver.

"Kezia!" cried Dolly in surprise.

"Well, blow me down. You sure are a sight for sore eyes, girl," said Barney, hurrying to help her down. "We heard you was teaching in Washington."

Kezia laughed. "And so I was — and will be again. But I thought I'd come and take a look at my folks back home. Need to see Aunt Ida too. Is she still around?" she added anxiously.

"She sure is. Made a fine gateau like old times for Nathan Jacques' party the other night," Barney told her.

"It's just so good to see you," said Dolly, taking Kezia's hand with genuine pleasure.

They had hardly been friends when Kezia, an escaped slave from the plantation, had arrived in Gorbydale. Eavesdropping at Overdale House, Dolly knew that Kezia had travelled from America with Robert and Jessie after her husband died in the Civil War. She knew that, because Kezia had saved Robert's life, she was warmly welcomed by his parents.

Invited by the elders of the Gorbydale chapel, Kezia had spoken movingly of her life as a slave and won the hearts of the townsfolk. Some, including Dolly herself, had treated her as a curiosity. Remembering this, Dolly felt ashamed. In the end, Kezia had confessed to Jessie that she felt like an outsider and wanted to return to America and be with her own people. Now here she was in her old home, and Dolly was so glad to see another face from Gorbydale.

"Is Clement about?" asked Kezia. "I heard in a letter from Jessie that you and he had been married."

"He's not here just now," Dolly told her and muttered, "thank goodness," under her breath.

Kezia heard the note of dissent and her eyebrows raised.

"Will you stay with us while Clement's not here?" invited Dolly. "We'd be glad of the company."

Kezia gazed round the house. Jessie had told Dolly that the ex-slave was Clement's half-sister, fathered by his father, though he would certainly not acknowledge her as such.

"Maybe I could," said their visitor. "Though I expect Clement would throw me out if he comes home. He'll be in no mood to welcome an ex-slave into his house. Thank you for asking. There would certainly be more room here than in the village." She hesitated. "But I'll be more comfortable with Aunt Ida. Besides, I haven't seen her in years, and I think she'd like the company."

"At least come and have some tea and tell me all your news," said Dolly, eager for some distraction from her gnawing problems.

Clement had bought some precious tea with his last gambling win, and Dolly rationed it carefully. A visitor from Gorbydale was a rare treat to be celebrated with her precious brew.

Kezia nodded with a grin. It would be a novelty sipping tea like a lady in the house where she was once a slave. Things had certainly changed since the war, though in many places she was just as badly treated.

Aunt Hattie bustled out with some drinks but refused to sit and gossip with them. "I'll catch up with you later," she told their guest with a secret smile.

They sat awkwardly at first, then Clemmie and Albert arrived. Kezia looked stunned when she saw the change in the daughter of the house. She held the troubled young woman's hands and gazed earnestly into her eyes. "Do you remember me, Miss Clementine?" she asked gently. "It's Kezia. I used to tidy your room. I used to serve your dinner to you. Remember you gave me your old blue dress?"

There was a faint flicker of recognition in Clemmie's eyes, and then she began to cry.

"Oh, you poor chile," said Kezia, taking her in her arms to comfort her.

If Clement had witnessed such a thing in the past, Kezia would have been beaten and dismissed from the house to the fields, but humanity had replaced convention in his absence.

"I'm so sorry you had to lose your mamma and papa. We all lost loved ones in that dreadful war. I lost my Abraham. You remember him? He looked after the horses."

Clemmie looked anxious and retreated back into her shell until Albert arrived to meet the visitor. He chatted happily to Kezia as she told him about her school in Washington and asked him about his lessons with Jeremiah. Clemmie watched their guest cautiously, as if trying to piece together some part of the past. As she and Albert wandered off, Clemmie glancing back, looking puzzled.

"That poor creature," said Kezia, shaking her head. "She was such a pretty thing and likely to marry some rich boy hereabouts. Now the rich boys are mostly dead or gone away, and poor Clemmie has had her wits destroyed by the war. What will become of her?"

"We'll look after her while we can," said Dolly with a sigh. She told Kezia of Delia's arrival and the unspoken threat that she would put her sister in an asylum. She mentioned the fire that followed.

"Did they find out who did it?" asked Kezia cautiously.

"They blamed some poor black boy who everyone says was innocent," Dolly told her. "I suspect that swine Clucas myself — if he acted alone."

Kezia bit her lip and fell silent for a moment. "I wouldn't be a bit surprised if it was that devil Clucas," she said, her voice filled with venom. "May he rot in hell, especially after what he did to me."

"To you?" echoed Dolly.

"He dragged me in the stables when I was nothin' but a girl and he…" Kezia stopped with a sob. She didn't have to explain to Dolly.

"He did that to you?"

"He did it to any girl when he got a chance. He was an animal, nothin' but an animal." Kezia bowed her head in shame. "My Abraham didn't think the worst of me, though. He said it wasn't my fault. He loved me despite what that evil Clucas done."

Dolly was silent for a moment. Then slowly she told the secret that she had never revealed to anyone, not even her mother. "Clement did much the same to me," she said quietly and deliberately. "Oh, it was my own fault. I was stupid enough to show him the way to the temple in the dark. You remember old Matthias's little white temple?" Kezia nodded. "I thought he'd give me half a crown for my trouble. Turns out he was after more than my help to find the way to some stupid folly. I must have looked willing enough. It was my folly he exploited without so much as by-your-leave. He forced himself on me and that was that. Next minute I had Albert on the way, and years later Clement comes and claims him as his son. Like a fool I insisted he marry me to make Albert legitimate. That's how I ended up here." Dolly shrugged.

"Why did you marry him after what he'd done?" asked Kezia in surprise.

"I expect at the time I thought it was better than skivvying for the Overdales. At least Albert has a future here, if I can get the plantation going again like it was. He'd have had no chance in life living down River Road. Kezia, you're the first person I've ever told. Please, I hope you won't tell anyone else?"

Kezia smiled and patted Dolly's hand. "I won't tell, if you don't tell," she said with a chuckle. "I tell you somethin', though; you will make a go of this here plantation. Folks in the village are sure of it. Barney's son Zeb that drove me here was tellin' me how you've brought the place back to life, despite ole Clement."

"I'm doing my best," admitted Dolly. Deep down, though, she feared that all her efforts would crumble to nothing if Clement found out about her and Nathan. He would certainly do that if she had a child. That fear continually nagged her thoughts. In the dark shifting shadows of the night, it haunted her waking moments and invaded her dreams.

"Life is very strange," said Kezia thoughtfully, relaxing back in her sagging chair and sipping her drink. "To look at us we have nothing in common, a black slave and a girl from a Lancashire cotton town thousands of miles away. Yet I have been to your home town and here you are in mine, and we have both been used cruelly by wicked men. And we have both made better lives for ourselves despite them."

"We're survivors," Dolly declared firmly, then shuddered when Clement's return plagued her thoughts yet again.

Kezia noticed. "Is Clement cruel to you?" she asked gently.

"Not cruel. He just ignores me, all the time. And I do mean all the time. He is kind to Albert, though; that's when he's not annoyed with him. Albert's such a gentle soul. And he loves playing with the village kids. Clement hates that. He thinks Albert should act the master and lord it over them. But Albert's not a bit like that, bless him."

Kezia finished her drink. "I'd better get going to see Aunt Ida," she said, rising from her seat. "She'll have heard I've arrived by now. Thank you kindly for the tea. And I think Albert gets a lot of his ways from you, Mrs Dolly. To tell the truth, I didn't like you much in Gorbydale, but I like you fine now. And I promise I'll never tell your secret. You a proper lady, Mrs Dolly."

Dolly laughed. "Some rag tag lady!"

"You are all right. Some man once called me 'remarkable'. You sure are remarkable too." Kezia didn't add that the man had been Robert Overdale on his first visit to the plantation years before, and she cherished the remark still. "Bye Hattie," she called into the house as she left.

Aunt Hattie came to wave her off. "Give my love to Ida. Don't forget there's always a bed here for you."

Kezia stayed for over a week before she headed back to Washington. She and Dolly were often seen together. They talked about so many things — their homes, their work and about Gorbydale and the people they knew there.

Dolly missed her when she left. She missed the company and the distraction from her niggling worries about Clement. He had still not appeared, and the longer he remained away, the more she dreaded his return. Then a welcome appearance on her bedsheet one morning relieved her of one worry. She would not be having a child.

CHAPTER 48: A FIGHT

Dolly was inspecting the cotton in her fields and glanced up when she heard the sound of hoofbeats coming towards the house. A stab of guilt immediately wracked her. How could she face Clement after what she and Nathan had done? She didn't regret it but felt that surely Clement would read her guilt on her face. Dolly took a deep breath, straightened up and listened. Then she recognised that there was more than one horse as the sound beat nearer. Peering in the heat, she thought she recognised one of the figures as Clement. She watched as Aunt Hattie opened the door to the visitors and gestured for her to come. On trembling legs, she headed towards the house. To her surprise, two men she had never seen before stood solemnly in the hall, their hats respectfully in their hands.

"Mrs. Duplege?" one asked.

"Yes," answered Dolly cautiously. "That's me."

"I'm afraid I have some bad news for you," continued the man. "The sheriff of Baton Rouge has sent me to see you. I am his deputy."

"Is it Clement?" she asked anxiously.

He nodded. "I'm afraid it is. We're mighty sure it's your husband. There was an accident on board one of the riverboats. Your husband and another man got into a fight, and your husband fell into the water. I hate to tell you, ma'am, that he got dragged down as the wheels turned round."

"You mean he's dead?" asked Dolly, her knees suddenly going weak.

"I'm afraid so, Mrs. Duplege," one visitor informed her.

Aunt Hattie saw her buckle and hurried to hold her up. "Fetch me a chair, in that room there?" she commanded one of the men.

He hesitated, surprised to be ordered by a black woman. Then he hurried away to do her bidding as there was no other choice.

"Where is his body?" asked Dolly, as she sank onto the chair.

The men glanced at each other and looked uncomfortable.

"The water was too wild," said the other man. "No one could save him. I'm afraid his body has not been recovered. It was some time before the engine could be stopped, and by that time he was lost in the water."

"Are you sure it was my husband?" asked Dolly faintly, anxious for an answer. "Are you sure there's not some mistake?"

The man nodded. "We're pretty sure, Mrs. Duplege. A man on the boat recognised him. He'd played cards with him many times before."

"And what about the man that pushed him overboard? Has he been arrested?" demanded Dolly, anxious to appear a grieving widow. She'd wished Clement dead and buried a thousand times, but now she was faced with the fact of his death, she felt sick, her legs weak. She hadn't expected to be so affected by the news.

"The man claims he was acting in self-defence," said the deputy. He reached into a pocket and produced a small pistol. Dolly recognised the pearl handle, the silver scrollwork on the barrel. She had seen that little gun many times beside Clement's watch by his bedside. "Did this belong to your husband?" he asked gently. "Do you recognise it?"

Dolly nodded. "Yes," she whispered. "That's Clement's pistol, all right. I'd know it anywhere."

"Sure is, mister," Aunt Hattie confirmed. "That's Massa Clement's gun right enough. Seen it many times."

"It fell on the deck from your husband's sleeve during the fight. I think that just about confirms that the victim was Clement Duplege," he said, turning to the other man.

Dolly nodded in agreement. "What do I do now?" she asked faintly.

"Well, as you know there's no body to identify," said the deputy. "The sheriff will write something to you. I guess you just tell the rest of his kinfolk. We're right sorry, ma'am."

"Might his body wash up along the shore?" asked Aunt Hattie. "I heard once of a cousin of mine that was washed up." She didn't add that he'd been escaping from men with dogs when he'd been drowned, though she told Dolly afterwards.

The men hesitated. "You do know there's alligators along the Mississippi," said the deputy cautiously.

Dolly shuddered and began to cry. It was less from grief than from the horror of her husband's fate. She was also overwhelmed by the huge wave of relief and, choked by her conflicting emotions, tears poured unabated down her cheeks. "So he's gone," she whispered. "Oh Aunt Hattie, he's gone, and I don't know what to do now."

"Don't you worry about a thing," Aunt Hattie told her, with a reassuring arm round her shoulder.

The deputy and his companion looked affronted by Hattie's familiarity, but said nothing as Dolly was obviously not bothered.

Jeremiah and Albert arrived with Clemmie in tow. They were surprised when they saw the visitors.

"These men come to tell us that Massa Clement's been killed in an accident," Aunt Hattie explained to them.

Seeing his mother's tears, Albert ran to comfort her. "Don't cry, Mam," he said.

"Your Papa won't be coming home anymore, love," she tried to explain through her tears. "He fell overboard into the big river and drowned."

"Like Clucas?" asked Albert.

She stared at him in surprise. He was so quiet at times, yet seemed to absorb everything around him. "Yes, something like that," she said.

"Poor Papa," said her son and began to cry along with her.

"Would you like a drink?" Aunt Hattie asked the two men. "You've come a long way with this awful news."

They hesitated, with a glance at the widow and her weeping son.

"That would be good," said the deputy.

Hattie led them all out onto the porch and left Dolly and her son in peace.

Jeremiah questioned the two strangers, hoping to discover more details, but there was little they could tell him. There had been plenty of witnesses to the initial argument and then the fight. A man had accused Clement of cheating, and it had escalated until a hard blow had knocked Clement overboard. They had all watched in horror as the giant wheel had mown him under the water.

"What should Mrs. Duplege do next?" he asked them.

"Now she's recognised Duplege's gun and there's no doubt he's our man, I reckon she should get a lawyer and claim his estate," the deputy told him. "I doubt his body will show up, so there's no buryin' to be done."

"Yes, she should claim his estate for her son," agreed Jeremiah. He chatted with the men for a while, gleaning some

313

news of the outside world, then went into the house to console Dolly and Albert.

The news of Clement's death spread quickly, and not only the villagers came to call with sympathy. Nathan arrived next day, and Dolly was glad to see him but they had no time to talk privately as some of the O'Neills came to pay their respects too. Old Ma O'Neill sat rigidly on a rickety armchair, her face a picture of grim judgement.

"I expect he got no more than he deserved," she said. "Folks say as how he riled up plenty of men with his gamblin'. They say that fine house in Baton Rouge was won from a poor man that blew his brains out. Say the man's widow was housekeeperin' for him and ran off with the money from sellin' it. Reckon you got a lucky escape, Mrs. Duplege — one way and another," she added, looking pointedly at Nathan.

"Now we shouldn't speak ill of the dead, Mrs. O'Neill," he chided her. "Reckon his maker will make the proper judgement on him. 'Judge not' the good book says."

"Reckon if more people read the good book, they wouldn't end up with the alligators," she snapped.

"Mother! Remember the child," scolded her daughter-in-law, glancing at Albert who was huddled next to his mother, sporting a black arm band on his suit. "That poor boy has lost his father."

The old woman curled her lip and went quiet. Dolly was anxious to speak to Nathan, but it seemed an age before her other visitors moved and he had to make his excuses to go.

"I'll show you to the door," she said.

"I'll call tomorrow," he murmured after they had said their loud farewells.

That evening she sat down and, with Jeremiah's help, wrote to Delia with news of her uncle's death. She was grateful that there was no funeral for Clement's niece to attend and that would be an end to their conflict. Dolly rightly doubted that Delia would come and claim her sister.

It was late afternoon the next day when she saw Nathan riding up the drive towards the house. Now wearing a black dress cobbled together from one of Aunt Hattie's old skirts and one of Clement's shirts dyed black, Dolly felt very dowdy. She had never lost her love of colour but had to wear the miserable outfit for decency's sake. "Mr. Jacques," she said formally with a small bow.

"Mrs. Dolly," he answered with a polite smile.

"It's nice of you to call."

"I said I would," he told her, settling down on a battered chair on the porch.

Dolly was grateful he hadn't sat in Clement's usual chair. Though her husband was dead, she felt his spirit would linger around his old home a while longer. She hadn't slept very well after a disturbing dream and had spent the rest of the sleepless night imagining his dripping body in the shadows. She had wished him dead, but the guilt that plagued her betrayal had nonetheless refused to go away.

Aunt Hattie automatically came out with a drink and lingered for a moment. Then Albert joyfully burst out of the house followed by Jeremiah now that their lessons had finished for the day.

"'Lo, Mr. Jacques," called Albert, waving as he raced off towards the village to see his friends.

Jeremiah shook his head in amusement. "I envy the young their carefree existence," he said. "I have tried to explain to him about his father, Mrs. Dolly, but he's too young to understand. I did try to explain about heaven and that the good

315

Lord judges men on their merits, but I'm not sure if my message got through."

"The good Lord would need a lot of patience to find Clement's merits," snorted Dolly.

"The Good Book does say 'judge not lest you yourself be judged'," Jeremiah reminded her.

Dolly chuckled. "I expect you're right, Mr. Leach. Doubtless Clement had many hidden merits — and kept them well hidden. But he did love Albert, though, and that might help him squeeze through the narrow gate."

Jeremiah lingered for a moment, then somehow sensed that Nathan wished for a private word with Dolly. "Excuse me while I go and prepare tomorrow's lessons for my pupil," he said. "I shall desist upon heaven and try measurements. I will go and ask Aunt Hattie if she has any string that I may knot into suitable lengths. Boys usually like messing with string."

Dolly smiled as he left. "He's an odd man, but he's got a heart of gold. Albert has really learnt so much from him. Clement wanted to send him away to school, but I don't know how he'd cope with a load of rough boys. I know the kids in our school in Gorbydale were a tough lot and showed no mercy to anyone what was different."

"Children can be cruel," admitted Nathan. He patted her hand. "Have you thought that you might have more children one day?" he asked quietly.

"I'm certainly glad that I'm not about to have one any time soon," she said. "Oh Nathan, I was so worried that I might be expecting a child. That would have taken some explaining to Clement if he'd come back."

"In a way I'm sad," he told her. "But you're right. A baby would have taken some explaining. But, Dolly, perhaps we could have some words in private. Shall we walk the fields?"

He was so serious that a feeling of dread poured over her. Was he about to tell her that their tentative relationship was at an end? When they were some way from the house he paused, took her hand, then carefully dropped it and stepped away from her. Her dread rose and paralysed her. Her breath froze into a cold hard lump in her chest until he spoke. "I know Clement is gone and that is an end to some of our worries. But, though I would wish it, we must not rush into anything."

Dolly stayed silent, her eyes wide and anxious in supplication. Surely he would not abandon her after all the cherished words he had said about 'risking plenty' for her and how precious their moments together in the stable had been.

"I'm a lot older than you, Dolly, and I've been a widower for a long time. But I know I can make you happy," he said earnestly.

Dolly laughed with relief. "Oh, you can certainly do that," she told him.

"But like I say, we mustn't rush into anything. If you're willing, and I hope you are, we could wait for a respectable time and get married. Would you like that?"

"Oh Nathan, I would love that above all things," said Dolly, tears of joy streaming down her face. She started towards him, but he raised a gentle hand.

"Don't forget, my dear, that you are newly widowed. If we do things in a rush, people will start talking."

"Oh, I don't care what people say," began Dolly eagerly.

"But I do," said Nathan solemnly. "You have your reputation and your son to think about, and I have one too. We don't want to bring shame on our families. We don't want folks to be gossiping in front of them. Dolly, my dear, we have all the time in the world."

"But can we still…?" she began, anxious to repeat her experience in the barn.

He knew immediately what she meant and smiled as he shook his head. "Do you think that's wise? What if you should fall for a baby? Much as I want to, I think we should be sensible. Time will come soon enough."

"Oh, very well," said Dolly, reluctant to be sensible. "If you're sure?" She hoped perhaps he would relent as time went on. Now she had tasted such fierce passion, she could hardly wait to taste it again.

She was all in a fever of longing for the next few days and wondered how she would cope with a prolonged bout of celibacy until Nathan decided a respectable time had passed. From Dolly's agitation, Aunt Hattie guessed that something was about to happen. She was right; something was about to happen, but it wasn't what they all anticipated.

CHAPTER 49: A LETTER FROM BATON ROUGE

"There's a letter here for you from Baton Rouge," Aunt Hattie called to Dolly some weeks later.

Dolly hesitantly took the envelope as Hattie went to make a drink for the dusty rider who had delivered it. "Jeremiah," she called, unwilling to open her letter without his presence. Her reading was improving all the time, but her confidence faltered when faced with such an official looking envelope. She gingerly opened it and read slowly. "It's from a judge in Baton Rouge. I have to go to court," she said, puzzled. "Delia Bartholomew has dis…"

"Disputed," read Jeremiah, looking over her shoulder.

"Disputed my claim — or rather Albert's claim to the plantation. She's called my Albert illegitimate. The cheek of the bitch. My Albert illegitimate! I'll sue her."

"You will of course have papers to prove otherwise," said Jeremiah confidently.

Dolly's heart sank. "Oh hell." She closed her eyes and her head fell on her chest in desperation. She felt sick as her hopes for her son began to blur and waver in her mind.

"You do have papers, though?" asked the schoolteacher.

"The thing is…" began Dolly. She flopped down hard in a chair and tried to remember. "The thing is we didn't get married 'til Albert was about four. I was the only one working in the family, and my Mam brought him up as her own. Her name's on his birth certificate." She glanced up at the schoolmaster, her voice wavering with fear. "When Clement came and claimed him as his son and we got married in

Liverpool, he said he'd done something at the lawyers to make Albert legitimate and change his birth certificate. They said they'd send on the papers, but I don't know if they ever did. Clement would have seen to all that."

"So you don't know if they sent the papers?"

Dolly shook her head and thought hard. "He must have put them somewhere safe. Surely he'd have made sure he had 'em when Delia came snooping round to try and sell the plantation to those carpetbaggers."

"How did he find out about Albert?" asked Jeremiah. "Did you keep in touch?"

Dolly gave a hollow laugh. "He didn't have a clue he had a son when he left Gorbydale. He just had his way with me and left me to it. It was that nosy Honora Darwen suspected I was in the family way. She watched me like a hawk, though I kept denying it. More fool me. They all knew Mam was too old to have a baby. But there you go. Clement said it was Honora that told him and he came and checked out Albert for himself. Unless Clement has some papers knocking about, I'm in trouble."

"Let us go and have a look then," suggested Jeremiah. "Have you looked through Mr. Duplege's papers?"

"I didn't like to," admitted Dolly. "It felt somehow like an intrusion."

"Come along then," said Jeremiah. "We'll look together for them now."

Dolly was still hesitant to go into Clement's room. She had only made a quick and uneasy visit to see if he had left any money there. They found a small leather case with some papers, one of them their marriage certificate from Liverpool and others receipts for horses including Albert's pony. But there was no sign of a birth certificate for Albert.

"We must write to Liverpool immediately," suggested Jeremiah. "They should be able to make a copy of Albert's amended certificate from their records. And we should write to Miss Darwen and ask her to confirm what she told Mr. Duplege."

"I don't have her address. She's training to be a doctor is all I know," sighed Dolly. She burst into tears. "Oh Jeremiah, what am I to do? I've worked so hard and it's all going to be lost. That Delia is going to sell the lot to some carpetbagger and Albert won't be able to claim his inheritance."

"There, there Mrs. Dolly," he said, patting her on the shoulder. "We are not beaten yet. There is plenty of hope, but we must get writing as soon as possible. Do you think that the folks in Gorbydale will have Honora Darwen's address?"

"Oh yes. She and Jessie Davenport — Jessie Overdale now — were as thick as thieves. Jessie'll have her address."

"I shall look in my case and find some decent writing paper. And we shall write to the judge and tell him it might take some time to gather our evidence together in the light of Mr. Clement Duplege's unfortunate early demise. I shall tell him how distraught you are. With a bit of luck he might delay the hearing for a month or two."

"Oh Jeremiah, what would I do without you?" said Dolly, hugging his arm and bursting into a fresh flood of tears. "I bless the day you came to our house."

"There, there, Mrs. Dolly," said Jeremiah, patting her hand. "Your case is a just one."

Buoyed by his confidence, Dolly began to make her plans. Together they assembled the addresses and wrote the letters: one to the court at Baton Rouge, one to the registry office in Liverpool and another to Jessie Davenport requesting Honora

Darwen's address. They also composed one to Honora Darwen to be sent as soon as they received her address.

"We must take Albert with us to Baton Rouge," decided Dolly. Now that she had lost some of the fear of visiting Clement's room, she had scoured his things to find some evidence for her case. Among his bits and pieces she found a gold locket. It was an unusual thing for a man to have, and she hesitated before she opened it. For a moment Dolly thought she heard footstep behind her, and in guilty fear she froze. Slowly she turned to find Clemmie staring at her, silent as a ghost.

"Papa's," she said quietly. "Grandmère's."

Dolly noticed she was staring at the locket. It was at that moment Albert bounced in.

"There you are, Clemmie. Aren't you coming out?"

"Papa's," she repeated, pointing at the locket. "Grandmère's."

Albert came to see what his mother was holding. "Is it another watch?" he asked, touching it gently. "Does it tinkle like Papa's?"

Clemmie bent and whispered in his ear. She was murmuring for quite some time, though Dolly could not hear.

"Oh right," said Albert cheerfully. "Clemmie says it's a locket. Her Papa gave it to her. It was her Grandma's."

"Grandmère," whispered Clemmie.

"Uncle Clement, I mean Papa, was minding it for her so she didn't lose it. There's a picture inside."

Dolly pressed a tiny button at the side of the locket and it sprang open.

"Oh, it's me!" said Albert gleefully. "Look, it's me! But who's that other boy?"

Clemmie whispered again and Albert looked disappointed.

"Oh, it's not me. It's Papa and Clemmie's papa when they were little boys."

"They must be Clement and Henri when they were children," said Dolly, staring at the tiny painted portraits. The youngest boy was a mirror image of Albert, his hair brighter than his brother's, though Clement's fiery mane had darkened with age. "Jeremiah, Jeremiah," she called excitedly. "Come and look what I've just found."

"Mrs. Dolly," said Jeremiah with a confident smile as he carefully held the locket. "This is indeed a treasure. This little picture of Clement is Albert to the life."

Dolly hugged Clemmie. "You're a great girl," she said warmly. She sincerely hoped that Clement had indeed taken the locket for safekeeping and not just as a trinket to be pawned for yet another gambling stake. "We must take this with us when we go to court. When they see Albert and this locket together, they are sure to be convinced."

"I suggest we take Miss Clementine with us too," Jeremiah told her. "Then they will witness the good care you have taken of her and that will be in your favour."

"You will come with me, won't you?" asked Dolly.

"I will indeed," he told her. "I know Billy Mason, an old pupil of mine in Baton Rouge who has trained in the law. I am sure he will help us for friendship's sake. You can be sure that Mrs. Bartholomew will have a good lawyer to state her case."

Dolly had an anxious wait for her letters. She would have loved to dispel the tedious time in Nathan's arms but, though he called often, he was scrupulously respectable at all times. All the same, rumours filtered round the plantations and the town.

"I think we should have a talk to David and Jassy," he told her one day. "My daughter-in-law keeps making little remarks. Why, only this morning she said 'Oh, so you're going to visit the widow Duplege again today' with a very knowing glance at me."

"What did you say?" asked Dolly.

"I told her that I was being neighbourly in your hour of trouble," he said with a chuckle. "I asked her if she would like to come too and help you in your hour of need. She suddenly decided she had a lot of chores to do. But I do think we should tell them a little of our plans."

"If you're sure," sighed Dolly. She had enough to worry about without Ma O'Neill informing the neighbourhood of her suspicions.

CHAPTER 50: A LETTER FROM DOLLY

Jessie was having a lazy morning in bed after a sleepless and uncomfortable night as her body swelled with her baby. She was surprised when Melissa hurried into the bedroom with a brief knock on the door. Her mother-in-law was usually very considerate of her privacy.

"It's a letter from America, Jessica dear," she said, bubbling with curiosity. "Do you think it's from Honora? I wonder when she'll be coming home. She should remember her duty here with Matthias so unwell recently and you about to have your child. It would be such a comfort to have her home."

Jessie had heard this argument so many times, she almost ignored it but decided to defend Honora once again. "You know, Mother-in-law, that she won't come home until she has finished her studies and only then when she is allowed to practise as a doctor in England," she said gently.

"Yes, yes I know, but…" said Melissa impatiently. "Anyway, is it one of her letters? I don't recognise the writing."

Jessie smiled and carefully opened the letter. Her eyes opened wide in surprise. "It's from Dolly Tate, well, now Duplege. Oh dear, she says that Clement has been drowned after an accident on a riverboat. They couldn't save him and he was washed away down the river. Poor woman. And she asks if we can send her Honora's address. I wonder what on earth that's for? Oh, she says she needs some information concerning Albert. She sends her love to her mother and asked would we be kind enough to pass it on, and she sends her regards and warm wishes to all of us here. Albert is well and thriving in the warm climate. What do you make of that now?"

"Very odd," decided Melissa. "Well, we must of course send Honora's address to her, and we can ask Maggie if there's any news she'd like to send too. I'll let you get up, dear."

Jessie smiled as her mother-in-law left the room in a swirl of activity. That was certainly a hint for her to rise from her bed. She reread the letter before she struggled to swing her feet onto the bedside rug. She felt listless and heavy now that her pregnancy was nearing its end, not to mention anxious that everything would be all right. "We'd better write to Honora and tell her about Clement and to expect a letter from Dolly," she told Melissa as she pondered over her letter at a small writing desk in her living room.

There was a tentative knock on the door, and Maggie tiptoed in at Jessie's call to come in.

"I told her to come and see you. I hope that's all right?" said Melissa.

"Of course it is," said Jessie, smiling at the maid of all work.

"I told her about Clement, and she's very upset for Dolly and Albert," murmured Melissa.

"I've had a letter from your Dolly, and I know Mrs. Overdale has told you about poor Mr. Duplege, Maggie," said Jessie. "I'm very sorry for her and I will write and send our condolences."

"Our Dolly never had much luck," said Maggie with a sigh. "Now I expect I'll never see Albert again." She began to sob, and Jessie rose with difficulty and put an arm round her. Maggie was certainly a lot cleaner since Cook had taken her in hand and insisted she had the odd bath in the kitchen outhouse.

"I'm sure you'll want to send her your condolences too. Tell me what you'd like to write and I'll put it all down for you."

"Perhaps say that we're sorry for her loss and that Albert's lost his Daddy. We know we can't be with her, but we'll be thinking of her just the same." Maggie paused to think. "D'you think that's all right?"

Jessie nodded. "Those are lovely sentiments," she said.

"It's a good thing our Dolly won't be short of money," said Maggie. "That's one blessing." She was blissfully ignorant of her daughter's struggles.

"Dolly wanted to know Miss Honora's address in Washington, but she's sent a message to you too, about Albert. Look, she sends you her love and says that Albert is well and thriving."

"Poor mite," said Maggie. "He'll have to grow up without a Daddy."

Jessie glanced at Melissa, sure that they were both thinking that Maggie's children might have been better people without Tommo's malign influence.

After she had added Maggie's heartfelt sympathy, she finished the letter with Honora's address. On Melissa's insistence, she added more sympathetic messages from the rest of the family, though she was unsure if Matthias and Robert would agree with the sentiments expressed in their names.

Once Jessie had sealed the letter, she wrote another to Honora warning her to expect a letter from Dolly and telling her that Clement had drowned in the Mississippi river. She hoped this would put her friend's mind at rest. Having someone like Clement lurking about and set on revenge must have been worrying indeed.

Later when the two men arrived for their midday meal, they heard of Clement's unfortunate death.

"Good riddance to bad rubbish," growled Matthias. "He cheated me out of hundreds with those useless Confederate dollars."

"I can't say I'm unhappy to hear of his passing," said Robert. "Not after he abandoned me at sea during that attack by the Union navy. What an odd coincidence that your brother was serving in that navy," he said to Jessie. "Still, you have to feel sorry for Dolly that she's lost her husband."

Despite their feelings the two men duly sympathised with Maggie on the loss of her son-in-law, when she came to serve the meal. She hurriedly dished out the stew and left with tears streaking her cheeks.

"I understood she didn't know him that well," said Matthias, puzzled. "Old Clement seems to have done a flying visit and grabbed her daughter and the lad and whisked them off to America. I don't suppose Tommo was too pleased to lose his meal ticket at the time."

"I expect she's feeling sorry for Dolly and Albert," Melissa told him.

"Maggie thinks she won't see Albert ever again," Jessie informed them. "I know I'd feel the same if I thought I wouldn't see my children again. She did bring him up as her own."

"Aye, I expect you're right," admitted Matthias. "Blood's thicker than water. I for one won't be sorry to see the last of that conniving, cheating…"

"We shouldn't speak ill of the dead, dear," said his wife.

Matthias snorted and didn't look convinced.

Annoyed with herself for feeling exhausted when she had only written two letters, Jessie flopped down on a settle by the French windows in her room. Lizzie had fed the children in the nursery as Matthias insisted and now they were playing outside in the sunshine on the terrace. Matty's walking was improving with the help of the braces on his legs, though his gait was still awkward and manoeuvring the heavy metal exhausted him. Helen was pushing round her doll's baby carriage on sturdy legs but including him in the game. Jessie knew her son was clever and perceptive in so many ways but was frustrated as to how to help him. As she tried to teach Helen the basics of reading and her numbers, Matty had surprised her by mastering a simple counting frame with bright wooden beads. His hands did not have the dexterity for writing, but he could move the beads with simple hand movements. Even Matthias had been impressed with his grandson's answers to simple sums.

Now the children spotted her through the windows and pressed against the glass to be let in. Lizzie opened the door as Jessie beckoned them. She felt too heavy to haul herself off the settle. Matty lurched through the door and trampled on her toes as he fell against his mother in his eagerness to see her. Jessie gave a cry as he fell heavily against her swollen belly. Lizzie's mouth fell open in alarm, but her mistress raised her hand to reassure her while hugging her son with the other arm to steady him.

"I'm fine, I'm fine," she said quickly. She felt anything but fine and wished with all her heart that her ordeal would soon be over, praying that this child would be fine too.

CHAPTER 51: HONORA WRITES

Honora wrote Jessie a long letter from New York, telling her that, now she had heard that Clement was dead, she was sleeping easier and walking abroad without forever glancing over her shoulder. She mentioned the letter she'd received from Dolly, hoping for a statement about the timing of her pregnancy back in Gorbydale. Dolly had also added a footnote in the hope that it would speed Honora's reply.

I think you will be relieved to hear of my husband's death. Some months ago I had a visit from a man called Bancroft who told me that Clement was suspected of your friend's murder in New York. At the time I told him that Clement was with me all the time we were in the city. When I thought about it later, he did leave me at times but I thought it was because he was gambling. I found a train ticket stub in one of his coat pockets after he died and it shows we left New York for Boston the day after the murder. I do know our journey was very quickly arranged. I hope this helps you.

These things were not total proof that Clement had killed Verity, but in Honora's mind they confirmed her suspicions.

Honora sat down and wrote a letter that might help Dolly prove Albert's legitimacy. She could not say positively that Clement had fathered the child, but she had calculated the dates and he was the likely suspect. She did not mention that the Tates had accused Arden Davenport of being the father and that he had vehemently denied it. Honora wrote that although she should have reported Dolly's pregnancy to her mistress Melissa, she felt sorry for the girl as Dolly was the only one of her family with a job. She stated that Dolly's parents had brought up the child as their own so that Dolly could continue to work. She read the letter through with relief and sent it off with a sense of closure.

Then Honora called on Verity's father with her news. He listened to her theory patiently, though did not seem convinced by it.

"So you say that you should have been the victim and not my dear Verity?" he said finally.

"I am sorry to say that I suspect it is so," said Honora humbly.

He snorted. "I expect this Dolly woman is hoping for the reward money," he said scathingly. "That's why she's finally come clean with this dubious evidence."

"There was no mention of the reward in her letter," protested Honora. "She has just lost her husband and, though he may have been a villain, he was the father of her child. I am sure she just wanted to set the record straight."

"We'll see," said Mr. Cain.

Honora was surprised that he seemed more concerned about his money than that his daughter's suspected murderer had himself been killed. "Perhaps you could use the money for a charity in Verity's name," she suggested. "Perhaps scholarships or bursaries for more young women to study medicine as Verity wished."

To her surprise he became angry. "And pray what good did it do her?" demanded Mr. Cain. "I indulged my daughter with that silly whim because, as my only child, I could deny her nothing. I know she was only studying medicine in honour of my profession because I have no son. Do you think I would encourage other young women in their folly? I think not, young woman. I will say good day."

Though she was being dismissed so abruptly, Honora paused to have her say. "Your daughter Verity would have made an excellent doctor," she said angrily. "She was clever and kind and she was skilful. With her small hands she could do the most delicate operations much better than some of the male students. You should be very proud of her. She would have been as good as you and even better had she lived. Good day, Mr. Cain, and I wish you and your money well."

He stared open-mouthed at her audacity as she stormed out of the room.

All her career she had been mocked and underestimated, but to see her friend treated with the same disdain, and by her own father, made her boil with anger.

Honora realised how low she had felt since pushing Arden away and Ben's rejection. Sometimes she had done the minimum work to get by. Now her determination to succeed as a doctor rose up with renewed vigour. She had been spared the ignominy of being murdered by Clement. Now she was determined to work hard to honour Verity and become the doctor she had always aspired to be.

CHAPTER 52: AN UNEXPECTED OUTBURST

The day that Nathan and Dolly were to speak to his son arrived. Nathan had primed the young couple that Dolly was to visit. He drove her over in his wagon, her hand trembling as she held tight to her seat.

"Don't worry," he told her. "It'll be fine. They'll be fine."

All the same, Dolly was nervous. Nathan deliberately hooked her arm into his as they entered the room. Jassy noticed this small intimacy immediately and threw David a look of resentment. Immediately Dolly knew this meeting would not go well, despite Nathan's reassurances.

"Dolly and I have something to tell you," he began.

"And I can guess what that is," snapped Jassy. "I'll bet my granny was right. You're gonna marry this whore. Her husband is hardly cold in his grave and she's got her claws into you. Mark my words, she'll steal this plantation away from my David when she has her little whore babies."

They all stared at her, amazed at her angry outburst.

"Jassy, that's enough," protested David.

"More than enough. I might remind you, young woman, that you are living in my house," said Nathan coldly. "And Clement Duplege hasn't even got a grave. You should know he was never a good husband to Dolly, what with his drinking and gambling and the Lord knows what else. We decided to tell you our plans because you're family, and we thought you should be the first to know. But not because we felt we needed your approval. Dolly and I won't be getting married for some time, at least not until an acceptable time has passed for decency's sake."

"Decency!" hissed Jassy under her breath. She looked defiant but fell silent when David glared at her, bewildered by his wife's belligerence.

"I'm sorry, Pa. I didn't expect that from Jassy. I'm sorry, Dolly, but I didn't expect…" he began.

"That's all right," said Dolly, lifting her chin with dignity. "But I can tell you that I have no intentions of stealing your plantation. In case you haven't noticed, Albert has one of his own, and a fine one it will be in time. Isn't that right Nathan?"

"Indeed it is. I had hoped our announcement would be a happy one," he said quietly, his piercing glance raking Jassy.

She bridled with indignation but fell silent.

"I've been a widower for a long time, David, you know that. I loved your mother dearly, but since she's been with the Lord, I've been very lonely at times. I hope you don't begrudge me a little happiness too before I meet my maker. I've admired Dolly since I first met her, although I didn't expect her to want to marry an old man like me."

"You're not so old," she reassured him, squeezing his arm.

"Older than you," he said with a smile. "Anyway, she has consented to be my wife and when a respectable time has passed, we'll be married. I wanted to tell you both, but I don't want you telling all and sundry about this. This is just for our family. And I don't want you to go telling that granny of yours," he told Jassy sternly. "Otherwise the whole county will know, and it's nobody's business but ours. You understand?"

She nodded her head sulkily.

"If somebody confronts me with it, I'll know it's you that talked, right?"

"Perhaps my mother?" she asked tentatively.

"Nobody," insisted Nathan sternly.

Ignoring his wife, David grabbed his father's hand. "Congratulations, Pa," he said, shaking it vigorously. "And you too, Dolly. I hope you'll be very happy. This is fine news. Surprising news, mind you. Who'd have thought a fine gal like you would fall for an old goat like my Pa?"

"Less of the 'old goat' my boy," said Nathan, laughing.

Dolly thought she heard Jassy snort behind them. "Thank you David," she said. "I'll try my best to make your father happy. You know I wouldn't do anything to harm the family. You've both been very good to me. Barney and I couldn't have revived the plantation without you. God knows I've had enough trouble in my life to want a happy and peaceful life now, for myself and for all of us."

"I know," he said. "Clement Duplege can't have been an easy man to live with."

"And a dangerous man too," Dolly told him. She did not confess that she had lived in fear of her life for many months, wondering if one day her defiance would find her face down in a creek like Clucas, or consumed in a fire as she suspected Delia was meant to be. But now by some miracle she was free and planning to marry a man who could make her happy.

"Well, Dolly my dear, I did not expect that little outburst from Jassy," Nathan confessed as he drove her home. "I suspect that old witch Old Ma O'Neill has been poisoning her mind against us. But it'll make it awkward living in a house together."

"I know," said Dolly with a sigh.

"Well, I've been thinking, and what I've decided is that we could build a house for David and Jassy down by that spring on the road to the O'Neill's place. It's on my land, and it'll be nearer to her folks. I'll suggest David calls it Jacinta Springs or something like. That'll please her, and she can have the run of her own house instead of rearranging mine. We'll have plenty of time to build it for them before we can get married. What do you say?"

"I agree to anything that makes you happy," she told him, hugging his arm in happiness.

She wished he hadn't imposed this ban of enforced celibacy on her. Now she had tasted the joys of intimacy, she was eager to continue. The memory of that liberating night filled her dreams.

CHAPTER 53: A DAY IN COURT

The date for the court hearing was fixed. Nathan insisted on accompanying Dolly as she travelled to Baton Rouge to face her accusers. He arrived on his wagon ready to drive her to the city. Barney and the other workers came to wish them well.

"We all prayin' for you, Mrs. Dolly," he told her, and some of the others said, "Amen."

Aunt Hattie had told her that they were all worried that Delia would win the case and that she would sell the plantation to the highest bidder. "We could lose our homes," she said anxiously.

"Then we'd be all out of a home," said Dolly. "The Lord save us all." She felt uneasy as she helped Clemmie aboard the wagon and, though the girl was docile enough, her anxious eyes continually checked that Albert was nearby.

Jeremiah had come too to introduce her to his former pupil and to keep an eye on Albert and Clemmie while Dolly was in court. Safe in her bag she had her letter from Honora giving dates for her pregnancy and the calculated time from Clement Duplege's visit to Gorbydale. She also had an amended birth certificate from the Liverpool Registry for Albert's birth. Luckily Clement had arranged it all before they left for America but, though the clerks had promised to send it on, it had never arrived. And round her neck she had the precious locket, surely proof of Albert's parentage.

Once again they stayed with Jeremiah's sister Margaret, who was glad to see them. Clemmie had been reluctant to go with them, but Aunt Hattie had made her look respectable in her newest dress. She had even persuaded the girl to wear a pair of old corsets to improve her figure and, despite her anxiety, she showed traces of the girl who had once danced carefree at the family parties. At the court they found a place in the gallery while Dolly, clothed in her miserable widow's weeds, and Lawyer Mason, Jeremiah's old pupil, went down into the courtroom.

Delia and Jonathan Bartholomew were already in court, though Delia refused to look at Dolly. She sat with her head defiantly raised while Johnny gave a brief and apologetic nod in Dolly's direction. They all rose when the judge entered. Glancing down at his papers, he summed up their contents.

"This here case is all about who is entitled to the Amiens Plantation situated in Picardy Creek, in the state of Louisiana. Mrs Dorothea Duplege here states that her son Albert is the heir of Clement Amiens Duplege and entitled to the estate. Mrs Delia Bartholomew, you maintain that this son of Mrs Duplege, previously Tate, is not the progeny of your Uncle Clement."

"I certainly do," said Delia, her nose raised in disgust. "He appeared from nowhere with that woman, and I know for a fact that my Uncle Clement was not married when he was last at the Amiens Plantation. So the child was obviously born long before they were married in England. That doesn't say it's his."

Dolly rose to her feet. "I have papers here to say that Albert is Clement's son. It's true that Albert was born out of wedlock, but my husband acknowledged Albert as his own when he found out about him. Do you think he would come all the way to England just to claim a child that isn't his?" she shouted angrily. "Albert is Clement's child all right. Just look at his hair."

Everyone in the court glanced up to the gallery, where her son's bright head was visible.

"I've letters to say that Albert is Clement's son from people that witnessed things."

"Mrs Duplege, do not interrupt this court," ordered the judge.

"Why, she's English, she's not even American," said Delia, sniffing loudly.

"His father was an all-Southern gentleman. My son may have English blood in him, but half of him is from the South too; the South that you readily deserted." Her voice rose as she ignored the judge's warning hand. "And the South you were willing to betray by selling my son's inheritance to a Northern carpetbagger to pay for your fine lifestyle in the North."

"Mrs Duplege!" protested the judge.

"And we are caring for your poor sister, driven witless by the cruel bombardment of Vicksburg by the Union soldiers and where she saw your poor mother and father die of starvation through the siege of the Union soldiers. You readily abandoned your sister when you saw how bad she was."

"I was affected by that fire at the hotel," protested Delia. "My arm was badly burnt."

The court all glanced at her arm, which seemed to be well healed and encased in the silken sleeves of an expensive gown.

The jury were Southerners to a man. There was a rumble of mistrust among them and they glared at Delia. She visibly shrank in the dock.

As Dolly had obviously waylaid the court with her indignant protests, the judge addressed her. "I have looked over these letters you mentioned, Mrs. Duplege," he said with a sigh. "The letter from Miss Honora Darwen is, I could say, a little insubstantial as to the time of when the er … deed was done and Albert was conceived."

"Well, we weren't going to perform such a private act in public, my lord," said Dolly, and everyone in court sniggered.

One of the jury laughed right out loud and received a stern glance from the judge.

"Quite," he admitted. "But you just call me 'judge', Mrs. Duplege. We leave all this 'my lord' business to you British."

"I'm very sorry," said Dolly humbly. "But it all happened in such a rush. I was very innocent, and Mr. Duplege was very persuasive."

"You can say that again," called one wit among the spectators. "He persuaded me to lose all my money in a card game."

A ripple of laughter echoed round the court.

"We'll have silence in this court, sir," the judge rebuked him. "So, Mrs. Duplege, it says in one of these letters that your mother and father brought the child up."

"Yes, that's true." Dolly gave a soulful sigh. "I was the only one of my family with work. With the war in America going on, there was no cotton and all the mills were closed. People were starving. If my employer had found out about my child, I would have been thrown out on the streets and we all would have starved." Her blue eyes widened and filled with tears, and she bathed the jury in their pathos. A hum of sympathy rose from the court.

"So when Mr. Duplege called to find his son, you must have seen it as a great opportunity."

"I wasn't sure at first. I knew that I would have to leave my beloved family behind after all they'd done for me. You can understand that my mother was heartbroken at the thought of having to lose Albert. My Dad was ready to kill Clement because of what he'd done to me. But Clement finally persuaded them that Albert would have a better life out here in

America and that we should get married to make his son legitimate. So I finally agreed." She was twisting and weaving the truth as well as any master weaver, but her whole way of life was at stake.

"Oh, and I've got this locket my lord, I mean judge. It belongs to Miss Clementine Duplege, my late husband's niece, Mrs. Bartholomew's sister. There's a picture inside of Clement and his brother when they were little boys. You can see that Albert is the spitting image of his Papa." She carefully untied the ribbon round her neck and, opening the locket, she had it passed to the judge.

He glanced at the tiny picture and then up at Albert with a nod. "Seems right," he acknowledged.

The locket was then passed round the jury, and one by one they glanced up at Albert and agreed.

"Let me see that," demanded Delia. "That picture could be of anybody." When it finally reached her, she stared down at the gleam of gold in her hand and her lip trembled. "I haven't seen this in years," she said quietly. "This was my grandmother's locket, and that is my father and Uncle Clement as children." She realised then that she had lost, but she was still defiant. "That doesn't mean that the child is Clement's. I certainly dispute that."

"But, Mrs. Bartholomew, like Mrs. Duplege has said, 'Is it likely that a man would travel all the way to England to claim a child that wasn't his?' Miss Darwen states in her letter that when she told Clement Duplege in Washington that he had a son, he was surprised. He didn't deny that he knew Miss Tate, as she was then. Surely he would have checked out that the boy was really his child before he married the mother and brought them to America. He could easily have left them abandoned and had other children after the war. Now in my judgement,

Mr. Clement Duplege was a shrewd man, as I think some of his gambling companions will testify."

"Sure will," called the wit from the court.

"I heard that too," said another.

"Why, he won that house in Baton Rouge in a card game," said a woman indignantly. "I was acquainted with Mrs. Domain who owned it, and her husband shot himself over the affair. It was a terrible business."

"So members of the jury, it is up to you to decide if the Amiens Plantation should be the property of young Albert Duplege or of Mrs. Delia Bartholomew. I'll let you talk among yourselves."

Dolly watched anxiously as the men murmured among themselves. They frequently glanced at her and up at Albert. It didn't take long for them to decide.

"The Amiens Plantation should go to the boy, your honour," said their spokesman. "We heard his mother is doin' a fine job bringing the old place back to life. Don't see why it should be sold to some carpetbagger to pay for some fancy Northern lifestyle."

The rest of the jury mumbled their agreement.

"Then I decide in favour of Albert Duplege and appoint his mother as his guardian until such time as he reaches his majority. I'm sure she will do her best by her son."

"Oh, I promise I will, judge," said Dolly joyfully.

There were congratulations all round except for Delia, who stormed out of the court hurriedly followed by her husband.

"Aren't you going to stop to say hello to Clemmie?" called Dolly, only to receive a malevolent glare from Delia as she departed.

"No love lost there," said someone.

"Well, Mrs. Duplege," said Billy Mason beside her. "You certainly didn't need any help from me. You won the hearts and minds of the court all by yourself."

"You gave me confidence," she said, smiling as he warmly shook her hand. "You and Jeremiah and Nathan and everyone."

Albert waved down at his mother.

"God bless the child," said a woman from behind Dolly and added in an undertone, "Let's hope he turns out better that his father."

Dolly turned to stare at her and she smiled.

"Hello, Mrs. Duplege. Do you remember me? We met at the dress shop. My name is Amelia Kay."

"Yes, I remember you Mrs. Kay," said Dolly cautiously. "You were a friend of my husband."

"Yes, an intimate friend," said Amelia with a smirk. "So the alligators got Clement after all, one predator devouring another. But I'm sorry for your loss."

"You sound it," retorted Dolly.

"But congratulations to you and your son," said Amelia and paused until Billy Mason had moved away to talk to Jeremiah. "It's a good thing the judge didn't know that Clement could father no other children after the war."

"How would you know a thing like that?" Dolly felt stunned.

"I have my informants," said Amelia smugly. "Clement wasn't the only one who could act the spy. Good day, Mrs. Duplege. And congratulations once again."

Despite her jubilation, Dolly was lost in thought as they drove back to Margaret's house. Was Amelia's revelation the reason why Clement had never tried to make love to her? He had been eager enough in Gorbydale. Had he had been too ashamed to confess he was impotent? Her life with him had certainly been one long mystery. But Dolly was content that at least the plantation had been secured for Albert.

Nathan drove them to Margaret's home, chatting happily about their plans for the future. Though Dolly gave him several warning glances, he seemed oblivious to their passengers. Jeremiah smiled and nodded and seemed to have already guessed what would soon be a reality for Nathan and Dolly. Albert nodded to sleep with the jolting of the wagon, and Clemmie squirmed with discomfort. They reached Margaret's house and she hurried out to hear the news. She was overjoyed at Dolly's fortune. As they settled to something to eat from a generous pot, Clemmie continued to wriggle and looked distressed.

"It's probably those corsets," decided Dolly. "I'll help you take them off once we've finished eating."

There were three bedrooms to the house, and Clemmie was sharing with Margaret while Dolly slept with her son and the two men bunked down together. Margaret showed Dolly and Clemmie to her room, and Dolly set about removing the offending garments. Their host left them to it. Aunt Hattie had certainly laced the corsets quite tightly, and Clemmie seemed to have swollen in the heat and the journey. She sighed with relief once they were removed. Dolly was about to throw them on the bed when she noticed some stitching had burst. To her surprise she noticed a gleam of gold showing through. She picked at the stitching further and to her astonishment pulled out some gold coins.

"Mama said for safety," said Clemmie shyly.

"Well, you certainly kept them safe. Clever girl," Dolly praised her and moved to another part of the garment.

She fingered along the seams until she felt something else irregular. With a small pair of needlework scissors she found on Margaret's dressing table, she cut the stitches. Delving further she pulled out some thinly rolled union dollars from the gaps she'd made. Finally she removed a long thin roll of paper. Carefully she unrolled it. It seemed to be a fragile end page of a bible and it was covered in handwritten script.

"The last will and testament of Henri Amiens Duplege…" She hesitantly read the spidery writing. For a moment she thought to ask Jeremiah to help her read the words but as she silently read the next part, she hesitated. *I leave my estate the Amiens Plantation to be divided equally between my two beloved daughters Delia Duplege and Clementine Duplege, the estate to be managed until their marriages by my brother Clement Amiens Duplege who will share equally in the profits*. It was signed with Henri's flourishing signature.

Dolly counted the money and there was almost a hundred dollars in notes and coin. She glanced at Clemmie, who had wriggled back into her clothes and was struggling to tie her sash. Did the girl realise the importance of the hidden bounty? Could she understand what the will would mean? But Dolly did. She knew very little of the law except how to avoid it, but she knew enough to suspect that Albert might lose the estate. The will of Clement and Henri's father had never been found, but Henri's wishes were plain enough. Determination and anxiety sharpened Dolly's brains. She remembered that a will should be witnessed. Henri's was the only signature. Despite Henri's wishes, Dolly felt morally entitled to act in her son's interest. She screwed the paper tightly into a ball and slipped it up her sleeve.

"Look at all this money that your Mama sewed in your stays," she brightly told Clemmie. "Your Dad, your Papa left all this money hidden inside them to take care of you. Isn't that wonderful?"

Clemmie stared at the money in vague recognition. "Mama said for safety," she repeated.

"And you're a great girl for keeping them safe. Let's go and tell Albert and Jeremiah and Nathan," said Dolly, quickly tying Clemmie's sash into a bow. "Won't they be pleased?"

They were all astonished when Dolly revealed what was concealed in the corsets. She stayed silent about the will.

"No wonder the poor girl felt uncomfortable," said Jeremiah, shaking his head in amazement.

As everyone examined the secret stash, Dolly quickly slipped the small paper ball into the stove. A quick flash of flame and her secret was safe. Margaret glanced at her.

"Ladies' things," murmured Dolly.

Margaret nodded and turned back to wonder over the money.

"To think of all the times you struggled to make ends meet," said Jeremiah. "And this cash was there all the time in the corset."

That night, with her son breathing gently beside her, Dolly stared at the dark ceiling and remembered that small burst of flame. What she had done was wrong. The plantation rightly belonged to Delia and Clemmie. Though the will had not been witnessed, Henri's wishes had been plain enough. Yet if she had shown that flimsy paper to anyone, she and Albert could have been thrown out of their home, all her hard work for nothing. The plantation would have been sold and Clemmie locked away in an asylum. Trying to block the disturbing thoughts from her mind, she lay restless with her conscience.

They had barely reached the plantation next day when they saw Zeb hurrying towards them. Far behind him on the track was Barney stumbling along. Dolly realised with sadness that he was getting frailer. It was hardly surprising with the hard life he had led. She jumped down off the cart and rushed to meet Zeb, anxious that something was wrong.

"What's the news from the court, Mrs Dolly? Are we to lose the plantation and our homes?" he asked, panting with effort.

Dolly burst into laughter. "No, no. We've won. The plantation is safe. We're safe."

Any qualms about what she had done vanished in a second. While she had been worried about losing her son's inheritance, all the village folk had been worrying about losing their homes and their livelihoods. "We've won. We've won," she told Barney as he caught up, struggling for breath.

"Praise the Lord, Mrs. Dolly," he gasped. "We was hoping and praying."

"Well, He heard your prayers," she said, laughing. She hugged Barney, to his surprise, while secretly praying herself. "Forgive us our trespasses."

CHAPTER 54: A NEW ARRIVAL

Despite her size Jessie had a desperate urge to tidy her rooms. She had asked Maggie to help in the last few months of her pregnancy, but the woman was more enthusiastic than effective. She was just dusting her mother Nellie's rosy bowl when the first twinge came. Jessie dismissed it. She was sure she had at least another two weeks to go before the baby was due. The severity of the second twinge made her sit down on the settle. When it had passed, she hauled herself up and went to pull the bell to summon help. It was an age coming, and she struggled instead to the door. Next moment Maggie burst through the door that led to the kitchen.

"Sorry Missis, I was just in the middle of peeling some potatoes," she excused herself.

"Can you send for Mrs. Connolly? No, now of course she's Alice Davenport on Weavers Row," said Jessie. "Quickly as you can."

"Is the baby...?" began Maggie, but there was no need for explanation as a puddle appeared by Jessie feet.

"Looks like it!" said Jessie, laughing despite her contraction.

"I'll get the Missis," said Maggie, hurrying off to find Melissa. She found her snoring gently in the parlour and hesitated before she roused her. "It's the baby, Missis," she wailed.

Melissa blinked in confusion.

"The Missis's baby's coming," explained Maggie. "I've got to go and fetch Mrs. Davenport."

"Mrs. Davenport is dead," said Melissa, still confused by her abrupt awakening.

"No, the new one, Alice Connelly as was."

By now Melissa was wide awake. "The baby! Oh, the baby! We must send for the doctor. Matthias will insist on it. Maggie, send for the doctor."

"But the Missis wants Mrs. Davenport," said Maggie, confused by the new orders.

The commotion downstairs brought Lizzie hurrying down from the nursery, where she had been mending the children's clothes while they took a nap.

"It's the baby. It's coming," wailed Maggie. "And Missis wants Mrs. Davenport and the other Missis wants the doctor."

Lizzie took charge of the situation immediately. As the eldest of seven children, she was used to confinements. "Go for Mrs. Davenport," she told Maggie, "and on the way stop at the stables and ask Myers' boy to go for the doctor."

Maggie nodded and hurried off as Melissa emerged from the parlour.

"Would you mind keeping an eye on the children, Mrs. Overdale, while I get Mrs. Jessica upstairs and into her nightie? They're asleep at the moment, but they might wake up soon."

"Yes, yes, that would be a good idea," said Melissa, happy to avoid any medical emergency. "I'll do that."

Lizzie knocked gently on the door of Jessie's parlour and went in. Her mistress was still resting on the settle staring out over the terrace and the garden. She'd watched Maggie and the groom's son hurrying down the drive on their errands and felt help would soon be at hand. She smiled up at Lizzie. "I expect you've heard all the palaver," she said.

Lizzie nodded. "Yes, and I think we'd better get you upstairs and ready," she said.

"Oh, I'll be ages yet," said Jessie, twisting awkwardly to make herself comfortable as another contraction wracked her body.

"Best be safe," insisted Lizzie. "The second one usually comes a bit quicker, and this will be your third really. Come on, I'll help you upstairs."

"What would I do without you?" said Jessie, smiling as she submitted to Lizzie's help. "Are the children all right?"

"Mrs. Overdale's keeping an eye on them," said Lizzie. "Don't worry about everyone else. Let's get yourself sorted."

Jessie sighed. "But I am worried, Lizzie. What if this baby isn't all right?" She began to cry softly. "I am worried."

"Everything will be fine," the nursemaid reassured her. "Matty wasn't expected. If he was, they'd have been quicker off the mark to help him into the world. This baby will be fine."

"I hope you're right," said Jessie, taking her arm. "Anyway, let's get upstairs. Will someone go and tell Robert, do you think?"

"Oh, I expect the word will travel fast enough," Lizzie laughed. "Probably Myers will go to t'mill with the news."

The baby arrived faster than anyone else. Alice hurried through the empty hall to hear a baby's cry. Dr. Braddock's nephew arrived in time to examine the cleaned up little boy with a neatly tied umbilical cord.

"I congratulate you ladies on a fine job," he told them. "I couldn't have done better myself."

An anxious Robert was admitted.

"You have a fine son, Mr. Overdale," said young Dr. Braddock, shaking his hand.

"Is he all right?" were the first words out of Robert's mouth. He blushed as he caught Jessie's eye. They both knew his words were a small betrayal of Matty.

"He's fine. All the fingers and toes you could ask for," said the doctor, smiling. "What will you call him?"

"Jacob," said Jessie firmly. "For my father. We can call him Jack, like Robert's grandfather, so as not to cause confusion."

She and Robert had barely discussed a name. She would certainly not call her son Augustus as Matthias had suggested, hoping for a wealthy patron. Melissa had often mentioned her father Jack, a master weaver, though usually Matthias scowled at his name. Robert had told her that his father had never seen eye to eye with the old man. But in that moment Jessie chose the name to suit both families and glanced up at Robert.

"Jack it is," confirmed Robert as he knelt beside his wife and new son. "Hello Jack," he said, taking a tiny waxy hand. "Welcome to the world. He's beautiful. And his Mama's beautiful too."

He tenderly kissed Jessie's damp forehead, and in that moment she forgave him for his query. She still felt guilty that it was the first question she had asked the doctor too.

Matthias was delighted with the new arrival. "A fine healthy boy, eh. I knew you could do it."

Jessie bit her lip to avoid saying something to spoil the moment.

"Yes, a fine boy to carry on the Invincible. Well done, my boy," he said, shaking Robert's hand vigorously.

Robert glanced at his wife and took a deep breath. "We'll see, eh?" he said. "He might want to be a fine gentleman, or be a scholar — or even go to Parliament."

"You're making great plans for little Jack and he hasn't even had his first sup of milk," Melissa chided them. "Come along now, Matthias, and let the poor girl rest."

Robert brought a chair and held his son, gazing at the soft pink face nestled in his shawl. "I told Lizzie to bring the children in when Mother and Father had left," he said. "Don't worry, she's told them to be very quiet so as not to frighten the baby."

"I hope they like him," said Jessie. "I hope they're not jealous."

"I've never had a brother or sister," said Robert. "Were you jealous?"

"You mean when Eddie arrived?" she asked thoughtfully. "Oh, I was at first. I was used to being the petted darling with two older brothers. When our little afterthought arrived, I had my nose pushed out and I was expected to help too. Of course I was jealous! But he was such a sweet little chap I soon grew to love him. He was a pest when I was growing up though, stealing my hairpins to make all sorts of gadgets. No wonder he wants to be an engineer like John and Arden."

"Is Eddie old enough to be a godfather?" asked Robert.

Jessie smiled at her husband. Sometimes he could do the nicest things. "I don't see why not. He's been confirmed. I was going to suggest Arden."

"We'll have them both," said Robert firmly. "We can arrange the christening for when Arden is back in port."

CHAPTER 55: PLANS FOR THE FUTURE

David and Jassy's house was rising steadily. The walls and the roof were in place, and Jassy was bubbling with plans. Though she had no glass in her windows, she had raided her mother's and Nathan's house for curtains. She had marked the furniture she wanted to take with her and been to Picardy Creek to find material for other soft furnishings.

Nathan put his foot down when she claimed the chiffonier. "That was my mother's and it stays," he said firmly.

Luckily Dolly had admired it when she and Nathan had been alone, so she would not get the blame for preventing its removal to the new house.

The cotton was growing steadily in the fields, and the men had some time to work on the house. There was also time for Nathan to visit Dolly, and she longed for his visits. She restricted her visits to the Jacques plantation to when she knew Jassy would be at her mother's. But despite her best efforts, Nathan steadily refused to repeat their one moment of bliss.

"We'll do it right," he told her sternly. "When the harvest is over, we'll have another party and announce our plans. What would people say if they saw a woman with child at the altar? Your name would be blackened."

"It's black enough anyway," said Dolly with a sigh. She knew what the people of Gorbydale had muttered behind her back, too afraid to say it to her face and confront Tommo Tate. The people of Picardy Creek already treated her with suspicion, and not only because of her connection to Clement. "But I expect you're right," she said with a sigh. "We'll have a fresh start, a clean slate."

To Dolly's relief, the house at Jacinta Springs was nearly finished. As Nathan had predicted, Jassy was thrilled with the idea of her own home named in her honour. The cotton harvest was ready to begin, and everyone on the three estates was focussed on the crop. Dolly hardly saw Nathan for the next couple of weeks. She and Barney and the rest of the village were working hard as they collected the fluffy cotton bolls into their sacks. Again there were opportunities for the Amiens workers to help with the Jacques' harvest. Of course there was talk among the workers.

"I heard folks say Mrs Dolly and Massa Jacques gonna jump the broomstick sometime soon," one of the young women teased Barney when Dolly was barely out of hearing.

"Hush your mouth woman," ordered Barney, with a quick glance towards Dolly.

She pretended she hadn't heard and glanced over to Albert and Clemmie doing their bit along one of the rows of cotton.

Although it was not quite a year since Clement's disappearance, Nathan was now anxious to be married. "I miss having the family round me in the old house," he told Dolly. "We'll announce our plans at the harvest feast and then get married soon afterwards."

Happy that those precious moments together at the last party were soon to be repeated, Dolly heartily agreed. She had hardly thought about Clement since his disappearance. She remembered her moment in court as the grieving widow. Then a small flash of flame in an old stove reminded her of other things too.

She knew she must say something to Albert and Clemmie soon. An unexpected announcement at the harvest supper would upset her son and the sensitive young woman who relied on him. Anxiously she waited for Nathan to call with news of when the party would be. She planned to tell her little family the day before, although Aunt Hattie already suspected. Hattie had dropped plenty of sly hints about the state of the Amiens mansion and how 'Mr. Jacques' house was a fine practical house'. His home was certainly smaller than Clement's with none of the pretensions to grand French architecture that the Dupleges had embraced.

Dolly was looking forward to living in a house with glass in all the windows. Although she had managed to have some of her home's windows repaired, the upper floor was uninhabitable with the shutters nailed closed. On dark nights the floorboards creaked and groaned like the moans of dead men. The slightest breeze rattled through the shutters. An uneasy Dolly felt as though the restless spirit of Henri was trying to reclaim his home for his daughters or that Clement's drowned wraith had returned and was trying to get in. Now she had seen Henri's will, she felt like an intruder and would be glad to move to her new home. Nathan had planned for Albert, Clemmie and Aunt Hattie to join her. Hattie was getting old now, but it would be no hardship for her to look after Clemmie's needs. Nathan already had a housekeeper who cooked for his family, but he would not abandon Hattie and Clemmie to live in the dilapidated Amiens mansion and Dolly loved him for it. Jeremiah was another matter, though. Nathan's house would not have an extra bedroom for a single man.

Dolly approached Nathan with the problem.

"I've been thinking about that too," he said. "Do you think Mr. Leach would object to educating negro children?"

Dolly hesitated. "I don't know," she said. "I've seen him showing the village kids his atlas with maps of America and the world. Some of them asked him where Africa was and he happily showed them."

"Only there's a small house nearby. It's empty at the moment, but it wouldn't take much to put it right. I wondered if we could build a schoolhouse beside it and Jeremiah could teach the children alongside Albert."

"I suppose we could ask him," said Dolly. "But after we make our announcement."

"He could live in the house anyway," decided Nathan. "Albert needs his lessons, and it's too far for him to go to school at the Creek. Some of those children in the town would eat him alive."

The weeks flew by and the cotton was ginned and baled. The wagons had headed for the port and Dolly could barely contain her excitement. Now that the harvest was finished, the workers were able to help David and Jassy move into their new home. Jassy was still cool with Dolly, though for their menfolk's sake they held a civil but uneasy truce. The day before Nathan's harvest supper, Dolly sat beside her son and Clemmie and began to explain their future.

"How would you like to go and live with Mr. Jacques?" she began.

The pair looked at each other. Clemmie's eyes opened wide with fear.

"I do mean all of us," said Dolly hastily. "You and Clemmie and Aunt Hattie too. We would have windows and proper bedrooms and beds and there's a pump for water."

"What do you think, Clemmie?" Albert asked his friend. "Sounds all right."

She nodded, happy that she was not about to be abandoned.

"Mr. Jacques and me are going to get married," Dolly told them. "He'll be your new daddy."

Albert looked thoughtful. "'Cos my old dad's gone to heaven?" he asked. "Aunt Hattie says he's with the angels."

"Er, yes," said Dolly, biting her lip. She could not envisage Clement with any angels.

"Oh right." Albert accepted the explanation without a murmur.

She had expected a barrage of questions from her son. He was an inquisitive little boy and, although he looked thoughtful for a while, he seemed to accept the situation without any trouble. He'd had plenty of disruption in his young life and seemed to cope in his own quiet way, but sometimes his mother remembered his plaintive cry of 'Mam, Mam' echoing round the Liverpool station as he was torn away from Maggie. She was thankful that Nathan had been especially kind to him and Clemmie whenever he called.

She approached Jeremiah and asked if she could have a word. "There will be an announcement at the party tomorrow," she told him quietly.

"About you and Mr. Jacques?" he said, smiling, and she nodded. "I had expected something like it. Congratulations to you both."

"We'd still want you to teach Albert. But there isn't much room at the Jacques house, as you know. There's a little house nearby if you'd like to take it."

"Yes, that would be fine," said the schoolteacher, nodding thoughtfully. "I did wonder if you would send young Albert away to school, and I'm sure my sister would give me a bed. But I'm sure the little house would be fine."

"Mr. Jacques wondered if you would be willing to teach the village children," she asked tentatively.

Jeremiah stared at her in surprise. "Oh, I'd never thought of that. I'd just assumed my salary would be for teaching young Albert." At least he hadn't chastised her for even asking such a thing. Jeremiah was thoughtful for a moment. "But would you mind your son being educated along with negro children? I know Master Clement would have objected strongly. People might talk."

Dolly shrugged. "He already plays with the village children. Clement wanted to send Albert away to school anyway."

Jeremiah went silent for a moment, deep in thought. "Some of the children are a bit wild," he said. "I've never taught a full class. I don't know if I could control them."

"They wouldn't have to go to school if they didn't want to," decided Dolly, remembering that her own schooling had been haphazard. "I expect the naughty ones wouldn't go anyway, but I'm sure there are many that want to learn. It's up to you. The little house will be yours anyway."

"Thank you, Mrs. Dolly," said Jeremiah. "I would be sorry to leave my home here. I've grown used to my young charge — and my older student."

"Yes, and I have to thank you sincerely for that," she told him. "Without you I'd just be an ignorant woman, robbed by my thieving husband of all the things we'd worked for."

"I must confess I lived in terror that day you took his watch to sell in town," said Jeremiah with a chuckle.

"I expect there's an alligator somewhere with the watch in his belly. I don't expect it chimes anymore, though. What a waste — of a gold watch, not a husband," said Dolly with a hollow laugh.

She unexpectedly kissed him on the cheek before she went to her bed. Dolly wanted to look her best for the next day.

CHAPTER 56: AN ANNOUNCEMENT AND A WEDDING

Once again, there was rising excitement as the loaded wagons trundled up to the Jacques plantation. Dolly glanced round the happy faces and wondered how they would look when Nathan made his announcement. She caught the eye of Ma O'Neill enthroned on her large armchair and refused to wither under that malevolent scowl. Nathan hurried to help Dolly down and other people noticed and exchanged meaningful glances. Most smiled, but Old Ma O'Neill remained grim-faced and muttered some comment to her daughter.

Nathan didn't wait long to make his announcement. When everyone had been welcomed and seated, he took Dolly's hand and led her to the top table. "I am sure many of you have noticed, but it may come as a surprise to some of you, that Mrs. Duplege and I have become good friends over the past few months of her troubles. I have asked her to become my wife, and to my great joy she has said yes."

There were cheers and clapping from the workers, though the O'Neill party were more restrained in their congratulations.

"I'm surprised that she wants to marry an old workhorse like myself, but there it is," he added.

"And I'm very happy to do so," called Dolly. "A good man is hard to find, and I know I've found a good one at last."

There were 'Amens' and cheers, and the party began with goodwill and happiness at the announcement. Everyone at the party knew or guessed how hard her life with Clement had been, though some begrudgingly muttered that she must have deserved it for having a child out of wedlock.

Albert slipped beside Nathan and tugged his hand. "Will you be my new daddy?" he asked.

"I'll be proud to, son," said Nathan kindly.

"Will you drink nasty whisky and roar like my old one?" questioned the little boy.

"Not if I can help it," Nathan told him with a chuckle.

Those around them caught a revealing glimpse into the child's life. Clement had been as kind as he was able to his son, but the boy had witnessed much in the treatment of his mother. Albert was not the robust, horseriding son that Clement had wished for, and the sensitive child had felt the intimation of his disapproval many times.

"Poor little boy," said Mrs. O'Neill, ignoring the rumblings of her mother-in-law's displeasure.

Everyone settled down to enjoy themselves and the food and entertainment on offer. Again the choir sang and band played.

"Would you like to dance, my dear?" asked Nathan.

"I don't know how to," confessed Dolly, who'd had little opportunity to try.

"Come on, you'll soon pick it up," said her husband-to-be, taking her in his arms.

Others joined them including, to Dolly's surprise, Clemmie and Albert, who jigged round in a novel fashion.

"I expect poor Clemmie went to plenty of balls when she was younger," said Dolly.

"Oh, the Amiens place was famous for them," Nathan told her. "We were never invited of course."

Dolly once more felt a stab of guilt that she had stolen the girl's inheritance, then guessed that Clemmie's fate would have been an asylum anyway. She dismissed the troubling thoughts from her mind. "I don't suppose you fancy coming out to the stables," she whispered in Nathan's ear.

"Behave yourself, woman," he chuckled. "You have a duty to your guests."

Dolly had never felt so happy. How could she have known, when she inveigled her way into Clement's life, that she would indeed find happiness, though not with the man she had married?

A month later Dolly Duplege and Nathan Jacques were married in a simple ceremony at the Jacques plantation in front of a small company of family and friends. Dolly wore lilac in a prudent gesture to her widowhood. Old Ma O'Neill declined to attend. After the ceremony and an enjoyable meal, the party dispersed. David and Jassy returned to their new house. Barney and Aunt Hattie escorted Albert and Clemmie home for a few days to allow the newly married couple some time together before the daily routine took over.

Nathan squeezed her hand as she waved goodbye to her tearful son. She had reassured him many times that she was not leaving him for good, though the memories of other farewells had entered his young soul and he could not be consoled.

"Don't worry, my dear," Nathan comforted her. "We'll go and collect them in a few days to put your mind at rest. I remember how miserable David was when we lost his mother."

"Thank you," she whispered, grateful for his kindness.

The child who he had once been, virtually abandoned to her mother, had entangled himself in her heart with his funny, kind ways. He had been all she had left on this side of the wide Atlantic. For an odd moment she felt homesick. She would have loved for everyone in Gorbydale to witness her happiness. Then her longing quickly disappeared as she turned to her husband and he stroked her cheek. Dolly was instantly filled with a more urgent longing.

A few days later, Albert and Clemmie were installed at the Jacques plantation.

Nathan was working with the horses when Dolly arrived with a cold drink for him. "Well, Mrs. Jacques, are you cornering me in these stables once again?" asked her husband with a chuckle.

"Not when there's a nice comfy bed upstairs," Dolly laughed.

"I've been thinking. You haven't had much of a honeymoon," said Nathan, straightening from the task he was doing.

"I'm just so happy to be here," Dolly told him with a satisfied smile.

"Perhaps you would like to go somewhere special sometime," he said. "Is there anywhere you'd like to go when Albert is settled?"

An unexpected wave of homesickness returned to her mind. She'd been so glad to leave her old home, and here it was lingering in her memory. "Not really," she said. "The only place I could think of would be my old hometown, but that's out of the question."

"Why?"

"Because there were things that happened there that I was glad to leave behind. Because I was nothing but a skivvy there and not a very good one at that."

"But your mother is there and still alive. Wouldn't you like to see her while she is still with us?"

It wasn't something that had crossed Dolly's mind. Maggie was skinny, but surely she was strong as an ox. She'd had to be to survive Tommo's onslaught. Dolly still felt guilty, though, when she remembered Maggie's heartbreak at losing Albert.

"Yes, I suppose I would," she admitted. "Albert certainly would."

"Then we'll do it," said Nathan. "I've been stuck on this here farm long enough, hearing about places round the world. I should like to see what becomes of my cotton. We'll go."

Dolly stared at him in surprise as a thousand excuses why she shouldn't return flooded her thoughts. She certainly didn't want Nathan to meet Tommo and have her old man trying to cadge money from him. She'd heard in a letter from Maggie (written with Jessie's help) that Seth was in Strangeways prison in Manchester after a drunken brawl, so that was one problem she wouldn't have to face. Yet how could she take her new husband to a place where she had been despised? She desperately wanted to stay where she was respected as the wife of an admired plantation owner; where the people of the Amiens estate looked up to her as the saviour of their plantation. But she remembered the haunting 'Mam, Mam' as Albert was dragged away from her mother.

"I'd like to meet your mother," said Nathan, almost as if he could read her thoughts. "We should go while she's still living."

CHAPTER 57: GOING HOME

Nathan was enthusiastic about his idea and, despite her reservations, Dolly agreed that they should travel to Lancashire. Albert loved the travel, especially now he was old enough to appreciate the new sights and sounds displayed before him. Secure in Nathan's loving care, Dolly too began to enjoy herself. She worried that she and Albert might again be seasick, but Nathan procured a cabin with a porthole, which helped. All the same, she was relieved to see the landfall in Ireland and excited when the port of Liverpool appeared. Nathan took great interest in the docks and the cargoes of cotton being unloaded.

After the meal at their hotel, they took a stroll around the city in the evening sunshine. Their walk took them towards the Flags where so much of the cotton trade was conducted. Dolly listened as Nathan chatted to Albert. He'd brought a guide book, lent to him by a helpful employee of the hotel and was explaining some of the buildings to the little boy. For a moment Dolly let her attention stray as she drank in all the sights she had so briefly seen on the first rushed visit to the city. Then she froze, and her hand tightened on Nathan's arm. The figure she had briefly noticed in the crowd vanished among the milling evening strollers.

"I think I've just seen Clement," she whispered in a fearful breath.

Nathan looked at her, full of concern. "That's impossible, my dear. You know that's impossible. Lots of people witnessed him drown. How could he possibly be in Liverpool? His body would be broken and battered, even if he'd survived. You mustn't be worried."

"But it was his height and his walk and…" She was sure she had recognised that lazy, ambling gait.

"The mind plays strange tricks on people when they lose someone," said Nathan gently. "I know I often thought I saw Marie after she'd died. I even called out once at the Creek, but the woman that turned round was not Marie. She was a right ugly dame too!" he said with a chuckle to lighten Dolly's fear. "You mustn't worry, my dear. Clement is truly dead and gone."

Though she knew Nathan must be right, the feeling that Dolly had seen her first husband persisted and she spent a restless night arguing with herself.

She nervously glanced around her the next day as they boarded a train to Manchester where they would be staying. The following day they took the train to Gorbydale, and Dolly had anxieties of a different kind. She was determined that Nathan would not meet Tommo.

"Mam will be at Overdale House," said Dolly. "We should go there. I don't want you to see the dump where I grew up. And I certainly don't want to bump into my father."

They arrived in a cab at Overdale house and knocked tentatively on the door.

"I used to work here a long time ago," Dolly told Albert with a faint smile. She was nervous of seeing her mother.

"It's a fine house," said Nathan.

They waited for some moments before the door was opened. A burst of voices and laughter washed over them as it opened, and a stunned Maggie stared at them in bewilderment.

"Mam!" cried Albert and rushed forward to crush Maggie.

Dolly was surprised how worn and grey her mother looked.

"Dolly! Albert! What are you doing here? It's baby's christening tomorrow. Are you invited?" gasped Maggie. "They never said."

"No, Mam, we've come to see you. This is Nathan, my new husband that I wrote to you about. We're on our honeymoon and we thought we'd surprise you."

Robert came to the door to find out what was happening. "Nathan!" he said, hurrying forward and grasping his old friend's hand. "What are you doing in Gorbydale? Why didn't you warn us you were coming? Come on in. Don't just stand there on the doorstep."

"We don't want to intrude," said Nathan, realising they had arrived at an awkward time. "We just wanted to see Dolly's mother."

Robert nodded politely to Dolly. "You're not intruding a bit. You're most welcome," he said, taking his old friend's arm. "Maggie, take their coats. Nathan, Dolly, come and meet the family. It's my boy's christening tomorrow. You arrived at a good time." He led them into the parlour. "Look who's here, everyone," he called. "This is Nathan Jacques, who grows our cotton, and Dolly too with her little boy."

"Albert," said Maggie proudly, with her grandson's arms still wrapped around her. Tears poured down her beaming face as she followed her daughter and Nathan into the parlour.

Everyone stared. Jessie came tentatively forward to greet her unexpected guests. "Hello Dolly," she said quietly. "How nice to see you again, and Albert too." She turned to Nathan. "Mr. Jacques. How good to meet you at last," she said warmly. "Robert often tells me how good you and your son were to him in America and how kind you are now whenever he visits. Please come and join us."

"Mr. Jacques," said Matthias, struggling from his chair to greet the visitors. "My lad's told me a lot about you. Very pleased to meet you. Er … Dolly," he said with a brief nod in her direction and something resembling a snort.

Melissa bustled up to be introduced. She greeted Dolly more civilly than her husband, but her formal greeting showed little warmth. "Would you make some fresh tea for our guests, Maggie?" she asked.

Hampered by Albert's embrace, Maggie hesitated.

"I'll ask Lizzie if she'll make the tea," suggested Jessie. "She won't mind as it's a special occasion."

Melissa nodded, her lips pursed in mild disapproval.

Then Helen bustled over to lay claim to Albert. "Come and see our new baby," she demanded. "He doesn't talk yet and he poos his nappies, but Mother says it won't be long before he's talking, if he can get a word in edgeways with me around."

The adults chuckled, and Dolly too asked to see baby Jack and cooed over the cot and the sleeping baby.

"You might have another one yourself one day," murmured Nathan beside her, as he too came to admire the infant.

Remembering her first foray into motherhood, Dolly gave him a tentative smile.

The visit went well, despite Matthias' obvious disapproval and Maggie hovering in the background, trying to be unobtrusive. Dolly sat by her mother and whispered her news, as Nathan and Robert chatted easily like the old friends they were.

"You must stay with us," decided Robert. "Honora's old room is free, and we can make up a bed for young Albert in the nursery. You've shown me such hospitality in the past. It will be a pleasure to return it."

"Aye, aye," said Matthias. "You'll be staying for the christening, won't you?"

"Yes, you must come," said Jessie, now that she seen her father-in-law's approval of their uninvited guests.

"Our clothes and baggage are in Manchester," Nathan told them. "But we would be honoured to return tomorrow for the christening."

"Then you can bring your baggage with you and stay for a few days," said Robert with a quick glance at his father for approval.

"Aye, we can show you round the mill on Monday after all this christening palaver is over," added Matthias, eager to show off the Invincible, always his pride and joy.

They left after they had taken tea, with promises to return next day.

CHAPTER 58: A CHRISTENING

The house was full when Dolly and Nathan arrived back at Overdale House. The family from Weavers Row were there. Jacob and Alice greeted the new guests kindly. Arden, who was to be one of Jack's godfathers, met Dolly's eyes and nodded briefly. They both remembered all the trouble she had caused him. Eddie, now a gangly raw youth, was to be a godfather too. John and Elsie and their two children were present, as was Jessie's great friend and stepsister Mary and her new husband Dilwyn.

Dolly had little chance to see her mother. Maggie was busy with the cook in the kitchen, preparing the food for the christening celebration. But after the visit to the church where baby Jack, the pride of the Overdales, was baptised and the christening feast consumed, Dolly slipped down to the kitchen to see her mother.

She warily greeted the cook, who had often given her a chastising whack with a wooden spoon for not attending to her duties. The woman scrutinised her fine clothes and looked as if she was about to make some caustic remark but obviously thought better of it.

Dolly drew her mother to one side. "Have you told Tommo I'm here?" she asked her quietly.

Maggie nodded hesitantly. "But I warned him that you wouldn't be happy to see him," she stammered.

"You're right there!" said Dolly, annoyed at her mother. "I wanted to tell you not to mention our visit yesterday. But it's too late now. You tell him I don't want him coming here and showing me up. I'll send him some money to keep him away and to keep his gob shut. D'you understand?"

Maggie nodded. "But you know what's he's like," she whimpered. "He won't take any notice of me. If I hadn't told him, somebody else would have and I'd probably get a crack for keeping quiet about you."

Dolly forgot her anger and was suddenly filled with pity for her mother. She gave Maggie a hug to reassure her. "Aye, you're right. I knew all along I shouldn't have come, but…" She had never expected to be homesick for Gorbydale, but in the heat and strange vegetation of Louisiana she had missed the clear heights of the hills around her native town. "Anyway, Nathan wanted to meet you. Albert wanted to see you, and I did too. I wanted you to see that he's doing fine."

That evening she stared over those hills from Honora's bedroom.

"Are you glad to be home?" asked Nathan, slipping his arms round her waist.

Dolly was silent in thought. She felt safe in Nathan's arms, safer than she had ever felt since she'd been a child, trying to protect her mother; safer than when she'd been trying to conceal her pregnancy from her father and everyone at Overdale House. She had rarely felt safe with Clement. She repressed a shudder when she remembered the figure slipping away at the Flags in Liverpool. "I'll be glad when we're back home," she confessed quietly. "Our home."

"We'll go home whenever you want," said Nathan. "I know you must feel uneasy here in Overdale House. But these are good people. They won't make you feel inferior."

"No, the Overdales know their manners with you here, but I can see old Matthias biting his tongue," said Dolly with a chuckle. "It must stick in his craw that his old skivvy is having her dinner at his table. Anyway, I know you want to see London," she added. "We'll go and see if the queen will invite us for tea."

Next morning Matthias hauled Nathan off to see his little empire and, after a leisurely breakfast, Jessie took Dolly up to the nursery to see the children. Helen was bossing the boys around in her usual manner.

"Have the children been good?" Jessie asked Lizzie.

The nursemaid gave a wry smile. "Master Matty and Albert have been very good," she said. "Miss Helen keeps forgetting her manners, though."

The two boys giggled as Helen was chastised. Her lip stuck out in a sulk. "He talks funny," she said, pointing at Albert. "I told him to talk proper."

"Albert has come all the way from America to visit us," Jessie told her truculent daughter. "You should be very nice to him and show him our hospitality."

Helen snorted and went to hide behind a picture book.

"Honestly, she's a right little madam," muttered her mother, shaking her head.

They were joined by Robert and Nathan, who had finished their tour of the Invincible. Nathan took a great interest in the two boys, who were leafing through a book together and laughing.

He quietly asked Matty a few questions and then beckoned Robert. "I noticed your boy peering at some of those children's books. He reminds me of myself when I'm trying to make sense of my papers." He reached into his pocket and pulled out a tortoiseshell case. From it he extracted a pair of pince nez. "See these here things, Matty," said Nathan, putting the tiny glass ovals on his own nose with a clip. "See if you can look through them too?"

"Is it magic?" asked Matty.

Nathan chuckled. "It could be. I find them magic when I want to see my accounts. Pity they don't make 'em balance." He placed the small glasses carefully on Matty's nose, and the boy glanced down at the book.

Matty's eyes widened with amazement. "Look!" he gasped, somehow expecting the others to be able to witness what he saw. "Just look. It is magic." He pointed to the picture book. "A big brown dog and an orange cat," said Matty hesitantly.

The family all knew he loved colours, but now it was obvious he could see the pictures much more clearly.

"I think there's your answer," said Nathan. "The boy needs glasses."

"Nathan Jacques, you are a genius," said Robert, laughing. "Jessie, Dolly, come and see."

They were delighted that such a simple solution would in future make Matty's life much easier. It was from that day on that he learned to read, and even Matthias was surprised by his grandson's progress.

Next day, after a tearful parting with Maggie, the guests left for London. Jessie was left to console Dolly's weeping mother. As Dolly passed the gate, she noticed a familiar figure. Tommo Tate gave a brief wave to his daughter. She did not order the cab to stop. She turned away and looked ahead, promising never to return. In Dolly's mind she had pictured herself returning in triumph to Gorbydale in her fine clothes, with her new husband and thriving son at her side. Instead she had endured an awkward few days among people who knew what she had been and how she'd behaved. She had only been accepted because of Nathan. She might act the fine lady in London, but it was back in Louisiana where she was loved and appreciated, and she longed to go home.

CHAPTER 59: FAMILY

The house was quiet now that the visitors had left, and Jessie was tired. She went gratefully to bed after her busy day. As she mounted the stairs, she heard the whimper of her baby son. First she changed for bed and, leaning over the cot, gently took Jack in her arms. Sitting back against the pillows, she slipped her nightgown loose and held the soft milky child to her breast. He gave a little sigh and began to suckle with little snuffles of pleasure. Matthias Overdale looked on this child as the heir to his fortune, not Matty with his sharp brain but wobbly body, nor Helen with her bold and bright willingness to tackle anything. So much was expected of this small suckling babe.

Robert came and stroked his son's head, smiling with a pride that unsettled her. It made Jessie feel that she was betraying her older children. She knew she would work tirelessly for them all but hoped she could at least make their paths as fair as she could.

Beside her, Robert lay back and stared at the ceiling. "It's nice to have the house back to ourselves," he said. "Though I was glad to show Nathan some hospitality. He's been very good to me in the past. Fancy him turning up with Dolly, though. I thought Father would explode," he added with a chuckle. He turned quietly thoughtful for a moment. "How strange that Duplege should drown in the Mississippi. It was the same fate he would have dealt to me that night at sea near Carolina. Perhaps there is some justice in fate."

She felt him shiver as he remembered how he himself had survived the cold sea despite the odds. "I think you might be right," said Jessie, carefully changing the baby to her other breast. "I told you of Honora's suspicions that he had accidentally murdered her friend instead of her."

"That can never be proved now, but at least Clement's death will put her mind at rest," said Robert. "It's a pity that his body has never been found, though," he added. "I hope for Nathan and Dolly's sake that his fate has indeed been sealed. That Clement Duplege could escape the devil."

"Surely not," said Jessie. "Nathan said there were witnesses who saw him dragged under the water."

"I suppose so," said her husband, but did not sound convinced.

Jessie finished feeding her baby and handed the sleepy child to Robert's waiting arms to settle him back in his cot. "I wonder what the fate of our children will be?" she murmured. "Let's hope that it's kind to them and that they deserve all that it brings them."

"Only time will tell," said Robert, kissing his wife. "Just as for most folks, I expect it will be a pretty mixed bag. At least our children will have a better start in life than some of the poor wretches down by the river."

Jessie felt gratified that now at least he recognised the suffering of the poor and had been instrumental in trying, along with his Uncle Eli, to alleviate some of the squalid conditions in the mean dwellings by the river. Once, he would have ignored them entirely.

She remembered that Dolly had been brought up down by the river in the crumbling, insanitary houses with a bully for a father and a criminal for a brother. Yet here she'd been a guest at Overdale House, where once she'd been a skivvy. She'd been very quiet and subdued on her visit. Dolly was now married to a decent and well respected man, and her son was heir to a large plantation. Fate had indeed taken some strange twists and turns in Dolly's life and in her own too.

Jessie remembered Amisha and wondered if she too would have had the courage to escape Taylor Walmsley's controlling ways if she'd married him. She laid her head on Robert's shoulder and he pulled her closer towards him. Matthias may see the future of his mill with baby Jack but, once he had left the world, the mill would be in Robert's hands. Jessie felt confident that her husband was a just man and he would do right by their children. Feeling a great contentment wash over her, she drifted off to sleep, ready to face the future and whatever it would bring.

A NOTE TO THE READER

Dear Reader,

Thank you for taking the time to read this book, whether as a continued journey from *Song of the Shuttle*, or the start of your Lancashire Cotton Saga adventure.

This book was in the final stages of editing, and the third already submitted for review, when Christine sadly and unexpectedly passed away in January 2020.

Christine always had a love of writing and, after attending creative writing classes, a tutor encouraged her to write short stories for magazines. To have her work in print in magazines (over 200 in various publications) was wonderful but to have a book, and be a published author, was a dream come true for her.

Christine's dedicated research into the cotton industry, American Civil War and the plight of all the people involved led to her first novel, *Song of the Shuttle*. This was initially a standalone story however, the characters had other ideas, and insisted on being part of a trilogy. Indeed, the Davenports and Overdales have been a part of our own family life for such a long time. It is a pleasure, and a great comfort, to be able to see this book completed and the saga continued.

We would love to hear your thoughts on this story so please take a moment to post a review on **Amazon** or **Goodreads**.

The Evans Family would like to give a special thanks to Sapere Books for their continued support in making Christine's dream a reality.

Rest in Peace Christine.

Sapere Books is an exciting new publisher of brilliant fiction and popular history.

To find out more about our latest releases and our monthly bargain books visit our website:
saperebooks.com

Printed in Great Britain
by Amazon

85259330R00214